An Orphan's
Journey

Rosie Goodwin is the million-copy bestselling author of more than thirty-five novels. She is the first author in the world to be allowed to follow three of Catherine Cookson's trilogies with her own sequels. Having worked in the social services sector for many years, then fostered a number of children, she is now a full-time novelist. She is one of the top 50 most borrowed authors from UK libraries. Rosie lives in Nuneaton, the setting for many of her books, with her husband and their beloved dogs.

Rosie GOODWIN
An Orphan's Journey

ZAFFRE

First published in the UK in 2021
This paperback edition published In the UK in 2021 by
ZAFFRE
An imprint of Bonnier Books UK
80–81 Wimpole St, London W1G 9RE
Owned by Bonnier Books
Sveavägen 56, Stockholm, Sweden

A CIP catalogue record for this book is
available from the British Library.

ISBN: 978–1–83877–352–6

Also available as an ebook and an audiobook

1 3 5 7 9 10 8 6 4 2

Typeset by IDSUK (Data Connection) Ltd
Printed and bound in Great Britain by Clays Ltd, Elcograf S.p.A.

Zaffre is an imprint of Bonnier Books UK
www.bonnierbooks.co.uk

For a very brave little girl that I am so very proud of
Emmy Reid
14th November 2009–20th November 2020
xxx

Prologue

December 1874

'Come on, girl, your dad will be home wi' no dinner on the table if yer don't get a move on, an' yer know what that means!'

'Yes, Ma.'

Pearl renewed her efforts as she struggled to peel the potatoes, daring to glance across her shoulder just once at her mother, who was sitting at the side of the dying fire with a glass of cheap gin in her hand.

At twelve years old, Pearl was small for her age, as were all her brothers and sisters. It wasn't surprising really, as both their mother and father spent most of the small amount of money that came into the house on drink, so they frequently went without food. But at least today they would eat. Once the potatoes had been softened in a pan of water, Pearl would mash them and smear the stale loaf she had managed to get from the baker's with dripping. It would be a feast, and her mouth watered at the thought of it.

At that moment, Matthew, Pearl's youngest sibling, a baby lying in the drawer on the floor next to her mother's chair, began to whimper and, sighing resignedly, Molly Parker lifted the infant none too gently, roughly yanking aside the dirty blouse she was wearing to allow him to suckle.

He must be practically drinking neat gin, Pearl thought to herself, *it's no wonder he's so sickly*. But she didn't dare voice her thoughts. Her mother might be small, but she could certainly pack a punch, which accounted for the many bruises that covered poor Pearl's arms and legs.

Molly Parker was only twenty-eight years old, and while she had once been pretty, the hard life she had led, the lack of good food and the countless beatings she had received from her husband meant that now she could easily have been taken for a woman in her fifties. She had married her husband Fred just over twelve years ago and Pearl had been born shortly after. They had been so happy back then, delighted at the birth of their first child – so much so that they had decided to name her after a precious stone. Fred had promised her the world, but all she had to show for their marriage were two downstairs rooms in a terraced house in a courtyard near the docks in the slums of Whitechapel, which they shared with two other families, cockroaches and a legion of rats. After Pearl was born, the children had come with frightening regularity, one a year, although not all of them had survived. Now, with all her dreams knocked out of her, Molly found her only solace lay in the bottom of a bottle of gin.

Ten minutes later, the potatoes were peeled and after adding salt to the water, Pearl crossed the room to place them over the dying fire, hoping they would cook through before it went out altogether. Yet again the coal store was empty and if her father hadn't got work on the docks today, they would face another cold night. As she carried the heavy pan, she stumbled and some of the water sloshed across the hard-packed earth floor.

'Mind what yer doin', you useless little sod,' her mother growled. 'Yer neither use nor ornament. Why did I have to 'ave a cripple, eh?'

Thankfully the infant in her arms stopped her from lashing out, but even so it didn't stop the flood of colour that poured into Pearl's cheeks. With her heart-shaped face, shock of silver-blonde curls and striking green eyes she was a pretty little thing, or so people said – but she had been born with one leg slightly shorter than the other, which made her walk ungainly, and her mother never let her forget it.

'Right, now get this place tidied up a bit,' her mother barked once the potatoes were safely hanging above the flames.

Pearl nodded, but as she looked about the tiny room she didn't quite know where to start. Her brothers and sisters sat lethargically on the bare floor, propped up against the walls, scratching at the lice in their hair, looking pale and wan. Pearl gave them an affectionate smile as she lifted a broom to start sweeping the floor.

But then her mother remembered something and started. 'Oh Lordy,' she said fearfully. 'I just remembered it's rent day. You'll 'ave to get 'em all out o' the way till the rent man's been an' gone. I can't pay him, so we'll have to pretend no one's home. That won't work if he hears any o' this lot. Go on, away wi' yer an' pull the curtains to afore yer go!'

'But, Ma, it's freezing out there. Davey an' Maggie have got a hackin' cough already an' they ain't got any shoes,' Pearl said worricdly, as she stared towards the grimy window.

'Wrap a bit o' that sackin' about their feet,' Molly ordered, pointing to the old sack that had held the last of the potatoes.

'But where can I take 'em in this weather?'

Molly's face hardened. 'Can't you think of anything for yerself? Take 'em up town an' let 'em look in the shop winders. They'll be all decked out fer Christmas and they'll like that. Now get a move on and less o' your backchat or you'll be feelin' me foot up yer arse!'

Pearl quickly wrapped the children in anything she could lay her hands on, including tying some torn sacking around their feet. Then she herded them towards the door. There was no sign of her other sister, Eliza. Just a year younger than Pearl, her sister was prone to daydreams and spent much of her time wandering around the streets. It meant that Pearl usually ended up doing most of the work in the house, but even so, Pearl loved her dearly, and worried about her when she was gone. For though Pearl was pretty, Eliza was turning into a true beauty, with her oval face, bright-gold hair and green eyes, and Pearl knew there were unscrupulous people in Whitechapel who would love to take advantage of her beauty. Now Pearl just hoped she didn't turn up at the house at the same time as the rent man – otherwise her mother would give her a clout round the ear.

Once they were outside, Pearl quickly shepherded her siblings through the twisting alleys that led to the docks, telling them encouragingly, 'We'll take a look at the ships first, shall we? You'll like that.'

None of her siblings looked very enthusiastic and Pearl couldn't blame them, but she fixed a smile on her face and urged them along until they came eventually to the docks, where ships of all shapes and sizes were bobbing at anchor. Some were being unloaded of their cargo by burly seamen, while others were being loaded as the sailors nimbly leapt over the ropes with barrels on their shoulders. There were also a number of ladies with pockmarked, painted faces wearing low-cut dresses standing against the walls, hoping to entice the seamen who had just returned from long journeys to part with some of their hard-earned wages.

Three-year-old Davey was whimpering with the cold by then, so after a time Pearl led them towards the city centre.

'I's 'ungry, Pearl,' nine-year-old Amy told her sister gravely.

Pearl squeezed her hand reassuringly. 'Never mind, pet. Mr Grimley will have been an' gone soon an' then we can go home an' get you all some dinner,' she said, trying to ignore her own rumbling stomach.

Mr Grimley was the rent man and much dreaded by his tenants. As Lil, the woman who lived on the floor above them, had once commented to Molly, 'I reckon that man 'as got a swingin' brick fer a heart. He chucked the Freemans out on the bloody street in the snow last year 'cause they couldn't pay the rent, but how were they supposed to when Bill Freeman had broke his leg unpackin' cargo at the docks? The poor sods promised him they'd catch up just as soon as ever Bill got back to work but he wouldn't have a bar of it an' out they went wi' her ready to drop her babby any minute an' another two little 'uns not even out o' bindin's.'

Pearl shuddered as she remembered, and prayed the same fate would not befall their family.

Soon, they came to a main road and as they strolled along the children gazed in awe at the smartly dressed people walking to and fro. The women wore fur stoles or thick capes and pretty bonnets, while the men sported top hats and heavy greatcoats.

'Is they rich, our Pearl?' eight-year-old Tom asked.

Pearl smiled dreamily, trying to imagine how it would feel to be dressed in such fine clothes. 'I suppose they must be – but look at this window 'ere.'

They all stopped as one to stare at a display of toys. There were wind-up train sets, dolls with pretty china faces and all manner of things to catch the young ones' attention.

'It must be nice to be rich,' Tom commented enviously, and the little sea of pale faces crowded about Pearl's dull brown skirt nodded in agreement. They were still standing there, gazing into the window, when a smartly dressed lady carrying a number of loaded shopping bags paused to smile at them. She was wearing a thick navy-blue woollen cape with a fur-trimmed collar and a beautiful bonnet with feathers that bobbed and danced in the breeze.

'Are you hoping for Father Christmas to bring some of them to you?' she asked kindly.

The children shook their heads in unison. 'Nah! Christmas Day is just anuvver day to us; we won't get nowt,' Tom told her sadly.

The smile slid from the woman's face, and after rummaging in her purse, she produced a shiny silver sixpence, which she held out to them.

Pearl frowned. They might be poor but she still had her pride. But before she could refuse it, Tom's hand had snaked out and grabbed the coin.

'Fanks, missus!'

'You're very welcome. Why don't you go to the cart at the end of the road and get yourselves a nice plate of hot faggots and peas? It'll warm you all up.' And then, without another word, she hurried on her way, feeling that she had done her good deed for the day.

'Can we?' the children piped up, as the kind lady was swallowed up amongst the crowd. Their mouths were watering in anticipation and Pearl didn't have the heart to refuse them.

'Well . . . it is nearly Christmas so I s'ppose we could,' she answered uncertainly. Usually when their mother sent them out begging, they had to hand over anything they were given to her, but then it was only spent on drink, as Pearl knew only too well, and the children had precious few treats.

Ten minutes later, they were sitting on the wall surrounding a frozen fountain, tucking into their feast, and Pearl couldn't help smiling to see them looking so happy. But all too soon they had licked the plates clean and it was time to move on.

As they continued along the street, admiring the displays in the shop window, feather-soft flakes of snow began to fall, and Amy started to whimper again. 'I can't feel me 'ands, Pearl. They've all gone blue. Can we go 'ome now?'

'Nor me,' Davey piped up.

Taking her thin shawl from about her shoulders, Pearl wrapped it about him. The snow was coming down thicker now, and within seconds Pearl's shoulders were soaked to the skin and her teeth were chattering as she led the children back the way they had come. Whether Mr Grimley had called or not, she couldn't keep them out in such weather any longer.

They had only just turned into the grim courtyard that led to their home when their mother's raised voice came to them.

'So where the bleedin' 'ell 'ave yer been all day if yer didn't get taken on to work?'

'In the Mermaid!' they heard her father's sullen voice answer her.

'Oh ar! An' what did yer use fer money then? It's funny that yer can find money fer drink, yet I have to 'ide from the bleedin' rent man!'

'The landlord put it on the slate fer me, so stop naggin', woman, else you'll feel the back o' me 'and!'

'That's it, yer cowardly bastard, 'it a woman,' their mother screeched. 'But think on afore yer do 'cause I may as well tell yer there'll be another bleedin' mouth to feed in a few months' time!'

As they tentatively approached the door, the children heard their father groan. 'Oh *no*! You are kiddin' me, ain't yer? That one there is only five months old, fer God's sake. The way yer turnin' 'em out we won't be able to move in 'ere soon. An' there's only Pearl who's old enough to work as yet, not that anyone 'ud want 'er wi' that gammy leg of 'ers.'

'Well, if yer didn't keep demandin' yer rights when yer come in pissed up of a night, there wouldn't *be* another on the way, would there?' their mother screamed back. 'An' it's 'ardly my fault that Pearl is a cripple, is it?'

They heard a dull thud then and the sound of something overturning, followed by a sob from their mother.

'Dad's hittin' Ma again,' Tom whispered fearfully, shrinking into Pearl's side.

Pearl was smarting from what she had just overheard, but some of the smaller children were crying now and she urged them ahead of her, keen to get them out of the biting cold.

'Don't worry. He'll fall asleep in a minute; he allus does when he's had a drink,' she soothed.

Sure enough, when they entered the kitchen, they saw that their father had stormed off into the other room that served as a bedroom, while their mother sat crying on the floor.

'Lousy swine. He'll 'it me once too often an' I'll swing fer 'im one o' these days, you just see if I don't,' she muttered, as Pearl helped her up.

The children had huddled together on the floor in one corner for warmth and after flashing them a reassuring smile, Pearl went and lifted the pan of potatoes from the fire and carried it across to the large wooden draining board that stood next to the deep stone sink. Unfortunately, their mother had let them boil dry and some of them had stuck to the bottom of the pan, but thankfully she was able to salvage most of them. Not that the children were hungry for once, but she wouldn't tell her mother that.

It was six o' clock before their father emerged from the bedroom to ask blearily, 'What's fer dinner, then? I'm starvin'!'

Molly glared at him but remained silent as Pearl carried a plate of cold mash and bread with dripping across to him at the old rickety table.

'I'm sorry it's cold but the fire's gone out an' we're out o' coal so I had no way o' keepin' it warm fer you.'

Some of the younger children had already drifted off to sleep on the itchy hay mattresses that were spread along one wall, but the older ones sat silently, afraid of drawing attention to themselves.

Their father fell on the food like a man who hadn't eaten for a month. Then he rose and snatched his coat from the back of the door.

'You lots is goin' to 'ave to pull yer socks up if yer wanna eat,' he growled. 'So, first thing in the mornin' I want yer out on the main streets beggin'. All the toffs will be doin' their Christmas shoppin' this week an' they'll no doubt dig deep in their pockets . . . Do you 'ear me?'

The only light in the room was from a cheap tallow candle on the table and the children stared back at him fearfully as the shadows flickered over his face.

'Yes, Dad!' they said in unison.

Satisfied, he stormed from the room, slamming the door behind him.

Eventually they all fell asleep, until there was only Molly and Pearl left awake. It was then that Pearl dared to ask, 'Did I hear yer aright, Ma? That yer goin' to 'ave another baby?'

Molly hugged herself as she rocked back and forth and nodded dejectedly. Pearl felt a stab of pity for her. The gin bottle was empty now and the thump she had received from their father had caused a large purple bruise to form across her chin and right cheek.

'Don't worry, we'll manage some'ow.' She reached out to stroke her mother's arm and, in a rare affectionate gesture, Molly patted her hand.

It was only when Pearl had gone to bed and Molly sat alone listening to the tick of the tin clock on the mantelpiece that she considered a suggestion Lil from upstairs had put to her the week before. At the time it had seemed so preposterous that Molly had waved it aside, but now she was at the end of her tether and she knew that she must give it some serious consideration.

She couldn't go on like this.

The very next morning, just as their father had insisted, the younger children were sent begging, and once they had gone Molly told Pearl, 'Go an' collect yer things together, girl. Yer goin' on a little holiday.'

'What?' Pearl's mouth gaped with surprise, as Molly gulped and squirmed uncomfortably.

'Well, the thing is, as yer already know there's gonna be another mouth to feed soon so . . .' She patted her flabby stomach and forced herself to go on. 'Lil told me about a scheme they've got goin' wi' the work'ouse an' the orphanages. See, it seems that some o' the older kids in them places are bein' transported abroad. Just think o' that, a life in the sunshine. No more cold or snow.'

Secretly, Molly very much doubted that Pearl would be chosen to go with her lame leg, but even if she wasn't, she

11

would at least be assured of a good meal each day and it would be one less mouth to feed and worry about. It was usual for the people thereabouts to send the younger children away to such places if things got too desperate, for the older ones could normally be sent out to earn a wage – but there was little chance of Pearl doing that and the younger ones could earn more begging; people had more sympathy for smaller children. She was only sorry that Eliza, the girl next to Pearl in age, who was always away with the fairies, wasn't there too, as she could have gone with her – but as usual she had wandered off early that morning.

Pearl was so shocked that she couldn't even answer for a moment, but eventually she found her voice to ask, 'An' what happens to the kids when they get there?'

'Apparently the settlers take 'em into their homes to help wi' the chores. I'm sure you'd soon find a place 'cause you can cook an' clean along wi' the best o' them. An' they have schools there an' all. Yer could learn to read an' write. You've always wanted to, ain't yer?'

This had come like a bolt from the blue and Pearl was so stunned when she realised that her mother meant it that she was rendered temporarily speechless. Eventually she blurted out, 'But I don't *want* to go away . . . this is my 'ome an' yer all me family!' Tears started to roll down her cheeks. It might not be the best of homes, but it was the only one she had ever known and the thought of leaving it was terrifying.

But Molly's mind was made up. 'It'll be fer the best,' she said gravely, guiltily looking away from the stricken expression on her daughter's face. 'You'll get the start there that yer'd never get 'ere, an' one day yer can come back an' see us all again. So go an' get your stuff together, an' I'll have no more arguin'.'

Somehow Pearl managed to do as she was told, despite the fact that she was blinded by tears. In truth there was very little to collect and soon she carried her small bundle to her mother, who had wrapped a shawl around her shoulders, ready to leave. Lil upstairs had taken the baby for now.

'B-but surely you ain't takin' me there *now*?' Pearl was panicking. 'I ain't even 'ad time to say goodbye to everyone an' it'll be Christmas in a few weeks' time. *Surely* it can wait till after then?'

'It's better this way.' Molly stroked a tear from her first-born daughter's cheek with her thumb. 'Come on, let's get it over wi'.'

And before Pearl knew it, they were striding through the fast-falling snow towards the workhouse and Pearl's new life.

Chapter One

Pearl and her mother had gone no more than a few steps from the house when Molly spotted Eliza coming towards them with her head bent against the snow. Like Pearl, Eliza was small for her age; added to this she had the disadvantage of being sickly, and most people thought her quiet, always lost in her own world. Although she was eleven years old, she behaved as a much younger child would, and as Molly's eyes settled on the girl, it came to her in a flash that this was the perfect opportunity to leave Eliza at the workhouse too. After all, Eliza could only ever be a burden – she couldn't be trusted to work, or even help out properly around the home – and with both of the older girls out of the way there would be two less mouths to feed. It would make things easier for Pearl too if she had someone close with her, she reasoned, trying to ease her conscience.

As if Pearl could read her mother's thoughts, she stared up at her. 'You can't send Eliza to the workhouse, Ma,' she muttered, deeply distressed. 'She ain't good wi' people she don't know an' she wouldn't cope wi' being sent away.'

'Rubbish! It might be just what she needs,' Molly told her. 'There'll be far more opportunities fer both o' yer in a new country an' you'll be company fer each other.'

Pearl was so horrified that she found she couldn't utter a single word as Eliza came abreast of them and her mother caught her arm.

'Come along wi' me an' Pearl now, there's a good girl,' Molly encouraged, as she turned her about and Pearl's heart dropped like a stone in her chest as she realised that this was exactly what her mother intended to do.

She still hadn't had time to come to terms with what was about to happen to herself, but the thought of Eliza being sent away from everything familiar was even worse. Eliza had a habit of wandering off, for she had no sense of danger whatsoever, and sometimes Pearl felt as if she spent half her life looking for her, but she loved her dearly all the same. She opened her mouth to protest, but one glare from her mother silenced her and her tears began to flow faster as Eliza slipped her hand trustingly into hers.

'Are we goin' somewhere nice?' Eliza asked hopefully, as she ran to keep up with her mother and sister.

'Aye, you are, pet.' Molly flashed her a smile, moving on quickly so the two girls followed meekly, knowing that they had little choice.

All too soon the bleak façade of Poplar Workhouse loomed ahead of them in the snow and Pearl was so frightened that she feared she was going to be sick. She had known other families who had sent their children here when their homes became overcrowded, and as far as she knew their families had never bothered to see them again. Sometimes Pearl had had nightmares imagining how the poor abandoned souls must be feeling, but at least they hadn't been sent far away as she and Eliza might be.

'*Please*, Ma let us come home. I'll find a job, *I promise!*'

But Molly merely strode on, her face set with determination. As the snow fell gently about them, they stopped in front of the huge wooden doors that were the entrance to the dreaded place. Only then did Molly hesitate, but only for a moment.

Taking a deep breath, she stroked their cheeks, then, with a catch in her voice, she nudged them towards the doors. 'Go on then, no use in standin' outside 'ere in the cold. Just tell 'em yer ma sent yer 'cause of overcrowdin'.' She turned then, and the protest that was on Pearl's lips was lost as she disappeared into the crowds of people milling about the pavements.

'But why are we 'ere, Pearl?' Eliza asked in a timid voice. Her big sister was crying and it frightened her.

With a huge effort, Pearl pulled herself together enough to force a weak smile to her face. Just for a moment it had occurred to her that they could run away, but then what would happen to them with nowhere to go? Eliza wasn't strong enough to endure sleeping in shop doorways and at least here they would have somewhere warm and dry to sleep and they might be given their first proper meal in days.

'We're goin' to stay 'ere for a while,' she told her sister brightly. 'An' we're goin' to be just fine. So come along o' me now.'

Taking a deep breath, she stepped forwards and rang the large bell that hung at the side of the door, and seconds later she heard the creak of bolts as it was swung open.

A young woman in what appeared to be a nurse's out-fit opened the door and looked at them enquiringly, before asking, 'Can I help you?'

Swallowing the lump that had formed in her throat, Pearl nodded. 'Yes please, miss. We, er . . . we needs to stay 'ere for a while.'

'Ah, then you're in the wrong place.' The young woman gave her a sympathetic smile, making Pearl feel a little more reassured. If all the people here were as kind as her, perhaps it wouldn't be so bad after all? 'You need to go further along to the door marked "Admittances". Can you read?' When Pearl remained silent she stepped outside and pointed down the street. 'You can't miss the door and they'll help you there.' And without another word she quietly went back inside and closed the door.

Eliza began to sniffle. 'I don't like it 'ere, Pearl,' she whim-pered. 'It smelled funny inside when that lady opened the door. Why can't we just go 'ome?'

Pearl opened her mouth to answer, but quickly snapped it shut again. In truth she didn't have an answer, so without a word she gripped Eliza's hand more tightly and began to haul her in the direction the nurse had pointed. Sure enough, they soon came to another entrance that looked even more forbidding than the first, and with her heart in her mouth Pearl approached it and once again rang the bell. This time she was answered by a stout woman of indeterminable age who looked none too friendly.

'Yes?' she snapped as she eyed the two girls up and down.

'I . . . that is, we . . . need to stay 'ere, please.'

The woman sighed but stepping aside quickly she opened the door wide enough to allow them to enter, before slamming it behind them to stop the cold air from entering. It didn't seem to do much good, for Pearl felt it was as cold inside as it was out and their breath hung on the air in front of them.

Glancing about, she found they were in what appeared to be a large entrance foyer, which was bigger than the whole of the sooty little terraced house she had been brought up in. A young, underweight girl in a drab brown dress was mopping the black-and-white floor tiles as if her life depended on it, but she didn't look up. There was a large, highly polished desk to one side of the door and the woman ushered them towards it and opened a large ledger.

'Names!' she barked.

'P-Pearl Parker, miss. An' this is me little sister, Eliza.'

'Ages?'

'I'm twelve an' Eliza is eleven.'

'Dates of birth?'

Pearl shrugged. 'I only know mine is sometime in December an' Eliza's is in October.'

'And the reason you wish to be admitted?'

Colour flamed into Pearl's cheeks and she bowed her head in shame as she mumbled, 'Me ma is to 'ave another baby an' . . .'

'Overcrowding!' The woman shook her head. 'If only these women would stop breeding like rabbits, this place wouldn't be so full,' she spat in disgust as she wrote in the ledger. 'Address?'

In a choked voice Pearl quickly told her.

'Right, sign your names there.'

'Please, missus . . . I, er . . . can't write,' Pearl mumbled in embarrassment.

'Yet another illiterate,' the woman snapped, to no one in particular. 'Then just make a cross next to the names I've written.'

Pearl hastily did as she was told.

'Wait there,' the woman told them. And with that she was gone, leaving Pearl and Eliza quaking with fear.

From somewhere they could hear screams, and as the young girl mopping the floor grew closer, she hissed, 'That's the lunatics yer can 'ear. They're locked up up there.' She nodded towards a sweeping staircase that led to the first floor, but before she could say any more, the sound of footsteps echoed hollowly on the tiles and she immediately turned her attention back to the job in hand.

The same mean-faced woman who had let them in appeared with another equally drably dressed woman beside her. 'Go with Mrs Bates here,' the first woman told them. 'And make sure you behave yourselves. When she has you ready and clean I shall come and tell you what your jobs will be.'

Pearl looked at her enquiringly. 'Jobs?'

Unused to being questioned, the woman scowled at her. 'Well yes, of course you'll be expected to work for your keep. This ain't a hotel, yer know! Now get off with you.'

Eliza was openly crying now and as Pearl dragged her along the corridor behind Mrs Bates, the woman snapped, 'Stop that snivelling at once. We don't tolerate that sort of behaviour in here, girl.'

Pearl's first instinct was to tell the horrible woman not to talk to her little sister like that. *Surely* she could see how frightened Eliza was? But the woman looked so forbidding that she merely gave Eliza's hand a reassuring squeeze instead.

At the end of the seemingly endless corridor they came to yet another staircase, this one nowhere near as impressive as the one in the entrance foyer. Opposite was a door and they followed the woman through it to find themselves in a room where a number of tin baths were propped against the far wall. A large boiler stood in a corner and nodding towards it, Mrs Bates told them, 'Fill one of the baths from out of there. I'll be back in five minutes.'

Both girls immediately leapt into action. Fetching one of the baths and standing it by the boiler, Pearl began to fill it with water with a bucket that stood to one side of it.

The water was very hot and once the bath was half full, she looked around for a pump or somewhere where she might find some cold water to cool it down. She was still looking about when Mrs Bates reappeared holding a bar of carbolic soap, a pair of scissors and a couple of threadbare towels.

'Is it ready?' she barked.

Pearl shook her head. 'Not quite. I can't find the cold water,' she explained.

By this time Eliza was so frightened that a puddle of urine had pooled on the floor between her legs. Back at home the most they had ever been able to do was wash in cold water; never in her life had she been totally submerged in a bath, and the sight of this one with the steam rising from it was enough to terrify her.

'How *disgusting*, you filthy little guttersnipe!' Mrs Bates lip curled with contempt and, leaning forwards, she cuffed Eliza's ear soundly, making the poor child howl with pain and shrink into her sister's side.

'She couldn't 'elp it; she's frightened,' Pearl said indignantly before she could stop herself, and that earned her a cuff about the ear too.

'That's enough of your lip or you'll feel the strap on your backside. Now strip off the pair of you. Who's going in first?'

'B-but it's too hot,' Pearl hiccupped as she pressed her hand against her stinging ear.

'Rubbish. Now get those clothes off or do I have to take 'em off for you?' Mrs Bates threatened.

Too afraid to disobey, Pearl hastily began to do as she was told until she stood there naked with her face glowing with embarrassment and humiliation. Hands on hips, the woman nodded towards the bath and Pearl warily climbed in, gasping as the hot water covered her feet. She watched as they turned bright pink from the heat, imagining blisters appearing. She was steeling herself to lower the rest of her body slowly into the water when Mrs Bates roughly pushed her in.

Before she could even fathom what had happened, the woman said nastily, 'Right, we'll get some o' that filth off you now.'

Grabbing a jug from a nearby table, she filled it with water from the bath and without warning tipped the lot over Pearl's head. Poor Pearl was coughing and spluttering, unable to catch her breath, but she had no time to react or object before Mrs Bates began to rub the carbolic soap into her hair. She was so rough that Pearl's head wobbled from side to side and her scalp felt as if it was on fire. The worst wasn't over, though, for next Mrs Bates produced a fine-toothed comb and began to drag it through Pearl's matted hair. Pearl was so shocked and humiliated that she could hardly breathe, and in that moment she hated her mother for leaving them there.

'Look at this, you're *crawlin'* with head lice,' the woman said triumphantly as she held up the comb. 'Let's make the job a bit easier, eh?' Now she was wielding the scissors, and before Pearl could object, she took a length of hair and hacked it off to just below Pearl's ears. Tears were rolling down Pearl's cheeks now but she was too afraid of what the woman might do next, and she was desperate not to upset Eliza anymore, so she just sat there trying not to cry out.

The torture seemed to go on forever but at last, her cheeks red with exertion, Mrs Bates sat back and smiled with satisfaction. 'That's got rid o' most o' the little buggers,' she said. 'Now get out an, you' – she pointed at Eliza – 'you're next, so strip off.'

Too terrified to do anything else, Eliza did as she was told. Thankfully the water had cooled a little by then and so getting into the bath was not quite such a painful experience for her. Although she did cry out in pain when Mrs Bates attacked her long, tangled hair roughly with the comb and then hacked at it too. Pearl watched on, helpless, wishing she could protect her sister but knowing anything she said would just make matters worse.

Eventually the two sisters stood side by side looking like two shorn little lambs, wrapped in the shabby towels Mrs Bates had thrown at them.

'Wait there an' don't move while I go an' get you some clothes,' she ordered.

Once she was gone Eliza sagged against her sister. 'I don't like it 'ere, Pearl,' she whimpered pathetically. 'I want to go 'ome.'

'We won't 'ave to stay for long,' Pearl answered with a catch in her voice. After the heat of the water, the room felt unbearably cold, and by the time Mrs Bates reappeared their teeth were chattering and they were shivering with cold.

'Get these on.' She threw them each a drab, ill-fitting brown dress exactly the same as the one the girl they had seen in the foyer had been wearing, and some underwear made of a rough cotton that made them itch.

'Shall we wash our own clothes now?' Pearl dared to ask.

The woman snorted. 'Wash them? Why, it's only the filth keepin' 'em together. They'd fall apart if they went into water. No, they'll be thrown away. Now get all this mess cleaned up and then you can both follow me. I'll show you where you'll be sleeping.'

Pearl hastily swept their shorn locks into a pile with the broom the woman threw at her then the two girls followed meekly. Pearl was shocked to see that her skin was now a soft pink, nothing like the grubby colour it had been, so she supposed that something good had come from the bath, although she wasn't looking forward to the experience being repeated. Her head felt lighter too now that her hair had been cut. Eliza's was already springing into soft little curls as it dried and Pearl hoped that hers would do the same. She had never realised what a pretty colour Eliza's hair was before and as she followed Mrs Bates through a labyrinth of twisting corridors, she tried to be optimistic. After all, once her mother realised that it was she who had done the cooking and cleaning, she was bound to have second thoughts about leaving them here. It had been Pearl who had looked after all the younger children too and she had an idea that her mother would soon tire of that. She was sure to have a change of heart and would come for them soon, wouldn't she?

Chapter Two

'This is the dormitory where you will be sleeping. That bed over there will be yours and this one here is for you,' Mrs Bates told the girls when they eventually stepped into a long, narrow room at the top of a steep staircase. There were rows of narrow, iron-framed beds down either side with a small locker between each one, and like the rest of the place it was bitterly cold. It was also very bleak-looking with nothing to brighten it whatsoever. Even so, Pearl noted that each bed had a pillow and a thin grey blanket folded on the end of it, and after sleeping on the rough hay mattresses they were used to, she was looking forward to sleeping in a proper bed. She also noticed that everywhere was spotlessly clean with not a speck of dirt to be seen.

'Please, missus . . . couldn't me an' Eliza sleep next to each other?' she plucked up the courage to ask.

Mrs Bates glared at her. 'No, you could not. We're not a fancy hotel, you know! We've had to cram two extra beds in here for you as it is, so just be grateful that we didn't turn you away and that you won't be sleeping in a shop doorway out in the snow tonight. Now come along, there's work to be done. You earn your keep in this place — we have no time for slackers!'

Still clinging to each other's hands, the girls followed her back down the stairs, worried they would never find their way back to the dormitory again. The place was absolutely enormous and they felt totally out of their depth. Pearl's limp was more pronounced than ever as she tried to keep up, and once on the ground floor they followed Mrs Bates through yet more corridors, until she paused to tell them, 'This is the laundry and where you'll both be working for now.'

As she opened the door, hot steam took their breath away and they had to squint to see through the fog. For a brief moment, Pearl was grateful for the warmth, but within seconds it was stifling. They found themselves in an enormous room. Huge, bubbling copper boilers stood along the length of one wall; against another were rows of deep stone sinks. Through a further door they could see sweating girls and women furiously feeding washing through massive mangles, and they both felt as if they had stepped into hell.

'I don't think Eliza will be strong enough to work in 'ere—'

Pearl's words were cut short when Mrs Bates grabbed her arm and yanked her deeper into the room. Instantly a woman in a uniform approached them and eyed the two newcomers through narrowed eyes.

'Yet more new inmates?'

Mrs Bates nodded. 'Aye, I'm afraid so. One a cripple an' the other a halfwit,' she said unkindly as she pushed Pearl none too gently towards her. 'Just make sure they earn their keep.' And with that she turned and strode away, leaving the girls at the mercy of the laundry mistress.

Mrs Flanders, as the woman introduced herself, was a plump woman with iron-grey hair, muscular arms and hands like hams.

'Right, you two, you can come over to these two empty sinks an' start scrubbin' the sheets before they go into the boiler,' she told them, leading them to the vacant sinks.

There were girls already scrubbing sheets at the sinks on either side of them, but they didn't even glance up as Mrs Flanders pointed to a pile on the floor and Pearl rightly guessed that they were too afraid to take their eyes off what they were doing. 'You open 'em out an' get any marks off 'em an' it'll be woe betide the pair o' you if you don't do it right,' she warned. 'There's plenty o' carbolic soap there an' a scrubbin' brush each. Just call me when you've done an' I'll come an' check 'em before they're put in the boilers.'

'Yes, missus,' Pearl said quietly, rolling her sleeves up. As the woman walked away, she snatched up a sheet and nodded at Eliza to do the same.

The first sheet she unfolded made her heave. It was covered in stale faeces and the smell was disgusting. The second she plunged the sheet into the sink the water turned a dirty brown, and glancing to the side she saw that the one Eliza had lifted wasn't much better; hers was covered in blood. Eliza stood vacantly staring at it until Pearl hissed, 'Get the brush and start scrubbing it before you get into bother.'

Minutes later Pearl had got the worst of the mess off the one she was doing, although it would definitely need to be boiled as there was no way she could get the stains out completely. But another quick glance at Eliza showed that her little sister wasn't doing so well. 'Come here an' wring this one out ready to go in the copper while I finish that one,' she whispered, but before Eliza could do as she was told Mrs Flanders bore down on them, her mouth set in a thin grim line.

'What's this then?' She grabbed a corner of the sheet Eliza was tackling and stared at it disdainfully. 'You've barely touched it, girl.' With that she brought her huge fist back and boxed Eliza's ear soundly, making the girl yelp with pain. 'You'll need to do better than this else it'll take you all day to do one sheet. Now put your back into it, girl, else you'll get another wallopin'!'

Pearl bit down hard on her lip as tears stung her eyes and she reached for another sheet; it broke her heart not being able to protect her sister, but she'd already got the measure of this place and it seemed the only way for either of them to get by was to keep quiet. Saying anything would surely only make things worse for both of them. Another girl gave her a sympathetic smile as she collected the sheet Pearl had just done in a large laundry basket and bore it off to the copper.

And so the rest of the morning went on. Within no time, both girls' clothes were clinging to them but Pearl was relieved to see that Eliza was at least coping. Sweat was running off them but they daren't slow down for fear Mrs Flanders would come back. At last a bell sounded and the other girls and women sighed with relief and stepped away from the sinks as they mopped their wet brows.

'Tidy yerselves up an' form an orderly line,' Mrs Flanders barked. Immediately the girls and women did as they were told. Pearl and Eliza tacked on to the back with no idea where they were going as another woman appeared to march them away. With Pearl struggling to keep up, they tramped through numerous corridors until they eventually found themselves in a cavernous room where rows of tables were laid out in straight long lines.

At one end of the room some women were standing behind a trestle ladling food into dishes and Pearl's mouth watered at the thought of finally being fed. She'd been up since dawn and hadn't eaten yet, and their hard work in the laundry had certainly built up an appetite. At least they weren't going to starve here, Pearl thought, her stomach grumbling, which was something, she supposed.

'This is the dinin' room,' the girl in front of her whispered and Pearl saw it was the girl who had been collecting the sheets in the laundry. 'I'm Susan, by the way.'

'I'm Pearl an' this 'ere is me sister, Eliza,' Pearl said in a hushed voice as the queue shuffled forwards.

'That'll be enough talkin' back there.' Mrs Bates was glaring at them and, too afraid to say anything else, they fell silent.

Once it was their turn, following the lead of the girls in front of them, Pearl collected a dish from the pile on the end of the table and gestured for Eliza to do the same. As they moved along the line the first woman unceremoniously dumped a spoonful of lumpy mashed potato on to it. The second woman threw on a single sausage and a third woman dolloped on a spoonful of overcooked cabbage. It could hardly be called appetising by any stretch of the imagination, but to Pearl and Eliza, who sometimes went without food for days at a time, it was a feast. They seated themselves next to the girl called Susan on one of the long benches and waited as the housemother, who was seated with the other staff at the centre of the table, stood up and said grace.

For the next few minutes nothing could be heard but the sound of cutlery scraping the dishes. Sliced loaves were laid out at intervals along the tables and both Pearl and Eliza had two slices each and a large glass of water, which they both glugged down. It tasted so much nicer than the water they got from the rusty outside tap at home.

'P'raps it won't be so bad 'ere after all,' Pearl whispered to Eliza, but she got no answer, Eliza was too busy eating.

Things got better still after lunch when Mrs Bates approached them to say, 'Go with Harper here.' That, Pearl realised, was Susan's surname. 'You will be allowed ten minutes fresh air out in the yard and then you will have classes for the next two hours before returning to work in the laundry.'

Pearl had always longed to be able to read and write, so after they had taken a short break in the freezing cold yard she was delighted to do as she was told and follow Susan and the other children to an enormous room where small desks and chairs were set in regimentally straight rows.

Behind a larger desk at the front of the room, a young woman was sitting writing. As the pupils trooped in, she raised her head to smile at them and Pearl knew instinctively that here was someone she was going to like.

'Good afternoon,' the woman said when they had taken a seat, and then for the sake of the new arrivals who had no idea who she was, she added, 'I am Miss Sweet and today we are going to focus on learning our alphabet.'

She stood and began to write letters on the large blackboard behind her. Pearl was beside herself with excitement; no one had ever taken the trouble to teach her anything before and she watched avidly, while Eliza sat daydreaming with a blank expression on her face.

'Now then, who can tell me what letter comes after C?'

A few hands went up and Pearl flushed with shame because she had no idea.

The time in the classroom seemed to pass in the blink of an eye and by the time Mrs Bates arrived to take them back to the laundry Pearl had written down the whole alphabet on the small slate in front of her.

'Very well done, Pearl,' Miss Sweet praised with an encouraging smile, sensing that here was a girl who was hungry to learn. Some of the lesson had been spent in the class reciting the alphabet and already Pearl could remember the letters right up to H, although Eliza was struggling and couldn't remember a single one in order. The letters she had copied were merely gobbledegook to her.

'She's so nice,' Pearl whispered to Susan as she followed her back to the laundry behind Mrs Bates.

Susan smiled, transforming her pinched little face. 'She's sweet be name an' sweet be nature,' she whispered back. 'Not like the rest o' the bleedin' staff 'ere, who'll give yer the strap for nuffin'.'

Susan was clearly a cockney through and through, and Pearl sensed that in her she would find a friend.

It was six o'clock in the evening before the girls were told they could stop work, and by then Pearl was aching in muscles she hadn't even known she had.

Eliza was sniffling. 'Me 'ands are all sore, Pearl,' she muttered miserably.

Her sister patted her encouragingly on the shoulder. 'It'll get easier as they harden up,' she promised. 'But don't get cryin' an' makin' a fuss now, else you'll get yourself into trouble wi' Mrs Bates. An' at least we 'ave some supper to look forward to.'

Eliza bravely blinked back her tears as she slid her small hand into Pearl's. She had never been strong and despite her brave words Pearl was worried about her. It was back-breaking work in the laundry. Even she had found it hard and she had no idea how Eliza would stand up to it.

Once back in the dining room, they were served stew and dumplings. Admittedly the dumplings were as hard as rock and the stew was thin and watery with just fragments of gristly meat and overcooked vegetables floating around in it, but Pearl and Eliza cleared their dishes in seconds. They were then given a dish of semolina pudding each and a glass of watery milk, and for the first time in days their stomachs were full.

'What happens after supper?' Pearl asked Susan.

Keeping a beady eye on Mrs Bates, who seemed to have eyes in the back of her head, Susan whispered back, 'We goes to the chapel fer prayers an' then we goes to bed.'

Pearl guessed that it couldn't even be seven o'clock at night but after the hard day they had had she didn't mind; in fact, she was longing to lie down and rest; her short leg was aching after being on it all day.

The chapel shocked her. It was quite beautiful with stained-glass windows that twinkled in the lights from the many candles that were placed at intervals about the room. A stern-faced nun, who reminded Pearl of a big black crow, led the prayers and when they were over they were all marched to the toilet block before being led back to their dormitories.

'Get yourselves changed now,' Mrs Bates told them. 'And don't let me hear any chattering. Lights out in ten minutes so be sure you are all in bed when I come back or it will be the worse for you.'

The girls instantly began to undress and struggle into the scratchy nightgowns they had been supplied with. It was bitterly cold in the dormitory and they leapt into their beds, pulling the thin grey blankets across them. Soon after Mrs Bates reappeared.

'Right, not a peep out of any of you till the morning or you know what will happen,' she warned. Then she picked up the one oil lamp in the room and left, leaving them in pitch-darkness.

Just as Pearl had feared, minutes later she heard the sound of Eliza softly crying. She was afraid of the dark and Pearl had always slept with her.

'P-Pearl . . . where are yer?' A little voice came from the darkness.

'It's all right, I'm here,' Pearl answered in a hushed voice. 'Try to get to sleep now, yer quite safe.'

'Shush, else you'll gerr us *all* in trouble,' another voice said irritably in the darkness, and for a while silence reigned.

Soon, soft snores were echoing around the room and Pearl realised that Eliza must have fallen asleep, but still she lay there wide awake; she ached in every limb and her hands were sore and throbbing. Yet, for all that, their first day there hadn't been all bad as far as she was concerned. For the first time in weeks she had come to bed without her stomach grumbling with hunger, she was lying on a real bed, with a real mattress – albeit thin and lumpy – and she had loved the time she had spent in the schoolroom.

She smiled to herself as she thought of Miss Sweet. She had soft blonde hair and the bluest eyes Pearl had ever seen, and her clothes, although prim, had been the sort that Pearl could only ever dream of wearing. She could still picture the blue of the material and the row of tiny buttons that ran from the waist to the neckline, ending in a neat lace collar, and she could hear the lovely swishing noise it made every time the kindly young woman moved. But then, she supposed, she shouldn't get too settled. As she had assured Eliza, their mother would be sure to come for them once she realised just how much Pearl had done for her and the younger children. On that thought, Pearl finally drifted off to sleep.

Chapter Three

The following morning the loud clanging of a bell brought Pearl springing awake. She sat up, completely disorientated by her unfamiliar surroundings. And then the aches in her muscles brought the memory of what had happened the day before rushing back. She glanced anxiously towards Eliza's bed, which was closer to the door. The other girls were already tumbling out of bed, but Pearl had no time to reach her sister, for just then the door opened and the light from the oil lamp Mrs Bates was carrying spilled into the room.

'All right then, you lot,' the woman barked. 'Let's be having you. Idle hands make work for the devil.'

Pearl climbed stiffly out of bed, every muscle protesting, and as she began to pull her clothes on, she was dismayed to see that Eliza was making no attempt to get up but was lying curled into a tight little ball, softly crying.

'Are you deaf, or what?' Mrs Bates said angrily as she advanced on Eliza and threw the thin blanket back. Her lips curled back from her face in disgust. 'Why, you filthy, disgusting little guttersnipe,' she snarled as she grabbed the child's arm and dragged her from the bed. 'Just look at the state of this bed! It's soaked through.'

'I-I'm sorry, missus,' Eliza whimpered, clearly terrified. 'I needed to wee but I didn't know where to go.'

Pearl made to go towards her as the woman shook her like a rat, making the poor child's teeth rattle, but Susan caught her arm.

'Don't . . . you'll only make fings worse,' she hissed and tears sprang to Pearl's eyes.

'Well *now* you'll find out what happens to *dirty* little creatures who dare to soil their beds,' Mrs Bates ranted, as she dragged Eliza towards the dormitory door. Once in the corridor she rammed the child roughly against the wall and warned, 'Stand there until I come back for you and don't even think of moving or you'll make things worse for yourself.'

Too terrified to do anything else, Eliza stood there trembling as the girls left the dormitory and filed silently past her, some of them sneaking her a sympathetic smile. Susan had to almost push Pearl past her and once in the toilet block where they were queuing to relieve themselves Pearl asked her anxiously, 'What will Mrs Bates do to her?'

Susan chewed on her lip for a moment as if she was reluctant to answer, but then realising that Pearl would soon find out anyway, she sighed. 'She'll be caned an' then made to stand there wi' the wet sheet over 'er 'ead fer the rest o' the day. She won't get no grub today eivver.'

'But that's cruel! She couldn't help it!' Two spots of angry colour flamed into Pearl's cheeks.

Susan shrugged as she nudged her towards an empty cubicle. None of them had doors and Pearl thought it was degrading to have to sit there with all and sundry being able to see what you were doing, but it didn't seem to bother the other girls. No doubt they were used to it.

Minutes later, the girls began to file down to the dining hall and Pearl fell into step beside Susan. The other girl was very slightly built, although her arms were muscled from the back-breaking work she did in the laundry. Her hair was chopped off to chin length, as was all the other girls', and it was a dull, mousy-brown colour. But her eyes were her saving grace, they were a lovely deep grey colour that reminded Pearl of pictures she had seen of the sea on a stormy day. And she was kind, which Pearl appreciated.

Once seated in the dining hall Mrs Bates said grace and then the girls tucked into dishes of unsweetened porridge washed down with tin mugs full of stewed tea. It was hardly tasty but it was filling and for Pearl, who was used to being hungry, that was enough.

'Do you think I could risk goin' back to the dormitory to check 'ow Eliza is?' she asked Susan miserably when they set off to begin work, but Susan shook her head vigorously.

'Only if yer wants to 'ave a taste o' what she's 'ad be now.' She gave Pearl a sympathetic smile and Pearl felt she had no choice but to follow her.

The day seemed to pass interminably slowly as Pearl fretted about Eliza. The only bright point in her day was when she had another lesson with Miss Sweet.

'That's very good, Pearl,' the young woman praised her as Pearl laboriously managed to write down the first five letters of the alphabet on her slate. 'We'll have you reading and writing in no time at this rate. But tell me, where is Eliza today?'

Tears welled in Pearl's eyes. 'Please, miss, she were scared, wi' bein' in a strange bed in a strange place an' she wet the bed so Mrs Bates 'as punished 'er.'

'I see.' Just for a moment, Pearl thought she glimpsed a flicker of anger in the teacher's eyes, but then she forced a smile back to her face and made her way back to her desk without comment.

It was not her place to comment on the way the children in the workhouse were chastised, Marianne Sweet thought, but she certainly didn't agree with it. She was from a very well-to-do family and had no need to work but, as she had told her father at breakfast only that morning, she enjoyed the few hours she spent teaching the children each day and it gave her a sense of worth. Her father had sniffed disdainfully, but she knew deep down that he was proud of her. The same couldn't be said for her mother, who was a terrible snob and believed that women need only be trained in how to make good wives and mothers. She had been parading an endless stream of suitors in front of Marianne for the last couple of years but, as yet, not one of them had appealed to her, and she had remained obstinately single.

Now she watched Pearl lean over her slate again. The girl was concentrating so hard on what she was doing that her tongue was in her cheek and she seemed oblivious to everything that was going on around her. She was like a little sponge, soaking up every bit of knowledge she could – unlike some of the other girls who made it clear they were only there because they had no choice. She was a pretty girl too, Marianne thought, or at least she would be if dressed in the right clothes and taken care of. Her hair, although it had been hacked off, had sprung into a halo of soft curls that framed her face and her eyes were a lovely shade of green that reminded her of spring grass. With a little shake of her head the young woman forced herself to concentrate on the rest of the class. She really shouldn't have favourites but sometimes it was hard not to.

For Pearl, the end of the lesson came all too soon and once the class was over the girls began to file back out of the room.

'Pearl, a moment please.'

Pearl hurried to the desk and looked at Miss Sweet worriedly.

'It's all right, dear, you haven't done anything wrong.' She smiled kindly. She was dressed in a pale-green gown today and Pearl was sure she was the prettiest woman she had ever seen.

'I couldn't help but notice that your hands are very sore.' Miss Sweet reached out and took Pearl's roughened hands in her own for a second. They were red raw and covered in weeping blisters from the long hours they had been submerged in scalding water. Dropping them hastily she told her, 'I shall bring you some lotion in tomorrow that will soothe them but . . . could we keep it between ourselves?'

'Oh yes, miss, thank yer, miss.' Feeling as if she was floating on a cloud, Pearl turned and ran out to catch up with the rest of the girls, but Miss Sweet's kindness stayed with her for the rest of the day and was a distraction from her worries about Eliza.

Until they returned to their room that evening, that was, when she found Eliza curled into a foetal position beneath the thin grey blanket on her bed. The rest of the girls had gone to the toilet block, but Pearl had risked coming back to the dormitory to check on her sister and bring her the slice of dry grey bread she had managed to sneak out of the dining hall for her. Now she was even more glad that she had.

The room was in darkness but even in the gloom she could clearly see how ghastly pale Eliza was.

'Eliza . . . are you all right?' Pearl tentatively reached out to touch her sister's face but the girl flinched away from her. 'Eliza, *please* speak to me?'

Eliza continued to stare blankly at the wall so Pearl gently peeled the blanket back, and the sight that met her eyes when she did made her flinch. From halfway down Eliza's back to just above her knees was a criss-cross of angry-looking weals. In places the cruel split cane that Mrs Bates had used had broken the skin and she was covered in congealed blood.

'Oh, *Eliza.*' Pearl was so upset and horrified that she didn't know what to say. As it was, she had no chance to anyway, for at that moment the door opened and Mrs Bates stood there, her face a mask of fury.

'Why aren't you in the toilet block with the rest of the girls?' she barked.

Pearl's eyes flashed as she stared defiantly back at the woman. She couldn't keep quiet this time; she had to say something. 'I wanted to see how my sister was,' she snapped back. 'And it's a good job I did. Look at the state of her – she needs a doctor.'

Mrs Bates was so angry that her face flushed a dull, brick red and she looked as if she was about to burst a blood vessel. 'How *dare* you answer me back like that, you little *hussy*!'

Stepping into the room she put the oil lamp she was carrying down on the nearest bedside locker and advanced on Pearl with her hand raised. Once close enough, she smacked Pearl about the ear so hard that Pearl's head bounced on her shoulders and she heard bells ring, but she wouldn't give the woman the satisfaction of letting her see her cry.

'Me sister *needs* a doctor,' she repeated doggedly as the woman reached out and grasped her arm in a cruel grip.

'It'll be *you* as needs a doctor when I've finished with you.' Mrs Bates yanked her back out on to the landing just as the first of the girls appeared on their way back from the toilet block. Pearl had a brief glimpse of Susan's frightened face, but then Mrs Bates had dragged her to the top of the stairs and was dragging her down them. With her weaker leg, Pearl struggled to keep up and at one point she slipped, but the woman continued on with Pearl's knees scraping painfully on the hard wooden steps. By the time they reached the bottom, blood was dripping from the scrapes and cuts but Pearl sensed that there was much worse to come. When they reached Mrs Bates's office, she was proved right. The woman threw her inside, slammed the door and, as Pearl lay in a heap on the floor, went to fetch a lethal-looking cane from her desk.

'Seems to me that both *you* and your sister need to learn a little humility and obedience,' she snarled, as she crossed back to Pearl and stood over her like an avenging angel.

The cane rose and whistled through the air and seconds later Pearl winced as it smacked across her bare legs. The pain was excruciating but still she didn't cry out, although she couldn't stop the tears from flowing. All she could think of was how terrified Eliza must have been when Mrs Bates was caning her, and her hatred of the woman began to grow from that moment. Again and again, the cane rose and fell until Pearl was sure she was going to faint from the pain. But then, mercifully, the blows stopped and, peering up at Mrs Bates through swollen eyes, she saw her standing breathless with a look of satisfaction on her face.

'You won't be so quick to cheek me in future, will you, girl?' There was an evil glint in her eye as she nudged Pearl with the toe of her boot. 'Now, get back to your dormitory and no loitering on the way else you'll feel more of the same. I don't want hear another peep out of you or your sister.'

Somehow Pearl managed to drag herself to her feet and stagger out into the hallway, leaving drops of blood on the floor in her wake. Then one by one she tackled the stairs, feeling as if she were climbing a mountain. After what felt like a lifetime, she made it back to the dormitory, and as she headed for her bed Susan's voice came to her through the darkness.

'Are yer all right, Pearl?'

'Y-yes. Go to sleep else you'll get in bother too,' she answered, managing to keep her voice level, despite being on the brink of yet more tears. Somehow, she managed to climb into the bed, but she was in so much pain that she couldn't bear the weight of even the thin blanket on her wounds so she lay on the top of it, shivering.

'*Oh, Ma, Ma where are you?*' she whimpered into the darkness, but the only answer was the sound of the other girls snores, while through the window she could see the snow softly falling. She had never felt so alone.

Chapter Four

'So where are Pearl and Eliza today, Freda?' Miss Sweet asked a girl sitting at a desk in the front of the classroom the next afternoon. Freda was well known for being a bully and a troublemaker and Miss Sweet wasn't fond of her at all. She was tall for her age with a spotty complexion and teeth that protruded over her bottom lip.

Freda glanced up at her and informed her with a hint of glee, 'Mrs Flanders sent 'em both, that's Pearl an' Eliza, to the infirmary when they got into the laundry this mornin', miss.'

'Oh? And why was that?'

'They both got a canin' off Mrs Bates,' Freda informed her. 'Eliza fer wettin' the bed an' Pearl fer stickin' up fer her. But Eliza couldn't walk very well this mornin' an' Pearl were burnin' up wi' fever so they both got a day off work.'

'I should think so, if they are as bad as you say they are,' Miss Sweet retorted, as her dislike for Freda grew. She did try very hard not to have favourites; all of the children in there were to be pitied, but Freda did nothing to endear herself. 'Thank you, Freda,' she said primly, silently cursing Mrs Bates. In the time she had been working there Mrs Bates had inflicted the same punishment on a number of children and she didn't agree with it at all. Of course, she realised that in such an establishment there had to be a code of discipline, but surely not to the extent that Mrs Bates doled it out?

As soon as the afternoon classes were over, Miss Sweet tidied her desk and collected her cloak and bonnet before setting off purposefully for the infirmary. Thankfully, she had met Sister May, who ran it, a number of times. Unlike Mrs Bates, she seemed to genuinely care for the people who were admitted so Marianne had no doubt she wouldn't object to her visiting.

'I've come to see how the Parker girls are,' Miss Sweet informed her when Sister May opened the door of the infirmary. She was tiny with bright eyes and a kind face and reminded Marianne of a little bird hopping about the place. But today she shook her head gravely, as she ushered her inside.

'Neither of them are at all well,' she answered truthfully. 'Eliza is completely traumatised. It's as if she's locked herself away in a world of her own, and Pearl . . . well . . .' She tutted. 'The poor child has a raging fever.'

'But she will be all right?'

The sister shook her head. 'It's in God's hands now. We're doing all we can. She had a severe thrashing but with this fever on top it could go either way . . .'

Miss Sweet frowned. 'May I see them?'

'Of course.' The sister led her to the ward where the children were lying in beds next to each other. 'But I doubt either of them will know you're here,' she warned.

At the sight of them Miss Sweet's temper rose, so much that she thought she was going to choke. 'This is quite *appalling.* Mrs Bates should be reported to the guardians,' she said, as tears pricked at her eyes.

The sister patted her arm. 'I quite agree, but both you and I know that nothing would come of it even if anyone dared to report it. Mrs Bates would just say that the children became aggressive with her while she was trying to reprimand them and she was simply defending herself. A nurse who used to work here did just that once and she was gone in no time. The guardians don't know half of what goes on here, that's the trouble.'

'Then perhaps it's time I spoke up and told them,' Miss Sweet replied, her eyes never leaving Pearl's flushed face.

'Hmm, and they would just find some excuse to finish you too, and then where would the children be? They rely on you to show them a little kindness during the time they spend with you; you're the only bright spot in their day unless they end up in here,' the sister pointed out.

Miss Sweet's shoulders sagged in defeat. She knew the sister was speaking the truth, and as she slowly left the ward, she had never felt so useless in her life.

Luckily Pearl's fever soon broke and she started to recover, but the sister allowed them both to stay in the infirmary for a few days. During that time, Pearl learned from the kindly sister just how huge the workhouse was. As well as the dormitory where she and Eliza slept, there was an isolation hospital, a ward where the lunatics were kept, the infirmary, the Gothic-style chapel, the dining hall, a nursery for the babies and numerous other dormitories that housed the boys and the older men and women who were separated the instant they entered the place. It seemed so sad to Pearl that families should be separated just because they had fallen on hard times, but that was the way the place was operated. She had also discovered that while the women earned their keep doing the laundry or cooking and cleaning, the men were put to work breaking rocks or picking oakum, which involved picking fibres from old hemp ropes. The resulting material was then sold to shipbuilders or the navy who would mix it with tar and use it to line ships.

Pearl and Eliza were finally released from the infirmary on Saturday evening.

'Well at least we don't 'ave to go to work tomorrer,' Susan said chirpily when she met Pearl leading Eliza back to the dormitory on Saturday evening after they were released. 'An' we get a crackin' nice dinner on Sunday an' all. The guardians come sometimes an' the housemuvver allus makes sure to put on a good show fer 'em. We 'as to go to chapel in the mornin' first, though, but after dinner we can do what we like wivvin reason. Some o' the kids get visitors on a Sunday. Do yer fink your ma will come?'

Pearl was shocked by how accepting her friend was of the place. She was sure that she would never be happy here no matter how long she had to stay.

'I don't know,' Pearl answered truthfully. She had prayed for her to come every single day while she lay in the infirmary but as yet there'd been no sign of her. 'But what about yours, will she come?' She realised that she didn't even know if Susan's mother was still alive and hoped she hadn't put her foot in it.

Susan smiled. 'Ner, she won't be able to, she's too ill. That's why I'm in this place; she'd never 'ave let me go uvverwise. She's really beautiful, yer see. We lived in a lovely 'ouse in Chelsea wi' servants an' everyfin' but then me dad died an' we 'ad to move to a smaller place before she took bad. But just as soon as she's better she'll come; I know it.'

'Ooh, your tongue should fester, Susan Harper,' Freda Swift mocked.

Susan's cheeks flamed but before she could say any more Mrs Bates appeared and all the girls fell silent.

'So what's this?' The stern-faced woman glared at them, putting the fear of God into each of them. 'Why aren't you all getting ready for bed? Come along now, unless you want to feel my cane on your backsides.' As her eyes momentarily rested on Pearl and Eliza, Pearl could have sworn she saw her smirk, but she wouldn't give her an excuse to punish her again so she merely looked away.

Ten minutes later, by which time the children were all in bed, the woman returned, collected the oil lamp and left the room without another word.

The instant she had gone, Susan leaned up on her elbow and grinned at Pearl. She had missed her and was pleased to have her back. Pearl was the only friend she had made since entering the wretched place. 'We can relax a bit now,' she told her. 'Mrs Bates will go off duty till morning an' Miss Hayes who takes her place ain't nowhere near as bad. She don't mind the girls havin' a little natter wivvin reason. So tell me, are you an' Eliza better now? We 'eard as you were really poorly.'

'We're better than we were,' Pearl said. 'Though it'll take a while for the wounds from the cane to 'eal. She laid into us good an' proper.'

'Hm!' Susan screwed her nose up. 'She's bleedin' wicked, that one is. I 'eard as 'ow 'er husband left her fer a younger woman so she 'ad to come an' work 'ere to keep 'erself. Yer couldn't blame 'im fer leavin' that old bag, could yer?'

Pearl couldn't help but grin into the darkness; Susan was a character and she liked her. All around them the girls were whispering and giggling but eventually the room grew quiet and they slept.

The next morning being the Sabbath, they were allowed an extra half-hour in bed, and after washing and dressing they made their way to the dining room, where they were served with the usual lumpy, bland porridge for breakfast – but at least if what Susan had told them was true, they had a nice dinner to look forward to.

After breakfast, they attended a service in the chapel and were then allowed into an enormous room where they mixed with the boys and the families that lived there. It was the only day the families could be together and it broke Pearl's heart to see them clustered close, chattering away to each other like a little flock of starlings and making the most of every moment. It brought home to her how much she was missing her brothers and sisters and a lump formed in her throat as she pictured them in her mind.

At lunchtime, they trooped back into the dining hall and just as Susan had said, some of the guardians of the workhouse were seated at the top table with the staff. Mrs Bates was simpering as she pandered to them and Pearl felt resentful, wondering what the guardians would say if they could see the state of her and Eliza's backs. Eliza was worrying her, for since the day Mrs Bates had caned her she had barely said a word. She just went about with her head down, doing what she was told with a blank expression, as if all the sparkle had gone out of her.

'Looks like we're gonna 'ave a lovely dinner today,' Pearl whispered encouragingly to her sister as they waited in the queue to be served. Some of the women who worked in the kitchen were already placing steaming trays and covered dishes full of food on the table in front of the staff and the guardians, and the delicious smell issuing from them was making Pearl's stomach rumble in anticipation. They were served with creamy mashed potatoes, slices of thick juicy pork, and cabbage and carrots, which for once hadn't been cooked to a pulp. Everyone carried their meals back to the tables, careful not to spill a drop, and once grace had been said they tucked in. There was apple pie to follow and Pearl thought she had never tasted anything so lovely in her life, but she noticed with concern that Eliza merely picked at hers.

'Wasn't that lovely?' she said when the meal was over and they were allowed back into the visiting room. Some of the boys and families were already there, some in little groups, others sitting alone staring expectantly at the door.

'Visitin' is allowed this afternoon,' Susan reminded them, and after finding a vacant table Pearl, too, sat staring at the door as if thoughts of her mother would somehow conjure her up. On the stroke of three the visitors began to trickle in, their eyes searching the room until they rested on the ones they had come to see.

'You expectin' someone?' Susan asked curiously.

'Er, not really.' Pearl didn't dare say that she was hoping their mother would come for them for fear of upsetting Eliza if she didn't show up, but deep down she was sure that she *would* come. She'd had a few days to realise just how much Pearl had done about the home now, so surely she would be ready to take them back?

But the minutes ticked away and still there was no sign of her.

'What time does visitin' finish?' she asked Susan after a while.

'Five o'clock, I reckon, an' then we 'ave to go fer another service in the chapel afore supper,' Susan informed her, although seeing as Pearl couldn't tell the time it didn't help her much.

Many of the children who never had visitors had congregated into little groups, casting envious glances towards the luckier ones who did, and suddenly Pearl wondered why Susan's mother hadn't come. Surely, if she was as lovely as Susan professed, she would at least visit her.

'Are you expectin' anyone?' she asked innocently.

Susan flushed. 'Ner, like I told yer, me ma's too ill to come, else she'd be 'ere like a shot.'

Freda, who was sitting on the next table, overheard what she had said and smirked, making Susan flush an even darker shade of red.

'Come on, let's go an' sit at that table over by the winder.' She walked off quickly and Pearl followed her with Eliza trailing behind. Now that Pearl came to think of it, Susan never seemed too happy when Freda was present, but she only gave it a passing thought. She was too intent on watching the street outside for a glimpse of her mother.

By four o'clock it was pitch-dark and the girls watched the lamplighter as he made his way along the busy street. The street lights cast pools of yellow on to the snow beneath them and it sparkled like shattered diamonds, but Pearl was too miserable to notice how pretty it looked, as hopes of her mother coming for them faded with each minute that passed.

Chapter Five

Bright and early the next morning found them back at work in the laundry. Neither Pearl nor Eliza's backs had healed, and some of the wounds opened up again and started to bleed as they heaved the heavy wet washing about. Eliza in particular was struggling to keep up with the workload, and more than once Pearl saw Mrs Flanders clip her sharply about the ear. Strangely, Eliza made no complaint. It was as if she had lost all feeling, and because Pearl was unable to help her, she had never felt more useless in her life.

By lunchtime, their hands were raw and weeping again and Susan stared at them sympathetically as they sat down to eat. 'Me ma used to say that your own piss hardened 'em up,' she whispered to Pearl. 'But seein' as we ain't allowed piss pots under the beds, that's no use.'

The salve that Miss Sweet had given to Pearl while she was in the infirmary was almost gone now as she'd been sharing it with her sister, so Pearl knew they would just have to put up with it.

'Try an' eat somethin',' she hissed to Eliza, who sat beside her staring at the congealing food on her plate, but it was as if the child hadn't even heard her and Pearl's spirits sank even lower. She tried to cheer herself up, thinking that they had their lessons to look forward to at least. But the next blow came when they arrived at the schoolroom shortly after lunch to find Mrs Bates standing next to Miss Sweet waiting for them.

'We've just realised that seeing as you're twelve, you don't need lessons anymore, and shouldn't have been allowed any in the first place,' Mrs Bates informed Pearl with a malicious grin. Miss Sweet had told her how well Pearl was doing and how much she enjoyed learning. 'So you can go back to the laundry and get on with work.'

Miss Sweet was wringing her hands together and Pearl could see that she wasn't happy with the decision, but on this she had no say. Rules were rules and unfortunately children in the workhouse were only educated until they reached their twelfth birthday. It was a shame, though, the kindly teacher thought, because Pearl obviously loved learning.

Without a word Pearl turned and left the classroom, her shoulders slumped, and within minutes her hands were once again immersed in hot, soapy water as she scrubbed at the seemingly unending pile of dirty sheets.

Eliza returned two hours later, and she too resumed her work without even glancing in Pearl's direction. Pearl realised that it would have been no hardship at all had it been Eliza who had been forced to miss the lessons. She had never shown the slightest interest in anything Miss Sweet had tried to teach them, but because she was only eleven she was still allowed to attend class. Pearl worried about Eliza, floating around like a spirit. Still, she decided, all she could do was be there to keep an eye out for her, and that was exactly what she intended to do.

Slowly the days slipped into one another and the girls resigned themselves to the monotonous routine. Nothing ever seemed to change, and each day was the same as the last. There had still been no sign of their mother and each night as Pearl lay in bed she fretted about her siblings back at home. Would their ma be feeding them? Would their dad still be rolling in drunk and knocking them about? She had no way of knowing, although she doubted things would have changed, so each night she fell asleep with her cheeks damp with tears.

On Christmas Eve, the mood in the workhouse lifted. Even Mrs Bates managed a smile or two and the girls were happy because they had been told that they would be allowed to finish work two hours early that day.

'Mrs Bates says we can go into the day room an' do as we please till supper,' Susan hissed to Pearl as they stood side by side at the deep stone sinks in the laundry. 'An' after supper we 'ave some carol singers comin' in to sing to us an' we'll all get a 'ot mince pie.'

Pearl turned her head to Eliza who was working on the other side of her. 'Did you hear that?' She smiled at her sister. 'And no work at all tomorrow. That's good, ain't it?'

But it was as if Eliza had gone deaf, for she didn't even acknowledge that she had heard her sister speak.

At last Mrs Flanders clapped her hands and the girls and women instantly stopped what they were doing. 'Right, that's it for today,' the woman told them. 'Work will resume at the normal time on Monday morning and make sure you're not late!'

Because Christmas Day fell on a Friday that year it meant that they now had three whole days off to look forward to.

'I wish Christmas Day could be on a Friday every year,' Susan said as they made their way in an orderly line to the day room. 'We allus get Boxin' Day off an' all, an' 'cause we don't work Sundays anyway it'll be almost like a little holiday.'

They were pleased to see that a fire had been lit in the day room and what with that and the vases of holly that someone had placed on the mantelpiece, it looked quite festive.

'This is a bit of aw'ight, ain't it?' Susan said appreciatively as she held her chapped hands out to the welcoming flames. 'An' just look frough the winder, the snow's comin' down fick and fast out there.'

'Yes, it is.'

Leaving the comfort of the fire, Pearl stepped over to the window and stared through the glass longingly. The lamplighter was ambling along lighting the gas lamps and the pavements were teeming with people intent on doing their last-minute Christmas shopping. One lady staggered past, carrying an unplucked turkey that was almost as big as she was, and once again Pearl wondered what her family would be doing. Had she been at home she would have been at the market now, waiting for them to close the stalls so she could get any bargains that were going.

It was then that a light tap on her shoulder made her whirl about and her mouth gaped as she looked up into the lovely face of Miss Sweet.

'Hello, Pearl. I stayed behind today to prepare the lessons for the children for after the holidays,' the young woman told her. 'But before I left, I just wanted to give you these.'

She pressed a slate, some lengths of chalk and a small book into Pearl's hands and told her, 'On top of the slate I've written your name, look. I want you to practise writing it yourself, and in the book you will find lots of small words that you can copy and learn. Just remember to pronounce the letters of the alphabet the way I taught you and you'll be reading and writing in no time.'

'B-but, miss . . . Mrs Bates said I weren't to have no more lessons 'cause I'm too old,' Pearl pointed out, with a look of consternation on her face.

Miss Sweet's lovely smile seemed to light up the room as she gave a small tinkling laugh. 'You're quite right, Pearl, she did. But there's nothing to stop you practising on a Sunday afternoon or in your spare time, is there?'

Now it was Pearl's turn to smile and it lit up her beautiful face. These were the most wonderful gifts she had ever received and she didn't quite know how to express her gratitude. 'Th-thank you,' she managed to mutter eventually past the huge lump that had formed in her throat.

'You're more than welcome.' Miss Sweet began to pull some soft-beige hide gloves over her slim fingers. 'But now I really must be going. My parents are holding a party this evening and I won't want to be late for that, will I? Merry Christmas, Pearl. Goodbye for now.'

Pearl stood and watched her until the door closed behind her and then the happy mood was shattered when Freda, who was sitting close to the fire, said spitefully, '*Ooh*, proper little teacher's pet, ain't yer!'

Holding back the sharp retort that had sprung to her lips, Pearl instead smiled sweetly, and turning away retreated to an empty table in the corner of the room to begin her first lesson.

'That were nice o' Miss Sweet to give yer them things, weren't it?' Susan commented as they hurried back from the freezing toilet block to their cold bedroom later that evening. They had loved listening to the carol singers and had been allowed to stay up a little later, and now they had Christmas Day to look forward to.

'Yes, it was.' Pearl had tucked them safely away beneath her few possessions in her locker earlier that evening. 'And I'll tell you somethin', I shall be writin' me name in no time, you just watch me.'

'I don't doubt it.' Susan chuckled, but was stopped from saying any more when Mrs Bates bellowed from behind them, 'That's enough of that chattering. Hurry along, girls!'

The two girls grinned at each other but did as they were told.

They woke the following morning to an eerie grey dawn to find the ice on the inside of their windows had formed a lace-like pattern. There was also a delicious smell wafting up from downstairs.

'That smells like sausage and bacon,' Susan remarked, sniffing the air like a bloodhound.

'It does,' Pearl agreed.

Today they could hardly wait to get down to the dining room where crisp, white cloths had been laid on the tables, and to go with the sausages and bacon were lovely fried eggs with golden-yellow yolks.

'Cor, just imagine havin' nosh like this every single day.' Susan sighed as she sliced into a fat, juicy sausage. Instead of the weak tea they were usually given, today there were glasses of frothy milk and Susan gulped hers down in seconds.

Then, when the meal was over, Mrs Bates stood up to announce, 'Make your way to the chapel for the Christmas morning service, and when it is over form an orderly queue in the main foyer where our dear guardians will give you each a gift.' She flashed a simpering smile at the well-dressed gentleman seated beside her as the girls piled out of the room.

'Pity one o' the guardians can't be 'ere all the time,' Susan whispered as they entered the chapel, and Pearl nodded in agreement.

The service that day was very enjoyable and they all sang hymns and admired the little nativity scene that stood by the altar. When it was time for them to line up for their presents Susan was almost hopping with excitement. The boys had been allowed to join them today and one mischievous-looking chap with lovely dark hair gave Pearl a cheeky wink when she caught his eye and she blushed furiously. She had seen him once or twice before on Sunday in the day room and had noticed him because, like herself and Eliza, he never had any visitors.

But then they were moving along the queue, and once they reached Mrs Bates and the gentleman guardian who had shared breakfast with them, he smiled at her and Eliza kindly.

'Good morning, my dears. Sisters, are you?' he asked, noting their matching pale-blonde hair.

'Yes, sir.' Pearl bobbed her knee respectfully as she had been told to do, while Eliza clung on to her hand.

'Then may I wish you both a very happy Christmas!' He handed them a small bag each, and seconds later they were jostled along as they made for the day room where they had been told they could relax until lunchtime.

'I wonder what it is?' Susan was feeling the bag as they headed for a window seat and the second she sat down she tore her bag open to reveal a short length of red ribbon and an orange. 'Cor, look at that!' She ran the ribbon through her fingers with a look of wonder on her face, before telling Pearl, 'Well go on an' open yours then, it ain't gonna bite yer.'

Smiling, Pearl did as she was told, to find a length of pale-blue ribbon and an apple in hers. In Eliza's was a ribbon in a deeper blue and a pear.

'Well, I don't know about youse but I'm eatin' mine now afore it gets nicked,' Susan said, peeling the skin from her orange.

As she bit into it she sighed with a look of pure pleasure on her face. She couldn't even remember the last time she'd had a piece of fruit and intended to savour every single mouthful. Pearl and Eliza did the same and soon even Eliza was smiling.

But even the rare treats couldn't quite wipe away the disappointment as Pearl's glance kept straying to the window.

She had been so convinced that her mother would come on this very special day but once again she had let her down and now, for the first time, she was forced to wonder if she ever *would* come. If she didn't, Pearl's fate would be the same as the three girls who had left the workhouse the week before. They were to begin lives in service in places that the workhouse had found for them, as they did for all the young people when they reached the age of fourteen. Until then she would be forced to continue slaving in the laundry.

It was a daunting thought, and suddenly some of the pleasure went from the day and a wave of homesickness washed through her. She might not have had the best of homes, but it had been the only one she had ever known and she was still struggling to come to terms with the fact that her mother had valued her and Eliza so little that she had abandoned them here.

Chapter Six

'So, expectin' visitors today, are you?'

Pearl had become so lost in her gloomy thoughts that she started when she realised that someone was addressing her, and she glanced up to find the dark-haired boy she had noticed earlier staring down at her.

'Oh, er, no . . . I don't think so,' she replied, all of a fluster. 'I was hopin' so, but now . . .' When her voice trailed away, the boy sat down next to her. Susan and Eliza were listening to a girl chattering away on the next table and hadn't even noticed that he had joined them.

'I ain't got nobody comin' either,' he said, stretching his legs out in front of him. 'It's just a shame as every day ain't like today in 'ere, ain't it. Oh, an' I'm Nick by the way. Nick Willis. What's your name?'

'I'm Pearl an' that girl there is me sister, Eliza,' Pearl told him awkwardly.

'Mm, thought as much.' He grinned, revealing a set of straight, white teeth. 'Yer look alike, did yer know that?'

Nick was at that curious age when he appeared to be neither boy nor man. He was tall and scrawny and his arms and legs appeared to be too long for his body. His hair was a lovely dark brown and reminded Pearl of the colour of nutmeg, but it was his eyes that caught her attention. They were a rich tawny colour that made her think of warm treacle, and he had a kind smile.

Pearl smiled back at him, starting to relax a little. She wasn't used to talking to boys other than her brothers but Nick seemed nice enough and seeing as he was on his own, she didn't really mind him joining them. No one should be on their own on Christmas Day, after all.

'So have yer been here long?' she asked timidly.

He shrugged. 'A good few years now. Me dad cleared off when I was a babby an' then me ma died so I ended up 'ere, but it ain't so bad if yer keep yer 'ead down an' do as yer told. I shall be out o' here anyway, when I's fourteen. I work in the gardens out back an' I'm hopin' they find a place fer me on a farm out o' the city. I'd like that. What about you? You ain't been 'ere long, 'ave you?'

'No.' Pearl shook her head. 'Just a short while.'

He studied her intently for a moment before asking, 'So why are you 'ere then? Parents die, did they? Or were yer livin' on the streets?'

Pearl felt her cheeks begin to glow, but luckily she was saved from having to answer when Susan spotted him and grinned.

'All right then are yer, Nick?' She had clearly met him before.

'Yeah, I'm fine, Susan.' Then by way of explanation he told Pearl, 'Me an' Susan used to live close to each other before we come in 'ere.'

'Oh!' Pearl was mildly surprised. Susan had given her the impression that she came from a very well-off area, but she didn't have time to ask questions because Mrs Bates appeared in the doorway then with yet another group of carol singers who had come to entertain them until lunchtime, and soon those that knew them were singing along to well-loved carols. Even Eliza seemed to be coming out of her shell a little and Pearl was thrilled to see her little sister looking more like her old self.

The rest of the day passed in a pleasant blur, and when they tucked into bed that evening their bellies were comfortably full and they were all in a good mood.

'Cor that turkey we 'ad at dinner time were luvly, weren't it?' Susan gave a contented sigh. 'If only we didn't 'ave to work in that bleedin' laundry it wouldn't be so bad livin' 'ere.'

Murmurs of agreement rippled through the other girls until Freda piped up, 'Ooh! 'Ark at *Lady* Susan. She thinks she should live in a posh 'otel.'

'Shut up, yer spiteful bitch!' Susan retaliated, her good mood gone. 'Trust you to go an' try an' spoil everyfin'!'

'What's all this noise in here?' Light spilled into the room as Mrs Bates appeared in the doorway with an oil lamp in her hand. 'Settle down now, girls. Christmas Day or not, it's past lights out, so I don't want to hear another peep out of you.'

'Yes, Mrs Bates,' the girls chorused, and as the door closed behind her they were left in darkness once more.

'She soon got back to 'er old self once the guardians were gone, didn't she?' Susan hissed but then silence fell. Soon there was nothing but the sounds of snores to be heard.

One cold, foggy Sunday afternoon early in January, as they all sat in the day room, Nick came to join them. He often sat with them now but today he seemed excited about something and they soon discovered what it was.

'Mr Fellows, our housemaster, came to see us yesterday,' he confided. 'An' he told me an' some o' the other lads that it looks like they're goin' to be shippin' another lot o' young 'uns abroad in the spring.'

Pearl instantly thought back to what her mother had told her about the possibility of having a new life in the sunshine, and her ears pricked up.

'So – what's it all about then?'

'Well, apparently this woman called Annie MacPherson started this scheme goin'. It's mainly kids from the Dr Barnardo's homes that get chosen to go but sometimes if there's room left on the ships they'll take a few from other orphanages an' the work'ouse. My mate got chosen last year an' I were hoping to go an' all but I never got chosen.'

'So where exactly do they go?' Pearl asked with interest.

Nick shrugged. 'All over the place, from what I've heard of it. Some go to Australia, some to New Zealand an' some to Canada. They go to live wi' the settlers there who take 'em on as workers.'

'Sod that!' Susan piped up. 'If that's the case we'd be as bad burned as scolded. It just means yer swappin' one place o' work fer another, surely?'

'Ah, but the difference is yer livin' in sunnier places an' I bet we'd get more freedom than we'd get here,' Nick answered. 'Anyway, you lot will probably be told about it soon an' all. Last year they took four girls an' four boys from here, all about round our age, so there's a chance fer all of us.'

'Well, I wouldn't go if they picked me an' they didn't pick Eliza too,' Pearl said heatedly as she glanced at her little sister.

Nick chuckled. 'Well, we'll just have to wait an' see, won't we?'

They went on to chat of other things and the subject was dropped.

Two weeks later, the girls were woken one morning to be told by Mrs Bates, 'We have six children in the sick bay with measles. If any of you feel unwell you are to tell me or a member of staff immediately. We don't want this to turn into an epidemic. It's really most inconvenient!'

'Silly cow,' Susan mumbled when she left the room leaving them to get dressed. 'As if *anybody* would choose to be bad, especially wi' measles. It can be a killer, can't it?'

'Yes, it can.' Pearl nodded as she pulled the drab brown dress over her head. She could remember all too clearly how the disease had killed a whole family of children in the terrace of houses where she had lived with her parents.

Later in the morning when they were hard at work in the laundry, she noticed that Eliza looked flushed. Initially she wasn't too worried; it was no wonder, really, when they were labouring over sinks full of steaming water. Even so, she kept a wary eye on her and when they finally broke for lunch, she knew that something wasn't right. Eliza's eyes looked unusually bright and she seemed to be even slower than she usually was.

'Do you feel all right?' she asked with concern as they made their way to the dining room.

Eliza shrugged. 'Just a bit tired, that's all.'

'Hm!' Pearl wasn't convinced so she watched her carefully for the rest of the day and was glad when they could retire to bed. Perhaps Eliza was just a bit under the weather and a good night's sleep would cure her.

But the next morning her worst fears were realised when she glanced towards her sister's bed to see an ugly red rash across her face. Still in her nightdress, she flew out on to the landing and shouted in a panic, 'Mrs Bates, come quick. I think our Eliza's got the measles.'

'Oh, not *another* one,' the woman groaned as she appeared from a small office at the end of the landing. Already the infirmary was full and during the night the first of the patients had succumbed to the illness and passed away. 'Right, let's get her out of there,' she told Pearl, with no hint of sympathy. 'The younger ones are coming down with it left, right and centre!' She allowed Pearl to bring Eliza out on to the landing, but then told her harshly to go back and get changed and carry on as normal as she led Eliza away to the sick bay. Pearl was beside herself with fear. Eliza was burning up with fever and so weak that she could hardly walk and Pearl didn't need a doctor to tell her that she was very seriously ill.

'She ain't that strong, I don't know if she'll be able to come through this,' she confided to Susan as they made their way down to the morning service in the chapel. 'And I'm not even allowed to go and see her. She'll be so frightened surrounded by people she don't know!'

'She's stronger than yer think,' Susan told her comfortingly as she squeezed her hand. 'She'll be outta there in no time, you'll see.'

Word filtered through to the laundry later that day that yet another inmate had died that morning and shortly after, they saw the staff and the vicar following a small coffin as they made their way towards the burial ground at the back of the house.

'Poor sod, whoever it were,' Susan muttered, but then Mrs Flanders bore down on them and they had to concentrate on their work.

When they finally got to their dormitory that evening it was to find two more empty beds. Another two girls had joined Eliza in the infirmary.

'Lord, they're droppin' like flies,' Susan said in her usual forthright way. 'There won't be room in the infirmary for all of 'em if it carries on like this.'

Pearl spent a sleepless night fretting about her sister and the second Mrs Bates entered the room the next morning to wake them she asked her, 'Have you heard how Eliza is doing, Mrs Bates?'

Mrs Bates glared at her. 'Do you *really* think I have time to keep running to and fro to the infirmary to check on *one* girl?' she spat nastily. 'Now get dressed, those of you that are still able will have to work extra hard to cover for those who are ill, so get to it!'

'Miserable old cow!' Susan said the second she left. 'It would serve 'er right if she come down wi' it; she might be a bit more sympathetic then.'

Sick with worry, Pearl could only nod in agreement.

During the following week, all lessons were called off for the younger children and no one was allowed in or out of the building as the staff fought to contain the disease within the workhouse. As things went from bad to worse, even the tradespeople who delivered the food were told to simply ring the bell and leave it on the steps. One of the dormitories in the boys' section eventually had to be cleared of those who were lucky enough not to have come down with the illness and turned into a temporary sick bay to accommodate those infected. But still Pearl had heard nothing of how Eliza was faring, or even if she was still alive.

Each morning at the early service in the chapel, the healthy girls would stare at the empty seats and wonder who would be next to go missing, praying hard for their friends and themselves. Although they hadn't been told, they were aware that many of the younger and older people had died by the number of cheap coffins that seemed to be arriving daily from the local undertaker. And then they were forbidden from even walking around the yard for the short time they had previously been allowed each day to get a breath of fresh air. That was no hardship, as although the snow had thawed it had been replaced by a thick, freezing fog.

'I feel like a bleedin' prisoner. This place is gettin' to be more like a prison than a work'ouse,' Susan complained.

Pearl nodded in agreement, although if truth be told she would have had no desire to escape even if the opportunity arose, not without Eliza.

Then suddenly, one morning during the first week in February, Eliza suddenly walked into the laundry as if she had never been away and tears of relief stung at the back of Pearl's eyes. Her first instinct was to fly to her sister and give her a big hug, but she knew that would only get her into trouble with Mrs Flanders so she simply continued with her work, although she couldn't prevent herself from continually glancing towards her sister. She had been thin before her illness but now she was almost skeletal and looked as if one good puff of wind would blow her away.

It was lunchtime before Pearl had the chance to speak to Eliza and at the first opportunity, she caught her in her arms and gave her a big kiss.

'How are you feeling? You've lost a lot of weight. Are you sure you're well enough to come straight back to work?' The questions poured out of her as Eliza stood quietly.

She shrugged. 'I's all right,' was all she said, and with that Pearl had to be content as she silently thanked God for sparing her. It seemed He had listened to her prayers after all.

Chapter Seven

It was four weeks later, early in March, and things had returned to relative normality, with many of the girls coming back to work safe and well again, when Pearl, Eliza and two of the other girls were called into the day room. As their names were called out, they glanced at each other fearfully, wondering what they had done wrong, before following Mrs Bates into the office where a well-dressed gentleman with steel-grey hair was waiting to speak to them. He was almost as far round as he was high, and wore a smart suit with a brightly embroidered waistcoat. As they filed in, he eyed each of them from beneath thick, bushy eyebrows that seemed to have a life of their own.

'So, young ladies,' he began when they were all seated. 'I am here to speak to you today about an opportunity that has arisen for the four of you to travel to climates new. There will also be four boys of similar ages to yourselves given the same opportunity. Mrs Bates here has kindly given me the names of the four she feels would be the most suitable to go, so you four are' – he lifted a sheet of paper and cleared his throat before continuing importantly – 'Freda Swift.' Freda's face was a picture of delight as she clasped her hands together. 'Susan Harper, and Pearl and Eliza Parker.'

Susan and Pearl stared at each other as if they could hardly believe their ears. Were they really being selected to go?

'Now, girls, you are being offered a golden opportunity to go and live in the New World. How do you feel about it?'

Eliza merely stared at the floor, while Susan and Freda nodded enthusiastically. Only Pearl looked troubled.

'Would we be allowed to come back 'ome if we didn't like it there? An' where exactly would we be goin'?' she asked tentatively.

Swallowing his annoyance, the man stared at her. Usually the children that were selected were so grateful that they fawned over him, but here was this impudent young pup daring to question him! 'In answer to your first question, my dear, I doubt very much whether you ever *would* wish to return here. And as for the second question – you will be going to live in Canada. You should think yourself very lucky that you are being given such a golden opportunity.' Now that the four girls stood before him, he could see why Mrs Bates had put their names forward. The girl he was speaking to was a cripple, her sister was clearly away with the fairies and the other two . . . well, they were so scrawny he doubted very much if they could work particularly hard. No doubt Mrs Bates simply wanted shot of them, but then that wasn't his concern. His job was to fill the berths on the ship and, truthfully, he didn't much care who filled them.

'But what about our ma an' our family?' Pearl dared to ask, and now she could see that he was annoyed.

'I doubt very much they will miss you,' he said in a clipped voice. 'Otherwise why would they have put you in here? No, I'm sure they will raise no objections to you going so I advise you to seize this chance of a lifetime with both hands. And now I really must be getting on. I have to meet the four boys who have also been selected to go and tell them the *good* news. I shall be back to give you all instructions as to when exactly you will be leaving and what you will require to take with you closer to the time. Good day.'

He picked up a rather grand hat and with a little bow in the girls' direction, he waddled from the room.

'Phew, well whadda yer make o' that then?' Susan whooped when Mrs Bates had shown him out. '*Canada,* eh! I can 'ardly believe it!'

'But what about your ma? What if she gets better an' wants you back 'ome?' Pearl asked.

Freda laughed, an ugly sound that made Susan's pale cheeks burn. 'Want her back? There ain't much chance o' that 'appening, is there, Susan?'

Susan's hands had clenched into fists of rage. 'Shut yer dirty bloody mouth.'

But Freda had no intention of being silenced. '*Her* ma is too busy entertainin' any bloke who can afford to pay 'er. She's a drunken whore! Ain't that right, Susan? That's why she got rid of yer in 'ere. She didn't want yer in the way!'

Angry tears had sprung to Susan's eyes, but as she made towards Freda the door opened and Mrs Bates entered the room again.

'What's going on in here, then?' She had expected to find the girls in good spirits but instead she felt as if she had walked into a war zone. She tutted. 'You ungrateful girls. Get back to work, all of you. Hopefully you will be leaving sometime in April, so just try to behave yourselves until then. Go on, be off with you!'

Head down, Susan stormed past her followed by Pearl and Eliza, who were very quiet, and Freda, who had a smug grin on her face.

It wasn't until they were in the dining hall that evening that they could talk again. 'Pay no heed to Freda. We all know how spiteful she can be. We didn't believe what she said about yer ma, honest!' Pearl whispered sympathetically.

Susan, who was usually the first to finish her meal, hung her head and pushed the food about her plate. It wasn't very appetising that night anyway: lumpy mashed potatoes and gristly gammon that was difficult to chew.

'Sh-she ain't as bad as Freda said,' she muttered.

Reaching beneath the table, Pearl found her hand and squeezed it. 'It wouldn't matter if she were,' she told her kindly. 'She's still yer ma an' you'll love her no matter what.'

'That's the trouble . . . I do.'

They fell silent then but none of them really enjoyed their meal that evening and Pearl was glad when it was time to go to bed. She had a lot to think about. Eliza hadn't said a word about going to Canada, but then Pearl realised that she probably hadn't understood what the man was telling them.

As she lay in the darkness, tears trickled down her cheeks. Deep down she knew that what the gentleman had told them was the truth. If her mother had *truly* loved her and Eliza, she would never have abandoned them the way she had. She could quite easily have come to visit them but she hadn't even bothered to do that, which told its own story. For the first time Pearl wondered if going to Canada wouldn't be so bad after all, for surely it couldn't be any worse there than it was living here in the workhouse? Admittedly she had grown accustomed to the back-breaking work in the laundry, and her hands had hardened and calloused so they no longer pained her as they had when she had first arrived, but they were still well used to feeling the flick of Mrs Flanders's cane whenever they did the least thing wrong. She lay trying to imagine a land full of sunshine, until finally she slept.

Early in April the gentleman, whose name, Mrs Bates informed them, was Mr Miller, again appeared. Once more they were singled out and led to the day room where he informed them that they and the four boys who had been chosen would be sailing to Quebec on *The Dunbrody* at the end of April. Pearl was pleased to hear that Nick was amongst them; they had become friends and she had been teaching him his alphabet on a Sunday afternoon as now she could proudly write her own name and quite a few little words. But still she held that tiny hope that her mother might oppose them being sent away, so she asked tremulously, 'But what if our ma don't want us to go?'

Mr Miller sniffed, setting his large grey moustache quivering. 'You need have no concerns on that score. All the parents who are still alive have been contacted, and yours has given her consent for you to go.'

Pearl felt as if all the air had been knocked out of her. So her ma knew and hadn't tried to oppose them going, or even bothered to come and say goodbye? Deep down she had believed this would be the trigger that would make their mother fetch them home, but now she realised there was no hope of that ever happening.

Blinking back tears, she raised her chin. 'Then in that case I'll look forward to it,' she said. 'But will we be allowed to go and see her to say goodbye?'

'If Mrs Bates has no objections, I can't see why not,' Mr Miller answered, looking towards Mrs Bates.

She frowned. 'Well, if I allowed it you would have to go on a Sunday afternoon,' she said shortly. 'I can't have you having time off during work hours.'

'Thank you, Mrs Bates,' Pearl answered and reaching out she squeezed Eliza's hand. It was something at least.

Over the following week, each of the children who would be sailing were kitted out with new clothes. They were very plain and drab, but serviceable and easily the best that Pearl had ever owned. They were even issued with black leather boots, very superior to the hard wooden clogs they wore about the workhouse. Even Eliza managed a smile when she saw the warm woollen coat they were given. Everything was slightly too big for them, but they didn't care. As Mrs Bates pointed out, they would soon grow into them. Most of them had never even had warm clothes before and they all wondered if this was an omen of wonderful things to come.

On the last Sunday of the month before they were due to set sail, Pearl and Eliza set off for home one sunny afternoon. It seemed that the world was slowly coming back to life after the long, cold winter, and Pearl smiled to see the new green leaves on the sparsely dotted trees opening to the sunshine.

They were under strict instructions to be back within two hours and as they marched along with Pearl gripping tight to Eliza's hand, she said, 'It'll be nice to see our ma an' all the kids again, won't it?'

Eliza shrugged, not much caring one way or another, and eventually they turned into the street where they'd lived, and there was little Amy playing marbles in the street. At sight of Pearl and Eliza, she let out a whoop of delight and flew towards them, throwing herself into Pearl's arms so forcefully that Pearl almost fell over.

'Pearl . . . I missed yer,' she said as she swiped her bare arm across her snotty nose. She was barefoot and looked even thinner than Pearl remembered and her heart sank. The weather was improving but there was still a nip in the air so what was she doing outside half naked? She could see the head lice rampant in her little sister's hair and her stick-like arms were covered in scabs.

'I missed you too,' she told the child, returning her hug. 'Where's Ma?'

Amy thumbed across her shoulder. 'In there, but she ain't in a very good mood.'

Pearl straightened. Good mood or not, she hadn't come this far to turn back without seeing her.

The minute she opened the front door, the stench of stale urine and filth hit her. The stained wooden draining board was piled high with whatever dirty pots her mother possessed and the floor was strewn with rubbish. But it was her mother who gave her the biggest shock. She was huddled in a chair beside the empty fire grate and she looked grievously ill as she rocked to and fro. She was pitifully thin apart from her swollen stomach, and Pearl realised that she must be close to giving birth again. Her head turned in Pearl's direction, but there was no welcoming smile. All she said was, ''Ave yer got any money on yer? I ain't had a drop o' gin since last night an' I'm gaggin' fer a drink.'

Eliza shrank into Pearl's side. Suddenly this place made the workhouse look like a hotel.

'Hello, Ma.' Pearl ignored the question as she crossed to the sink and began to pump water into it. There was no way of heating it so she would just have to do the best she could with cold.

As she rolled her sleeves up and plunged the pots into the water to soak her mother asked again, ''Ave yer got any money?'

'No, I haven't,' Pearl snapped as she took up the broom that stood in one corner. Judging by the state of the place, it hadn't been used since she and Eliza left. 'And even if I had I wouldn't give it yer to waste on drink. Where's Dad?'

'Huh! That *lousy* bastard. I ain't seen 'ide nor 'air of 'im fer over a week now.' Her mother blinked back tears of self-pity. 'I's beginnin' to think he's got hisself a fancy woman.'

Pearl began to sweep the floor, noting the many rat droppings amongst the rubbish. 'So why don't you get yerself an' the kids down to the soup kitchen then?' she asked, smiling at the other children who were sitting quietly against the wall with their thumbs jammed in their mouths.

'And where's the baby?' She had only just noticed that one of her siblings was missing.

'The measles done fer 'im a while back – snuffed 'im out just like that.' As her mother snapped her fingers, Pearl felt tears burn at the back of her eyes. She wasn't really surprised. The children were so neglected that they had little strength to fight off any illness. She was just relieved that the others had survived, for now at least.

'I think you ought to go an' tell the parish that you've nothing in to feed the kids,' Pearl suggested as she glanced into the empty food cupboard. All it contained was mice droppings.

'I ain't goin' beggin' fer charity.' Her mother bristled.

'No, but you don't mind sending the little 'uns out beggin', do yer?' Pearl snapped.

Her mother's mouth gaped before she ground out, 'Ooh, *hark* at you. Yer think yer the bee's knees now as you're goin' to live in another country, don't yer?'

'I don't *have* to go,' Pearl pointed out. 'If I was to come home I could at least make the place look half decent again an' see as the kids are fed.'

Her mother's lip curled as she looked at her with contempt. 'Oh yes, an' then there'd be more of yer fer me to worry about again, wouldn't there? Look at the pair o' yer! One a cripple an' one an idiot. No, yer best off where yer are out o' my way.'

Pearl's lip trembled as she stared at the woman who had given birth to her; she suddenly seemed like a stranger. 'Come on, Eliza,' she coaxed as she rolled her sleeves down and buttoned them back up. 'We ain't needed here anymore. Goodbye, Ma.'

Her mother sniffed but made no reply as slowly Pearl bent to kiss her siblings before leading Eliza back out into the street.

Her mother hadn't even wished them well. No good luck . . . nothing, which finally brought home to Pearl just how little she and Eliza had meant to her. Pearl supposed that even though her parents were still alive, she and Eliza were orphans now and only had each other.

'Come on sweet'eart,' she whispered, giving Eliza's hand an encouraging squeeze. 'We've got to go an' prepare ourselves fer our new life.' And she walked away without looking back.

Chapter Eight

The following week, the girls were instructed to go for a medical in the infirmary.

'It's to make sure that none of you have any contagious diseases and that you're fit enough to travel,' Mrs Bates informed them shortly.

They lined up in the corridor until the doctor called them in one at a time. It wasn't much of a medical, as Susan remarked on their way back to the laundry.

'All 'e did were look in me mouth, me eyes an' me froat.'

'Same here,' Pearl agreed. The time to sail was fast approaching and she could still hardly believe that they really were going.

A few days later they were each issued with bags to pack their new clothes into and Susan was delighted with hers.

'I wonder 'ow many uvvers will be goin',' she said, but no one seemed to know, so all they could do was wait patiently for more news.

And then at last, during the third week in April, Mr Miller paid them another visit. 'You will be sailing a week on Friday with the morning tide on *The Dunbrody*,' he informed them. 'Very early in the morning someone will come to escort you to the docks. And that is really all you need to know for now.'

'But what will 'appen to us when we get there?' Susan queried.

Mr Miller sighed with annoyance. 'There is accommodation arranged for you all until you are placed wherever you are going.'

'But will we all be able to stay togevver?' Susan asked, showing the first hint of nerves.

He raised his eyebrow. 'I should think that would be highly unlikely. I doubt very much that a family would need all four of you, but you'll just have to wait and see, and be grateful for any opportunity you are offered.'

Susan scowled and crossed her arms across her skinny chest. It had only just occurred to her that they might be separated when they got there and she didn't like the thought of that at all. Pearl was the only real friend she had ever had.

'Now, do you have any more questions?' Mr Miller asked sarcastically and when Susan's hand shot up again, he frowned impatiently.

'Yes, 'ow long is it gonna take fer us to get there on the ship?'

'That very much depends on the weather conditions,' he answered truthfully. 'But as a rule, it should take between four and five weeks.'

Pearl gulped. That sounded like an awful long time to be on a ship, but she didn't say anything, knowing it couldn't be changed and not wanting to worry the others, least of all Eliza.

Soon after, Mr Miller left with strict instructions that they should be ready early on the day of departure.

'Don't you worry on that score, they will be, sir,' Mrs Bates told him as she showed him out, and Pearl had the feeling that she could hardly wait to get rid of them.

The atmosphere in the dormitory had changed towards them now. Those that hadn't been selected to go were envious and Pearl found herself wishing the time away until they could leave. Once or twice she had tried to get Eliza to talk about how she felt about them going, but all her efforts had come to nothing as Eliza had simply shrugged. It was almost as if she didn't care what happened to herself anymore. Pearl just hoped that a fresh start might bring her sister back out of her shell.

The time seemed to pass quickly, and suddenly it was the night before they were due to leave. They had done their last shift in the laundry and Pearl was glad about that at least. Mrs Bates ordered them to take a bath when the rest of the girls had retired to bed and it felt strange to Pearl to think that this was the last time she would ever bathe there. *Will we be able to have a bath on the ship?* she wondered, and then shuddered as she thought back to that first night when Mrs Bates had so cruelly bathed them and cut their hair. Pearl's hair had grown quite a lot since that first night and the blonde waves now shone with cleanliness. Then they were ordered to pack their clothes, leaving out only the things they would be wearing the next morning.

'There will be no time for breakfast before you go. No doubt they will give you some once you're on board the ship,' Mrs Bates informed them, not really caring if they starved. She was glad to see the back of them; Eliza was neither use nor ornament, Susan and Freda were lippy little creatures, and Pearl had a defiant air about her that irked Mrs Bates every time she set eyes on the damn girl. Pearl had not shed so much as a tear during her caning, and added to this, she was a cripple. Admittedly she was a worker and had earned her keep but as far as she was concerned it was goodbye to bad rubbish, which was why she had selected the four of them.

As she lay in bed later that night, Pearl's only regret was having to leave behind her younger siblings, but there was nothing she could do about it, so she could only pray that they would survive their mother's neglect.

It was a shock when a member of staff came to rouse them in the early hours of the following morning. Pearl was surprised that she had managed to get any sleep at all and tumbled out of bed bleary-eyed. All four girls shrugged themselves into their clothes before catching up their coats and bags and being led down into the foyer. Through the window they could see a cab waiting for them, the horse that pulled it pawing restlessly at the ground, and Susan's eyes grew wide with excitement.

'Ooh, I ain't never been in a cab before,' she said and Mrs Brewer, one of the kinder members of staff, smiled at her indulgently as the girls struggled into their coats. Thankfully Mrs Bates was still tucked up in bed. She hadn't even bothered to get up to say goodbye to them.

'Now, let's have a look at you. Have you all brushed your hair and put your brushes in your bags?'

Four heads nodded in unison and, smiling, she ushered them towards the door where the gentleman who had been sent to escort them to the docks stood waiting.

'Good luck, my dears,' Mrs Brewer said. 'Off you go and make the best of this opportunity and may God go with you.'

'Eeh, I feel just like gentry,' Susan said as they clambered into the waiting cab and settled back against the worn leather swabs. And then they were off, the horse's hooves making a clip-clop sound on the cobblestones as it rattled towards the docks.

Once they were there, a thick sea mist rising from the quay made it look like everyone was floating and they were surprised at the number of people milling about. The streets had been quiet due to the early hour, but in contrast the docks were teeming with people and activity. The girls were also astounded and somewhat in awe of the enormous boat sitting at anchor that would take them to their new life.

'Bleedin' 'ell! Would yer just look at that!' Susan croaked. 'How can sommat so big stay afloat . . . especially when all this lot get on it?' For the first time she looked apprehensive. Even Freda was quiet for once.

The gentleman who had come to fetch them nudged them forwards through the jostling crowd towards the gangplank. When someone stood on Freda's foot, she yelped, but still they were urged forwards, their bags gripped tightly in their hands until they stood at the end of the longest queue of children they had ever seen. Further down the ship stood another gangplank and they could see burly seamen rolling barrels and carrying huge crates of food up it.

'I shall leave you here,' the gentleman told them, as he took four folded documents from his pocket and handed one to each of them. 'When you reach the end of the queue there will be someone to take your names. Just give them these documents. But now I must hurry to fetch some of the other children who will be travelling with you from the Dr Barnardo's home. Hopefully you will be sailing this morning with the turning of the tide. Goodbye and good luck.'

It was so noisy that he had to shout to be heard and all Pearl could do was give him a grateful but nervous smile. It was still dark, although the dawn was just breaking, and she wondered how long it would be before they finally got on board – the queue seemed to be going down painfully slowly. Ahead she could see children of all shapes and sizes being ushered up the gangplank. Some of them were smiling, but others were openly sobbing and having to be urged along. Pearl gripped Eliza's hand, needing the support as much as offering it.

Suddenly all Susan's excitement was gone and she looked afraid as she stared at the enormous ship that stretched the entire length of the quay.

''Ere, what'll 'appen to us if we get seasick?' she asked anxiously.

Pearl smiled at her encouragingly. 'There's bound to be a doctor on board so we'll be fine,' she said, although she was feeling more than a little nervous herself. Even Freda had gone quiet and as usual Eliza was off in a world of her own, apparently oblivious of the adventure they were about to embark on.

Very, very slowly the queue inched forwards until they came to the bottom of the gangplank where two men with large clipboards stood waiting.

'Names,' the taller of the two asked, and Pearl haltingly told him as the other three hung back, happy for her to take charge. He ran his figure down the list in front of him then nodded and asked, 'Boarding passes, please.'

They handed him the documents they had been given and were then ushered on to the gangplank where Susan hung on to the rope rail for dear life. 'I ain't much fer this,' she said, staring down at the churning water beneath them, which was visible through the planks. It was a dirty brown colour and covered in floating debris that slapped relentlessly against the sides of the ship as if it was trying to find a way inside.

'Just keep going; we'll be all right.' Pearl urged them on.

At last they reached the top and stepped on to the wooden deck where two ladies were waiting for them. At that moment a large seagull swooped dangerously close to Susan's head and she instinctively ducked.

'Bleedin' 'ell. It's dangerous on 'ere,' she complained.

'Less of that bad language, if you please,' one of the ladies scolded as she stepped towards them. She was actually quite young and pretty with dark curly hair, Pearl noticed. 'Follow me and I'll show you to your quarters.'

The four of them stayed close together as they followed her across the deck, which was so much larger than any of them had imagined it would be.

Eventually they came to a door and they followed the woman down a steep wooden staircase that seemed to be little more than a ladder. Once at the bottom they found themselves in a long, low corridor with numerous doors leading off it. Each door was clearly numbered and after what seemed like a long time the woman stopped in front of door 22 and threw it open. They entered a low-ceilinged, narrow room with bunks beds built from floor to ceiling along each side. There was a small porthole at the end, but seeing as it looked out on to the seaweed-encrusted wall of the quayside, at present it was very dark and gloomy. There were two girls already storing their small bags beneath two of the bottom bunks, both looking as nervous as Pearl felt. They looked to be about the same age as them and Pearl rightly guessed that they had been separated into age groups.

'Right, girls, you can choose whichever bunks you like,' the woman told them. 'There will be twelve girls to a room when the others arrive so just remember your door number. You'll find the toilets at the very far end of this corridor should you need them, but for now I would like you all to stay in here until the ship sets sail. It's fairly hectic up on deck getting everyone aboard, as you've seen, but hopefully we'll be setting sail within the next two or three hours. You can all come up on deck then, should you wish to, and later on this morning you'll be shown around so that you know where the dining cabin and things are.'

With that she closed the door, and Pearl quickly chose two beds close together for herself and Eliza, and placed their bags on them.

'It's a bit bleak, ain't it?' Susan said glumly as they sat on their bunks.

'Ah well, we'll just 'ave to make the best of it. After all, it ain't everybody that gets to sail in a big ship, is it?' Pearl said, hoping to raise everyone's spirits. 'I'm Pearl, by the way, an' this here is my sister Eliza.'

'I'm Nancy,' said the girl, who they would soon discover was the youngest of the group, with a smile. She was clearly excited about the new life they were going to, but the other girl remained quiet and so Pearl too fell silent. They sat listening to the hum of furious activity on the deck high above them. Beyond the door they could hear the sound of footsteps on the bare wooden floors as yet more children were shown to their sleeping quarters, and the raised voices of adults shouting instructions. Through the thin walls dividing the cabins they could hear the muted sounds of girls chatting as the rooms filled up and then the door opened and the final six girls entered to join them.

Introductions were made, but Pearl had forgotten half their names within seconds as her thoughts turned to the siblings she had left behind, especially the baby she'd never even met – she and Eliza didn't even know if it was a brother or a sister. She could only pray yet again that they would survive. There was nothing she could do to help them now.

Slowly it grew slightly lighter in the cabin but with the porthole facing the dock they couldn't see much, even as the mist cleared and a pale watery sun appeared in the sky. Suddenly Susan turned pale and gripped the side of her bed as she gasped, 'I reckon we're off. I'm sure I just felt the ship move.'

Before anyone could reply the door opened and the same young woman they had seen earlier, told them, 'We're leaving the docks now. If any of you would like a last glimpse of England follow me up on to the deck.'

Despite Pearl trying to convince her to come with them, Eliza chose to stay where she was, but the rest of the girls hurried after the kindly woman and very soon they were up on deck again, gazing towards the rails where girls and boys clamoured for their last sight of home. The ship was very slowly picking up speed as it left the docks and Pearl felt a lump form in her throat.

If I ever come back here, it will be once I have made something of my life, she promised herself as she stood and watched the land slowly slip away. This would be the start of her new life, in the New World.

Chapter Nine

The first night on the ship was surprisingly comfortable and it was nice to wake the next morning knowing they didn't have to face a long day in the laundry.

'I wonder what we'll get fer breakfast?' Susan said with a yawn and a stretch, thinking of her stomach as usual.

The young lady who had shown them to their cabin had introduced herself as Miss Walker and explained that they would go to the dining cabin in sittings and that she would fetch them when it was their turn the next morning. The girls could understand that they couldn't all possibly be fed together – there were hundreds of children aboard, let alone the crew and the people who had gone along to organise them. Susan was just worried that they might run out of food.

'Did you see how much they were carrying aboard while we were waiting to get on? There was enough to feed an army fer months!' Pearl had tried to reassure her.

'Ah, but warrabout fresh water?'

Pearl sighed. 'They've already explained that we'll be stopping at different ports along the way. And anyway, we'll be washing ourselves and our clothes in sea water,' Pearl pointed out.

'Hm.' Susan still wasn't convinced as she collected her towel and they headed to the washroom. Once there they had to wait their turn to reach the sinks which they filled with jugs of water from a barrel standing on the corner.

'Our clothes are gonna be stiff as boards if we 'ave to wash 'em in salt water,' Susan complained, and Freda glared at her. She was back to her old sarcastic self and Pearl just hoped they could get through the voyage without too many squabbles.

When their turn came to eat, they were pleasantly surprised at the food. Thick, juicy sausages, crisp rashers of bacon and doorstep wedges of fried bread.

Things got even better when Miss Walker told them they could attend a talk that had been organised for them once the dining room had been cleared. Until then they were free to take the air on deck providing they didn't hang over the rails or get in the sailors' way.

Pearl held tight to Eliza's hand as they wandered along, marvelling at the huge sails that were flapping in the wind. Some of the children were already suffering from severe bouts of sea sickness and were confined to their cabins, but thankfully none of the girls from the workhouse had been ill as yet, although one of the girls from the Dr Barnardo's home who was sharing their cabin had.

As they were staring out at the vast expanse of sea, Nick came racing towards them with a broad smile on his face.

'This is a bit of all right, ain't it?' He grinned. 'It's like bein' on 'oliday, I imagine, an' the breakfast were grand.' He rubbed his stomach appreciatively and Susan giggled. 'The bunk beds are comfy an' all, ain't they? Are yer goin' to the talk when everyone 'as finished eatin'? Mr Briggs, who's keepin' an eye out fer the lads in our cabin, told me they're goin' to be tellin' us what we can expect when we get there.'

'Yes, I'll be goin',' Pearl confirmed enthusiastically. 'It'll be nice to know what to expect. Better than goin' back to our cabin just yet anyway; one o' the girls in there 'as gone green wi' seasickness an' the place stinks.'

'Mm, I wondered what them buckets under the bunks were for.' Susan grinned. 'An' it ain't even as if we can open a winder.'

When they all eventually piled into the dining room where the tables had been organised into neat rows, Pearl was entranced as she listened to Miss Walker tell them of the new land they were going to, although Susan wasn't too happy with some of what they were told.

'I didn't know they 'ad grizzly bears there.' She shuddered. 'Imagine comin' face to face wi' one o' them, eh? I don't much like the sound o' the grey wolves either, nor them cougars.'

Pearl laughed. 'I doubt they'd hurt you if you didn't hurt them,' she said stoically.

Now that she no longer had to work each day, Pearl intended to spend some of her free time practising her alphabet on the slate that Miss Sweet had given her. She had offered to help Susan learn her alphabet too, but Susan wasn't that interested. Already the sallow look was disappearing from her cheeks and she was looking forward to her new life.

Pearl was beginning to relax too and even Eliza didn't seem so tense, although she was still quiet, but then she had never had a lot to say for herself so there wasn't really much change there. Still, Pearl lived in hope that now they were on the way to a new life her sister might come out of her shell.

By the time they went to bed that evening, the girls were all in a mellow mood. Admittedly the smell was still not too pleasant in their cabin, despite the fact that they had propped the door open earlier in the day, but the sound of the old ship creaking and groaning was surprisingly calming and with that and all the fresh sea air, Pearl slept like a top.

The days slid easily one into another, and for the first time in their lives Pearl and Eliza were treated kindly. Even the captain had a ready smile for the children he saw on deck and the grown-ups organised endless things to entertain them so they wouldn't get bored. When the sailors were swabbing the decks, the children were confined to their cabins, and they would chatter and gossip, especially Nancy, who was coming out of her shell now. All in all they suddenly had a great deal of time on their hands and the majority of them took full advantage of the fact. As well as practising her letters, Pearl loved to lean on the rail watching the boat slice through the clear blue water and Nick often joined her.

'I could get used to this way o' life,' he chuckled one day as the sun shone down on them. Because of the time spent outside, Pearl's hair had turned a lovely platinum-blonde colour and now that it was growing longer it framed her face in soft curls. Nick secretly thought she was the prettiest girl he had ever seen, although he didn't tell her that, of course. She was still just a kid as far as he was concerned, whereas at fourteen, he considered himself to be almost a man. 'I wonder what this place we'll be staying at till they find us work will be like?' he mused. Miss Walker had told them about it that day.

Pearl was as curious as he was. 'Well, it sounds like a type of children's home,' she answered.

'Hmm, but then we ain't all little kids, are we?' Nick was actually amongst the oldest travelling to Canada. 'I reckon we'll get chosen fer jobs first, bein' amongst the oldest,' he mused.

Pearl nodded. 'Probably. I bet the littler ones will stay in the home till they're a bit older, but we'll soon find out.'

They stood side by side staring out across the calm waters until Freda came to stand beside them, batting her eyelids at Nick. It was obvious she'd developed a crush on him, although, could she have known it, he didn't particularly like her. He'd heard the way she spoke to the others, especially Susan, and he didn't like it.

'All right, Nick?'

'Mm, yes, ta,' he answered shortly and without a word turned and walked away, quickly followed by Pearl who didn't spend a moment longer than was necessary in Freda's company.

Later that afternoon, some ball games were organised for them on the deck, followed by a supper of cottage pie and vegetables in the dining room. The older children were amongst the last to sit down to their meal, but there was always plenty of food left and Pearl wondered how the cooks managed it.

She felt content as she snuggled down in her bunk that evening and stared dreamily at the star-studded sky through the small porthole, and soon she drifted into a peaceful sleep.

But it didn't last long as in the early hours of the morning, Pearl started awake. The ship was juddering and swaying alarmingly and she realised they were experiencing their first storm. Outside the porthole jagged flashes of lightning were lighting the sky and deep rumbles of thunder seemed to be rocking the boat as it rose and fell on the high waves like a cork.

'Gawd love us! What the bleedin' 'ell is goin' on?' Susan had just woken and was gripping the edge of her bunk for all she was worth. Two of the girls started to sob, and clambering out of her own bunk Pearl made her way unsteadily over to Eliza, wrapping her protectively in her arms while some of the other girls were violently seasick into buckets put in the cabin for just such a time.

'Ain't it bloody typical. I fought it were too good to last,' Susan complained chokily. 'There we was 'aving the time of us lives an' now we're gonna end up as bleedin' fish food.'

Her words made some of the other girls cry even harder as the ship lurched and shifted.

'Come on, you lot! Panickin' ain't goin' to help us, is it? Just hold tight an' I'll bet it'll all blow over in no time. The sailors know what they're doin' an' they won't let us sink,' Pearl told them sternly.

There was no answer save for the sound of people vomiting and once again the acrid smell was overpowering. Suddenly there was another loud crack of thunder and the heavens opened and a deluge of rain lashed against the porthole as if it was trying to get in. At that moment there was a tap on the door and Miss Walker entered, hanging on to the door handle for dear life as the movement of the ship threw her from side to side.

'Underneath your mattresses you'll find a strap, girls,' she told them, trying to contain her panic. She was still in her dressing robe and with her hair loose about her shoulders she looked very different to the neat and tidy young woman they were used to seeing. 'Tie them around yourselves and don't attempt to get out of your bunks until I come back to tell you to. And try not to be frightened. I'm sure this ship has survived many a storm,' she ended tremulously. The girls instantly began to rummage beneath the thin mattresses and Pearl stopped to help Eliza into hers before climbing up and doing her own. Soon they were all strapped in but it didn't stop them from being afraid. Some of them were still vomiting but now they were merely leaning over the side of their bunks and the smell made Pearl feel nauseous too.

'I just want yer to know, Pearl, that I fink the world o' yer,' Susan said solemnly as tears trickled down her cheeks. 'I ain't never 'ad a proper friend afore.'

'Oh, don't talk like that,' Pearl scolded. 'We'll be back in calm waters in no time, you'll see.'

But despite her brave words, she wasn't so sure. What if none of them made it to the new life they had been promised? What if they all ended up in Davey Jones's locker never to see the light of day again? She fell silent and prayed as she had never prayed before.

As the endless night wore on, the girls could hear shouting as the sailors above tried to steer the ship through the storm. Eventually the cabin grew lighter as dawn streaked the dark sky and after what seemed like a lifetime, the ship began to feel a little steadier.

'I think we're through the worst,' Pearl whispered hopefully but Susan didn't hear her. As terrified as she was, she had fallen asleep through sheer exhaustion. Some of the other girls were sleeping too although some were still crying and praying aloud. In the light filtering in through the porthole Pearl could see that the cabin floor was awash with vomit and the sight made her stomach revolt.

At last Miss Walker appeared again, dressed this time, and smiled at them, though she looked thoroughly tired out.

'The worst is over, girls, but please stay where you are for a while longer. It's pandemonium up on deck. One of the masts was damaged during the storm so goodness knows what time they will be able to prepare breakfast. Are you all all right?' Her eyes fastened on the youngest girl in the room. Nancy was lying unnaturally quietly with her hand flopping limply across the side of the bed and when Miss Walker had waded through the disgusting mess on the floor to get to her, her face paled. She hurried away, only to return minutes later with a burly sailor, who lifted Nancy from her bed and bore her away as if she weighed no more than a feather.

'What's wrong wi' Nancy, miss?' Susan enquired worriedly.

Miss Walker merely shook her head. 'I have no idea, Susan, but just lie patiently for a while longer.' And with that she was gone.

The minutes ticked away and slowly the boat stopped rocking and things were calm again.

'Phew, that wcrc a close 'un,' Susan declared as she unfastened the strap holding her to the bed and sat up. Some of the other girls did the same. They all looked pale and frightened but at least they had survived.

It was well after eleven o'clock in the morning before they were allowed to head for the dining hall but after the night they'd had none of them were really hungry.

'I'm so sorry, girls, but I'm afraid Nancy didn't make it,' Miss Walker told them sadly when they entered the room. 'There will be a short memorial service for her later this afternoon.'

'What!' Susan sputtered. The girls were horrified. Nancy had been such a sweet young girl.

'The doctor thinks she had a weak heart that had probably never been detected,' Miss Walker said.

Many of the girls, including Freda and Susan, began to cry, but Pearl stood in stunned disbelief as a picture of little Nancy's smiling face flashed in front of her eyes. She couldn't believe she would never see her again and tears started to slide down her cheeks. She had seemed so alive, so excited to be on board and to have this opportunity. To think that flame had gone out and she was dead was terrible. She was only a couple of months younger than Eliza, just eleven years old.

'But why can't we wait till we get to Canada to bury 'er?' Susan asked in a shaky voice. She didn't like the thought of Nancy being tossed over the side of the ship into a watery grave, and she'd heard that's what happened with burials at sea.

'I'm afraid it wouldn't be wise,' Miss Walker told her gently. 'And so if any of you wish to attend the service to say your goodbyes be on deck at three o'clock. Meanwhile,

I suggest you get some mops and buckets and clean your cabin up. I'm afraid everyone is far too busy trying to put right the storm damage to help you.'

In a melancholy mood the girls went to do as they were told.

Chapter Ten

The girls spent the next few hours cleaning the cabin as best they could. Dirty bedding was taken up on deck and left to soak in huge barrels of sea water, and the floor was mopped as thoroughly as they could manage, but the smell persisted, so the girls escaped back up on deck again where the air was clean, although the sky was still leaden.

'I 'ope we ain't in fer another storm,' Susan said fretfully as she stared up at the dark clouds. Nancy's tragic death had affected them all badly and suddenly all the fun had gone from the adventure they were embarking upon.

'I shouldn't think we are,' Pearl said, hoping to reassure her. 'And anyway, we'll be docking in the Bay of Biscay in the next couple of days to stock up on supplies. I'm sure the captain would put off sailing from there if he thought there was a risk of us running into another storm.'

Nick ambled up to join them, his face grave. 'We heard in the lads' quarters about what 'appened to little Nancy,' he said solemnly. 'What a shame; she were a nice kid, weren't she?'

'Yes, she was.' Pearl swiped a tear from her cheek and they stood in silence, staring out across the vast expanse of sea suddenly longing for a sight of land.

At three o'clock, everyone assembled on deck for Nancy's burial. A short plank had been fastened to the rail that jutted out across the water and a sailor carried Nancy's body, wrapped and tied securely in sailcloth, across to it and laid it on top.

The priest took his position to one side and solemnly began the service, 'Unto Almighty God we commend the soul of our sister departed, Nancy Bell, and we commit her body to the deep; in sure and certain hope of the Resurrection unto eternal life through our Lord Jesus Christ; at whose coming in glorious majesty to judge the world, the sea shall give up her dead . . .'

His voice droned on as tears spilled down the cheeks of many of those present. Even the captain, who had taken off his hat as a mark of respect, looked to be damp-eyed. It seemed so sad that such a young girl who had her whole life in front of her should be snuffed out so quickly like a candle in the wind. And then the plank was lifted slightly and Nancy's little body plummeted into the water below and slowly sank out of sight.

'That's it then.' Susan swiped a trail of snot from her nose on the sleeve of her dress as they all trooped into the dining hall. It was done.

They sailed into the Bay of Biscay two days later and the children watched in fascination as the sailors lowered the gangplanks and began to bring on board fresh food supplies. Pearl had a yearning to run down the gangplank after them and feel dry land beneath her feet, but of course they weren't allowed to leave the ship as the captain was keen to set sail again while the weather was in their favour. And so, some three hours later, they were off again, and the excitement slowly began to rise once more because they all knew that the next stop would be their destination and their new homes.

As the wind filled the sails, the port slowly became smaller and soon there was nothing but sea to be seen again. The sailors had obligingly strung some lines up across one corner of the deck and the girls took advantage of them when they washed out their clothes in the big barrels and hung them across the lines to flap in the breeze; it was nothing like doing the laundry back at the workhouse.

'We'll be itching again with the salt in these when they dry,' Susan complained, but Pearl didn't mind. At least they would be clean.

'Why don't we hop in the barrels an' have a bath afore we empty the water?' she suggested, but Susan didn't seem too keen on that idea. She'd never been that meticulous about hygiene.

'Well, I'm going to; pass me that soap,' Pearl instructed and before Susan could object, she'd stripped down to her underwear and disappeared around the back of the barrel where she wouldn't be seen as she hopped in.

'Ooh, it's cold,' she giggled as she dunked her head beneath the water. She began to rub the coarse soap into her hair until she'd worked it into a lather.

When she emerged dripping some minutes later, she shook herself like a dog and dried herself roughly on her dress before slipping it back on and grinning.

'That's lovely; I feel all tingly an' clean now,' she declared, and soon other girls were doing the same, and laughter and curses filled the air as they disappeared beneath the water, only to reappear seconds later coughing and giggling.

'Go on,' she urged Susan. 'We ain't none of us smellin' too sweet an' it feels really nice.'

Somewhat reluctantly Susan followed suit, and by the time they all went into the dining cabin for their meal their hair was shining and their faces were glowing.

Thankfully the rest of the journey passed uneventfully and as they neared their destination, excitement began to mount.

'I 'opes I get set on in a big posh 'ouse,' Susan said thoughtfully as they sat over dinner one evening. 'Then I'll get to wear a really posh uniform an' be a maid to a proper lady.'

Miss Walker had informed them that they would be travelling to Galt in Ontario where they would stay in what she termed 'a holding home' founded by Annie MacPherson until they were found a position. They knew that the settlement they were heading for was a thriving community where many of the settlers had bought parcels of land and established farms, and the town was growing and becoming prosperous.

'Miss Walker says Galt is right on the Grand River an' all,' Susan went on enthusiastically. 'That'll be nice won't it? We could per'aps learn to swim in us free time. I just 'ope we get placed close to each other.'

Pearl giggled. 'Well, that surprises me seein' as yer don't even like to have a bath.'

Susan sniffed disdainfully. 'That's different,' she said primly. 'Swimmin' is 'avin' fun.'

Pearl glanced at Eliza who was sitting quietly beside them, staring off into space as usual. Following the storm, she had developed a cough and Pearl was concerned that it seemed to be getting worse. But still, she comforted herself, she was sure to get better once they were off the ship and on dry land again.

At last, during the second week in June, a cry came from the crow's nest. 'Land ahead!'

Everyone scrambled to get to the rails, and sure enough, far in the distance they saw a land mass. They had been told they would dock at Port Mississauga in Ontario, and now the excitement reached fever pitch as the land drew closer.

'We should be docking this evening,' the captain told them when he came to stand amongst them. The voyage had claimed poor Nancy's life, but he was painfully aware that it could have been much worse. During the previous voyage, a case of dysentery had broken out and claimed the lives of eleven people. He stared at the bright-eyed children gazing with delight at the far distant land and felt infinitely sad. They were all going to uncertain futures with no one to care what became of them, unlike his own two children who he missed greatly but who he knew were cossetted and pampered back at home. But then he supposed that he had at least got them there safely and surely nothing could be worse than the lives some of them had led back in London? Many of them had been rescued from what amounted to little more than child slavery in the matchbox industry and the rest were from various orphanages and workhouses where they worked long, tedious hours for their living. His eyes rested on Pearl and when she smiled his heart ached. Both she and her sister, with their lovely silver-blonde hair and deep-green eyes, were going to be beauties in a few years' time, if he was any judge.

'Captain, you're wanted, sir!' A voice sounded behind him, and with a last smile at the children he went about his duties. Very soon what became of them all would be in the lap of the gods. He could only pray that life would be kind to them.

Dusk was settling across the landscape as the children prepared to disembark early that evening.

'Are you quite sure you have everything, girls?' Miss Walker asked from the cabin doorway. Eleven heads nodded and she smiled as she ushered them past her and up on to the deck. The sailors were busily manhandling the gangplank into place and as Pearl peeped down at the sea swirling far below, she was surprised to see how blue and clear it was; nothing at all like the sludgy brown water back at the docks in London.

She squeezed Eliza's hand and smiled at her. 'All ready for this, are yer?'

Eliza merely stared blankly back at her as Pearl led her forwards. It was time to start their new life; there could be no going back now.

Chapter Eleven

'Here we are then; this is where you'll be staying. For now, at least,' Miss Walker informed them, as she ushered them into a building made entirely of logs that was unlike anything the girls had ever seen. Inside, though, it was surprisingly spacious and comfortable. She led them into a long, narrow dormitory with beds placed against each wall.

'Choose which beds you'd like to sleep in and leave your things on them then come along to the dining room for some food and a drink; I'm sure you must all be hungry. I'll be back in five minutes to show you where it is.' Miss Walker smiled at them and slipped away.

Pearl yawned. After disembarking they had travelled for hours by train and across rugged country in a convoy of horse-drawn carts to get there and they were so tired that some of them were almost asleep on their feet. Pearl had watched the passing scenery with interest to begin with, keen to get a picture of her new home country, but then tiredness had claimed her and she had napped for most of the way. If truth be told she was still exhausted and would have liked nothing more than to just curl up in one of the beds – they did look surprisingly comfortable – but Eliza had eaten hardly anything for days and she was keen to persuade her to eat something at least. Her sister's cough seemed to be getting more persistent, and Pearl had decided that she would speak to Miss Walker about it at the earliest opportunity.

Most of the girls had perked up considerably now that they had finally arrived at their temporary home and they were keen to look about.

'Just look at them trees,' Susan said, peering out of a window. 'I don't fink I've ever seen any so big.' She threw her bag on to the bed next to Pearl's and looked around, excitement shining in her eyes. Canada, with its vast, open spaces and forests, was a far cry from the crowded, sooty streets of London and she already had a feeling that she was going to like it here. Freda, on the other hand, didn't look very enamoured of anything.

'It's like bein' dumped in a wilderness,' she whined. 'Look, there ain't even no street lights 'ere. What if a bear walks in?'

'I doubt that will happen; we do have doors, yer know, and I'm not sure a light would stop 'em,' Pearl told her with a chuckle as she took her brush from her bag and started to tidy Eliza's hair.

They had been told that the boys would be in a similar building next door and she was looking forward to finding out what Nick thought of their new home. Knowing how much he loved the outdoors, she had no doubt that he would love the place.

True to her word Miss Walker was back within minutes and led them to yet another enormous log cabin that served as a classroom for the younger children and a dining room for the residents there. Nick was already seated at a table by a large window with some of his friends, and he winked at Pearl and gave her a cheery wave. There was a large trestle table where two women in long white aprons were dishing out food and soon they were all seated with steaming dishes of pork chops and mash, and glasses of creamy milk in front of them.

'Well, it's nice to know we ain't gonna starve at least, even if there is a chance we could get eaten by bears,' Susan said cheerfully as she tucked in. She never refused food yet she was stick thin and Pearl wondered where she put it all.

Even Eliza ate a little of her meal which pleased her older sister no end.

'If any of you would like to do a little exploring do go ahead,' Mr Briggs, the young man who had accompanied the boys, told them when the meal was over. 'But please stay within sight of the home until you know your way around a little more. It would be awful if we had to send out a search party the first day we got here. The rest of you are free to return to your rooms and rest, if you prefer.'

'I'm off fer a look round,' Susan told them. 'Anyone fancy comin'?'

'No thanks, I reckon I'll go an' 'ave a lie-down.' Pearl stifled another yawn as she took Eliza's hand and led her outside. Dusk was falling and all that could be heard was the sound of the birds in the trees. It was hard to believe that the town of Galt was only a short distance up the rough road.

Mr Briggs and Miss Walker appeared and made off in the direction of the large woods behind the home for a stroll.

'Hm, they look like a couple o' love birds, don't yer think?' Susan grinned, then wondered off to join a couple of the other girls who were going for a walk, while Pearl and Eliza went back to the dormitory. Once there, they lay down on their beds and within seconds, they were fast asleep.

The next morning, after visiting the bathhouse, the girls again made their way to the dining room. Susan beckoned them over to her table to tell them, 'Miss Walker says people will start to arrive today to see if any of us are suitable fer the positions they 'ave. I just bloody 'ope no one chooses me fer laundry work! I 'ad enough o' that back at the work'ouse!'

They ate a hearty breakfast and were then led into a large room which also served as a classroom for the older children. Eventually people began to arrive and walk amongst them, eyeing them up and down.

'I feel like a cow on show at a cattle market!' Susan hissed to Pearl.

Some of the people were extremely well dressed, while others were clearly farmers and their wives. Pearl saw one such man and his wife approach Nick and the boy sitting next to him. She couldn't hear what was being said but it was obvious that Nick was happy from the broad smile on his face. Minutes later the man went off to speak to Mr Briggs and Nick came bounding over to them like a young deer.

'I'm goin' to work on a farm.' He punched the air with exhilaration. 'Can yer believe that, eh? It's just what I dreamed of.'

Pearl was pleased for him but she knew she would miss him. 'Will you be far away?' she asked.

He shook his head as his eyes strayed to his new boss. 'Only about two miles out o' town as the crow flies, apparently, so 'opefully we'll still bump into each other from time to time.'

His new employer was signing some forms and minutes later he approached Nick. 'So are you ready, boy? I've got the cart outside.'

It was the first time Pearl had heard a Canadian accent and she liked the way his words seemed to roll together.

'Yes, sir,' Nick answered as he gave the girls one last smile and followed the man from the room.

'Good luck,' Pearl called after him but through the window she could already see him clambering on to the back of the cart, still smiling broadly as the farmer and his wife took the front seat.

When she turned back, Pearl noticed a woman was speaking to a scowling Freda and soon after the woman approached Miss Walker.

'Looks like you've found a place too,' Pearl said as Freda glowered at her.

'Oh, yeah, workin' in a smelly butcher's shop,' she grumbled.

The room was full of people now and Pearl held tight to Eliza's hand praying that they might be chosen to go somewhere together. She knew Eliza would never cope on her own.

Soon a dainty, very well-dressed woman in a fancy bonnet trimmed with peacock feathers stepped into the room and began a conversation with Miss Walker. She was attractive and looked to be in her mid to late thirties and Pearl watched as Miss Walker's head nodded in answer to the questions the woman was asking. Shortly after the woman began to wander around the room and as her eyes fastened on Eliza she suddenly stopped directly in front of them.

'Are you two sisters?' she asked in a refined English accent, her eyes fixed tight on Eliza.

Pearl nodded and answered for both of them. 'Yes, missus, we are an' we'd like to find a place where we can work together, if possible.'

'Hm, I see.' Her eyes flicked briefly to Pearl before returning to Eliza. 'And are you good at housework?'

'Oh yes, missus. We're both *real* good at cleanin' – *an'* washin' an' ironin',' Pearl assured her eagerly. She had no idea who the woman was but from her clothes and the way she spoke she clearly wasn't a farmer's wife. As the woman stared thoughtfully at Eliza's blank face for a second, Pearl detected a deep sadness in her eyes, but then seeming to reach a decision the woman went to seek Miss Walker out again.

After a while she came back to them and said, 'I have decided to give you both a trial. 'You,' she said to Pearl, 'will be trained to be a maid, and you' – her voice softened as she smiled at Eliza – 'will be working in the kitchens. Does that sound suitable?'

'Oh *yes*, missus.' Although the woman spoke very well, she didn't seem to be unkind and Pearl was just relieved that she and Eliza could stay together. At that moment Eliza started to cough and the woman frowned.

'Have you had that cough for long, my dear?' she enquired as she reached out to gently touch the girl's hair, but Eliza simply hung her head and remained silent.

Pearl hastily told her, 'She's had it fer some time, missus, but it is gettin' a bit better.'

The woman shook her head and sighed as she turned her attention to Pearl. 'I can see I have a lot of work to do with you to bring you up to standard, starting with some elocution lessons. Your grammar is quite appalling.'

'Elecru what?' Pearl looked worried.

'Elocution lessons; teaching you how to pronounce your words and speak properly,' the woman explained patiently. 'But now I really must go. Someone will be here to fetch you and your sister later this morning and when you get to my home the housekeeper will tell you what to do and what will be expected of you both.'

'Yes, missus,' Pearl answered soberly and with a bow of her head that set the feathers on her hat dancing, the woman swept gracefully from the room.

'Cor, she were posh, weren't she?' Susan whispered enviously as they watched the woman climb into a beautiful horse-drawn carriage. 'Are you an' Eliza really goin' to work fer 'er?'

'It looks like it.' Pearl gulped.

Susan giggled as she mimicked the woman, trying to copy her accent. '*Ho your electrocution is appalling!*' But then becoming serious she said sadly, 'I shan't arf miss yer, though. I kept finkin' we might be found a place togevver but never mind. This place can't be that big so we're bound to see each uvver from time to time, ain't we?'

They put their arms about each other until Miss Walker approached them to tell Pearl, 'Well, you and Eliza have certainly fallen on your feet there if you keep your noses clean. That was Mrs Forbes, the wife of the richest man for miles about. They have a beautiful house right on the banks of the river on the other side of the town and Mr Forbes owns at least half of the town by all accounts.'

'Really?' Pearl was shocked.

'Really,' Miss Walker assured her with a smile. 'But now run back to your room and pack your things. Some-one will be coming to pick you up very shortly and you don't want to get off on the wrong foot by keeping them waiting.'

Pearl gave Susan one last hug. Then, hoisting Eliza to her feet, she led her back to their room.

Shortly before lunchtime as they sat ready and waiting with their small bags on their laps, a horse-drawn cart arrived to take them to their new place of work. A lot of the children who had arrived with them had already left, mainly the boys who had been snaffled up as farmworkers, but sadly Susan was still there waiting to be chosen.

'You look after yersen's now,' she said with a catch in her voice as she gave Pearl a quick hug.

Miss Walker ushered them outside and introduced them to the tall man who was waiting for them.

He grinned at them. 'I'm Will Masters. I work for Mr and Mrs Forbes in the stables. Hop on, girls, and I'll have you back in no time.'

Pearl noticed the way his eyes seemed to linger on Eliza for a moment, much as Mrs Forbes's had done, but she didn't have too long to think on it because it was time to say goodbye.

Miss Walker gave them both a quick kiss on the cheek and Pearl managed to give Susan a last wave and then they were off, clip-clopping along to the next chapter in their lives.

Chapter Twelve

For a while they rode along in silence and soon found themselves on the main road that led through the town. Pearl was shocked at the size of it. She had imagined it would be a very makeshift kind of place with little more than log cabins and ramshackle buildings dotted here and there, but in fact it seemed to have everything. There was a smart-looking barber's shop with a long red-and-white striped pole fastened above the door and next to that was a butcher's displaying all manner of meats on big marble slabs in the window. There was a lady's dress shop with elegant gowns on mannequins in the window, and a menswear shop that seemed to sell everything from socks and cravats to smart suits. The wonderful smell of fresh-baked bread wafted out to the street as they passed the bakery, and over the road from that was a fishmonger. There was a bank and a post office as well as a general store and a hardware shop, and Pearl realised that the place was nowhere near as uncivilised as she had expected it to be. Admittedly it wasn't as busy as the London streets she was used to, but even so there were a fair number of people going about their business, and the air and streets felt cleaner. Some of them were very fashionably dressed while others looked like farmers' wives or women out shopping for food for their families.

'So, from London, are you?' Will asked as he urged the horse along, interrupting her thoughts.

'Yes,' Pearl told him.

'Hm. Lost your folks, did you?'

Pearl was too embarrassed to tell him that her mother had abandoned them to the workhouse so she merely nodded. Eliza was cuddled close to her, holding her hand as if her life depended on it, and Pearl gave her a reassuring squeeze.

'It's much busier here than I thought it would be,' she told Will.

He nodded. 'Oh, this place is thriving. We've got quite a good little community going here now. The master, Mr Forbes, owns a lot of the larger businesses hereabouts. He owns the sawmill as well as a number of the smaller shops in the town, but his biggest building is his shipping business. He owns most of the ships that sail in and out of here and has a huge shipbuilders' business on the banks of the river not far from the house.' He smiled as he motioned to the densely wooded areas around them. 'As you can see there are trees everywhere you look so he makes a fortune in timber alone. The lumberjacks cut them down and then the wood is transported all over the world.'

'Is he a nice man?' Pearl dared to ask.

Will looked thoughtful for a moment. 'I'm not so sure nice is how I'd describe him,' he answered as honestly as he could, flicking a lock of his thick, fair hair back from his forehead 'He expects a fair day's work for a fair day's wages, but he's not bad as bosses go.'

'And what about Mrs Forbes?'

Will smiled. 'Now she is a true lady,' he informed her. 'Although she's not been too well for a while. There was a tragedy in the family last year and she's only just started to get out and about again.'

Pearl longed to ask him what had happened but didn't quite dare to.

He went on, 'The master is a fair bit older than her and he worships the ground she walks on so he's been worried sick about her. No, I doubt you'll have any trouble with her or the master if you do your work and keep your head down. It's the son as you have to worry about. Master Monty.' He scowled as Pearl looked at him enquiringly.

'Oh? What's wrong with him then?'

'He's a cocky little sod!' As soon as the words had left his lips, Will looked guilty. 'Sorry, I shouldn't have sworn in front of you girls, but just the thought of that lad can get my back up. He's been spoiled rotten by his mother. His father tries to keep him in check, admittedly, but the young tyke treats the staff like dirt and I've come close to landing a thump on his chin more than once, I don't mind telling you – although I'd rather you didn't repeat that.'

'Of course not.' Pearl grinned. She liked Will and felt that she had possibly made at least one new friend in her soon-to-be home.

They drove on in silence for a while as Pearl looked about with interest at the surroundings. There were so many new varieties of trees to look at as well as flowers – not that very much of anything grew where she'd grown up. One plant in particular that grew in small, spiky purple clusters beneath the trees caught her eye and she asked Will what they were.

'They're the floss flower, or ageratum. They attract a lot of butterflies and insects,' he explained.

'And why do those trees over there look as if they've got snow on their branches?'

Will looked towards the copse of trees she was pointing at. 'Ah, they're the cottonwoods. They shed thousands of tiny seeds that collect on the branches in clumps that look like snow.'

Pearl was beginning to realise that she had a lot to learn about this brand-new country she had come to. They had come to the outskirts of the town now and were passing beneath trees that blotted out the sun and formed a canopy above them when Will told her, 'We're almost there; you'll see the house and the Grand River in a minute.'

Pearl leaned slightly forwards, gripping tight to the edge of the narrow bench seat, keen to get a glimpse of their new home and suddenly they came out into the sunshine again and Pearl smiled as a lovely house loomed into sight. It was set well back from the road down a long driveway and looked like some of the grand houses she had seen in London. It was made of brick with two wide, smooth marble steps leading up to two massive wooden doors in the centre of the building. Above was a decorative portico supported by two marble pillars, while on either side of the door, tall windows framed by heavy drapes glinted in the sunshine. A couple of men were hard at work scything the smooth green lawns that surrounded the house, and here and there flowerbeds ablaze with colour were dotted.

Will glanced at Pearl's face and seemed to guess what she was thinking. 'It's impressive, isn't it? It was built with bricks from the master's brickworks some years ago when he an' the mistress first came here, an' no expense was spared. An' if you think the outside is nice yer should see the inside! The mistress has had things brought from all over the world to furnish it. There are handmade rugs from Turkey, furniture from France and paintings by famous artists. O' course us outside workers don't get to look inside very often but if you're going to be working in the house, you'll see it all.'

The horse was approaching the portico now and Will urged it around one side of the house into what she realised was a large yard with stables. Beyond that she could see an orchard and what looked like a vegetable garden. Crisp white sheets were flapping on a clothesline strung across the yard and once Will drew the horse to a halt she hopped down before turning to help Eliza.

'Go into that door there and Mrs Veasey the housekeeper will sort you out.' Will pointed across the yard.

Pearl gave him a nervous smile and thanked him for fetching them, then watched as he led the horse away. He was so nice and she would have liked to ask him a little about himself but she didn't dare, not till she got to know him a bit better at least. Then she squared her shoulders and gripped Eliza's hand. 'This is it. Let's go an' meet our new gaffers, eh?'

The door was opened as they approached it by a large, rosy-cheeked woman who asked, 'Are you the two new girls who've come to work here?'

119

When Pearl nodded, she ushered them into the largest kitchen Pearl had ever seen. On an enormous scrubbed table that ran down the centre of the room was some pastry that the woman had clearly been rolling before she answered the door.

She dusted the flour from her hands and, after wiping them down the front of a voluminous white apron, she asked, 'So you're Pearl and Eliza, are you?'

Pearl nodded; her mouth dry.

'So which is which? I believe it's Eliza that'll be helping me in the kitchen.'

'This is Eliza,' Pearl piped up, as she gently nudged the girl forward.

The woman frowned. 'Is it now? And can she not speak for herself then, hinny?'

The woman had an accent that Pearl had never heard before. As Pearl would later discover she was from South Shields in the north of England.

Eliza suddenly started to cough and crossing to the sink the woman filled a glass with water from a large pitcher and carried it back to her. 'Get some of that down you, lass,' she urged as Eliza took it from her and she looked at Pearl again with a question in her eye.

'Eliza's quite quiet, an' she hasn't been too well,' Pearl explained in a small voice.

'Hm, well sit yourselves down at the end of the table there an' I'll get you both a bite to eat till Mrs Veasey comes to tell you what will be expected of you.'

The girls obediently did as they were told, and soon the cook placed two plates full of fresh-baked bread and lumps of cheese in front of them, along with two glasses of milk. 'We have our main meal in the evening but this should keep you going till then,' she told them, then went back to rolling her pastry.

As they ate, Pearl examined the room. On the wall behind her was the largest dresser she had ever seen full of china cups, plates and dishes that were so fine she could almost see through them. An enormous range stretched almost the length of the other side of the room, and next to that was a cosy inglenook fireplace with a worn leather wing chair and a stool set at the side of it. On the wall overlooking the garden was a large enamel sink and a huge wooden draining board, and everywhere was so clean Pearl felt she could have eaten her dinner off the floor.

Behind Eliza a green baize door led into what Pearl assumed was the main house. They had almost finished their meal when it swung open and a middle-aged woman in a smart pale-grey bombazine gown appeared. She had a chatelaine about her waist from which numerous keys dangled and her fair hair was swept up into an elegant pleat on the back of her head.

'Ah, you've arrived. Good afternoon, girls. I am Mrs Veasey, the housekeeper. Excellent, I see Cook has fed you. So if you would like to bring your bags, I'll show you where you will be sleeping and explain your positions to you.'

Pearl hastily rose from her seat, dragging Eliza with her. Clutching their bags, they followed the woman through a door at the end of the room that Pearl hadn't noticed, and up a flight of very steep wooden stairs that set Eliza coughing again, and was difficult for Pearl with her leg. She was trying not to limp; this seemed like a great opportunity and she didn't want the woman to think she wasn't capable.

Eventually, they came to a very long landing with numerous doors leading off it and, pointing to the end one, Mrs Veasey told them, 'That will be your room. You're lucky that you'll be able to share.'

When she threw the door open, Pearl and Eliza stepped past her into their new bedroom. She guessed that they were in the loft space as one side of the ceiling sloped but as she peeped through the window she gasped with pleasure.

'Oh, Eliza, look, down there. It's the river that Will told us about. But just look how wide it is! It's almost as big as the sea. We could perhaps go for a swim in it on our days off.'

The woman frowned and shook her head vehemently. 'I don't think that is such a good idea. *Please* don't ever say such a thing in front of Mrs Forbes.'

Pearl stared at her for a moment and the woman relaxed again. 'Right, I'll leave you both to unpack, then come down to the kitchen and I shall sort out some uniforms for you.' She inclined her head and left in a rustle of skirts, closing the door gently behind her.

'Phew, what was all that about?' Pearl mused, although she didn't really expect an answer. Eliza rarely spoke nowadays unless she had to. 'She were fine till I mentioned swimmin' in the river, weren't she? I wonder why that was?'

As she looked around at their bedroom, she was pleasantly surprised; although it wasn't large, it was clean and cosy. There were two iron beds with pillows and blankets neatly folded on the end of each one, and cream muslin curtains fluttered in the breeze at the open window. A large chest of drawers stood at the end of one bed, while a mahogany washstand with a pretty flowered jug and bowl was at the end of the other one. Between the beds was a small table on which there was a tallow candle in a brass candlestick.

'I think we're goin' to be all right 'ere, Liza,' she said happily as she began to bundle their meagre possessions into the drawers. 'But now let's go down an' see what these here uniforms we've got to wear are like, eh?' With an encouraging smile, she took her sister's hand and they made their way to the kitchen to begin their duties.

Chapter Thirteen

Pearl discovered that she was to have two uniforms. One for cleaning out the hearths before lighting the fires first thing in the mornings and for doing housework, and the second much prettier one for answering the door and serving tea and coffee to Mrs Forbes's visitors.

'The last maid left because of Master Monty's bullyin'. He near broke the girl's spirit and she went eventually,' Mrs Drew, the cook, told Pearl later that afternoon as they enjoyed a tea break.

'How awful,' Pearl said, glancing at Eliza, who was peeling potatoes at the kitchen sink for the evening meal. 'Did she run away?'

'Huh!' Mrs Drew huffed. 'No, she didn't, God bless her. She went back to her parents, even though she needed the work, the poor little lass!' Then, realising that she had probably said too much she stood up and said sharply, 'But that's enough of that. We'd best get back to work. You can go through to the dining room and set the table for the evening meal. There'll be three people dining tonight and you'll find the tablecloth, cutlery and everything you'll need in the big sideboard in there.' When Pearl looked dismayed, she frowned. 'Did you hear me, girl?'

'Y-yes, Cook,' Pearl answered falteringly. 'But the thing is . . . I ain't never laid a *posh* table afore. We only ever had spoons at home.'

'Oh, Lord help me! Come on and I'll show you.'

As the cook led her into the hallway, Pearl's mouth fell open. The walls were covered in a rich, damask wallpaper and hung with beautiful gilt-framed pictures and mirrors. The black and white tiles on the floor were so shiny that she could see her face in them, and multi-coloured rugs were scattered across them. The dining room was even more luxurious, and Pearl gasped. 'Cor! I reckon I'll be scared to touch anythin' in here, it's all so grand!'

Cook grinned. 'I don't know about touch anything; you're going to have to get used to cleaning it all, my girl. But now, take note of what I'm doing.' She took a snow-white linen cloth from a drawer on the long mahogany sideboard and threw it across the matching table, around which twelve chairs were arranged. 'There will only be the family dining tonight so we'll just set three places at one end,' she told Pearl as she deftly placed the table mats on the cloth and withdrew a handful of gleaming silver cutlery. 'This knife and fork is for your starters, see? Next to that goes the knife and fork for the main course, and you put the soup spoon and the dessert spoons like so.'

Pearl scratched her head in bewilderment. There were so many of them and so much to remember.

'Next you put out the wine glasses and the water glasses.'

In a surprisingly short time, the woman had the table laid as she wanted it and she smiled with satisfaction as she asked, 'Got it?'

Pearl chewed on her lip uncertainly. 'But how do they know which is which?'

'You always start at the outside with the cutlery and work in.' The cook demonstrated, but Pearl was still unsure. 'But now that's enough of standing about, run a duster round this room while I go and start preparing the meal. You'll find all the cleaning things you'll need in the cupboard in the kitchen I showed you. And don't skimp on the polish either. The mistress likes to be able to see her face in the furniture, so be sure to use a little elbow grease.'

Pearl nodded and followed her back to the kitchen before returning to the dining room, armed with everything she would need. Now that she was alone, she had a little more time to look about and as her eyes settled on a portrait in a gilt frame that took pride of place in the centre of the wall next to the table, her breath caught in her throat.

It was of a young girl and she looked so remarkably like Eliza that Pearl was stunned. She had the same green eyes and blonde curly hair, although hers was somewhat longer than Eliza's, but most striking of all was that they had the same perfectly oval face. In many ways, Pearl looked a little like the girl as well, but as her face was heart-shaped, the similarity wasn't as glaring. She stood for a full minute admiring it, but then started guiltily and crossing to the sideboard she began to polish it as if her life depended on it. *I'll ask Cook who the girl in the portrait is when I go back to the kitchen*, she promised herself, as she got on with her chores.

By the time she had worked her way around the room, carefully moving all the ornaments and trinkets before polishing, the place smelled of beeswax and lavender and she straightened and looked around with satisfaction at what she considered a job well done. When she was quite happy that she hadn't missed anything, she made her way back to the kitchen, just as the door leading out to the stables slammed open on its hinges and a youth with a sour expression on his face appeared. He had obviously been riding if the whip in his hand and the jodhpurs he was wearing were anything to go by.

'Send some tea through to the day room immediately,' he told Cook shortly, and she scowled at him as she looked down at the mud his boots were trailing across her clean kitchen floor.

'How many times have I to ask you not to come in this way, lad?' she scolded.

'And how many times do I have to remind *you* that this is my parents' house and I can go wherever I like in it! And may I also remind you that it's Master Monty to you!' he shot back disrespectfully. He noticed Eliza and Pearl then, and peered at them in turn.

So this is Monty, the young master of the house, Pearl thought. He was tall and slim and Pearl guessed probably a couple of years older than herself. His hair was dark and straight and his eyes were a toffee colour, but there was no warmth in them and she took an instant dislike to him.

At that moment Mrs Veasey appeared and she too frowned as she looked at the state of the floor. 'I suggest you take your boots off before you go into the hall, sir,' Mrs Veasey told him. 'I'm sure your mother would be none too pleased should you ruin any of her lovely rugs.'

He narrowed his eyes for a moment but then dropped on to the nearest chair, yanked his boots off, threw them across the room and stormed out into the hallway.

The cook shook her head and tutted in disgust. 'It's about time someone taught that young man some manners,' she muttered, as Pearl hurried past her to put the polish and the dusters away. 'Pearl, would you take those boots outside to the pump and wash the worst of the mud off them? I just hope the poor horse is all right. He's a cruel young devil is Master Monty! Will said Spirit was all of a lather when he took him back to the stables yesterday.'

Pearl did as she was asked, suddenly wondering if she and Eliza had ended up in such a good place after all. The young master had stared at them both as if they were dirt beneath his feet, but then she was used to being looked down on. She remembered the looks she would get from people when her mother had sent her out begging on the streets, and the way the staff at the workhouse had treated her, and she supposed so long as the mistress was kind to them she could put up with her son.

The rest of the afternoon was spent doing any jobs that the cook asked her to and eventually she told her, 'You'd best nip up to your room and change into your best uniform now, Pearl. You'll wear that for waiting on table or answering the door to visitors.'

Pearl was only too happy to do as she was told. The uniform was a pale dove-grey dress with a tiny white lace collar over which she was to wear a frilled broderie anglaise pinafore and a matching mop cap. Once she had put it on, she stared at her reflection in the tiny cracked mirror over the washstand and smiled. It was the prettiest outfit she had ever owned, although the dress was a fraction big and slightly too long. Even so, there was a broad smile on her face when she went back downstairs.

For the next half an hour, Cook and Mrs Veasey taught her how she was to serve the meal.

'You just carry the dishes in and place them carefully in the middle of the table,' Mrs Veasey instructed. 'The mistress will serve them and you never speak unless you are spoken to and only then to answer. Oh, and don't forget to bob your knee when you leave the room after asking if there is anything else they require. Do you understand?'

'I think so.' Pearl's head was spinning. There was so much to take in but she hoped she'd soon get the hang of it.

Once the family were seated in the dining room a little bell – one of many that hung in the kitchen in a row on a brass pole – tinkled, indicating that the family were ready for the meal to be served.

'I shall serve the first course tonight. It's soup,' Mrs Veasey told her as she lifted a steaming tureen. Pearl's eyes widened; she wasn't sure she'd be able to lift that tureen alone and with her limp she might splosh the soup everywhere – she just had to hope they didn't eat soup too often. 'Then you can help me serve the main meal. But I shall only help you for this evening to make sure that you've remembered everything I have told you, so just watch me and pay attention.'

She disappeared and returned soon after. They waited then until the bell tinkled again to tell them that the first course was finished and Mrs Veasey took a large wooden tray and hurried off to collect the dirty soup dishes, which she passed to Eliza to wash.

'Now, Pearl, we are ready for the main.'

'Yes, missus.' Both she and the housekeeper each took a large dish of steaming vegetables and set off down the hallway. When they entered the dining room, they found Mr and Mrs Forbes and their son already seated, and with a polite nod Mrs Veasey approached the table and laid her dish down. Pearl quickly did the same, trying to keep her eyes away from the portrait of the golden-haired child, before they hurried back to the kitchen. It took four journeys to fetch all the food in. As well as the vegetables, there were dishes of roast and mashed potatoes and a large leg of pork covered in crispy crackling that made Pearl's mouth water. Finally, Mrs Veasey carried in two different bottles of wine while Pearl followed with a large gravy boat. Mrs Veasey looked at Pearl expectantly. Suddenly remembering what she was to do, Pearl blurted, 'D'you want anythin' else, missus?'

Mr Forbes glanced up with a look of surprise on his face as Mrs Forbes tried not to smile.

'No thank you, Pearl,' she said with an amused twinkle in her eye. 'When we are ready for the second course we shall ring.'

Pearl awkwardly bobbed her knee and almost fell over in the process as Mrs Veasey hurriedly shooed her out of the room closing the door gently behind them.

'Goodness me. Whoever was that?' Mr Forbes enquired as he started to carve the meat.

His wife grinned. 'That was Pearl, our new maid. She came here with the latest batch of children from the orphanages and workhouses in London. She's a bit of a rough diamond admittedly but I'm sure she'll do well with a bit of coaching.'

Her husband shook his head. 'Let's hope you're right, my dear. I dread to think what your guests will think of her accent.'

'She has a younger sister too, who will be helping Cook in the kitchen,' his wife informed him. 'She's such a sweet little thing, I'm sure you'll like her.'

'I doubt I'll even get to see her,' he answered as he placed a slice of the succulent pork on each of their plates, and she supposed he was right. He was always so busy working, which was why he was so happy to leave the running of the house to her.

Monty, meanwhile, looked on with a sulky scowl on his face and wolfed down his meal.

'That Mr Monty is a sour-faced devil, ain't he?' Pearl said to Mrs Veasey as they made their way back to the kitchen.

The woman sighed. Pearl seemed to be a good little worker, she had to admit, but there was a lot of work to do with her before she was ready to admit visitors, and it was a shame about her limp.

'You really shouldn't pass such comments about members of the family, Pearl,' she scolded. 'And certainly, *never* outside of these four walls. A good maid should always be loyal to her employees.'

Pearl apologised, even though as far as she was concerned, she'd only said the truth, but she didn't want to get into bother on her first day so she said nothing more. *But he is a sour-faced devil an' I don't like him one bit!* she said to herself, as she helped Eliza dry the dishes.

Both girls were tired and Pearl's hip was aching when they were allowed to retire to their beds that evening, but all in all Pearl felt that their first day in their new job had gone quite well, even though being on her feet so much had started Eliza coughing again.

'It's nice to think we'll get to have every Sunday afternoon off, ain't it?' she said to her sister as they snuggled down into their beds. 'Wi' a bit o' luck we'll be able to meet up wi' Susan an' Nick. I wonder how they're gettin' on in their new jobs? An' the missus an' cook seem all right an' all. An' Mrs Veasey, if it comes to that.'

But the only answer was the sound of Eliza gently snoring, so after snuffing the candle out, Pearl snuggled down under the blankets and within seconds was fast asleep.

Chapter Fourteen

On their first Sunday afternoon in their new home, after helping Eliza to wash and dry the dinner pots, Pearl set off to explore. Eliza had said that she wanted to stay and rest, and although Pearl would have preferred to have her sister with her, she headed for the town, hoping for a glimpse of Susan or Nick.

It was a warm day and Pearl enjoyed being out in the fresh air. As she moved along, she admired the miles of woodland that climbed up the hill on the other side of the river. Having lived in the slums of London, she had never seen so many trees in her life, but better still were the clusters of bright-yellow anemones – known as windflowers and archangels – that grew beneath them. Soon the town came into view; it was very different to the first time she had seen it as it was very quiet and all the shops were shut. There was a saloon bar open though, and as she passed it, the sound of music and laughter drifted out to her.

Pearl concentrated on looking for the bakery where she believed Susan had gone to work. She'd given Susan's description to Will and he had said he'd seen her briefly the day before when he went into town and she had asked him to let Pearl know where she was. Luckily, just as Pearl spotted the place, Susan emerged from an alley that ran down the side of it.

'Pearl!' Her face broke into a wide grin at the sight of her friend and she flew towards her, her pleasure at seeing her plain to see.

'So 'ow 'ave yer been in yer first week?' the girl enquired as they fell into step and continued on towards the docks.

'Not bad. I gets to wear a really nice uniform when I'm servin' at table but the one I wear fer lightin' the fires an' cleanin' ain't so posh. But what about you? How have you got on?'

Just for a second Susan's smile slipped, but then she said cheerily, 'Oh, not so bad really. I mean it's bloody 'ard work! I 'as to be up at five of a mornin' to light the ovens an' then I barely stop all day. Even after all the customers are gone I ain't finished 'cause I 'ave to clean the place ready fer the next day. Still, I gets plenty to eat so that's sommat, ain't it?'

Pearl turned her head to look at her more closely and after a moment she asked soberly, 'An' how did yer get that bruise on yer cheek? It's a beauty an' I'm surprised yer don't have a black eye with it an' all.'

Susan's hand rose self-consciously to stroke her swollen cheek as she shrugged. 'Aw, I just whacked it on the oven door but it's fine. It'll be gone in a few days. But tell me about the Forbes family. I've 'eard tell they're ever so posh an' ever so rich. Are they kind to yer?'

'Well, Mrs Forbes is kind,' Pearl told her as they arrived at the docks where an enormous ship was being unloaded. 'I ain't really seen much of the master, but Monty, the son, ain't so nice. In fact, he's horrid! He nearly pushed me over in the yard yesterday as I were gettin' the washin' in. He treats all the servants like dirt 'cept fer Mrs Veasey the housekeeper 'cause she soon puts him in his place if he so much as sets a foot wrong.' As they perched their backsides on some barrels by the quay, Pearl went on, 'I've got an idea Master Monty is about to be sent away to finish his schoolin' in England. I over'eard Mrs Veasey an' the cook talkin' about it while I were makin' the fire up yesterday. It seems he's upset his dad in some way but I don't know what he's done. To be honest, I'll be pleased if he does go; I can't stand him. But what about Nick? Have yer heard how he's goin' on? Or Freda at the butcher's?'

'Not a word.' Susan sighed. 'The farm 'e's workin' on is about two miles out of town from what Mrs Belling, me boss, says. She's all right as it 'appens but I ain't so keen on 'im.'

'Why is that?'

Susan wiped her nose on the sleeve of her faded dress and shrugged. 'Oh 'e's, er . . . yer know? A bit touchy-feely, like. But don't worry I can 'andle 'is sort, an' it's only when 'is missus ain't about. The dirty old bleeder.'

Pearl looked so dismayed at this information that Susan couldn't help but grin. 'I told yer, don't worry. I'll give 'im a good kick in 'is old man if 'e comes it too thick. An' as fer yer other question, far as I know Freda's none too pleased about workin' at the butcher's 'cause she told me she always fancied working in a baker's. Now I've met the gaffer I almost wish she'd got my job instead!'

Pearl couldn't help but chuckle. Susan was a law unto herself, despite the fact that she was only a scrap of a girl. They went on to talk of other things until the light began to slowly fade and Pearl said, 'I reckon I'd best be gettin' back to check on Eliza. What are you goin' to do wi' the rest o' your day off?'

'Eat an' sleep,' Susan said decisively, as they strolled back in the direction of the baker's shop.

Once there they gave each other a hug, and then with promises that she would be back the same time the following Sunday, Pearl set off back to the Forbeses' grand home.

There was a carriage at the bottom of the steps outside the front door when she arrived but thinking nothing of it, she set off around the side of the house for the servants' entrance. As she entered the kitchen, Cook, who was sitting at the side of the fire with her feet on a stool and a glass of ale in her hand, told her, 'The mistress has called the doctor in to have a look at Eliza. She's worried about her cough. He's with her now, I reckon, if you want to go up and check.'

Pearl was off up the stairs like a shot from a gun and was just in time to find the doctor speaking to Mrs Forbes on the landing. They both glanced up as they heard her and Mrs Forbes smiled.

'Ah, Pearl, here you are. The doctor has just examined Eliza, I was a bit worried about that cough of hers, but thankfully he says it's nothing to worry about. She has a weak chest and just needs rest and this tonic he's prescribed.'

'Thanks, missus,' Pearl mumbled as relief flooded through her. She wasn't sure what she would do were anything to happen to her little sister, they had always been so close.

The doctor bid them good day then as Mrs Forbes said, 'Going on what he said, I've decided I'm going to move Lizzie into the main house until she's completely recovered.'

It took Pearl a moment to realise that Mrs Forbes was talking about Eliza. She found it strange to hear Eliza addressed as Lizzie. She had never had her name shortened to that before. She was a bit saddened at the thought of them being separated, but knew it was for the best.

'I shall also tell Cook that she won't be helping in the kitchen for the foreseeable future,' Mrs Forbes continued. 'I also thought . . . well, this is just a thought, but my husband has decided that our son should finish his education in England so he will be leaving for London next month. As we booked the tutor he has here for the next two years, I've decided that he may as well teach you and Lizzie for a couple of hours each day. How does that sound to you? And you can join Monty for some lessons starting tomorrow.'

Pearl's face lit up as she nodded with her eyes shining. 'I'd love that, missus! I can already write me own name.'

'In that case, I shall go and have a room prepared for Lizzie immediately.' She swept along the landing in a rustle of silk skirts, then suddenly paused and turned back to say, 'Oh, and once Monty has left, I shall be giving you both elocution lessons. I'll discuss with Mrs Veasey what time is best. I really can't have you addressing my visitors speaking as you do.'

Pearl awkwardly bobbed her knee; she could never quite seem to get the hang of it. 'Thanks, missus.'

'Thank you, Mrs Forbes,' the woman corrected her. 'We may as well start as we mean to go on.'

And then she was gone, leaving Pearl to wonder how she and Eliza had got so lucky with their employment. *But then I've never worked in a posh house before*, she thought. *Per'aps all posh folk treat their staff this way?*

She went into the bedroom to find Eliza sitting in bed, propped up with pillows, looking considerably brighter than she had for some long time.

'The missus is movin' me to a posh bedroom in the main part o' the 'ouse,' she immediately told her sister, and again Pearl was shocked. It was the most Eliza had said without being questioned for months.

'I know, she just told me.' Pearl crossed to the bed and tenderly stroked her little sister's soft blonde curls.

'An' the missus calls me Lizzie. That's nice, ain't it?'

'It is, so just make sure as yer do all she tells yer,' Pearl warned. 'We're both goin' to be having lessons wi' Mr Monty's tutor an' all, though I don't suppose you'll be so chuffed about that.' Unlike Pearl, Eliza had never enjoyed the lessons at the workhouse and she very much doubted she would like them now. 'Anyway, I'd best get yer few things packed afore the missus comes back fer you.'

'She told me I won't need nothin'. She's got all new stuff fer me,' Eliza told her and Pearl frowned – they'd only just got their uniforms and they were brand new. Why would the mistress go to all that trouble for a little kitchen maid?

Shortly after, Mrs Forbes returned and, taking Eliza by the hand, she led her away. Pearl watched them go feeling strangely lonely. All her life she and Eliza had slept together and it would be odd to have a room all to herself. Even so, if it meant Eliza getting properly well again, she knew it would be worth the separation.

Settling down on the bed, she took out her slate and chalk and practised her letters. Eventually it began to grow dark so, putting her slate aside, she rose and stretched and made her way down to the kitchen for her supper.

She had reached the bottom of the servants' stairs and the door leading to the kitchen when she paused with her hand on the doorknob as she heard Mrs Veasey and Cook in deep conversation.

'I'm telling you no good will come of this, it isn't natural,' Cook said, sounding worried. 'Whoever heard of a servant being treated like a member of the family they're supposed to be working for?'

'Well, I think we know why it's come about, don't we?' Pearl heard Mrs Veasey answer. 'The mistress is even calling the child Lizzie, and just when I thought she was beginning to get a little better. I feared this would happen the minute I clapped eyes on the child. The likeness she bears to poor Elizabeth is quite uncanny. Still, there's nothing we can do, although I fear the master might have something to say about it.'

Pearl frowned. Who was this Elizabeth that Eliza was supposed to look like? It must be something to do with the portrait of the little girl that hung in the dining room. Taking a deep breath, she turned the handle and entered the room. Instantly the two women stopped speaking.

'Ah, had a nice rest have you, pet?' the kindly cook said. 'Come and sit down, there's some fresh bread and cheese for your supper. The rest of us ate earlier on.'

Pearl sat at the table and then blurted out, 'Cook . . . who was Elizabeth?'

The two women looked startled, but the cook replied, 'She was Mrs Forbes's daughter. A lovely little lass she was, but she died in an accident early last year. The poor mistress has never quite got over it. In fact, at one time we feared for her sanity, the poor love.'

'Is that her in the portrait hangin' in the dinin' room?'

The cook gave a nervous little cough before nodding. 'Yes, that was her. That was painted shortly before she died.'

'She looked a little like Eliza, didn't she?'

It was Mrs Veasey who answered this time. 'Yes, I suppose she did, and now that Eliza won't be working for a time, I'm afraid it will put more work on your shoulders.'

'I don't mind that.' Pearl began to saw a slice off the loaf of bread on the table. 'I'll work twice as 'ard as I already do if it means Eliza gettin' better.' She already had to be up with the dawn to clean out the fireplaces and get the fires going but she meant what she said. Eliza was all the family she had left and she meant everything to her.

'You're a good girl,' Mrs Veasey said softly. 'But if you find the extra work too much for you, you must say and the mistress will have to get someone else in. But let's see how we get on, shall we?'

Pearl frowned. 'But where is Eliza? Has she already had her supper?'

'Er . . . yes she has. She dined with the family earlier,' Mrs Veasey informed her.

'Dined with the family?' Pearl looked shocked. Eliza barely knew a fork from a spoon so she could only imagine what a mess she would have got into trying to work out which cutlery was used for which course. And her clothes – they certainly weren't grand enough to wear in a formal dining room, especially as the family always changed for dinner, but then she supposed Mrs Forbes knew what she was doing.

The first night alone in her room was strange. It wasn't that long ago that she had been sharing a straw mattress on the floor, cramped in with all her siblings, and now she found herself alone in this room, in another country. She lay there listening to the soughing of the wind in the trees and the wildlife until she eventually fell into an uneasy doze hoping that Eliza was feeling better than she did.

As usual, she was up bright and early the next day and once the fires were lit, she hurried through to the kitchen to put the kettle on the range to boil and prepared the cups and the teapot. Cook loved a cup of tea when she first appeared and they usually had ten quiet minutes before starting the breakfasts. The family would eat first and then the staff, and Pearl hoped that Eliza would be joining them.

After she and Cook had drunk their tea, she shot off to lay the dining room table, and this time she paid particular attention to the child in the portrait. There was an uncanny resemblance to Eliza, she had to admit, although this child was dressed in satin and lace and was plumper than her sister had ever been. She laid three places as usual but as she was heading back to the kitchen Mrs Veasey informed her somewhat frostily, 'Go back and lay another place, please, Pearl. Mrs Forbes has just informed me that Eliza will be dining with the family again this morning.'

'Oh! Right, missus.' Pearl turned and scurried back to lay another place, wondering if this was to become a common thing now. She hoped not, because she was missing Eliza already.

It was very strange to serve the family breakfast with her sister sitting beside them. Pearl had almost dropped the steaming tureen of porridge she was carrying when she first entered the room and saw Eliza sitting at the table. She had looked so different that Pearl had had to look twice to recognise her. Her hair had been washed and brushed and rested on her shoulders in soft springy curls with a blue satin ribbon tied amongst them. The dress she was wearing was blue too and her face was freshly washed. Pearl wasn't sure whether she was allowed to speak to her or not but decided against it when she saw the faces of Mr Forbes and Monty. Mr Forbes looked decidedly uncomfortable, while Monty looked angry and kept glaring in Eliza's direction. Mrs Forbes, however, was cheerful and smiled at Pearl.

'Place it in the centre of the table,' she told her. 'And I'll serve it while you bring in the rest of the food. You can put it all over there on the sideboard. And then that will be all for now, thank you, Pearl.' She turned her attention to Eliza then and as Pearl bobbed her knee and quietly left the room, she heard the mistress say, 'Come along, Lizzie, this is very good for you. It will build your strength up. Try to eat just a little bit for me, won't you?'

Pearl felt a lump form in her throat. Eliza hadn't looked at her once, but then she supposed she was too nervous to, so she instantly forgave her.

Once again, she found Cook and Mrs Veasey with their heads together when she entered the kitchen, but they stopped speaking the second she appeared and Pearl guessed they had been talking of the situation. She couldn't really blame them, and without a word she began to take the rest of the meal through to the family, although how four people were supposed to eat so much in one sitting, she had no idea. There had been times back home when the whole family hadn't had as much food in a whole month between them. There were rashers of crispy bacon, fat juicy sausages, devilled kidneys, mushrooms and tomatoes and a whole tray of eggs as well as slices of golden-brown toast.

When the meal was over, Monty left the table without a word and slunk away, and Mrs Forbes told Eliza kindly, 'You did well this morning, dear. If you continue to eat good nourishing food, we'll have you fit as a fiddle in no time. Why don't you go up to your room and rest for a while? You'll find some lovely story books in there.'

Eliza nodded and scurried away, and as soon as she was gone Zachariah Forbes rose from his seat and crossed to place an arm about his wife's shoulders as she stood staring out across the garden.

Zack was a tall, handsome man with a smattering of grey in his dark hair and moustache that made him look distinguished. Although he looked to be a good few years older than his wife, he still had a muscular physique and prided himself on keeping fit, but now he looked gravely concerned.

'Darling . . .' he began, choosing his words carefully. 'Are you quite sure that you are doing right by paying so much attention to this child?'

His wife stared up at him from deep-blue eyes that could always melt him. 'Why, Zack, don't you like Lizzie?'

He looked uncomfortable as he licked his dry lips. '*Of course* I do, she seems to be a perfectly nice child, but . . . Well, you must remember you've been quite ill over the last year and I would hate to see you going back to how you were just when you were showing such signs of improvement. I thought the girl's name was Eliza? Is it right to call her Lizzie?'

Shrugging his arm away she turned to face him, her lovely eyes flashing. 'What you mean is I shouldn't call her by the name we called our daughter! But don't you see the similarities? Elizabeth – Eliza, and the similarity in looks. I truly believe that this child has been sent to us to help me come to terms with our loss. Of course, no one could take the place of Elizabeth but if I can help this child, I will feel like I have a purpose again, especially now you are sending Monty to England!'

He took a deep breath. 'Under the circumstances, don't you think that is for the best? You admit he is beyond our control. I'm afraid you have spoiled him shamelessly and the way he thrashed that young maid was unforgivable. And it wasn't the first time, she told me. It cost me a pretty penny, I don't mind telling you, to get her to return to London and keep her mouth shut.'

'But Monty denies hurting her,' she responded hotly. 'It is only her word against his and I choose to believe my son!'

'Then you have more faith in him than I do.' Zack shook his head sadly. 'This school I have found for him will be the making of him, you'll see. When he comes back in a few years' time, he will be a man, and hopefully a responsible one.'

His wife pouted and flounced away, and realising that he was wasting his time, Zack slowly made for the door. 'I shall be back for dinner this evening. I have a busy day ahead at the shipyard. The new ship that the men have been building is almost completed and I want to oversee the final touches to it. I was hoping that Monty would join me following his lessons, but once again he has shown no interest. Goodbye, my dear.'

Once alone Emmaline sank down on to a dining room chair and stared at the portrait of her late daughter with tears in her eyes, just as she did every single day. It was still hard to accept that she was really gone; that she would never see her or hold her again and the pain was still raw. But something about little Eliza had touched her deep inside and right or wrong she knew that this child was going to become her incentive to carry on. There had been so many times when she had wanted to die. Dark days when she had been too grief-stricken to even get out of bed. She knew all too well how close she had come to being shipped back to London and put in an asylum to recover. Only the devotion of her husband and dear Mrs Veasey had prevented it. But now she felt she had something to live for again.

Chapter Fifteen

'So what's up wi' your face then?' Susan asked in her usual forthright way when Pearl walked in to town to meet her the following Sunday afternoon. 'Yer look as if you've lost a shillin' an' found a tanner.'

Pearl gave her a wry smile. 'There's nothing *wrong* exactly but . . .' She went on to tell Susan about Mrs Forbes's sudden interest in Eliza as they wandered along the main street.

'Hm,' Susan said when she had finished. 'An' 'ow is Eliza respondin' to this sudden interest?'

'Well, that's the strange thing. She seems to be thrivin' on it. She's come right out of 'er shell already an' I know I should be glad about that, but she don't seem to 'ave time fer me anymore.'

'Sounds like sour grapes to me 'cause the missus is showin' 'er favour instead o' you,' Susan said bluntly.

Pearl flushed and shook her head in denial. 'It ain't that at all . . . it's just that Eliza don't even hardly speak to me anymore, only when her has to. I know she's always been quiet, but we always felt close and now it feels like she's getting more distant.'

They had come to the gates of the churchyard and on an impulse Pearl suggested, 'Let's go in an' have a look, shall we? I reckon this must be where Mrs Forbes's daughter is buried.'

'Huh! An' unless yer knows where the grave is it'll be like lookin' for a bleedin' needle in an 'aystack,' Susan grumbled. She had never been keen on churches, they were cold and draughty places as far as she was concerned, and graveyards gave her the shivers: all those dead folk lying there. But she followed Pearl through the lychgate anyway, and they began to wander amongst the tombstones. As they came to the shelter of a large tree, one in particular caught their eye. It was a beautifully carved marble angel and easily the biggest in there.

'This is it!' Pearl pointed at the name etched into the stone beneath it.

'What does it say?' Susan asked, interested in spite of what she had said. In actual fact this was a very nice church as churches went. It was built of red bricks that had mellowed in the sun to a warm golden colour. A heavy oak door marked the entrance and beneath the spire, lovely stained-glass windows depicting saints from times gone by sparkled in the sunshine.

Pearl narrowed her eyes. She'd been practising her reading on the boat but she still struggled, though she was sure her lessons with Master Monty's tutor would help her improve further.

'Eliza-beth . . . Jane . . . Forbes,' she read haltingly. 'Beloved . . . dau-gh-ter and . . . sis-ter, tak-en far too soon.' There was more written but Pearl couldn't manage to read it nor the date that she could see was written there.

'Poor little sod,' Susan said. 'Mrs Belling the baker's wife were on about it in the shop the uvver day. I 'eard 'er when

I took a tray o' bread up. From what I could catch of it she drownded in the river.'

'Really?' Pearl looked surprised.

'What? Yer mean yer live there an' yer didn't know?'

'Nobody talks about it,' Pearl told her solemnly. 'I s'pose they don't want to upset the missus.'

Susan nodded in agreement. 'Yer could be right. Apparently, she went a bit . . . yer know' – she tapped her head – 'doolally fer a time. But anyway, let's get away from 'ere shall we? These places give me the creeps. 'Ow's about we walk down to the river; I ain't 'ad chance to get a proper look at it yet.'

Neither had Pearl so, happy to oblige, she followed her friend away from the docks and back along the winding path and to the main road where they headed towards the woods.

Once there, the trees formed a canopy above them and Susan glanced about in the gloom nervously. 'Yer don't suppose there's snakes or bears in 'ere, do yer?' she whispered.

Pearl giggled. 'Well, if there are, they're probably as scared of us as we are o' them. Come on, don't be a scaredy cat. I'm sure I can hear the river already. It can't be far through here.'

She was proved to be right when some minutes later they emerged from the trees to find themselves on the banks of the river.

'Bloody 'ell, look 'ow wide it is,' Susan breathed. 'Yer can barely see the uvver side. An' look 'ow fast it flows. If your missus's daughter fell in there it's no wonder the poor fing drownded. Yer wouldn't stand a chance against that current would yer?'

'No, I don't think yer would,' Pearl agreed as they began to stroll along the riverbank.

They had gone some way when Susan suddenly remembered something and grinned. ''Ere you'll never guess who I saw t'other day? It were Nick. He came into town for food for the animals wi' the farmer 'e's workin' for.'

'Really?' Pearl smiled as she thought of him. 'An' how is he?'

'Well, 'e ain't too 'appy as it 'appens,' Susan told her. 'He reckons the farmer is a slave driver. ''E's up wi' the lark an' ain't allowed to go to bed till it's dark, so I fink farmin' ain't turnin' out to be quite what 'e'd hoped, poor sod.'

'That's a shame.' Pearl was sad for him. She went on to tell Susan about the lessons she was now having with Monty's tutor.

'It's just for an hour every weekday,' she explained. 'But me readin' is comin' along lovely an' I'm learnin' me numbers an' all now. Mr Jackson, Monty's tutor, is smashin'. Quite young, I reckon, probably in his early twenties. But Monty ain't too happy about me an' Eliza joinin' in.' She chuckled. 'Still, he's due to sail fer London to his new school next week an' hopefully once he's gone it'll make things easier. The missus is in a right two an' eight about it, I don't mind tellin' yer. She's walkin' about wi' a face on her like a wet weekend but personally I'll be glad to see the back of him. He's a nasty piece o' work. Once he's gone she says she'd going to start me elec . . . elect . . . Well, anyway teachin' me how to speak proper like.'

Susan giggled; she couldn't imagine Pearl speaking in a posh voice and thought Mrs Forbes might have quite a task on her hands to achieve it, although she didn't like to say it.

'And have you heard how Freda is gettin' on?' Pearl asked then and Susan nodded.

'I 'ave, as it 'appens. She left the butcher's an' got took on by a farmer but never lasted a week there afore the farmer's wife dumped 'er back at the 'ome. Her boss reckoned she were bone idle, which don't surprise me, an' she's still waitin' to find another position, so I 'eard.'

They spent another leisurely hour strolling and chatting but eventually they headed back to the town where they parted, promising to meet up again at the same time the following week.

Pearl was almost at the drive that led to the Forbeses' house when she suddenly became aware of a horse's hooves galloping up behind her and, turning, she was shocked to see Monty bearing down on her. The horse was frothing at the mouth as Monty whipped the poor creature to make it go faster.

'Out of my way, servant!' he shouted as he flew past and Pearl just had time to jump aside.

'Idiot!' she shouted at his retreating figure as she shook her small fist at him, but he rode on without even looking back.

Will won't be pleased when he sees what state the poor horse is in again, she thought as she dusted down her skirt and set off. *But at least he'll be gone next week an' it's good riddance to bad rubbish far as I'm concerned.*

She found Cook and Mrs Veasey in the kitchen when she entered and told them, 'Master Monty just come chargin' after me on 'is horse like a bat outta hell! If I hadn't jumped outta the way I'd be flat as a pancake.'

150

'Oh, Pearl, your grammar really *is* atrocious,' Mrs Veasey sighed, ignoring what she'd said about Monty. 'From now on the mistress says that I'm to start correcting you and so is Cook here, so be warned.'

Pearl flushed with indignation. What was wrong with the way she spoke? And what did she have to gain by learning to speak posh like they did? Even so, she supposed she should at least try, although she knew it wasn't going to be easy. 'I were only tellin' yer about Monty's bad be'aviour,' she mumbled, crossing her arms across her flat chest.

'No, Pearl . . . I *was* only telling *you* about Monty's bad be*ha*viour,' Mrs Veasey corrected. 'Now try again.'

Pearl sniffed. 'I were . . . *was*, only trying to tell yer . . . *you*, about Monty's bad be*ha*viour,' she repeated slowly.

Mrs Veasey smiled approvingly. 'That's much better. You see you *can* do it when you stop to think. Let this be the start of the lesson.'

Pearl let out a deep sigh. She'd have to watch her step in future.

The following week, the house was in turmoil as Monty prepared to leave to start his new school in London. His mother had insisted that his father should travel with him to see him properly settled and they were to sail with the tide early the following morning on one of Mr Forbes's own ships. The hallway was full of trunks containing Monty's clothes and the books he would need. The ones they hadn't been able to obtain would be bought by his father when they arrived in London.

'Promise me you won't leave him until you are quite sure he has settled,' Pearl heard Mrs Forbes implore her husband as they sat at dinner that evening. And then the poor mistress broke into tears again.

'Anyone would think we were sending him to prison rather than to one of the best schools in England,' her husband said softly as he handed her his handkerchief. Her own flimsy little lace-trimmed one was quite sodden.

Monty meantime sat silent, his face angry and resentful. He was well aware that his easy life was about to finish, for the next few years at least, but what could he do other than go along with it? He knew his mother didn't want him to go, she had made that more than clear, but his father wasn't as easy to twist around his little finger.

'The time will fly by, son, you'll see,' he told Monty now. 'It's high time you knuckled down to some serious work now. And then when you come home, you'll be able to take over some of the businesses here for me.'

Throughout all this Eliza sat silent, although she was secretly relieved he was going. With him out of the way she would have the mistress all to herself and she couldn't think of anything nicer. She was starting to like being pampered and spoiled. Only the day before Mrs Forbes had taken her to her own dressmaker in the town and had her fitted for two new dresses. She had even let Eliza help choose the patterns and the material for them and she could hardly wait to have them. How grand she would be then with matching ribbons in her hair. Pearl was sure to be quite green with envy. Better still, the night before, Mrs Forbes had entered her room and tucked her in and kissed her goodnight. Her own mother had never done that and now Eliza intended to make the best of it.

The meal was a miserable affair and no one ate much. *What a waste*, Pearl thought as she carried the barely touched leg of lamb back to the kitchen. Unbidden her thoughts flew back to her family in England and she wondered how they were faring. No doubt her ma would still be drowning her sorrows in gin and her dad would be passing every penny he could get his hands on over the bar of the nearest inn, but it was her siblings that she worried most about, though she knew that she couldn't do anything to help them. Her ma had made sure of that when she had Pearl and Eliza shipped off to Canada without so much as a goodbye.

'Eeh, what a waste of time cooking that was,' Cook grumbled when Pearl slid the untouched lamb on to the table before returning for the vegetables. 'But never mind, I can save the meat pie I'd cooked for our dinner till tomorrow and we'll have this tonight; I know Will loves a bit of lamb so it won't go to waste.'

As a result, when Pearl eventually went to bed that evening she was feeling comfortably full, but the room still felt very lonely without Eliza.

Pearl was up first thing in the morning as Mrs Forbes wanted breakfast prepared early so that her husband and son wouldn't set sail on an empty stomach.

'I'm glad I don't have to get up at this unearthly hour *every* day,' Cook groaned – usually the kitchen was warm and Pearl had a pot of tea mashing for her by the time she had to put in an appearance. The next hour was hectic as the family pecked at their breakfasts while Will was packing Monty's luggage on to the carriage. And then at last it was time for them to go and Mrs Forbes clung to her son on the steps of the house, sobbing as if she might never see him again.

'I shall miss you *so* much,' she wept as she covered his face in kisses and he blushed a dull, beetroot red. 'Please promise me that you will take the very greatest care of yourself. Write regularly, and if there is anything at all you need, let us know immediately.'

'Yes, Mother.' Monty untangled her arms from about his neck and escaped into the carriage where his father sat waiting for him.

'Safe journey,' Emmaline called, waving her handkerchief as Will urged the horses forwards. 'Goodbye, my darlings.'

Monty sat staring sulkily out of the window with his arms crossed while his father waved back. They stayed watching and waving until the carriage was out of sight over the horizon.

'Oh, if only Zack had let me go the docks to see them off,' Mrs Forbes sobbed to Mrs Veasey. 'But he said it would be too upsetting and we would be better saying our goodbyes here.'

'And I believe he was quite right.' Mrs Veasey placed a comforting arm about her shoulders and turned her around. 'Now come inside and I'll get Pearl to fetch you a nice fresh pot of tea.'

Emmaline cried on and off for the whole of that day, even paying little heed to Eliza, but the next day, true to her word, when Pearl had completed the housework, she was sent for.

'Right,' Mrs Forbes told Pearl with a bright smile. 'I think it's time we had a go at turning you and Eliza into young ladies now.' Eliza, who was already in the drawing room, scowled while Pearl merely sighed resignedly. She really didn't have much say in the matter if it was what her mistress wanted, so she supposed she may as well get on with it.

'I want you to repeat after me. How now brown cow.'

And so, the first lesson began.

When it was over Pearl rose to leave but Mrs Forbes stopped her. 'Pearl, I hope you don't mind me asking but what caused your limp? Was it an accident of some kind?'

'Oh no, missus, I mean, ma'am. I were born wi' . . . with one leg shorter than the other.'

'I see.' Mrs Forbes tapped her lip thoughtfully before eventually saying, 'In that case, I think it might be remedied. Tomorrow morning, I shall take you to see the shoemaker in town. Be ready to leave by ten o'clock.'

'Yes, ma'am, thank you, ma'am.' Pearl shot out of the door with a smile on her face. Could there really be something done to improve her limp? She could only live in hope.

Chapter Sixteen

'Nick . . . I thought it was you!' Pearl ran forwards and without thinking threw her arms about the boy's neck, making him blush furiously.

'Give over,' he objected. 'I'm pleased to see you an' all, but there's no need to go all soppy on me!'

'Sorry.' Pearl giggled as she stepped away from him. It was the first time she had seen him since they'd started their new jobs and she thought he looked tired.

He was standing outside the blacksmith's and thumbing across his shoulder he told her, 'One o' the gaffers horses needed shoein' so I've brought him in. I've got a list o' stuff to get 'ere fer the farmer's wife while he's bein' done an' all. Per'aps yer could tell me the best places to get 'em?'

He held the list out to her and she nodded. 'Ah well, as luck would have it, I'm just on the way to the haberdashery shop to pick up some embroidery silks for Mrs Forbes. That's where you'll get the darning wool from. Come on and I'll show you where it is.'

As they started off side by side, he stared at her curiously from the corner of his eye. 'Here – I thought there were somethin' different about yer an' I've just realised what it is; yer talkin' all posh now! An' you ain't limpin'! What happened?'

Pearl grinned as she pulled her shawl more tightly about her shoulders. It was now early October and bitingly cold. 'Well, I'm trying to,' she told him. 'The mistress and Mrs Veasey have been giving me lessons but I still forget from time to time and revert back to my old way of speaking. And as for my limp, Mrs Forbes took me to see the shoemaker and he's made me a built-up shoe for this foot so that this leg is the same length as the other. It's wonderful, I don't have to limp anymore.'

'Well, it's great regardin' the limp but as for lessons on how to speak, there were nothin' wrong wi' how you spoke before,' he said huffily. 'Yer sound all different now. But 'ow are you? Yer look a bit tired.'

'I am,' she admitted. 'When we first went to work for the Forbeses, Eliza was working in the kitchen but then Mrs Forbes decided she wasn't well enough and since then I've been doing her job as well as my own.'

'So is Eliza still not well then?'

'Oh, she's really well now, thank goodness,' Pearl assured him. 'The trouble is since their son Monty left to go to school in England Mrs Forbes has got a bit obsessive about our Eliza. She almost treats her like a daughter and Eliza is taking full advantage of the fact.'

She looked so sad as she told him that Nick was shocked. 'But she were always such a timid little thing.'

'She's just quiet and doesn't enjoy the lessons like I do, but she's got to be quite sly now,' she said regretfully. 'She can play Mrs Forbes like a fiddle and barely speaks to me anymore. Not that I'm not pleased for her,' she added hastily. 'It's nice to see her being so looked after. But that's enough about us. Susan told me that you haven't been having it easy. How are you getting on?'

Hands in pockets, Nick shrugged and she noticed how much he had grown in the last few months. He was still stick thin but decidedly taller than she remembered him. 'I reckon I'm gonna change jobs in the new year,' he confided. 'I quite fancy workin' at the shipyard. Farmin' ain't what I imagined, but I'd love to work on the ships. Better still, I'd like to sail in 'em one day, but we'll see.'

They had arrived at the haberdashery by then and smiling, Pearl told him, 'Here we are. What colour wool does your boss want? I'll come in and help you, if you like. I have to go in anyway.' And so together they entered the shop.

At that moment up at the house, could Pearl have known it, Mrs Veasey was having a word with her mistress. 'I'm a little concerned about Pearl,' she told her.

Mrs Forbes frowned as she sat at her ornate escritoire writing a letter home to her parents in London. 'Oh, and why is that?'

'I'm afraid having to do her own job and Eliza's is proving rather too much for her,' Mrs Veasey said with a note of concern in her voice as she chose her words carefully. 'You see, when she first took on Eliza's job, we all thought it would be temporary, just until Eliza had got over her dreadful cough but . . .' Her words trailed away.

Mrs Forbes flushed. 'I don't feel that Lizzie is strong enough to resume kitchen duties yet,' she answered tartly. 'And even if she was, I enjoy her company. She keeps me amused. What is wrong with that?'

'Oh, nothing at all,' Mrs Veasey hastened to assure her. 'And Pearl has never complained – she's a hard-working girl. But the thing is, ma'am, the master is due back any day so there will be more work and . . . well, people are beginning to talk . . . you know? They can't understand why you would take an orphan under your wing.'

'So let them,' her employer snapped. 'As my mother would say, while they are talking about me they are leaving some other poor beggar alone. What I wish to do in my own house is my own affair. However . . .' She looked slightly guilty. 'Pearl is a good little worker and doing amazingly well at her lessons and I don't want to overwork her, so perhaps you could arrange another kitchen maid to take Lizzie's place? I don't want it said that I'm a slave driver.'

'Very well, I'll look into it straight away,' Mrs Veasey said primly and turning about she left the room without another word.

'So how did you get on?' Cook asked the second she walked back into the kitchen.

Florence Veasey shook her head. 'It seems that she has no intention of Eliza resuming work in the kitchen, so she's told me to employ another kitchen maid. It's something, I suppose, and at least that will take some of the work from Pearl's shoulders.'

The cook tutted. 'That little madam is getting too big for her boots,' she said angrily. 'Why, only this morning I heard her shouting at Pearl to come and do her hair immediately. She treats her like a servant but they're sisters, for goodness sake! I think Madam Eliza has forgotten that. Between you and me, I think the master has his concerns as well. The way she treats that lass is a little disturbing. Anyone would think she was the daughter of the house!'

'I agree, but as there's nothing we can do about it we just have to get on with things. Meanwhile, I'll go and see if Miss Walker can recommend a new kitchen maid.'

In the hallway, with her ear pressed up against the green baize door, Eliza fumed as she listened to the two women speaking about her. *They just want to spoil things for me 'cause they're jealous*, she told herself as she crept away. *But I won't let them!*

Three days later, the new kitchen maid that Mrs Veasey had appointed arrived and at sight of her Pearl's mouth dropped open. 'Freda,' she said. 'How are you?'

Freda sniffed as she sat at the table drinking tea with Cook before being shown to her room. 'I'm all right, I suppose. You 'ave to be, don't you?' she answered indifferently.

'So do you two know each other?' Cook asked. If they did, they certainly didn't seem too pleased to see each other.

'Yes, we were in the workhouse back in England together and we came here on the same boat,' Pearl said, and making an effort she gave Freda a smile.

'In that case when Freda's finished her tea, you could perhaps show her up to your room,' Cook told her. 'She'll be sharing with you.'

Pearl's heart dropped like a stone. As lonely as she was without Eliza, she didn't relish the thought of having to share a room with Freda again. She had always been so spiteful and unfriendly, but perhaps she had changed now? Pearl could only hope so.

'So that will be your bed there,' she told Freda shortly after she had shown her up to their room.

Freda sniffed as she looked around. 'It ain't exactly posh, is it!'

'It's comfortable enough,' Pearl answered as she straightened the cover on her own bed. 'But I'll leave you to unpack now. I have to go and lay the table for lunch.'

'Ooh 'ark at Miss La-di-da!' Freda said maliciously.

Refusing to be goaded, Pearl quietly left the room with a sinking feeling in the pit of her stomach that things might not be quite so harmonious in the Forbes household from now on. It was bad enough with Eliza acting like she owned the place, but something told her things were about to get worse.

Once the lunch dishes were cleared away, it was lesson time, Pearl's favourite time of the day, and they trooped into the drawing room to find Mr Jackson waiting for them.

Like Eliza, Freda wasn't at all keen on being educated, but Pearl still loved it and soaked up everything she was taught like a sponge. Recently they had been learning about the kings and queens of England and Pearl had enjoyed it. Now he was teaching them about Greek mythology and she loved that even more. She was enchanted with characters such as the beautiful Artemis, the daughter of the legendary Titaness Leto and Zeus, the king of the gods, and fascinated with all the gods of ancient Greece. Mr Jackson had sent for some books on the subject from England to help them with their learning, but as yet Pearl was the only one who had shown any interest in reading them.

'Ah, Mrs Forbes informed me that there would be another pupil joining us. Welcome, Freda,' Mr Jackson said as they entered the room, but Freda merely scowled and sat down looking disinterested before they had even begun. Eliza didn't even attempt to speak to her and looked down her nose at her.

The next two hours passed in a blur for Pearl as, entranced, she listened to Mr Jackson speaking about the mythical gods, and when he finally glanced at the clock and called an end to that day's lesson, she sighed with frustration. She could quite happily have listened to him all day.

Eliza rose and skipped off to find Mrs Forbes, looking very pretty in a new blue cotton dress sprigged with tiny rosebuds. She didn't even glance in Pearl's direction, but Pearl was used to that now. Still, it was lovely to see Eliza looking so well. She had gained weight and her hair, which had grown well past her shoulders, danced as she moved.

'So what's goin' on wi' her then?' Freda asked as she and Pearl went back to the kitchen. 'I 'eard as how the mistress 'ad adopted 'er and treated her like her own daughter.'

'Well, that isn't quite true,' Pearl informed her. 'Mrs Forbes hasn't formally adopted her but she has taken her under her wing, which can only be a good thing for Eliza. She looks so well now.'

Freda raised a curious eyebrow. 'But what about you? Ain't you jealous that you ain't treated the same? I would be if I were in your position.'

'Not at all; I'm just happy to see Eliza being well looked after.'

They went into the kitchen and Cook smiled at Freda. As she had just remarked to Mrs Veasey, she was grateful to have more help. Freda wasn't the prettiest of girls but she felt sorry for her, and intended to take the girl under her wing. Mrs Veasey, on the other hand, hadn't taken to Freda at all. If she wasn't much mistaken the girl could turn out to be a bit of a troublemaker, and she intended to keep a close eye on her.

'Right, Freda, perhaps you could start preparing the vegetables for the dinner this evening and then I'll give you a lesson on making a fruit pie,' Cook told the newcomer with a warm smile. 'And, Pearl, you could go and give the drawing room a good dust and polish before you lay the table in the dining room, but mind you're careful with the mistress's knick-knacks. They come from all over the world and some of them are priceless.'

Pearl just wished that she wouldn't keep reminding her of the fact. It made her so nervous when she had to dust them.

As she made her way back to the drawing room, Pearl found Eliza sitting on a pretty gilt chair in the hallway looking at the pictures in one of the storybooks Mrs Forbes had bought for her.

'Why don't you come and help me do some dusting?' Pearl suggested with a smile.

Eliza scowled at her. '*I'm* not a servant. That's *your* job,' she answered imperiously.

Pearl was cut to the quick but she didn't let the hurt show. She simply nodded and went on her way without another word. Every day Eliza seemed to grow a little further away from her, but there was nothing she could do about it.

'Eliza, that was cruel to speak to your sister like that,' she heard Mrs Veasey scold as she entered the drawing room, but Pearl quietly closed the door and didn't hear her sister's reply.

That evening when she retired to bed, Pearl turned her back on Freda who was already tucked up in her own bed and had a hasty wash in the bowl on the washstand. She then slipped into her nightdress, but when she came to turn the blankets back, she was dismayed to find they were sodden.

As she glanced towards Freda lying in the light of the guttering candle, she saw that she was grinning.

'Oh, sorry about that,' she said with a sneer. 'I forgot to tell yer I had a little accident an' spilled some water from the jug when I were gettin' washed.'

The washstand was nowhere near the bed and Pearl knew there was no way this could have happened accidentally, but she bit back the retort that sprang to her lips and swiped the wet blankets into a pile on the floor before heading off to the linen cupboard to get some dry ones, as Freda turned to the wall.

Once she was finally in bed, she lay watching the shadows dance in the corner of the room, and felt sad. She had hoped when coming to this house that she would be happy, but first she had lost Eliza and now she had Freda to contend with, and somehow she knew that things could only get worse. Freda had always been spiteful and manipulative, but she already had Cook eating out of her hand and she wondered where it was going to end.

Two mornings later Pearl lifted the heavy breakfast tray from the kitchen table and headed to the green baize door to take it into the dining room where the family were waiting to eat.

Freda was sitting at the end of the kitchen table cleaning some silver cutlery and Pearl made to pass her when suddenly her foot connected with something and the tray she was carrying flew into the air before crashing to the ground. Food and broken crockery spilled across the tiles and Cook was furious.

'You clumsy little devil. I shall have to start cooking all over again now; everything is ruined and the mistress won't be pleased to be kept waiting. And just look at all those breakages! For two pins I'd get Mrs Veasey to make you pay for them out of your wages. Why can't you be more careful and look where you're going!'

'I *was* looking,' Pearl said, red-faced. 'I tripped over something.'

'Hm, fresh air by the looks of it,' Cook grumbled as she slammed a clean pan on to the range. 'There's nothing I can see that you could have tripped over, you've just got two left feet! I would have thought you'd be less clumsy now you don't have to limp!'

As Pearl's eyes rested on Freda, she saw a malicious gleam in her eye and suddenly she knew exactly what had happened. Freda had stuck her foot out and tripped her up on purpose. Not that she could prove it and Cook could see no wrong in the girl. Her lips set in a grim line she bent and began to pick up the spoiled food and broken pots from the floor.

She was still clearing up the mess when Mrs Veasey entered the room and raised her eyebrows. 'So, what's happened here then?'

'Pearl were clumsy an' dropped the tray, missus,' Freda piped up before Pearl had a chance to open her mouth.

'Accidents do happen; it isn't the end of the world,' the woman said coldly as she bent to help Pearl. It was clear that Mrs Veasey hadn't taken to Freda, so Pearl felt that she had at least one ally, which was something.

Later that morning when Freda was busy in the laundry room and Pearl was cleaning, Mrs Veasey asked the cook, 'So how is Freda doing?'

'Aw, the lass is doing really well,' Cook answered with a smile. 'Between you and me I feel sorry for the poor little soul. She's such a mousy little thing and I don't think she's had anyone to love her in her life.'

'That's as maybe but then neither have Pearl nor Eliza,' Mrs Veasey pointed out.

'Aye, but Eliza is certainly getting her share of the attention off the mistress now, isn't she?'

Mrs Veasey nodded. 'Yes, I have to agree with that. I actually feel quite sorry for Pearl, though; they are sisters, after all. She must feel very abandoned and left out.'

'Hm, but we all know what Eliza's attraction is, don't we? She's by far the prettiest of the two, and the double of poor

Miss Elizabeth into the bargain. Even so, no good will come of this obsession the mistress has with her, you just mark my words. The little madam has come right out of her shell now and is almost ruling the roost. The poor mistress dotes on her.'

Mrs Veasey nodded; she had a sinking feeling that Cook could just be right.

Chapter Seventeen

'Crikey, girl, have you got that fire going?' Cook asked as she entered the kitchen one cold and frosty morning.

'Yes, Cook, it's been lit for the last 'alf . . . I mean *half* an hour,' Pearl answered as she lifted the heavy soot-blackened kettle to pour water into the thick brown teapot. Once it was filled, she put the tea cosy on and bustled away to prepare the cups while it mashed. Cook always enjoyed her cup of tea before she started the breakfast each day, although it wasn't clear why this was still a task for Pearl since Freda had joined the household.

The snow had started to fall thick and fast some days before and already it was becoming difficult to leave the house. Pearl had seen snow many times before at home, but never anything like it was here. Back in London it turned to slush almost as soon as it settled because of the many feet that trampled across it, but here there were not many people to disturb it and it came down faster than she'd ever seen. The thick, white carpet grew deeper by the day. Only this morning, Pearl had struggled to open the back door and Will had cleared it for her when he appeared from his rooms above the stables.

The kitchen door opened and Mrs Veasey appeared, looking rather pale and gaunt. She hadn't been well for some time now, although the doctor, who the mistress had insisted she should see, was unable to determine what was wrong with her.

'It must be some sort of virus,' he had said and prescribed her a tonic, not that it appeared to be doing her much good.

Mrs Veasey took a seat at the table and gratefully accepted the tea that Pearl offered her as Cook asked, 'Are you feeling no better, Florence?'

'Oh, I'm not too bad.' Mrs Veasey smiled as she took a sip of the steaming drink, but then instantly clapped her hand across her mouth and lifting her skirts fled outside into the snow, to the toilet that was positioned across the yard.

'Well, if that's what she considers not too bad I dread to think what bad is,' Cook muttered, deeply concerned. Freda joined them then and the atmosphere changed instantly, as the cook motioned her to a chair. 'Come and sit down, pet,' she urged. 'And get this nice hot drink inside you. It'll set you up for the day.'

Pearl drained the rest of her cup and took it to the sink, before heading for the dining room. It was time to lay the table ready for the family's breakfast and she was glad of an excuse to escape from Freda. She was surprised when she entered the room to find the mistress there, already up and dressed, and she hesitated in the doorway.

'It's all right, Pearl, you may come in and go about your business,' she told the girl as she turned from the window. She had been moping about the house for days. Pearl thought it was probably because she was missing her son and she was proved to be right when Mrs Forbes confided, 'I am trying to persuade my husband to take me to London for Christmas so that I can share it with Montgomery at my parents' home in Chelsea. It just doesn't seem right not to spend Christmas with him. There is a ship sailing in two days, which would get us there in plenty of time for Christmas if he agrees to it.'

'That'll be nice, ma'am,' Pearl mumbled, not sure what she should answer.

'And of course, if we do go, I would take Lizzie with us, and you too, to look after her on the boat. I'm afraid I have never been a very good traveller. How would you feel about that, Pearl?'

Pearl was shocked, but after a moment she answered, 'I would like that very much, ma'am. Perhaps while we are there, I could have a short time off to go and visit my family?'

'I'm sure that could be arranged,' Mrs Forbes agreed as Pearl threw a snow-white cloth across the highly polished table. 'I will let you know when my husband has made his decision.'

Once the cutlery had been laid, Pearl almost skipped from the room in her excitement. She had often wondered if she would ever see England again, or her family for that matter. Deep down, she knew that after the way they had abandoned them at the workhouse, her mother and father probably never gave her or Eliza a thought, but it didn't stop her thinking of them and it would be wonderful to see her brothers and sisters again. Her mind began to race. She had saved every penny of the wages she had received since working for the Forbeses and while it didn't amount to a great deal, perhaps she would be able to get the children a small present each?

As she was carrying the food through to the dining room, Eliza and Mr Forbes joined Mrs Forbes and Pearl heard the mistress ask, 'So, have you given any more thought to us spending Christmas in London, darling?'

Pearl saw Eliza's ears prick up, although she didn't say anything as Mr Forbes crossed to the dishes and began to help himself to the hot food.

'Well, I must be honest; I have a great deal of work on at the moment and I was rather hoping we could spend Christmas here, especially as I've not long been back.' Mr Forbes glanced across at his wife and seeing her downcast expression he sighed. He found it very hard to deny her anything. 'But I suppose . . . if it means so much to you the men could probably manage without me . . .'

'Oh, Zack, you're just *too* good to me.' She hurried over to him and much to Pearl and Eliza's embarrassment began to rain little kisses all over his face.

'But I *would* have to come back on the first ship in the new year,' he warned, knowing he was lost. 'And that would mean you would probably have less than two weeks there by the time we arrive before we have to set off back here again. Are you quite sure it's worth all that travelling? You know you've never been fond of sailing, my love.'

'Oh, I'm *quite* sure,' she told him, smiling prettily. 'I've missed Monty *so* much! And now I really must go and see Mrs Veasey about the packing. There is so much to do if we are leaving the day after tomorrow.' Lifting her silken skirts, she skittered towards the door, breakfast forgotten, as Mr Forbes shook his head and carried his plate to the table with a resigned sigh. He was well aware that his wife could play him like a fiddle but even so he wouldn't have changed a single hair on her head.

'Aw well, at least that means we'll all have a nice peaceful Christmas,' Cook commented when Mrs Veasey told her of the family's plans shortly after. 'I'm surprised they're taking Pearl and Eliza though.'

Mrs Veasey, who was still feeling very under the weather, shrugged. 'I must admit I was somewhat surprised too. I think I'll get Pearl to do hers and Eliza's packing. The mistress has already dragged half of her wardrobe out on to the bed so I've asked Will to fetch the travelling trunks down from the attic for me. If you saw the amount of things she's planning to take you would think they were going for a year at least. Still, it's not my place to question, is it?'

Pearl entered the room at that moment with the rest of the dirty breakfast pots piled on a tray and Mrs Veasey told her, 'Forget the cleaning duties for this morning, Pearl. Instead I would like you to pack whatever you think Eliza might need for your journey and her stay in London. It must feel very strange to be going back to your place of birth.'

Pearl nodded in agreement as she gingerly placed the tray on the table. 'It does, to be honest. I didn't expect to be going back there for many a long day, let alone so soon, but I'm not complaining and it isn't as if we're going for long, is it?'

Will appeared in the doorway then. 'Right, that's all the trunks fetched down from the loft. I've left them on the landing for you so when they're ready give me a shout and I'll come in and bring them all down for you.'

Pearl smiled at him, realising that she would miss him while they were away. He'd become a friend to her in the time they had been there and whenever Freda's spiteful behaviour became a little too much to bear, he was always a shoulder to cry on. She guessed he must be at least eight to ten years older than her, but he was a handsome chap and she wondered why some girl hadn't snapped him up – not that it was any of her business, she reminded herself.

'Must be off now,' he told them as he headed for the kitchen door. 'The damned rats got into the chicken coop last night and killed at least four of our good layers.' Because of the open woodland surrounding them rats were a constant problem, despite Will's best efforts to get rid of them.

Freda, who had just heard of the trip Pearl and Eliza were about to embark on, stood at the sink angrily smashing the dishes into the water with a grim expression on her face. It didn't seem fair to her that Pearl got to go. She could understand Eliza going, for everyone knew that the mistress doted on the girl and hated to let her out of her sight, but surely she was big enough to look after herself without having her sister there to mollycoddle her? *Still*, she thought, *at least wi' them out of the way I'll 'ave Cook all to meself and I won't 'ave 'alf as many pots to wash if we ain't got that spoiled lot to pander to!* And so, she decided, there just might be some consolation to them going after all.

The rest of the day passed in a blur for Pearl as she helped with the packing and by early evening the hallway was full of trunks and boxes ready to be taken to the ship.

When Mr Forbes arrived home, his mouth fell open at the sight of them. 'What's all this?' he asked his wife as she appeared in the doorway of the drawing room.

She hurried over to him and grinned as she slipped her arm through his. 'It's our packing, of course.'

'But, darling, why do you and I need so much luggage? There must be enough clothes packed here to last us for a year at least.'

'It isn't all ours, silly!' She giggled girlishly. 'Some of it is for Lizzie and Pearl. And of course, I've also had to pack all the presents I've bought for the family.'

'Lizzie and Pearl?' He looked astounded as he drew her into the drawing room and closed the door behind them. 'But I thought it would be just you and me going. Why do you need to take them? They came here to be maids.'

Emmaline pouted. 'But I can't leave Lizzie behind and if I take her, I must take Pearl to look after her.'

He frowned as he began to strum his fingers on the tabletop. This obsession she had with Lizzie was beginning to concern him now. At first, he hadn't minded it because it seemed to have taken her mind off the death of their daughter a little, but now it was becoming worrying. Why, he wouldn't be at all surprised if she wanted to legally adopt her next.

'Look . . .' he began tentatively, choosing his words carefully. 'I can understand why Lizzie appeals to you. She has a look of our Elizabeth about her but . . . darling, we have to accept that Elizabeth has gone. She can never come back and no one can take her place.'

'Don't you think I *know* that!' Her eyes were full of tears now.

Mr Forbes felt wicked but it had needed to be said. 'I suggest that we go to London alone,' he said a little more gently. 'I can understand why you took Lizzie under your wing. She was ill when she first arrived and you were concerned about her, but she is completely recovered now, so if we left her here it might be a good time to let Mrs Veasey train her to help about the house?'

'*No!*' Emmaline's eyes were blazing. 'I've become fond of her and she is like a little companion to me when you are working. It would be just too cruel to suddenly demote her to being a servant again.'

'But her sister is,' he pointed out.

Emmaline shrugged. 'Since coming here Pearl has known nothing else and she seems to be perfectly happy with the arrangement, so why should the way I treat Lizzie trouble you? And anyway, you don't understand; when I'm with Lizzie I don't think so much about . . . about . . .'

For a moment her husband's chin sank to his chest but then he sighed deeply, and as he looked up at her again, Emmaline saw the raw pain in his eyes. 'It troubles me because . . . because I think you are trying to replace Elizabeth.'

'Of course I'm not,' she snapped with a toss of her head. And then in a softer tone she told him, 'I really don't want to be here without Monty and Elizabeth at Christmas. Please try to understand. Having Lizzie to fuss over keeps my mind off . . .' Tears were coursing down her cheeks and as always he felt himself weakening. He hated to see her so unhappy and he had to admit that she had perked up considerably since Lizzie had arrived.

'Very well, if it means so much to you then the girls may come,' he said resignedly and she smiled through her tears as she hurried away to put the finishing touches to the packing, leaving him with a sick feeling in the pit of his stomach as he wondered where it was all going to end.

Chapter Eighteen

'You're to be my maid on the journey,' Eliza told her sister imperiously the next morning as they waited in the hallway for Mr and Mrs Forbes to join them. Will had already made two journeys down to the docks with all their luggage and when he returned, he would be taking them to board the ship.

'How can I be your maid when I'm your sister?' Pearl snapped, although looking at how Eliza was dressed, anyone could have believed that she really was her maid. Eliza was wearing a beautiful red coat and bonnet trimmed with black braid, and her blonde hair was in ringlets, while Pearl was wearing her plain black cape and a staid grey dress. Not that she wasn't grateful for them – they were the best she had ever owned – but they weren't in the same league as the clothes Eliza was wearing.

'When we get to London, Mrs Forbes says she's gonna take me to buy me some more new clothes,' Eliza informed her as she preened in the hall mirror, and Pearl couldn't help but smile.

For the first time in her life Eliza was being spoiled. Could she really begrudge her that? After all, it was common knowledge that Eliza was a quiet, timid little thing, so she probably didn't mean to hurt her when she put on airs and graces.

'That'll be nice,' Pearl said as Mrs Forbes appeared wearing a rather splendid travelling gown in green velvet with a matching hat trimmed with feathers.

Mrs Veasey, Cook and Freda had come into the hallway to see them off and as Mrs Forbes pulled on her soft kid gloves, her husband placed a thick fur cape about her slim shoulders.

'I hope you all have a wonderful Christmas and we'll be back as soon in February as we can,' she promised them. 'Oh, and there's a little gift for each of you to open on Christmas Day.'

'Thank you, ma'am,' her staff chorused.

At that moment Will drew the carriage to a halt outside and Mr Forbes ushered them all towards the door. They were already slightly late but seeing as he was the owner of the ship they were to sail on, he knew there was no fear of the captain going without them. It was snowing heavily as they raced from the door and climbed into the carriage, and the minute they were inside Mr Forbes tucked a thick woollen travelling rug across his wife's legs and they were off, waving from the carriage window as the horses trotted down the drive.

As they were driving through the town, Pearl glanced towards the bakery, hoping for a sign of Susan, but she was nowhere to be seen. Sadly their departure had been so rushed that she hadn't had time to tell her they were going away but at least she had asked Will to let her know and Susan would then tell Nick if she saw him.

'I don't feel so good, Pearl,' Eliza whimpered as she lay on her little bed in the ship's cabin. They had only been at sea for a few hours but already she had turned an alarming shade of grey. It wasn't surprising really; the sea was choppy and even inside it was so cold that their breath was floating like lace on the air around them.

Pearl hastily fetched a bucket and a damp cloth to cool Eliza's forehead and thankfully after a time she fell into an uneasy doze. Shortly after Mr Forbes knocked on the door to tell her that his wife was very unwell too and poor Pearl had to do the same for Mrs Forbes.

Some holiday this is turning out to be, Pearl thought with a wry grin as she mopped her mistress's forehead. But at least she herself felt reasonably well, which she supposed was something to be grateful for. She dreaded to think what would have happened if she had been seasick too.

It was not a good passage; both Eliza and Mrs Forbes had been ill for the whole of the journey and despite Pearl's best efforts, both of their cabins smelled of stale vomit. So one day when Mr Forbes came to tell Pearl that they were almost in London, she sighed with relief.

They finally docked two days before Christmas Eve and Pearl hastily packed the trunks. Both Eliza and her mistress had worn few clothes because they had spent the majority of the time confined to bed, and now they both looked thin, pale and ill.

'I shall get a cab to take us straight to my mother-in-law's house and arrange for the luggage to follow on,' Mr Forbes told Pearl, when she went to inform him that they were all ready to disembark. He was desperately concerned about his wife, but hoped that once she set foot on dry land again, she might start to recover. Hopefully seeing her son would act as a tonic too.

It was late afternoon and already dark when he led them down the gangplank, but even so, Pearl had a sense of coming home and was not sorry to be back in London. Within minutes they were settled in a cab and as the horse set off at a trot she stared out at the familiar streets. The main streets were busy with smartly dressed people doing their last-minute Christmas shopping, and the lights from the gaily decorated shop windows spilled out on to the pavements.

'Ooh, everywhere looks so pretty, don't it?' Eliza whispered. She was already regaining a little colour in her cheeks and was clearly beginning to feel better.

Mrs Forbes smiled at her indulgently, 'You mean, doesn't it?' she corrected the child, but Eliza was too busy watching from the window to take much notice.

At last they pulled up outside a smart town house that was three storeys high and looked very grand. It was in a part of London that Pearl had never visited before. Mr Forbes helped them down on to the pavement and paid the cabbie.

'Here we are then.' He smiled. 'I don't mind betting it will be a surprise for them to see us. Our letter telling them we were coming probably won't have got here yet.'

They climbed three steep steps to a large door, on either side of which stood two topiary trees in glazed pots. Mr Forbes rang the bell and when a maid opened the door she beamed and exclaimed delightedly, 'Why, Miss Emmaline . . . Sorry, I mean, Mrs Forbes. We weren't expecting you. The family will be so thrilled to see you. Come in out of the cold.'

'Thank you, Millie.' Mrs Forbes clearly knew the woman well and she gave her a warm smile. 'Would you tell my parents that we are here please?' she asked as she unbuttoned her coat.

But there was no need to, for at that moment a door leading off the spacious hall opened and a smart woman, who looked like an older version of Emmaline, appeared. Her face lit up as she hurried forwards to hug her and she gasped, 'Why ever didn't you tell us that you were coming, darling?' Before her daughter could reply, she rushed on, 'But never mind. It will take the maids no time at all to get your room ready for you. What a *wonderful* surprise.' It was then that her eyes came to rest on Eliza and Pearl who were standing quietly, and raising an eyebrow she asked, 'But who are these girls, dear?' As her eyes lingered on Eliza, she frowned.

'Oh, sorry, Mother, I should have introduced you.' With a smile Emmaline took Eliza's hand and drew her forwards.

'This is Lizzie, I've been . . . looking after her. And this is Pearl, her sister, who is our maid.'

The woman sucked in a shocked breath but managed to plaster a smile on her face. 'Then you must go with Millie, girls. I'm sure our cook will find you a nice hot drink and something to eat.'

'But, Mother, you don't understand . . .'

Emmaline made as if to take Eliza's hand again – but her mother hastily grabbed her elbow and bore her towards the room she had just come from, saying to the maid, 'Once you have the girls settled would you bring a tray of tea through, please, Millie? And tell Cook there will be an extra two for dinner.'

'But Lizzie isn't a maid and she always eats with Zack and me . . .' Pearl heard her mistress protest, as her mother bundled her ahead of her before closing the door firmly behind her.

Eliza looked quite put out and pouted, but Pearl nudged her ahead of her as they followed the maid to the kitchen.

As Emmaline and Zack entered the drawing room their son, who was sitting in a wing chair by the fire, looked up.

'Oh, Monty, darling, I've missed you *so* much,' Emmaline cried as she raced across to him and threw her arms around him.

Looking embarrassed he squirmed out of her grasp. 'Mother . . . I didn't expect to see you this holiday.'

'I know but as Christmas grew closer, I couldn't bear the thought of us spending it apart,' his mother told him with tears in her eyes.

Monty glanced towards his father, who hadn't given him the same rapturous welcome, and they nodded stiffly to one another.

Plonking herself on the arm of his chair his mother asked excitedly, 'So, how is school, darling? You must tell me all about it.'

He shrugged as colour rose in his cheeks. What was he supposed to say? That he had been bullied and picked on because he was the new boy? That he was made to clear up the older boys' mess and teased mercilessly. 'It's all right, I suppose,' he mumbled.

His mother instantly looked concerned. 'Are you quite sure? You don't seem too enthusiastic about it.'

'He's not properly settled in yet. He'll be fine,' her mother told her firmly as Millie wheeled in a tea tray loaded with tiny pastries and cakes and a bone-china tea service.

She began to pour the tea into the dainty cups, and Monty stared at his father resentfully. It had been agreed before he left Canada that he should spend any school holidays with his grandparents in London because it was too far to travel home each time, but even that small respite from the chaps at school had its drawbacks. He had always been able to wrap his mother around his little finger but his grandmother was a different kettle of fish entirely. Back at home he had free rein to do as he wished, so long as he spent a few hours each day with his tutor, but Laura Kennedy-Scott always wanted to know where he was and who he was with, and even though he was on holiday she insisted that a certain amount of time each day should be spent on homework, so all in all staying with her wasn't much better than being at school. His grandfather was no better and sometimes he wondered how he would bear it.

But still, he consoled himself, in a few short years' time he could leave school and please himself what he did. He knew he was a huge disappointment to his father who had always hoped that he would show an interest in the many businesses he owned, but that had never appealed to Monty. He wanted to see the world and have freedom to come and go as he pleased. *And why shouldn't I?* he asked himself. His parents and his grandparents were wealthy, so the way he saw it they should be happy to finance him.

He took the cup and saucer his grandmother offered and sank back into his chair, wishing that he could become invisible.

His grandmother turned her attention back to her daughter. 'You look dreadfully pale, darling,' she commented, sipping daintily at her tea. 'Was it a bad journey?'

'Dreadful,' Emmaline admitted, although she was feeling better already now that she had seen Monty.

'And how long will you be staying?'

It was Zack who hastily told her, 'Only until shortly after Christmas, I'm afraid. I have rather a lot of work on at present but Emmaline was so set on coming. I didn't like to disappoint her.'

His mother-in-law nodded. She knew what a hard-working man her son-in-law was. She also knew that he could rarely deny her daughter anything, which was to his credit. The year before, following the death of her granddaughter, she had spent some months in Canada with them to help care for her daughter. She had feared for her sanity at one point but was pleased to see that she did seem to be a lot better now.

'And now tell me, who are the two girls you brought with you?' she questioned. It had given her quite a turn when she had first set eyes on Eliza. She was remarkably like Elizabeth and she hoped that Emmaline wasn't trying to replace her late daughter with this girl. If that was the case then she considered it to be extremely unhealthy; she didn't want her daughter to slip back into the dark place she had been in.

'They came over some time ago on an orphan ship from London.' Emmaline smiled. 'I took them both on as maids as one of ours had had to leave because . . .' She flushed as she glanced at Monty who instantly looked guarded. 'Anyway,' she rushed on. 'I took the two of them because they were sisters. It seemed cruel to split them up, but Lizzie . . . well, her name is actually Eliza, was ill and so I took her under my wing until she was better, and she's turned out to be a great comfort to me.'

'But the other one still works as a maid?' Her mother glanced at Zack, who lowered his eyes, and she knew instantly that he was no happier with the strange situation than she was.

'Well . . . yes, Pearl does,' Emmaline admitted, as she saw Monty frown. She had always suspected that he was jealous of Eliza, just as he had been jealous of his little sister when she was alive. Thoughts of Elizabeth brought a lump to her throat and rising hastily she said, 'I think I'll go upstairs and freshen up now, Mother, if you don't mind. I'd like to change for dinner before Father gets home.'

'Of course.' Her mother smiled and once she had left the room, she gave her son-in-law a meaningful look. 'I think you and I should have a little chat later on, dear.'

He nodded. 'Yes, I think we should.'

And excusing himself, he followed his wife upstairs.

Chapter Nineteen

In the kitchen, all was hustle and bustle as the cook and the kitchen maid put the finishing touches to the family's evening meal. Maids hurried in and out as they rushed to prepare a room for their guests and set the extra places at the dining room table.

'It's a good job I put a large joint o' beef in to roast,' the rosy-cheeked cook grumbled. 'I just wish people would let us know when they were comin' instead o' just turnin' up out o' the blue. Although I must admit, I'm lookin' forward to seein' the young mistress again. Poor soul. What she had to go through last year when she lost poor little Miss Elizabeth don't bear thinkin' about.'

Eliza was still sulking because she hadn't been allowed to join the family in the drawing room and was holding on to Pearl's hand for dear life, feeling totally out of her depth. Pearl was sorry that her sister was feeling sad, although it was nice to have her to herself for a while again. Cook was wondering why these two girls, who had been introduced to her as sisters, were dressed so differently. The younger one was dressed exactly as she would have expected Miss Elizabeth to be, had the dear little soul still been alive, and while the older one clearly took pride in her clothing, she was dressed as a maid. As yet she hadn't had time to question them, but she planned to just as soon as dinner was over.

'Will I be goin' in to dinner wi' Mrs Forbes?' Eliza whispered, forgetting all the grammar lessons Mrs Forbes had taught her in her nervousness. Unlike Pearl, she didn't like being back in London one bit and was afraid they might somehow end up back in the workhouse again.

Before Pearl could answer, Cook shook her head. 'No, you'll be eatin' in here with the rest of the staff,' she informed her. 'Only the family eat in the dinin' room. But don't worry, you'll not starve. I've made us all a lovely steak an' kidney pie.'

Eliza scowled in confusion. Back in Canada Mrs Forbes had made her feel as if she *was* part of her family, but now she didn't know what her role was again.

Pearl gave her sister's hand an encouraging squeeze. They were both worn out after the long journey and all she really wanted to do was sleep in a proper bed without being tossed about like a cork in a bottle by the high waves.

Eventually Millie and another maid carried the family's meal through to the dining room and when all the courses had been served and the mountain of dirty dishes had been cleared away, the staff finally sat down at the enormous scrubbed oak table to eat. There were so many of them that Pearl knew it would take a while before she remembered all their names as they introduced themselves. There was Millie who had admitted them, who told them that she was the parlour maid. There was Cook and Rachel, the kitchen maid, who seemed to spend half her life at the sink washing pots from what Pearl could see. Then there was Miss

Sophie Thomas, who was the mistress's lady's maid and Mrs Brookes the housekeeper. Esther, a scrawny little girl who was no further through than a matchstick, was the scullery maid; and Bridget, a plump Irish girl with a broad accent, was the laundry maid. The male staff were Jimmy, who was the groom, and Bert, the gardener. Pearl wondered why a house where only two people normally lived could possibly need so many staff.

The enormous steak and kidney pie that Cook had made for them was delicious and it was served with fluffy mashed potatoes, Brussel sprouts and green beans covered in a thick, creamy gravy. This was followed by apple pie and custard and Pearl, who hadn't realised she was hungry, tucked in, although she noticed that Eliza barely ate a thing. But then she did look tired, Pearl decided, and after a good night's sleep she would hopefully be as bright as a button.

Once the meal was over, Pearl volunteered to help with the washing up and finally when all the pots were washed and dried, Cook thanked her and told Rachel to take them up to the room they would be sharing in the servants' quarters. Again, Eliza didn't look too happy with that, and she followed the two older girls up the narrow wooden staircase with a frown on her face.

'This'll be your room,' Rachel told them, as she threw a door at the end of a long corridor open. 'Cook got Esther to make the beds up fer you earlier on. Oh, an' yer can 'ave this candle, if yer like. You'll each find there's a chamber pot under yer bed should yer need to go in the night, but make sure as yer take it out to the toilet an' empty it first thing then rinse it under the tap. Mrs Brookes is a stickler fer that sort o' thing.'

'Thank you, Rachel.'

As the girl quietly left, Pearl looked about the room, which like her room in Canada had a sloped ceiling. There was a washstand with a jug of hot water and a towel that someone had kindly placed there for them. There was also an old chest of drawers and a rather rickety chair, but other than that and the two small beds, the room was bare and very cold.

'So where will I hang all my new dresses?' Eliza said petulantly as she stared around.

'It looks like they'll have to hang on those nails on the back of the door,' her sister replied, as she hurriedly looked for their nightdresses in the small trunk they had brought. 'But I won't be unpacking them tonight. I just want a wash and to snuggle down in bed.'

Plonking herself on the edge of the bed, Eliza pouted and crossed her arms. The bedroom she was used to back at the Forbeses' house was much prettier than this one, and she had always had a small fire burning in the grate to keep her warm.

'Mrs Forbes won't be pleased when she knows they've sent me to sleep in this 'orrible room,' she grumbled. 'Back at their 'ouse she always had a stone hot-water bottle put in my bed to make sure I was warm.'

'Well, you're not at their house now, are you?' Pearl answered, more sharply than she had intended, as she hastily undressed and began to wash herself. She knew very well about the stone hot-water bottle as it was often her responsibility to put it there – not that Eliza seemed to care. 'I suggest you just make the best of it for tonight. Anywhere is better than being on that ship, surely?' Crossing to her bed, she hopped in, and pulled the blankets up to her chin.

Once she'd heard Eliza do the same, she blew the candle out, and within minutes she was fast asleep.

They were woken early the next morning by a tap on the door. 'Wakey-wakey rise an' shine,' Rachel called softly and then they heard her footsteps recede along the landing.

Soon after, washed and dressed, the girls went down to the kitchen to find Cook busy preparing breakfast for the family.

'Well, don't just stand there gawpin',' the cook told them. 'Come an' start washin' these dishes. Rachel is busy preparin' the mushrooms.'

Pearl happily rolled her sleeves up and did as she was told, although Eliza didn't look too happy about it. She had grown used to being pampered by Mrs Forbes back in Canada and she wasn't at all keen on being set to work again.

The next hour passed in the blink of an eye as the staff rushed about, laying the table in the large dining room and making sure the fires were lit. Then as the family made their way to breakfast, Eliza glimpsed Mrs Forbes behind her mother in the hallway, as the maid opened the door to carry a steaming tray of sizzling bacon through to them. Eliza's eyes filled with tears; she was feeling very abandoned. This wasn't turning out to be the sort of holiday she had expected it to be at all. She had thought that Mrs Forbes's mother would dote on her as her daughter did, but up to now that hadn't been the case at all.

Mrs Kennedy-Scott spotted Eliza peeping into the hallway and as she followed her daughter into the dining room, she frowned. *As soon as breakfast is over I shall have a good talk with Emmaline*, she decided. Thankfully, Emmaline looked a lot better after a good night's sleep and her mother was determined to keep her busy. They could go shopping this morning, for a start. Her husband would be off to his office after breakfast and Zack had mentioned that he wanted to visit the woodyard that he owned where the timber he sent from his sawmill in Canada was delivered. That just left Monty, and she was sure that he was more than capable of keeping himself occupied for a time.

After breakfast the men took their leave of the ladies and, pouring them both another cup of tea, Emmaline's mother said, 'I thought we might go and do a bit of shopping this morning, darling. It isn't often we get chance to spend any time together so I think we should make the most of it.'

Emmaline nodded absently as her eyes went to the door, and her mother immediately guessed she was thinking of Eliza.

It was the ideal opportunity to voice her concerns, so she began hesitantly, 'I was thinking that the two girls you brought with you could be a great help over the holidays with so many extra people in the house. I've already suggested to Mrs Brookes that the older one could act as your lady's maid and the younger one could help out in the kitchen.'

Her daughter looked dismayed as she sipped daintily at the tea her mother had passed her. 'But Pearl wouldn't have any idea what to do as a lady's maid,' she pointed out. 'And Eliza . . . well, I'm not at all sure that she's strong enough yet to resume kitchen duties.'

Her mother waved her hand airily. 'Rubbish. I'm sure the older one would jump at the chance to better herself; she seems to be very bright and polite. And the younger one will be fine, so stop worrying.'

Emmaline still wasn't happy with the idea, but her mother was a force to be reckoned with when she set her mind on something, so she fell silent until it was time for them to go and put their coats and bonnets on, while the groom fetched the carriage around to the front door.

After they had left the house, Mrs Brookes went to the kitchen to tell the two girls about her mistress's decision.

'Pearl, Mrs Kennedy-Scott thought that during your stay you could act as Mrs Forbes's lady's maid.'

Pearl, who was in the process of clearing the staff's dirty pots from the table, stared at her open-mouthed. 'But Mrs Brookes, I ain't . . . I mean, I have never done that before. I wouldn't know what to do.'

The kindly housekeeper smiled at her. She'd taken a shine to Pearl, although she wasn't so sure what to make of her sister. 'Don't worry about it, I'll tell you what you need to do and you'll learn as you go along,' she promised. Then, turning her attention to Eliza, she told her, 'And we thought, seeing as we have a lot more people here for Christmas than we'd reckoned on, that you could be a great help to Cook in the kitchen.'

The cook nodded in agreement. 'She would that,' she agreed, although Eliza didn't look too enamoured of the idea.

'Good, that's sorted then.' Mrs Brookes rubbed her hands together and, turning to Pearl, she said, 'If you come along with me, I can give you some idea of what will be expected of you while your mistress is out.'

Pearl nodded and followed her upstairs to her mistress's bedroom, where Mrs Brookes looked at the mistress's clothes that were strewn about. 'It's the duty of a lady's maid to always keep her mistress's clothes in good order,' she explained as she picked up the gown Emmaline had worn the previous evening. 'If any clothes that are left about are clean, then you hang them neatly away. If they are dirty, you take them to the laundry where they will be washed and ironed before being returned to you. Every morning, you will help your mistress to get dressed and do her hair for her, and it will also be your job to help her undress and change for dinner. When she wishes to bathe, it is also your job to see to the running of the bath and to make sure that she has everything she needs to hand – soap, towels and whatever. How does that sound?'

Pearl bit her lip as she shifted uncomfortably from foot to foot. 'But I've never done anyone's hair before, only Eliza's,' she said worriedly.

'Oh, don't get worrying about that. I'm sure your mistress will show you how she likes it done, and you know the old saying: "practice makes perfect". Everyone has to start somewhere and this could pave the way to you getting a very good job in the future. You never know, if Mrs Forbes is pleased with you, she may even ask you to continue to be her personal maid when you get back to Canada. Think what a step up that will be from being a housemaid. But now I'll leave you to get on.'

And with that she swept from the room, her bombazine skirts swishing as Pearl began to sort through Mrs Forbes clothes and tidy them away.

It was mid-morning before she entered the kitchen again with an armful of Mrs Forbes's dirty laundry that she had worn on the ship.

'Bridget will take them for you,' Cook told her, nodding to the little laundry maid who had just come in from the laundry for a tea break. 'And there's fresh tea in the pot if you want one.'

Eliza was chopping onions on a big wooden block and Pearl wasn't sure if the tears on her cheeks were due to the onions or the fact that she was once again being forced to do a menial job. Pearl was painfully aware that she had come out the lucky one for now, and she felt so sorry for her little sister that she almost wished they could change places.

'Haven't you finished them onions yet, girl?' Cook snapped at Eliza and Pearl saw her sister glare at her mutinously. But there was nothing Pearl could do about it; for now at least, Eliza was just going to have to get on with things whether she liked it or lumped it.

Chapter Twenty

After a morning of trailing from one shop to another and making numerous purchases, Mrs Kennedy-Scott finally took her daughter to lunch in a lovely restaurant close to Oxford Street, by which time snow had started to fall in thick flakes.

'I think you'll find the food is delicious here,' she told her daughter. 'Your father brought me here for our anniversary.' Emmaline had been unnaturally quiet all morning and as she handed her a menu she asked, 'So, why don't you tell me what is troubling you? Something clearly is.'

Her daughter shrugged as she pretended to study the menu.

Her mother sighed. 'Would this be anything to do with Eliza by any chance?' The colour that flooded into her daughter's cheeks was her answer. She took a deep breath, before saying gently, 'Look, I know that Christmas can't be an easy time for you, darling. We all miss Elizabeth. But taking Eliza under your wing isn't the answer, believe me. I can see why you are drawn to her, of course. The first time I saw her I got quite a shock because of the likeness. But you have to realise that no one can take Elizabeth's place and it isn't healthy for you to try and replace her.'

'I wasn't *trying* to,' Emmaline denied heatedly, as she blinked back tears. 'I just . . . I suppose I just felt sorry for her because she was so unwell when she first came to me, that's all.'

'I can quite understand that.' Her mother reached across the table and gave her hand a gentle squeeze. 'But you have to understand that she is quite well again now, and Pearl is her sister. It wouldn't be right to go on treating them so differently. So, from now on, I want you to promise me that you will let Eliza return to the role you first employed her for. It wouldn't do to let her get ideas above her station.'

They were interrupted by the waiter who was waiting for their order and so the conversation came to an abrupt end, but Mrs Kennedy-Scott felt deep down that this wasn't the end of it – not by a long way.

'Goodness me, is there anything left in the shops?' Emmaline's father laughed as the two women sailed through the door, loaded down with bags later that afternoon.

His wife smiled. 'This isn't all of it, I'm afraid, darling; there is still more to be delivered – but then it *is* Christmas, and it isn't often I get to go shopping with my daughter nowadays.' She dropped the packages unceremoniously on to the floor as the maid rushed forward to help her off with her coat. 'And I could almost kill for a cup of tea! The problem is my head still thinks I am twenty-one, but my body tells me otherwise.'

'I'll see to it straight away, ma'am.' The maid smiled as her mistress took the hat pin from her hat and smoothed her hair.

'Thank you, Sophie. We'll have it in the drawing room.' From the corner of her eye she saw Emmaline watch the maid as she headed for the kitchen, no doubt hoping for a glimpse of Eliza, but she didn't say anything and followed her parents into the drawing room, where a welcoming fire was blazing up the chimney.

'I have a feeling you may end up being here longer than Zack had planned,' Mrs Kennedy-Scott said, as she glanced towards the window where they could see the snow still falling thickly. 'Surely no boat will sail in this?'

'Of course it will,' her husband said fondly, although he would have quite liked to have his daughter around for a little longer. It had been such a lovely surprise when she had turned up so unexpectedly. He had even finished work early to spend some time with her, only to return home to find she and his wife had gone off on a shopping spree.

'Is Zack still at the woodyard?' Emmaline enquired as she warmed her hands at the fire.

He nodded. 'Yes, as far as I know, but he did say he would be back in plenty of time for dinner.'

Andrew Kennedy-Scott was tall with dark hair that now sported a spattering of grey about the temples, but he was still a very good-looking man who adored his wife and daughter. When he and Laura had first married, they had dreamed of having a horde of children, but sadly his wife had almost died having Emmaline and the doctor had strongly advised against them having any more, which only made their daughter all the more precious to them.

He looked closely at her, pleased with what he saw. The untimely death of their beautiful little granddaughter had

197

almost driven Emmaline to insanity. She did look better now, although there was still a haunted look in her eyes, but then Andrew supposed that was to be expected. Elizabeth had been a charming little girl who captured the hearts of everyone who met her and they had all been heartbroken when she died. His grandson, however, was a different kettle of fish altogether and Andrew struggled with him. Monty had never made a secret of the fact that he was jealous of his sister when she came along, and in nature he and Elizabeth had been as different as chalk from cheese, so much so that sometimes Andrew had wondered how two such different personalities could have come from the same womb. Elizabeth had been like her mother: sweet and kind, whereas Monty had always had a cruel streak – not that he ever showed it openly in front of his grandfather; he knew that Andrew would never have stood for it. As he thought of him, he asked, 'So where is Monty then? Did he go shopping with you?'

Laura laughed as the maid wheeled in the tea trolley. 'Don't be silly. Can you imagine Monty wanting to trail around the shops?' And then, looking at Sophie, she asked, 'Would you happen to know where my grandson is, Sophie?'

'Yes, ma'am. He said he was going out for a walk about an hour since.' The words had barely left her lips when they heard the front door opening and, seconds later, Monty entered the room with a sullen expression on his face.

'Ah, here you are.' Emmaline smiled warmly at him. 'We were just asking where you had got to. Did you have a nice walk, darling? I hope you wrapped up warmly; it's bitterly cold out there and I don't want you coming down with a cold. Did you go to meet a school friend?'

He scowled at her as he crossed to the fire. 'I don't *have* any friends here,' he said sullenly. 'All my friends are back at home.'

'Don't speak to your mother like that,' his grandfather scolded with a frown, and without a word Monty turned and left the room, slamming the door resoundingly behind him. 'Cheeky young pup, it's no wonder he's made no friends if he speaks to people like that!'

Emmaline chewed nervously on her lip. 'I just wonder if we've done the right thing,' she whispered.

'You most certainly have,' her father assured her. 'That school will teach him some manners, if nothing else. But let's not talk about it anymore. Why don't you show me what you've been spending my and your husband's money on?'

An hour later Emmaline went upstairs to find Pearl putting away the rest of her things. The room was immaculate and Emmaline smiled at her. 'I hear you're to act as my lady's maid while you're here?'

'Yes, ma'am.' Pearl awkwardly bobbed her knee as Mrs Brookes had advised her to. 'And I promise I'll do my best, although I've never done anything like this before.'

For the first time, Emmaline looked at her closely. She had always been so enamoured with Eliza that she had never really taken a lot of notice of Pearl. She was actually a very attractive girl with the same soft blonde hair and green eyes as her younger sister, but whereas Pearl, with her heart-shaped face, was pretty, her sister was beautiful.

'I'm sure we shall get along famously,' she assured her, as she took the pins from her hair, and then she couldn't help but ask, 'And how is Lizzie?'

'She's fine, ma'am. She's helping Cook in the kitchen.'

'Hm.' Emmaline sat down at her dressing table and began to brush her hair. She couldn't see Eliza being too happy about that, but her mother had made it more than plain that at least for the duration of the visit there wasn't much she could do about it. 'Good, well I think I'll have a rest now. At about five o'clock could you run me a bath and perhaps come back to help me get dressed for dinner?'

'Yes, ma'am.' Pearl once again bobbed her knee, almost tripping herself up in the process, but once she reached the door she paused to ask nervously, 'Please, ma'am . . . I was wondering, if you don't need me for a while, if I could perhaps nip out to do a bit of shopping? I'd like to get some little presents for my family and perhaps over Christmas I'll get time to deliver them?'

Emmaline's kind heart went out to the girl. She was aware of how her family had dumped her and Eliza in the work-house. Even so, it appeared that Pearl still had feelings for them, so how could she deny her request?

'Of course you may,' she answered kindly. 'Just be sure to be back in time to run my bath.'

Pearl's face lit up as she smiled and scurried away. It would give her about an hour, but if she kept her shopping to a minimum she might just about manage to get to her old home and back in time. On entering the kitchen, she found Eliza down on her hands and knees scrubbing the kitchen floor. It was obvious that there would be no chance of her going with Pearl, so she went to her room and put on her cloak and bonnet and outside boots, then took her meagre savings and tucked them safely into her pocket before hurrying off.

The shops were teeming with people, as she had known they would be, and the atmosphere was cheerful as everyone wished each other a merry Christmas. The shopping took hardly any time at all. She bought a bag of sweeties for the children and a pretty lace-trimmed hankie for her mother and another for Eliza – then, after gauging that she would still have time to make the visit, she set off for her old home.

It felt strange to be back in the familiar maze of twisting dark alleys where she had lived and it came to her just how poor the area was. She had never really noticed before but now she had seen another side of life. Thin children with gaunt faces and dressed in little more than rags were list-lessly kicking a stone up and down the lane when her home came into view. They eyed her bonnet, warm dress and cloak curiously, never imagining for a moment that she had once been one of them.

The first thing she noticed as she approached the house was that there were no curtains at any of the windows, and she wondered why her mother would have taken them down. Admittedly they had been little more than rags, but at least they had given them a measure of privacy.

Even so, she was smiling as she reached for the doorknob – but to her surprise, she found the door was locked. She hammered on it and when there was no response she went to peer through the dirty window. The room was quite empty apart from various pieces of rubbish that were strewn about.

'Is that you, Pearl, me luvvie? Eeh! It is an' all. Yer look so grand I nearly didn't recognise yer!'

Whirling about, Pearl found herself staring into the kindly face of Lil, her old neighbour. The woman's expression became solemn then as she told her, 'I'm afraid the 'ouse is empty at present, luvvie. There's a new tenant movin' in straight after Christmas be all accounts.' She shifted her basket from arm to arm as she avoided Pearl's eyes.

'But where are my family, Lil?' the girl asked.

The woman sighed regretfully. 'They've all gone, luvvie, every last one of 'em apart from Amy.'

'What do yer mean . . . *gone*? Gone where?'

'It were the influenza took 'em last month. The little 'uns went first, then yer ma an' da followed 'em wi'in days of each other. I'm so sorry, luvvie! There's nowt worth 'aving left in there now. Yer know what they're like round these parts, scavengers went in even afore they took the bodies away like a pack o' bleedin' vultures!'

Pearl was so shocked that she had to lean heavily against the wall to keep herself upright. She felt as if all the air had been sucked out of her lungs. 'I . . . I see,' she muttered eventually. 'And so where is Amy now?'

The woman shrugged her thin shoulders. 'All I know is she got offered a post as a kitchen maid somewhere in the Midlands. Young Gracie Hewitt from up the lane already worked there an' she got 'er the job apparently.' She reached out a hand and patted Pearl's arm, wishing that there was something she could say to bring her comfort but knowing there wasn't. Her parents may not have been the best in the world but they were all the poor girl had had and she felt heartsore for her. 'Look, why don't yer come in an' I'll make yer a nice cup o' tea?' she offered.

But Pearl shook her head. 'Thanks, Lil, but I won't, if you don't mind.' Then suddenly she pushed the bag of sweeties into the woman's hand, telling her, 'Give these to the children for Christmas; I won't be needin' them now.'

'Are yer sure?' The woman stared at the gift in amazement. She couldn't even remember the last time she had been able to afford to buy treats for them.

Pearl merely nodded.

'Then thank yer kindly. They'll be much appreciated. You just take care o' yourself now, eh?' She almost wished the girl a happy Christmas too, but realised it wouldn't be appropriate in the circumstances and clamped her mouth shut.

'Do you suppose . . . if ever you manage to catch Gracie when she comes home to see her parents that you could ask her where she and Amy are working now?' Pearl asked in a shaky voice. She could hardly believe that at the tender age of ten Amy was already working in a kitchen, although she was grateful to Grace for helping her.

'O' course I will,' Lil responded, although she knew the chances of that happening were slim. Gracie didn't come back to London much and if she did it wasn't likely that Lil would know about it until she had gone again. Still, she supposed she could always ask Gracie's parents if they had the address of where she was working. She didn't say that though because she didn't want to raise Pearl's hopes. She watched as Pearl walked away with her eyes downcast, before shaking her head sadly. From where she was standing, she secretly thought that being shipped off to

Canada on the orphan ship was the best thing that could have happened to Pearl and Eliza. They certainly hadn't had much of a life until then. With a sigh she entered her house.

All the way back to the Kennedy-Scotts', Pearl felt as if she was in a daze as she tried to digest the news. Her family all gone, just like that. Pictures of the little ones' faces flashed in front of her eyes. Davey, Maggie, Tess, little Tom and the new baby she'd never even met. Their lives over before they'd barely begun. It was a lot to take in, and what would she tell Eliza? She shuddered. She had been so shocked that she hadn't even thought to ask Lil where her family were buried, but then she supposed it was best that she hadn't. No doubt they would have gone to paupers' graves with no one to pay for the funerals. And Amy . . . her dear Amy. At least she was still alive somewhere, but how would she ever find her? Lil had said that she was somewhere in the Midlands but even Pearl knew that the Midlands covered a vast area. She could be anywhere, so the chances of ever seeing her again were slim. From now on it would be just her and Eliza. Swallowing the lump in her throat, she moved on.

Once back at the house she took her cloak and bonnet up to her room then slipped to the family's part of the house and headed for the bathroom to run the bath for Mrs Forbes. It was a large, spacious room with an enormous roll-top bath against one wall. The tap on it was connected to a pipe that led to a large copper in the kitchen that pumped up hot water, and beneath the plug hole was yet another pipe that drained the dirty water away. Pearl had never seen anything so luxurious in her life and would have enjoyed it had she been in a happier mood, but as it was, it was taking all her effort to concentrate. Next to the bath was a chair on which were a pile of fluffy towels and once the bath was run and everything was ready, she went to tap on Mrs Forbes's door. She found her employer dressed in a pretty dressing robe trimmed with feathers.

'Ah, Pearl, did you get everythi—' The words died away and the smile on her face faded as she noted how pale Pearl looked and she asked, 'Are you all right, dear? You look awfully pale. Are you feeling unwell?'

'No, missus . . . I mean, ma'am. It's just . . .' Pearl took a deep breath. 'It's just . . . I just found out that all my family has passed except for one sister. They all died of the influenza a while back.'

'Oh, my goodness. How awful for you.' Mrs Forbes could still remember how she had felt when Elizabeth had died and didn't quite know what to say, but eventually, she muttered, 'If you would like to go to your room and rest . . .'

'No, ma'am. Thank you, but I'd rather keep busy,' Pearl told her with a lift of her chin. 'And your bath is all ready for you if you'd like to come with me.'

Solemn-faced, Emmaline followed her along the landing to the steamy bathroom. She had desperately wanted to ask Pearl how Eliza was faring without her in the kitchen but now clearly wasn't the time.

Chapter Twenty-One

It wasn't until late that evening after she had helped her mistress to prepare for bed that Pearl was able to pass on the news to Eliza when she got to their room. She told her what had happened as gently as she could, and Eliza listened, showing no emotion whatsoever, and when she had finished she just shrugged.

'They didn't care about us anyway,' she said matter-of-factly and with that she turned to the wall and within seconds was sound asleep.

Pearl shook her head. She had a feeling that she would never truly know Eliza if she lived to be a hundred. Since arriving here and being banished to the kitchen, Pearl feared that her sister was slipping back into the quiet world she had lived in after they had first been admitted to the work-house. In Mrs Forbes's care, she had seemed to blossom like a flower, so much so that Pearl had sometimes wondered if Eliza really was as gentle as people had taken her for, but now she seemed sullen and resentful again and the worst of it was, Pearl was painfully aware that there wasn't a single thing she could do about it.

She washed quickly in the cold water in the bowl, pulled on her nightdress and slid into the cold bed, where she finally gave way to the tears she had been holding back. Her family was gone, and she had never felt more alone in the world than she did now.

It was late on Christmas Day as Pearl was carrying yet another tray of hot mince pies to the drawing room that she almost bumped into Monty in the hallway.

'Get out of my way, *servant!*' he snapped angrily and Pearl felt the colour burn into her cheeks.

'I *beg* your pardon. I didn't see you,' she retaliated heatedly.

His top lip curled back from his teeth as he pinched her arm spitefully. 'Don't you *dare* to answer me back, slut! When in the presence of your betters you should be seen and not heard!'

Pearl glared at his retreating back, her arm throbbing. When they had been in Canada, she had always been aware that Monty had resented the attention his mother had shown to Eliza, but now it appeared that he had transferred his dislike to her too. Back there, she had Freda's spite to contend with and now it seemed that here she would also be up against a bully. With a sigh, she went on her way.

Things did not improve over the next few days, and at every opportunity Monty went out of his way to be spiteful to her, but only when there was no one about to see it.

'Why don't you run and tell my mummy what I've done to you and we'll see who she believes?' he goaded one afternoon when he had tripped her up in the hallway, causing her to drop a tray of tea things she was fetching from the dining room. Some of them were broken and Pearl knew that she would be in trouble with Cook now.

'I don't need to tell tales, I can stick up for myself,' she said hotly, although he was at least a head taller than her. 'Why don't you go and pick on someone your own size?'

As she bent to retrieve the broken pots, he looked astonished. Not one of the maids they had ever employed had dared to answer him back before. 'Why you . . . you . . . for two pins I'd smack your dirty little face. Who do you think you are to speak to me that way?'

He advanced on her threateningly, but Pearl had had enough. Both of the men had gone to visit Mr Forbes's woodyard and the ladies were out at a friend of Mrs Kennedy-Scott's taking afternoon tea, so Pearl knew there was little chance she and Monty would be observed. She also knew from when she had grown up in the lanes that the only way to deal with a bully was to stand up to them, and she intended to do just that now. Enough was enough!

Just before he reached her with his fist clenched, she rose gracefully and when he was within reach, she lifted her knee and kneed him as hard as she could in his most private parts.

Monty yelped in agony as he doubled over clutching himself and Pearl went back to what she had been doing. 'I shall tell Cook that you're responsible for these being broken,' she informed him calmly. 'And if you *ever* come near me again, you'll get more of the same, so just be warned.' And with that and a cocky nod of her head she sailed off to the kitchen.

'The little devil! Spoiled rotten he is,' Cook grumbled when Pearl told her what had happened. 'He's bad through an' through that boy is, and he'll come to a sticky end if he don't mend his ways, you just mark my words! It's no wonder he's got no friends at the school.'

When the ladies arrived home later that afternoon Pearl went upstairs with Mrs Forbes to help her into a robe before she took a nap. Emmaline had deliberately avoided asking about Eliza because she knew that Pearl was grieving for her family, although to the girl's credit it had not affected her work.

But now she could wait no longer, and as she sat at her dressing table, while Pearl removed the clips from her hair, she suddenly blurted out, 'How is Lizzie coping in the kitchen, Pearl? Is she missing me? The poor darling must wonder what is happening but my mother feels . . .'

Her words trailed away as she realised that it wasn't really the done thing to speak to Pearl of her mother's feelings. The girl was only a maid after all, although with each day that passed, Emmaline was growing more fond of her. Pearl never complained and did whatever was asked of her to the very best of her ability. She was very polite and had come so far in the short time since Emmaline had employed her. Emmaline's instincts told her that Pearl was to be trusted, and would keep her confidences. Monty's tutor back at home was always telling her how clever the girl was and how quickly she could grasp things once they were explained to her. She could now read and write almost as well as Emmaline could and her grammar had certainly improved vastly.

Now after taking out the last of the pins, Pearl picked up the hairbrush and answered, 'She's doing all right, ma'am. Thanks for asking.'

'*Really?*'

When Pearl nodded, Emmaline fell silent. Her mother had made her solemnly promise that once they were back in Canada, she would make Eliza stay in the job she had been employed to do. But oh, she did miss the girl, she couldn't deny it.

Before they knew it, it was New Year's Eve and once again all was hustle and bustle as the staff rushed about preparing for the party that was to take place at the house that evening.

'I shouldn't be surprised if half of the people you've invited don't turn up in this weather, my love,' Andrew warned as he sat behind a newspaper at his desk in the study. It was the only downstairs room where he could get a bit of peace and quiet at present, and his wife had joined him in there.

'I fear you could be right, darling.' She glanced towards the window, where the snow was still coming down like a thick white curtain. 'But then I intend to make the most of it however many come. Emmaline and Zack will be going home in a few days' time and I wanted them to have a special night to remember. Who knows how long it will be before we see them again?'

Laying his paper down, he came to stand behind her and placed his arms about her waist. 'And how do you think Emmaline is now?'

She sighed. 'Much better, I think, but I've had to nip the obsession she seemed to have with the little blonde servant girl in the bud. I fear Emmie was trying to replace Elizabeth and we both know that that could only have ended in disaster.

She must allow herself to grieve properly without looking for distractions, otherwise she'll never get over her loss.'

'Actually, I don't think any of us will ever do that,' he said sadly. 'We simply learn to live with it and carry on. But come – we mustn't be maudlin today. It's almost the start of a brand-new year and Elizabeth wouldn't have wanted to spoil it, God bless her.'

'You're quite right as always,' his wife said softly, and they stood in silence staring out at the snow as they thought of the little granddaughter they had adored.

'It's beautiful isn't it?'

Pearl hadn't heard her mistress quietly enter the room and her voice made Pearl start and step quickly away from the stunning gown hanging on the door of the armoire that she had been admiring.

'Y-yes, ma'am. It really is,' she muttered, feeling embarrassed.

'It was ridiculously expensive,' Emmaline confided as she stroked the soft velvet of the skirt. 'But my husband insisted I should have it.'

The dress was a rich red trimmed with silver braid and silver embroidery about the low-cut neckline and around the bottom of the three-quarter-length sleeves. It fitted tightly into the waist and the skirt was full, falling in gentle folds that shimmered in the light. Pearl was sure it was the most beautiful gown she had ever seen, and could hardly wait to see her mistress wearing it. But first she must wash her hair and take her bath, which Pearl had readied for her.

Almost an hour later, Emmaline sat at the side of the fire as Pearl rubbed at her hair, and at last it was time to start getting ready.

'I thought I would wear my hair up tonight,' she informed Pearl. 'We can put it up in curls on top and tease some ringlets out.' She laughed as she saw the look of dismay flit across Pearl's face. Dressing her hair was still the one thing that Pearl hadn't quite mastered, and she sometimes wondered if she ever would. Emmaline's hair was so thick and wavy that it seemed to have a mind of its own. 'Don't worry, we'll do it between us and I'm sure it will be fine,' Emmaline told her kindly.

She watched in the mirror as Pearl followed her instructions with her tongue in her cheek as she concentrated, and half an hour later, they both smiled as they studied the end result.

'Wonderful,' Emmaline praised. 'And now I think it's time to get into my gown.'

Pearl helped her into her undergarments before fitting a tight girdle over the silk drawers, giving her mistress an hourglass figure. Then came the short silk chemise and the huge hooped underskirt that would give her new gown it's shape. Next came the gown itself, and Pearl found she was all fingers and thumbs as she did up the numerous tiny buttons that ran from the tight waist right up the neckline at the back. Beneath it the mistress wore silver silk shoes and Pearl couldn't help but be a little envious as she looked at them. She was very grateful for the built-up boots that Mrs Forbes had bought for her – at least when wearing them she didn't walk with a limp – but she would never be able to wear anything as dainty as these.

Finally, Mrs Forbes took a velvet box from the drawer of her dressing table and when she snapped the lid open Pearl gasped. Nestled inside on a bed of silk was the most beautiful pearl necklace and matching earrings that Pearl had ever seen.

'These were also a gift from my husband for our last wedding anniversary,' Emmaline told her, as she carefully lifted them from the box. 'And I thought they would complement the gown. What do you think, Pearl?'

'I think they're just beautiful, ma'am,' Pearl breathed as she took the necklace from her and fastened it about her neck. Emmaline fastened the earrings herself and at last she was ready. She gave a little twirl as she examined herself in the mirror.

She laughed girlishly. 'So, will I do?'

Pearl nodded emphatically. 'Oh *yes*, ma'am. You look *really* beautiful!'

The opalescent pearls perfectly matched the soft glimmer of the velvet and Pearl thought her mistress looked just like a princess who had stepped from the pages of a fairy story book.

'Thank you, my dear. Why don't you go and see if there are any little last-minute jobs you can do for Cook in the kitchen? I've no doubt she will be in a panic by now. And don't forget, it's the staff party tomorrow when you can all let your hair down. You've certainly earned it over Christmas.'

'Yes, ma'am, thank you, ma'am.' Pearl bobbed her knee and left the room, leaving her mistress to dab expensive

French perfume on her wrists before going downstairs where the first of the guests were just arriving.

Just as Emmaline had predicted, Pearl found organised chaos in the kitchen as the maids scuttled about like busy little ants carrying trays of food through to the table in the dining room. It made Pearl's mouth water just to look at it. There were platters full of roast beef, pork and gammon, pickles, pork pies, potatoes and pies of all shapes and sizes, as well as baskets of freshly baked bread and rolls. On another table were tiny individual jellies in all the colours of the rainbow that gleamed like jewels under the crystal chandeliers, and big jugs of fresh cream. There were rich-looking cakes, trifles, mince pies and pastries, and Pearl wondered just how many people had been invited as plate after plate was rushed through.

'There must be enough food to feed an army there,' she muttered.

Cook smiled. 'Oh, it'll go, believe me. The men will soon start to put it away when they've 'ad a drink or two. It seems to give 'em an appetite.'

Within no time at all, if the noise coming from the hallway was anything to go by, the party was going with a swing and now the maids rushed in and out filling trays with glasses of champagne before rushing out again.

'Phew! That's me done for the night,' Cook declared, sinking into the wing chair at the side of the fire and kicking her slippers off. 'Eliza, put the kettle on, there's a pet. Me throat is parched and I'm dying for a cuppa.'

Pearl watched as Eliza sullenly did as she was asked. Her ringlets had disappeared now and her hair was pulled back and tied with a ribbon at the nape of her neck. Cook had soon decided that the clothes she had arrived in were inappropriate for working in the kitchen, and now she was dressed in a drab, grey dress that had once belonged to one of the other kitchen maids who had worked there. Pearl felt a stab of sympathy for her. Once again, her young life had changed, but perhaps when they set off back to Canada their mistress would take her under her wing again. For her sister's sake, she half hoped that she would, despite the fact that she had enjoyed having Eliza to herself again for a while – albeit she had been quiet and bad-tempered. But they would just have to wait and see.

Throughout the evening, they each took it in turns to peep around the kitchen door so they could catch a glimpse of the beautiful dresses the women were wearing as they sailed past, and it was soon agreed that the young mistress looked the most stunning.

'Yer did a fair old job of puttin' 'er 'air up,' Bridget, the little Irish laundry maid, said admiringly and Pearl preened with pleasure. 'It's just a shame as they 'ad to let 'is lordship attend,' she said cuttingly, as they watched Monty sneak a glass of champagne from one of the maid's trays. 'He's a spiteful little so-an'-so,' she went on. 'He come in the laundry room when I were up to me elbows in suds t'other day and upended the washtub just fer the spite of it! Took me ages to mop it all up, it did, an' the rotten little bugger just laughed like 'e'd done somethin' funny.'

'He's sick in the head,' another one agreed. 'Nothing at all like his little sister was. Now she were a sweet little thing, but I reckon he were jealous of her.'

At last the grandfather clock in the hallway chimed twelve o'clock and suddenly everyone, even the kitchen staff, was turning to the person closest to them and giving them a kiss and wishing them a happy New Year. Unfortunately for Pearl, she was just returning from the dining room with a pile of empty platters when suddenly she was swung round to find herself face to face with Monty. His eyes were glazed and she knew instantly that he was drunk. She could remember seeing the same look in her father's eyes a million times before. Clutching the platters, she glared at him and he laughed.

'Aw well, seein' as you're the only one close, I suppose you'll have to do,' he said – and before she could stop him, he had grabbed her and thrust his tongue into her mouth.

There was nothing she could do to prevent it. One of his hands was behind her head holding her close, but she knew she would be in serious trouble with the cook should she drop the platters so she merely tried to pull away as she retched.

'Ugh! That was *disgustin'*,' she spat when she finally managed to break away – and completely forgetting all the lessons on etiquette that the mistress had taught her, she turned and fled to the kitchen.

'I swear I'll get my own back on 'im one o' these days,' she growled, reverting back to the way she used to talk as she wiped her hand across her mouth, trying to rid herself of the disgusting taste of him.

Mrs Brookes, who had witnessed what had happened, shook her head. 'Don't worry, dear. He'll meet his match,' she said and sighed. She could quite easily have reported what had gone on to her mistress but she was fretting already because it was only days away from her daughter's departure. It was also only days away from Monty returning to school, so she decided it would be best to say nothing for now. Hopefully he'd get his comeuppance eventually. His type always did.

Chapter Twenty-Two

'Oh, darling, are you *quite* sure it's safe to set sail in this weather?' Mrs Kennedy-Scott asked as she glanced anxiously at the stormy weather beyond the window. 'I can't believe that you're really going again. It seems like only a moment since you arrived.'

'I know, it has gone quickly, hasn't it?' her daughter agreed, as Zack placed a thick, fur-lined cloak about her slender shoulders. 'But I've really enjoyed it. Thank you so much for having us.' In truth anything would have been better than having to stay in the house in Canada where the ghost of her little daughter haunted every corner. And of course, it had been wonderful to spend Christmas with Monty, although he hadn't seemed overly excited to see her and his father. But then she supposed that was just his age. All teenagers were notoriously moody and hopefully the expensive school he was attending would make a man of him.

The groom was loading the last of their trunks and boxes on to the top of the carriage and Emmaline noticed that they seemed to be leaving with far more than they had come with, thanks to the many shopping trips she had been on with her mother. Just then, Pearl and Eliza came from the kitchen, dressed in their outdoor clothes and clutching the bags they had brought with them.

'Ah, here you are, girls. Go and hop into the carriage and have a safe journey,' Mrs Kennedy-Scott told them, and once they had gone her face became solemn as she addressed her daughter again. 'Don't forget what I told you. Once you get home, you must let Eliza return to her duties in the kitchen. And don't think I won't know if you try to do otherwise, because Zack will be keeping an eye on you too!' Her face softened then and she caught her daughter to her with tears in her eyes. 'Have a safe journey, darling, and remember, we love you very much.'

'I love you too,' Emmaline answered in a choked voice. Then she hugged and kissed her father, before turning her attention to Monty, who was standing with his hands behind his back and the usual sullen expression on his face.

'Are you quite sure you have everything you need for your new term?' she asked for at least the tenth time.

'Oh, for goodness sake,' her mother laughed. 'Stop worrying. If there's anything he needs we're still here and he won't go short of anything, I promise.'

Monty allowed her to kiss him on the cheek as, looking slightly worried, Zack pointed out, 'The captain will be waiting for us, darling, and you know what a stickler he is for sailing on time. If we miss the tide we'll have to wait until this evening.'

The sailors had been busy all day loading the ship with food and stock for the shops back in Canada. None of Mr Forbes's ships ever sailed without being fully loaded.

Emmaline was ushered outside and into the carriage, where the two girls sat quietly waiting for them and then she was hanging out of the window waving through the snow until her parents disappeared.

'Thank goodness for that; I thought you were trying to freeze us all,' Zack said.

Emmaline closed the window with tears glistening on her lashes and leaned back against the squabs, as the horses picked their way across the snowy cobblestones.

The cabins aboard the ship were just as cold as they remembered them and they instantly added some more layers of clothing, painfully aware that the journey ahead was not going to be at all pleasant.

As the ship set sail and the lights of London began to fade into the distance, Pearl stood watching them through the tiny porthole in their cabin with tears in her eyes, while Eliza lay curled up in a tight ball on her narrow bunk. It was incredible to think that she had arrived full of excitement at the prospect of seeing her parents and siblings again, only to find that they were all gone now. All except Amy, that was, and she knew the chances of ever seeing her again were slim. There would be nothing to tempt her back to the place of her birth anymore and it was a sobering thought.

Within hours, the ship began to rise and fall on the choppy sea and both Eliza and Mrs Forbes became ill again. Pearl found herself rushing between them with buckets and bowls as they vomited, offering what comfort she could. *Here we go again*, she thought with a rueful smile.

It was so bitterly cold over the next few days that the deck and the rails of the ship froze solid, and the poor sailors had to wear thick leather gloves and rubber-soled boots to stop them slipping over the sides. Both Eliza and Mrs Forbes were still feeling desperately sick, although because their stomachs were empty at least they had stopped vomiting.

'Come along, Pearl,' Mr Forbes said one evening when she had finished helping Mrs Forbes to wash and change her nightdress. 'The ship's cook told me earlier that he was cooking stew and dumplings this evening. Just what the doctor ordered to keep the cold out, eh?'

At the mere mention of it, Mrs Forbes turned an alarming shade of green again, but knowing there was nothing more that could be done for her for now, he nudged Pearl towards the cabin door. 'We're going to try to eat something, otherwise we'll be ill too and we won't have the strength to look after the invalids.'

Seeing the sense in what he said, she followed him to the dining room, where they found some of the sailors tucking into plates piled high with food. Even Pearl was feeling sickly by then but, determined not to give in to it, she did her best to eat as much as she could when he carried a steaming plate back to her. Surprisingly she did feel much better with something inside her stomach, and as Eliza was fast asleep when she got back to the cabin and Mr Forbes had assured her that he would look after his wife, she clambered into her own bunk and, despite the tossing and turning of the ship, was asleep in no time.

From then on, the endless days seemed to roll one into another. The storms they encountered were so bad that some days none of the women dared venture from their bunks, where they would lie praying that they were not about to sink. The ship was tossed about like a feather in the wind, and Eliza and Mrs Forbes were so ill that Pearl feared they might not make it. But worse still was the bone-chilling cold. Even wrapped in blankets they lay shivering, their teeth chattering and their hands and feet so numb that it was almost as though they were no longer attached to their bodies. They discovered that one of the sailors had been swept overboard to his death and they wondered how many more might follow him as the men struggled to keep the ship afloat. It was only because of the captain's expert skills that they hadn't all been lost already.

At last, late one afternoon when Pearl had resigned herself to being lost at sea, a shout came from above and minutes later the door flew open and Mr Forbes stood there hanging on to the handle to keep himself upright as he told them joyously, 'They've sighted land. We're almost there. We're going to be all right.' There had been times when even he had had his doubts, for it was the worst journey he had ever been on.

'Thank God,' Pearl muttered, gripping the side of the bunk. She had been so busy trying to stop herself being thrown out of it that she hadn't even been able to read any of the books Mrs Forbes had packed for her.

'Don't try and get up to start the packing until we dock,' Mr Forbes warned her. 'Once we've anchored, I'll send someone up to the house to get Will to come and fetch us in the carriage and you can do it then.' And then he was gone, and Pearl lay there crying tears of relief and offering up a silent prayer of thanks.

It was pitch-dark by the time they finally anchored, and Pearl cautiously clambered out of her bunk and began to pack her own and Eliza's things. Next she went along to her mistress's cabin and helped her to dress, which was no mean feat as the poor woman was so weak she could barely stand. Once she was dressed, Pearl began to pack her clothes, and minutes later a burly sailor appeared to carry all their luggage up on to the deck for her.

'I thought we were all going to die back there,' Mrs Forbes told her in a small voice.

Pearl nodded. 'So did I for a while, ma'am,' she admitted. 'But we're back now and once Will arrives, we'll have you home in no time.'

'And how is Lizzie?'

Pearl shook her head. 'No better than you have been, to be honest, but I'm sure once she's back on dry land she'll be fine again.'

Soon after that the sailor returned to take them all to wait in the dining cabin, but he had to practically carry both Mrs Forbes and Eliza up the steep steps. The ship's cook made them all a hot cup of tea but after the first sip both Eliza and Mrs Forbes were sick again, so they pushed the mugs aside.

At last Will appeared and they breathed a huge sigh of relief.

'Welcome home,' he said cheerfully. He had so many layers of clothes on that he looked almost twice his size and they soon discovered why when they ventured out on to the deck. All they could see was a vast white world. A path had been roughly cleared to give access to the dock and through the town, but drifts ten foot high were piled everywhere they looked and it was so cold that it took their breath away.

'Be careful,' he warned, as he led them towards the gangplank, which was treacherously slippery. 'This is like a skating rink, so hold tight to the rails.'

They did as they were told, breathing a sigh of relief when they eventually reached the carriage. The poor horses had thick blankets across their backs, but already Pearl could see there was ice forming on their manes and tails. It hurt to breathe, so they climbed in as quickly as possible. Mr Forbes said that the luggage could be delivered later and now all they wanted to do was get home as quickly as possible. The journey back was unpleasant as the poor horses slithered on the ice, and as they turned into the drive leading to the house they stopped abruptly and stubbornly refused to go another step, despite all Will's coaxing.

'I'm afraid you're going to have to walk from here,' he apologised as he came to open the carriage door. 'I shall have to leave the carriage here and lead the horses round to the stable one at a time. They're too afraid of the ice to venture any further.'

The men helped Mrs Forbes and the girls down and, slipping and slithering and holding tight to one another, they set off for the house. The snow was coming down thickly again now and Pearl had never seen anything like it.

It seemed to take a lifetime, but at last the house was in sight and as they staggered towards the door, Mrs Veasey threw it open and ushered them inside, where the welcoming warmth instantly made their clothes start to steam.

'Pearl, go through to the kitchen,' she ordered. 'And let's get the rest of you into the drawing room by the fire.'

Pearl immediately did as she was told, taking Eliza with her, and although Mrs Veasey looked surprised, she didn't comment.

'It's nice to have you back,' Cook said warmly when they first entered the room, but like Mrs Veasey, she looked mildly surprised to see Eliza in there. The mistress had barely let the girl out of her sight before they'd gone away, so she wondered what had changed.

Pearl dragged Eliza over to the warmth of the fire, aware that Freda, who was peeling vegetables at the table, was glaring at them. There was one person who certainly wasn't pleased to see them back. Even so she forced a smile as she said, 'Hello, Freda, did you have a good Christmas?'

Scowling, Freda kept her eyes firmly fixed on the potatoes she was peeling. Now that the family were back it would mean a lot more work again, and she wasn't too happy about it. 'Yes, we did,' she mumbled.

'Good, and have you seen anything of Susan or Nick?'

'How was I supposed to get out in this weather?' Freda snapped. 'Cook said as no one were to venture outside unless it were strictly necessary. It'd freeze yer to death in no time out there.'

'Yes, I suppose it would,' Pearl said distractedly as she began to take off her outer clothes. The feeling was just beginning to return to her fingers and toes now and they were throbbing.

Freda glanced at Eliza thoughtfully and asked, 'So what's she doin' in 'ere? I thought the missus kept 'er close.'

'Oh, er . . . I'll explain later.'

Pearl saw Eliza's face fall, but she had no need to explain as it turned out because minutes later Mrs Veasey came back into the room to tell them, 'Mrs Forbes has just informed me that Eliza will be working in the kitchen again from now on and she has other duties in mind for you, Pearl, which she will explain to you later.'

Ignoring the gloating look that flitted across Freda's face, Pearl answered, 'Yes, Mrs Veasey.' The housekeeper was clearly pleased to have her mistress back.

It was almost an hour later when Pearl was summoned to Mrs Forbes's bedroom. Despite the atrocious weather, Mr Forbes had ventured out to inspect his sawmill, and she found her mistress lying on her bed fully clothed. Mrs Veasey had plied her with hot sweet tea, but it clearly hadn't done much good as yet. She still looked ghastly and her face was the colour of bleached linen.

'Ah, Pearl.' Her voice was as weak as a kitten's.

Unsure what she should say, Pearl simply nodded as she crossed to throw some coals on to the fire blazing in the small grate.

'I was wondering if you'd mind helping me get undressed,' the woman went on. 'I'm still not feeling too well and think I'll lie down for a few hours.' As she spoke, she swung her legs over the side of the bed, as Pearl wiped her hands on her dress and went to fetch her mistress's nightdress and dressing robe. 'Actually, I also wanted to ask you how you would like to become my lady's maid full-time? You did a wonderful job while we were in London and although Mrs Veasey has always helped me dress for special occasions, I find I quite liked being pampered. What do you think?'

After finding out about the deaths of her family and the atrocious sea journey, Pearl had had little to smile about for some time but now, she positively glowed with pride. 'I'd love that, ma'am,' she told her with a wide smile. It was a huge step up from being a housemaid, and she could hardly wait to see Freda's face when she found out. She wasn't going to be happy with the new arrangement at all.

'In that case, as soon as the shops are able to open again, we must see about getting you some more suitable clothes,' her mistress told her, as Pearl eased her gown over her head and began to unlace her stays. 'Something a little more fitting for your new position, I think. And perhaps when you're not needed Mrs Veasey could start to teach you how to manage the household accounts. She's been talking of returning to England to her family for some time now and even though you're still very young, it would be nice, if or when she does, if you could step into her shoes without me having to train someone else. I've already put the idea to her and she thinks you would do very well.'

Pearl nodded enthusiastically, wondering if the day could possibly get any better. Just this time yesterday she had feared for their lives and now here she was back on dry land with a promotion she could never have dreamed of. Susan and Nick would be so pleased for her when she told them, although she was convinced Freda would not be any too happy about it, but that added to her excitement. Freda was such a jealous, spiteful girl, although she seemed to have Cook wrapped around her little finger.

Minutes later she helped Mrs Forbes back into bed and, after crossing to close the curtains on the snowy landscape, she picked up the clothes Mrs Forbes had been wearing to take them down to the laundry. They smelled disgusting, although that was hardly surprising considering how seasick the woman had been.

'There's just one thing, ma'am.' Pearl paused at the door, the smile gone now as she asked, 'Now that Eliza is to be working in the kitchen again, where is she to sleep?' Before the trip to London she had had her own pretty little room close to Mrs Forbes but she clearly wouldn't be allowed to sleep there now.

'Oh . . . I hadn't thought of that.' Mrs Forbes frowned as she leaned back against her lace-trimmed pillows. 'I think perhaps you could ask Mrs Veasey to find her a room in the servants' quarters with you.'

Pearl nodded. 'In that case would you mind very much if she were to share with me? I have Freda in with me at present but I'm sure she would much rather have a room of her own.'

Mrs Forbes stifled a yawn and waved her hand impatiently. 'Yes, yes, that will be fine, providing Freda doesn't mind.'

Pearl hurriedly left the room and headed for the kitchen, where she found that Cook had gone for a short lie-down while the meal was cooking.

'So, little Miss Eliza ain't in favour wi' the mistress no more then,' Freda gloated with a nasty grin, the second Pearl entered the room.

Pearl bit her tongue to stop herself from retaliating. 'Actually, now that she's better, the mistress just thought she would be able to return to her kitchen duties,' she answered calmly. 'Which, I'm sure you'll agree, will make it much easier for you if there are two of you to help Cook. It also means that Eliza will be joining us upstairs, so I wondered if you'd like to have a room of your own so that Eliza can share with me again?'

Freda just shrugged, so Pearl went on, 'Of course if you'd rather stay where you are . . .'

'No . . . no I'll 'ave me own room,' Freda said hastily.

'Good. But there's something else I need to talk to you about. The mistress just told me that she wishes me to become her lady's maid.'

Freda was so shocked that her mouth gaped and she almost dropped the cup she was holding. '*You! A lady's maid!*'

'That's right.' Pearl stood across the table from her. 'I shall be starting straight away.'

'Yer *jammy* devil,' Freda said jealously. 'I swear if you fell in the Thames you'd come out wi' a pocket full o' fish! How did yer manage to smarm yer way round 'er to bring that about?'

Pearl was getting heartily sick of her attitude by then, so she answered cryptically, 'The same way *you* smarmed round Cook to become her blue-eyed girl, I suppose.'

And with that she turned on her heel and flounced off to her room, taking Eliza with her.

Freda followed a short time later to find all her belongings placed neatly on the landing outside the door of the room

Mrs Veasey had allocated to her. Muttering, she snatched them up and, striding into her new room, began to throw them into the drawers.

No one ate much that evening as they were still feeling quite unwell and just wanted a good night's sleep.

'Eeh, I don't know why I went to all the bother of cooking,' Cook grumbled, as the food was returned from the dining room virtually untouched. Mrs Forbes hadn't even bothered to come down but had requested a tray be sent up to her room.

'So how long does this weather last here?' Pearl asked. She was longing to see Susan and Nick again, but knew that she wouldn't be allowed to go until the conditions had improved. No one could survive for long in that snow.

'It all depends,' Cook told her. 'It could be over in a couple of weeks or it could last for months. I've known us be completely snowed in here for weeks at a time.'

Pearl sighed glumly. It looked like she was going to have to be patient.

Chapter Twenty-Three

It was the middle of March before the thaw came, causing floods as the Great River came dangerously close to bursting its banks as the snow melted into it.

Pearl couldn't help thinking of back home in the springtime. In England, the spring flowers would be pushing their way through the earth and delicate green buds would be unfurling on the trees. Thoughts of England always made her think of her sister Amy, and she wondered how she was faring. Other than that, though, Pearl was content. She had settled well into her new job and much preferred having Eliza as her roommate, although she still had to endure Freda's spite during the day. There had been no shortage of food thanks to Cook. The large pantry was always stocked with fruit and vegetables she had pickled during the warm weather and the smoke house was full of preserved meat hanging from large hooks in the ceiling. As the ships also still brought in fresh supplies on a regular basis, none of them had suffered – apart from Mrs Veasey, who appeared to have taken a turn for the worse again and was at present confined to bed.

'I just can't understand what's wrong with her,' Mrs Forbes said to Pearl one morning as she was brushing her hair – Pearl was quite good at it now. 'The doctor is at a loss too. All he can do is recommend a tonic, but that doesn't seem to be doing her any good at all, poor soul.'

Pearl nodded. 'She doesn't seem to be getting any better,' she agreed. It was her who usually took up food to the poor woman – not that she was eating much now, so Cook had begun to prepare nourishing chicken soups to try to tempt her. 'And she's so weak,' Pearl went on. 'I'm making sure that she has as much liquid as she can manage but even that is making her vomit now.' She could have added that she had seen traces of blood in her chamber pot when she took it away to empty it too, but she didn't want to worry the mistress any more than she already was. Only that morning the pains in Mrs Veasey stomach had been so bad that it had taken Pearl all her time to wash and change her, and more worrying still was the fact that over the last couple of days she seemed to have been having mild seizures. She was forgetful too, but Pearl supposed that this was because she was in so much pain.

'I wonder if putting her aboard a ship and getting her to a hospital in England would help?' Mrs Forbes mused as Pearl began to pin up her hair.

Pearl shook her head. 'To be honest, I don't think she'd survive the journey in the state she's in now, ma'am,' she said sadly.

They all missed Mrs Veasey, but Pearl, in particular, wished she would get better, if only for Eliza's sake. She had hoped that once they got back from England Mrs Forbes would take an interest in Eliza again, but as yet that hadn't happened and Eliza had gone back into her shell. Cook seemed to have little patience with her, which didn't help the situation, although Freda could still do no wrong in her eyes and got away with murder. The second Cook left the room, Freda would make Eliza do the jobs that she should have done. It hadn't been so bad while Mrs Veasey was up and about as she had made it abundantly clear that she had no time for Freda and wouldn't stand for her spiteful ways, but now that she was ill, Eliza's life was worse than ever. But then, Pearl thought, Mrs Veasey had frequently criticised Eliza for trying to get out of doing her fair share of work, so maybe it wouldn't have made much difference. Because of this Pearl visited the kitchen as often as she could, but she couldn't be there all the time and she wished there were more she could do to help her little sister.

Her thoughts were interrupted as Mrs Forbes told her, 'I was thinking the roads might be safe enough to venture into town today. We could visit the dressmaker and get you measured for those new gowns I promised you.'

Pearl's face lit up. She was now thirteen years old and the dresses she owned were becoming dangerously tight across the chest, as well as being far too short. 'That would be lovely, ma'am. Shall I ask Will to get the carriage ready for us?'

When Mrs Forbes was dressed, Pearl skipped downstairs with a happy smile on her face wondering if there might be time when they went into town to pay Susan a quick visit. It had been such a long time since she had seen her and she missed her. She entered the kitchen to find Eliza down on her hands and knees laboriously scrubbing the kitchen floor and the smile instantly slid from her face.

'Isn't that *your* job?' she asked Freda coldly.

The girl grinned. 'It were till *she* got set on,' she said scathingly. 'But seein' as she's younger than me it should be 'er as does it now.'

Pearl's hands clenched in frustration. She knew that if she were to complain to Cook she would take Freda's side, and seeing as Mrs Veasey was so unwell there was nothing she could do about it either. Not that Pearl thought she would have. For some reason she had never seemed to take to Eliza either. With a toss of her head, she snatched her cloak from the back of the door and crossed the yard to the stables to find Will.

He was in the stalls rubbing one of the horses down, and Pearl stood for a moment enjoying the smell of fresh hay before telling him that his mistress wanted the carriage brought round.

'Right you are,' he said cheerfully. 'It'll do 'em good to get out for a trot. Poor things have been penned up in here for far too long. But then we all have. Just leave it with me an' tell Mrs Forbes I'll have the carriage round the front in a jiffy.'

'Thanks, Will.' As Pearl hurried across the yard, she found Eliza throwing the dirty water out.

'Are you goin' out?' the girl asked enviously as she swiped her wet hands across the front of her apron and Pearl felt a pang of guilt as she looked at Eliza's rough hands. Hers were as smooth as silk now and she wondered at how their situations had changed so quickly.

'Yes I am, as it happens. Mrs Forbes wants to take me into the town to get me measured up for some new dresses.'

Eliza pouted as she glanced down at her own drab work dress, then with a shrug she walked back inside without another word. Pearl hurried after her, relieved to see that there was no sign of Freda.

'Look, I've been saving my wages and by Christmas I'll have saved enough to buy you a new dress too,' she said, hoping to cheer her sister up. But Eliza merely sniffed and went about her work, without so much as looking at her sister again.

Half an hour later, Pearl and Mrs Forbes set out for the town and Pearl felt light-hearted to be free again. It had been a very long, hard winter, far worse than any she had ever experienced back home and she couldn't wait for spring to arrive. The roads were still slippery with slush and the horses had to tread carefully but eventually they reached the town all in one piece, much to Will's relief. He was always afraid that one of the horses would hurt their legs but thankfully they had managed the journey admirably.

'Give us about an hour, please, Will,' Mrs Forbes instructed him, and doffing his cap he clambered back on to the carriage and urged the horses on.

Pearl and Mrs Forbes spent a pleasant half-hour with the dressmaker, choosing patterns and material for two new gowns, after which the kindly little woman had measured almost every inch of Pearl. By the time they were finished, Pearl was beaming and could hardly wait for them to be made. One was to be a fine silver-grey wool for the colder weather and the other dress would be made from a lemon-coloured cotton trimmed with a darker braid that would be perfect for the warmer weather. They would both have full skirts and Pearl knew that she would feel like a real lady when she wore them.

'Right, we're all done here,' Mrs Forbes said after glancing at the clock. 'And we still have at least half an hour before Will comes back, so if there's anywhere you want to go, by all means do. I still have a few things to get but I'll meet you back here.'

It was the ideal opportunity to visit Susan, so Pearl set off for the bakery with a spring in her step. The smell of fresh-baked bread met her the second she stepped through the door and to her delight her friend was laying out a batch of fresh loaves on the counter. Susan glanced up as the little bell above the door tinkled and she beamed when she saw who it was.

'*Pearl!* Eeh, I've missed yer *that* much!' She was round the counter like a flash and before Pearl knew it, she was being enveloped in a bear hug that almost squeezed the air out of her.

'I've missed you too.' Pearl laughed as she finally managed to hold Susan at arm's length. Thankfully there was no one else in the shop and the baker was busy in the kitchen, so Susan could steal a few moments to talk to her.

'Oh, I've got so much to tell you,' Susan told her. 'Fer a start off Miss Walker who brought us here is gettin' married in June to that nice Mr Briggs, who come over wiv the boys. Nick told me . . . he called in t'other day an' he's now work-ing at Mr Forbes's boatyard an' lovin' it. He's stayin' at the 'ome we stayed in when we first got 'ere fer now but 'e seems a lot 'appier than he was workin' fer the farmer. But that's enough about what's been goin' on 'ere. Tell me all about yer 'oliday in London.'

And so Pearl told her about her promotion to lady's maid and that Eliza was now working in the kitchen again. Then, with tears in her eyes, she told her about the death of her family. Susan clucked her tongue sympathetically and gave her hand a little squeeze. Finally, she told her about how poorly Mrs Veasey was.

Susan shook her head. 'Poor sod, what d'yer fink is wrong wiv 'er?'

Pearl shook her head. 'I have no idea. Neither does the doctor if it comes to that, but she seems to be getting worse every day. The smell in her room is appalling and her mind seems to be going too. It's a mystery.' But then she smiled again and changed the subject when she told Susan, 'This is the first time I've ventured out since we got back. The weather hasn't allowed me to but hopefully we should be able to start meeting on Sunday afternoons again soon. But now tell me about you; how are you?'

For the first time she noticed how pale Susan looked, and was that a bruise on her cheek?

Susan looked fearfully across her shoulder then lowering her voice she confided, 'No better at all 'ere, I'm sorry to say. I got this' – she patted the bruise on her cheek – 'when the randy old devil come down a few nights ago when his missus were asleep. He thought 'e were goin' to 'ave 'is way wiv me but 'e soon left wi' a flea in his ear an' a good swift kick up the arse!' She bit her lip then. 'Trouble is, I don't know 'ow much longer I can fight 'im off! I've asked Miss

Walker to find another position fer me soon as she can.' Seeing the worried look on Pearl's face she forced a smile again and hurried on, 'But don't you get frettin' about it. I'll be fine.'

At that moment, the baker appeared in the doorway and after glaring at her he barked, 'Why ain't you set the rest o' them loaves out yet? I don't pay you to stand about chattin', you know!'

'Keep yer 'at on! I've nearly finished, ain't I?' Susan answered rebelliously as she hurried back to the large basket and began to slam the loaves on the counter.

Taking this as her cue to leave, Pearl turned to the door. 'If the weather is a bit better, I'll meet you on Sunday afternoon,' she promised and hurriedly left the shop.

Soon after, Will returned with the carriage and all the way home Pearl was quiet as she worried about Susan. However, the second they set foot through the door Cook rushed to meet them, wringing her hands and looking flustered.

'Pearl, you'd best run out and ask Will to fetch the doctor before he puts the horses away,' she told her with a hint of panic in her voice.

'Why, what's wrong?' Mrs Forbes asked.

'It's Mrs Veasey. Freda just took her a drink up and came down to say she's taken a turn for the worse. I went up to check and the poor soul is in a right state.'

Pearl rushed outside again to find Will while Mrs Forbes lifted her skirts and shot away up the stairs. Sure enough, she could see at a glance that Mrs Veasey was desperately ill, and tears came to her eyes as she dropped on to the side of her bed and took her hand in hers.

'Oh, my dear Florence,' she muttered brokenly as she stared into the woman's feverish face. 'Please don't leave me. It was you who got me through when we lost Elizabeth and over the years, I have come to regard you more as a friend than a housekeeper.'

But Florence Veasey seemed to be beyond hearing as her head rolled from side to side on the pillow and she gasped for breath. She was ghastly pale and her eyes were feverishly bright. For the first time Mrs Forbes also noticed that small warts and lesions had erupted on her skin and the smell of loose faeces was so overpowering that she almost vomited.

It was nearly an hour later by the time the doctor could get there, and by then Pearl and Mrs Forbes had washed the poor soul and changed her nightclothes and bedding yet again, not that it had seemed to help the smell in the room much. They both hurried out on to the landing, leaving the doctor to examine her.

It was some time before he joined them to tell them, 'I'm afraid there is nothing more I can do. It appears that her organs are slowly shutting down. I believe it is just a matter of time now. All you can do is sit with her and comfort her as best you can. I'm so sorry.'

Mrs Forbes dabbed at her streaming eyes with a white lace handkerchief, hardly able to believe what he was saying. But then, straightening her back, she called on every reserve of courage she had and said calmly, 'Thank you, doctor. Rest assured, we shall do all we can for her.'

And for the rest of the day that is exactly what she did. She sat tenderly mopping her friend's fevered brow with a cool flannel and dribbling water on to her dry lips as she talked soothingly to her, refusing to even go down for her evening meal. Then, as the staff were sitting down to their dinner in the kitchen, Florence Veasey gave a big sigh and quietly passed away.

Emmaline Forbes wished that she had encouraged the dear woman to return to England when she had first suggested it. But it was too late for regrets now, for who knew if she might not have become ill wherever she was.

She was buried in the small churchyard close to the grave of Mrs Forbes's little daughter with only a simple holly wreath to mark the spot, for it was too cold as yet for fresh flowers to grow there. The whole household mourned her passing, apart from Freda, who had never made a secret of the fact that she despised the woman.

Once the funeral was over, Pearl was busier than ever because as well as her duties as lady's maid she now had to take on the running of the household, answering the door to visitors, serving tea to the family and all the other jobs that Mrs Veasey had done.

By mid-April the long hours were taking their toll on her and Mrs Forbes began to worry. 'I think you are doing too much,' she told her one afternoon. 'I've been thinking of taking on a parlour maid to take some of the weight off your shoulders.'

For the first time in days, Pearl really smiled. 'In that case, ma'am, I think I know just the person!'

'Excellent, then you must bring her to meet me,' Mrs Forbes said and Pearl could hardly wait to pass on the good news to Susan.

Chapter Twenty-Four

June 1879

Pearl entered the drawing room and grinned to herself when she saw Mrs Forbes standing at the open window staring towards the town. Her mistress had been like a cat on hot bricks ever since news of the ship's arrival had reached them the day before because she was hoping for some letters from her son. Pearl was now sixteen years old and had the house running like clockwork. It hadn't always been that way, for following Mrs Veasey's death she had discovered she had a lot to learn. But patience and determination had paid off and now, could she have known it, Mrs Forbes held her in high regard.

Turning towards her, the woman smiled. 'Ah, Pearl, did you want to discuss the menus?'

'Yes, ma'am, if you can spare the time.'

They sat down together and slowly went through each day's meals until Pearl was satisfied that she knew exactly what supplies she would need to order. As she neatly wrote a list, she was unaware that her mistress was observing her with a smile on her face. Pearl was still not overly tall but over the last few years her figure had developed into that of a young woman's and that, added to the beautiful blonde hair that she now wore in a smart plait on the back of her head and her striking green eyes, made her very attractive indeed – although she seemed to be totally unaware of the fact.

From the first day she had arrived there following her interview with Mrs Forbes, Susan had also been an asset to the household and Mrs Forbes considered herself to be fortunate to have such a devoted staff. Within days of taking up her new role, Pearl had allocated Freda and Eliza their own specific jobs to do. Freda was now in charge of cleaning the house and lighting the fires each morning while Eliza helped Cook with whatever needed doing in the kitchen. Cook had been none too pleased with the decision initially because she made no secret of the fact that she favoured Freda, but even she had to admit that giving the girls their own separate duties made for a more peaceful kitchen, so in time she had accepted it.

Susan too had grown in all ways and now that she wasn't constantly having to look over her shoulder to make sure that the baker wasn't behind her, her confidence had grown. But the same couldn't be said for Eliza, who never seemed to smile or show much of an interest in anything, despite Pearl's best attempts to please her. She was now fifteen years old and whereas Pearl was attractive, Eliza was truly stunning. Already on the rare occasions when Pearl managed to tempt her into town, the young men flocked around her like bees to a honeypot, but to Pearl's relief she never showed any interest in any of them. The only boy she had ever seemed to like was Nick, but he had been away for most of the last two years now and Pearl still found that she missed him. After being taken on at the master's shipyard, his interest had progressed from building the boats to sailing in them and he had been off on numerous adventures, sailing the high seas and visiting many parts of the world. Nick posted letters to them occasionally, which Pearl would read and reread until they almost fell apart.

Now, happy that she had all she needed from her mistress, Pearl rose to leave the room, just as there was a knock on the front door.

The mistress was instantly all of aflutter as she said excitedly, 'Oh, I bet that's the postman. Would you answer it, Pearl?'

'Of course.' Pearl hurried away and returned minutes later with a happy smile on her face as she handed a letter to Mrs Forbes. She knew that the dear lady had been hoping for a few letters from her son, but as Pearl was learning she was usually lucky to get even one. Monty certainly wasn't the best at letter writing, as his mother had discovered within months of him going to school.

Mrs Forbes sank on to the velvet sofa to read it and Pearl crept away to leave her in peace to enjoy it.

'I have the menus for next week,' Pearl informed Cook. 'And I've written the order out but is there anything else you need?'

'Give it here and let's have a look, pet,' Cook answered, dusting flour from her hands and taking a pair of steel-framed spectacles from her seemingly bottomless apron pocket. She had just perched them on the end of her nose when the kitchen door leading to the hall suddenly flew open and the mistress appeared, waving her letter.

'It's Monty . . . he's coming home next month,' she told them breathlessly. She was delighted at the prospect but she wasn't so sure his father would be. She knew Zack had wanted him to continue his education for another year but then she was sure she could convince him that this would be for the best. Perhaps he could start to train Monty to help with the businesses now that he was older?

Cook raised her eyebrow as she glanced at Pearl. Neither of them had very fond memories of the young man, but they didn't want to spoil the mistress's pleasure. Even now she still had dark days when she grieved for her daughter, and having her son home might be just the thing to finally perk her up again. And anyway, he'd been away a long time, so hopefully he would have grown up.

'Then perhaps we should plan a little party as a homecoming for him?' Cook suggested.

Mrs Forbes eyes gleamed as she nodded. 'Oh, what a wonderful idea, Cook. Yes, I think that would be lovely. I shall start to make a list of people to invite straight away.' Then as something occurred to her, she frowned. 'It's strange that my parents didn't inform us of his intentions though, isn't it? I have at least one letter a month from them and they didn't mention a thing in the last one, although he stays with them most weekends . . . Oh well, perhaps he's only just decided,' she ended with a grin and turning about she tripped away.

'That's a turn-up for the books,' Cook said wryly as the door closed behind Mrs Forbes. 'Let's hope that he comes back a better person than when he went away, eh?'

Pearl wasn't so sure that would be the case. 'Between you and me, I'm dreading Monty coming home,' she admitted to Eliza as they got ready for bed that evening. But Eliza merely shrugged. Pearl wasn't surprised; Eliza didn't really show much interest in anyone, so she doubted whether she'd care if he came home or not.

The following Sunday afternoon, Pearl and Susan ventured out to walk by the river as they did most weekends.

'So, tell me about Monty?' Susan said as they strolled along. 'I know you were never keen on 'im when yer first came 'ere.'

'No, I wasn't. He was horrible to me when I went to stay in London at his grandparents' home that year,' Pearl confided.

'Ah, but he's a lot older now so 'e's probably calmed down,' Susan pointed out optimistically.

Pearl could only hope she was right – but suddenly all thoughts of Monty fled as she looked up and saw a tall figure striding along the banks of the river towards them. There was something vaguely familiar about him and as he grew closer Pearl exclaimed, 'Isn't that Nick?'

Susan followed her gaze and grinned. 'Well, whoever it is they've certainly got Nick's walk, but if it is 'im 'e ain't 'alf grown.'

They stopped and as the figure drew closer, they both gave a cry of delight and ran to meet him.

'Nick . . . I *thought* it was you.' Pearl was the first to reach him and, laughing, he swung her up and about as if she weighed no more than a baby, before doing the same to Susan.

'Crikey, you've grown some,' Susan chuckled, for he seemed to be at least a head taller than she remembered him.

'I should hope I have,' he laughed back. 'And you two have changed as well. You were little girls the last time I saw you but I come back to find that you're both young women now.'

Pearl felt herself blush as she studied him. She remembered him as a lanky youth, thin as a rake and all gangly arms and legs, but what a change two years had wrought. He towered over both her and Susan and he had filled out. She could discern his muscly arms through the sleeves of his coat and he sported a beard that was the same dark colour as his hair, which was curling on his collar.

Seeing that Pearl was staring at him, he self-consciously stroked the growth on his chin. 'Excuse this. We only docked early this morning and we've been busy unloading the ship ever since. Hopefully I'll have time to get to the barber's tomorrow.'

'I-it suits you,' Pearl muttered, wondering why she suddenly felt shy in his presence. She never had before. But back then he had been just a boy; now he had returned as a very attractive young man and it was as if she was meeting him for the first time.

'So how do yer like a life on the ocean waves?' Susan laughed. 'Have yer got to visit lots o' nice places?'

He nodded. 'Yes, although we don't often get to see much of them. We usually get where we're going, unload, load back up again and then we're off once more. I've been to Australia, Africa, New Zealand – all over the place really.'

'Ooh, it must be *luvvly* to see the world.' Susan sighed enviously and he laughed. Susan was taller but still stick thin, whereas Pearl had curves in all the right places now. And her eyes were still the lovely sea green he remembered.

They spent the next half an hour chatting pleasantly until Susan asked, 'So where are yer off to next and when?'

'We'll be taking a ship full of timber back to England next. It's being loaded even as we speak and I think we're set to sail the day after tomorrow.'

'So *soon*?' Susan said mournfully as Pearl blushed again. 'And when will you be back next time?'

He shrugged. 'Your guess is as good as mine. It all depends on what's waiting to be transported when we get back to England. They just tell us where it's going to go and we do as we're told.'

'But don't you get fed up of never 'aving any time at 'ome!'

'Home?' He raised an eyebrow. 'But I don't have a home, do I? We were sent here on the orphan ship but I never really considered it to be my home.'

'But yer could make it yer 'ome,' Susan pointed out.

He shook his head, 'No, I reckon if I ever leave the sea, I'll make my home somewhere back in England. But what about you two? Are you settled here now? Can you see yourselves staying here?'

'I never really fought about it,' Susan admitted. 'Wharrabout you, Pearl?'

Pearl sighed. 'I suppose I've always thought I'd go back to England too eventually,' she told them. 'I think it's because my sister is still there somewhere, though I doubt I'll ever find her. Our neighbour told me that she was

248

working somewhere in the Midlands but that's a big place, and that was years ago now. She could be in Birmingham, Coventry . . . anywhere really. Young Gracie Hewitt who used to live in our alley got her a position with her somewhere apparently.'

'So why don't you give me the address of this neighbour of yours and if ever I'm in London I'll go and see her and try to find out a bit more for you?' Nick suggested. 'If I had any luck, I could write to you and let you know where she is.'

'Oh, that would be lovely if you could,' Pearl said gleefully as hope surged through her. 'I've got to come into town in the morning to get a few things for Mrs Forbes, so I could write it down for you and give it to you then?' she told him breathlessly.

Later as she and Susan made their way home, Pearl had a wide smile on her face and wasn't sure whether it was the prospect of Nick finding her sister for her, or pleasure at seeing him.

'It were nice to see Nick again, weren't it?' Susan said innocently as she peeped at Pearl's glowing face from the corner of her eye. 'An' 'e's turned out to be a bit of a looker, ain't 'e?'

'Has he? I hadn't really noticed,' Pearl responded, but Susan had her own thoughts regarding that. She had seen the way Nick could hardly take his eyes off Pearl and the way Pearl had blushed prettily every time she so much as looked at him, but she didn't comment. It was just nice to see her friend looking so happy.

The following morning when Mrs Forbes had written down the list of things she wanted Pearl to get for her in the town, Pearl put her bonnet and cape on and popped into the kitchen to ask, 'Is there anything you need Cook, while I'm in the town?'

Susan grinned as she glanced at her friend's smiling face. 'Someone's lookin' 'appy today,' she said. 'An' I must say yer lookin' very nice.'

'Am I?' Flustered, Pearl fiddled with the ribbons on her bonnet. She had just retrimmed it with some ribbon the mistress had given her, and this would be the first time she'd worn it since. She'd been saving it for a special occasion. 'Well, I must be off,' she said, avoiding Susan's eyes as she shot away, much to her friend's amusement.

Pearl saw Nick just leaving the barber's shop as she walked into the town. His beard was gone now and, freshly shaved with his hair neatly trimmed, he looked handsomer than ever.

What's wrong with me? she asked herself. She had never felt like this with anyone before and couldn't understand why her heart had started to thump again.

Nick looked her way as she approached him with a basket over her arm and he beamed thinking again how pretty she was now.

'I, er . . . brought my neighbour, Lil's, address for you . . . just in case you ever get chance to go and see her.'

All fingers and thumbs, she fumbled in her pocket for the piece of paper she had written the address on and handed it to him.

'Thanks.' He tucked the paper into his pocket before asking, 'So what are you up to now?' He liked the bonnet she was wearing, he decided. The colour of the ribbons matched her eyes.

'Oh, I've got a few things to get for Mrs Forbes, then she's given me the morning off,' she answered. 'Her son is coming home from school in England and she's writing out the invites for the party she's arranging to welcome him home.'

'Isn't he the one that you and Eliza weren't keen on?'

She nodded. 'Yes. I'm just hoping he'll be a bit nicer when he comes back, but I'm not holding my breath.'

They walked on in silence for a few moments as Pearl headed to the post office with a letter to Mrs Forbes's parents that she'd asked her to post.

'I'll tell you what, I'll do your errands with you, then we could go for a cup of tea if you like, in that nice little café along the main road. I haven't got anything else to do.'

She smiled at him. 'I never say no to a cup of tea. I might even get you to treat me to a scone. They're particularly nice from there.'

'That's typical of you women, trying to get a bloke to part with his hard-earned cash,' he teased. They were at ease in each other's company again now and he couldn't think of a nicer way to spend the morning than with her. It was funny when he thought about it, he was no virgin and had had many girls in many ports, as most of his shipmates had, but he had always been able to leave them and never give them a second thought. *You're goin' soft, lad*, he scolded himself. He'd promised himself that he would never become attached to anyone and yet there was something about Pearl that drew him to her like a moth to a flame. Not that anything could ever come of the attraction. He was a sailor and who knew when he might dock here again. It could well be another two years away and by then a beautiful girl like Pearl would probably have a string of young men after her; he was surprised she didn't already.

They went to the post office and then the haberdashery shop and once she had everything on her list, Pearl told him with a smile, 'That's it, I'm all yours – for the next hour or so at least.'

Soon, they were tucked in seats at a window table in the café with a steaming pot of tea and a plate of scones in front of them.

'This is all very civilised,' Nick said as Pearl poured tea into delicate china cups through a small tea strainer. For some reason he couldn't seem to stop smiling. 'We're lucky to get tin mugs on board ship.'

'Then just enjoy what time you have left on dry land. Tomorrow will be here before you know it,' she told him wisely, and she went on to tell him all about what had been happening in her life for the last two years and what her life in Canada had turned out like.

It was a shock when Pearl glanced at the clock on the wall sometime later to see that they had been sitting there for over an hour. 'Oh, dear, look at the time. Mrs Forbes will think I've got lost. I shall have to go.'

'Must you?' Suddenly the thought of saying goodbye with no idea when he might see her again was unbearable – and could he have known it, she felt exactly the same.

'I'm afraid so.' Lifting her bonnet, she popped it back on, covering up her glorious fair hair, and after leaving a generous tip on the table he followed her outside.

'I could walk some of the way back with you, if you like?' he suggested and was rewarded with a smile.

'I'd like that, thank you.'

They walked through the town without speaking until, once they were on the road that led to the house, he gently took her arm and told her, 'I've enjoyed this morning, Pearl.'

'So have I.' She was shocked to find, now that she was standing so close, that she only reached up to his shoulders.

'Perhaps the next time I come back, we could do it again?'

She stared up into his wonderful dark eyes. With the sun in them they reminded her of the colour of treacle.

And then suddenly, before he could stop himself, he bent his head and kissed her. Pearl gasped as emotions she had never known she had burst into glorious life; the feeling was so wonderful, she felt almost as if she could have flown away.

It was he who pulled away first, looking guilty. What was he thinking of? He would be gone the next day so why was he leading her on? He knew it wasn't fair and yet he hadn't seemed able to stop himself. 'I'm sorry, I shouldn't have done that,' he whispered.

'Why not? I didn't stop you, did I? And I enjoyed it as it happens.'

He was looking uncomfortable now as he kicked at a loose stone in the road with the toe of his boot. 'Er, right, I'd best be off. Look after yourself.'

'I will,' she whispered and she stood and watched him until he was out of sight.

Chapter Twenty-Five

It was the middle of July and a beautiful day when Pearl threw open the windows in Master Monty's bedroom to let in some fresh air. The bed was freshly made up and everywhere smelled of lavender polish. She glanced around and once she was happy that everything was ready for his arrival, she went downstairs to find Mrs Forbes prowling up and down the drawing room like a caged animal.

'I do hope the ship hasn't been delayed,' she said for at least the tenth time in as many minutes, as Pearl plumped up the pillows on the small gilt sofa.

'I'm sure it won't have been, ma'am. If there had been any storms at sea, Mr Forbes would have heard about it from the other ships that have been docking here. They've all been on schedule.'

'Yes, yes, you're quite right, of course they have. It's just that . . .' Mrs Forbes's hand rose to her throat. 'I think I've been fretting a little. What I mean is, Monty has been away for such a long time now. What if we don't know each other anymore when he gets back? What if we are like strangers?'

'I'm sure that won't be the case,' Pearl assured her, as she ran an expert eye around the rest of the room. There was a large vase of freshly cut flowers on a small table and another in the hall, and they filled the house with their perfume. Everywhere looked perfect, so all they could do now was wait. Will had taken the carriage down to the quay to wait for the ship over an hour ago, but then they all knew that it might still be some time before it arrived.

'I'll just go and make sure that all is well in the kitchen, ma'am,' Pearl said and hastily took her leave. The mistress's pacing was making her nervous and she just wanted the homecoming to be over now. The house had been in chaos for days and she would be glad when things went back to normal.

She found Cook seated on a chair by the open door and the table covered in an array of freshly baked cakes and pastries. 'Mistress said as I was to cook all his favourites, so I have,' she grumbled. 'An' I just hope he appreciates it.'

Eliza was washing a lettuce at the sink to add to a large bowl of salad, and Freda was outside, hanging a load of clean sheets on the line in the yard.

'Still not 'ere?' she asked when she'd finished.

Pearl shook her head. 'Not yet, but I hope he won't be much longer for the mistress's sake. She's like a nervous wreck, poor soul.'

'Huh! I would 'ave thought 'is dad would 'ave took a day off to welcome 'im 'ome an' all,' Freda commented disparagingly.

Cook and Pearl exchanged a glance. Unlike his wife, Mr Forbes didn't seem to be too happy with the fact that his son was returning, but then, it was he who had sent him away in the first place. Cook had confided to Pearl some time ago that she thought the master held his son responsible for his daughter's death, and when Pearl had looked shocked she had hurried on to explain, 'They were both of them banned from going anywhere near the river but Master Monty took her down there one day and when she fell in he was unable to save her. No one could have with those currents. That river has been known to sweep full grown men to their deaths. Even in good weather when the top looks calm, the currents beneath are treacherous. Anyway, I don't think the master ever forgave him.' Cook had shaken her head sorrowfully. 'She was such a lovely little lass,' she'd said, as she'd sniffed back a tear. 'Always got a smile on her face and the sweetest nature, but her brother was always jealous of her. In fact, I sometimes wondered if . . .' Realising that she had almost said too much, she had shaken her head, but Pearl had already formed her own opinion. Could it be that Monty had played some part in what had happened to his sister?

Eliza was just adding some tomatoes to the salad bowl when they heard the sound of the carriage returning.

'Ooh, I bet this is Monty,' Freda hooted as she wiped her nose on her apron. She was now almost seventeen but still skinny and plain, which perhaps went some way to explaining why she seemed to be so jealous of Pearl and Eliza.

'I'd better get to the door just in case it is,' Pearl said – but she was too late, because as she hurried into the hallway the front door crashed open so hard that it bounced off the wall and Monty stood there glowering.

'Some homecoming this is,' he said peevishly. 'When I have to let myself in.' He stopped speaking as his eyes lit on Pearl, and for a moment he was speechless. Surely this wasn't the scrawny little cripple kid that he used to torment? But he had no time to think anything else, because the next second his mother came hurtling out of the drawing room and launched herself at him, almost knocking him off his feet, even though he was much taller than her now.

'Oh, my darling boy, you'll never know how much I've missed you,' she gushed. 'But come in – you must be hungry and thirsty. Pearl, could you have some tea and food sent in on a tray for him to keep him going?'

'Yes, ma'am.' Pearl turned around, glad of a chance to escape, but she could almost feel his eyes burning into her back as she set off down the hallway. He had changed a great deal in looks, in fairness, and was now a nice-looking young man, but if his entrance was anything to go by, his nature hadn't improved.

Cook prepared him some ham and salad sandwiches and, after adding a pot of tea and some small cakes and pastries to the tray, Pearl carried it through to him.

'Oh, thank you, just leave it there. That will be all thank you, Pearl,' Mrs Forbes told her, and without once looking in Monty's direction Pearl hurried out again.

'She's certainly grown up,' Monty remarked as his mother began to pour the tea.

Mrs Forbes grinned. 'Have you looked in the mirror lately, darling? I'll think you'll find you have too. But now come on and tell me all you've been up to. How are your grandma and grandpa?'

He sighed. He hadn't been home for more than a few minutes and already his mother was driving him mad with her constant chatter. Still, he supposed it was better than having to attend that school anymore. Had he not left when he did, he knew that he would have been expelled, so far better for his parents to think he had come home because he wanted to. And after seeing Pearl, there were perks to being here, he decided. She had turned into a very comely young woman. With a smirk, he took the tea his mother offered and helped himself to a cake as he thought about the fun he and Pearl could have.

'So, you're home then,' his father remarked rather unnecessarily, when he met Monty at dinner that evening.

'I would say that was rather obvious,' Monty replied sarcastically.

'Cook has made you your favourite roast dinner, look, darling,' his mother butted in nervously. She had hoped that her son and her husband would get on better after being apart for so long, but they certainly hadn't got off to the best of starts. They had only been together for five minutes and they were bickering already.

As she hurriedly began to pile Monty's plate with succulent roast beef and vegetables, her husband raised his eyebrow and remarked, 'I'm sure Monty is quite old enough to serve himself now, darling.'

She gave a nervous giggle. 'Of course, you are right,' she said to placate him. 'But I'm afraid old habits die hard. It's so strange to see him as a young man now.'

'Hm, which leads me to what I wanted to say to you.' His father looked at Monty. 'Now that you are, as your mother says, a young man, I think it's time you started work.'

Monty didn't look at all enamoured of that idea. 'Doing what?'

'Well, there are a few choices. I could set you on at the sawmill, or perhaps you'd prefer to work at the shipyard?'

'Doing what?' Monty repeated, and his insolent tone made his father frown.

'Obviously wherever you start, you will have to begin at the bottom, as I did, and work your way up, so that you know what all of the jobs entail.'

Monty looked horrified. 'But surely the boss's son should have a managerial role?' he argued.

'That's not how it works,' his father said solemnly. 'Imagine how the rest of the workers would react if you suddenly turned up giving them orders just because you are my son. No, I'm afraid anyone that works for me must know all the jobs inside out. I've always prided myself on being able to do anything that I ask my workers to do, and many a time I've worked with them if we've been a man down.'

Monty didn't look too happy with that idea at all. He had imagined as the boss's son that his days from now on would be spent doing whatever he liked with a good allowance to spend, but it appeared that his father had other ideas.

'Oh, and I ought to warn you that I've stopped your monthly allowance now that you are no longer at school,' his father continued, as if he had been able to read his mind.

'*What?*' Monty looked horrified. 'So what am I supposed to live on?'

'Money that you have earned.' His father gave him a stern glance. 'It's time to join the real world. You've had the best education that money could buy and now we'll see if it was worth all that it cost me. And don't look so horrified. You've had it easy compared to how I had it. I started out with nothing and built my businesses with my bare hands. There was no one to help me, so think yourself lucky. Just think about what you'd like to do and let me know. I thought you could start work next week when you've had a few days to settle back in.'

Monty scowled as he leaned over his plate and the rest of the meal was eaten in an uncomfortable silence. It was hardly the homecoming he had hoped for.

Later that evening as the staff sat in the kitchen enjoying a cup of cocoa before going to bed, Freda joined them. She had been banking down the fires in the drawing room and the dining room and now her face was flushed. 'Phew, I just met Master Monty,' she gabbled with a dreamy look in her eye. 'An' 'e's *so* 'andsome.'

'Huh, handsome is as handsome does,' Cook said. 'And I'll make my decision on that when he's been home awhile. I have to say though, of the little I've seen of him since he got back, he's still as cocky as he was before he went away.'

Much to everyone's surprise, Freda tossed her head. She never usually disagreed with Cook, but it was clear that she was smitten with Monty. 'Well, I like 'im *wharrever* any o' you lot say about 'im,' she said and left the room, slamming the door behind her without even waiting for her cup of cocoa, which wasn't like her at all.

The next morning Pearl was sitting in the office working on the household accounts when Monty appeared in the doorway and gave her a disarming smile.

'Oh, sorry to disturb you. I didn't expect to find anyone other than my father in here,' he apologised.

'Mr Forbes is at the mill today,' Pearl informed him politely. 'But he gave me permission to work in here when he was away.' She closed the ledger hastily. 'But of course, I can work somewhere else if you wish to use the room.'

'Oh, no, no, I wouldn't dream of disturbing you,' Monty assured her, with a sickly, false smile. 'I only came in to choose a book. I'm not used to sitting about and thought I'd read for a while.' Crossing to the huge bookshelf that took up almost all of one wall he pretended to browse the titles, although in truth he couldn't stand reading. It had always seemed such a complete waste of time to him, but he wanted to impress Pearl.

'It's quite all right. I've actually almost finished anyway, and I should be going to check if Mrs Forbes needs anything.' She inclined her head and without another word left the room.

Monty scowled. He wasn't at all used to girls ignoring him; in fact the ones back in London had never been able to get enough of him, especially when they knew that he had money in his pocket. It was one of his former school friends who had first introduced him to the delights of the brothels, and since then he had lost count of the girls he had bedded. He had even had two girls fighting over him one night, but he could see that he was going to have to try a different tack if he was to win Pearl over. The girls he was used to were trained to sleep with whoever had the money to pay for the privilege, but Pearl was probably one of those soppy girls who believed in love and romance. *I can do that*, he told himself with a grin. *At least until I've had my way with her and then she'll be like putty in my hands. Perhaps I could get her a little gift? All girls liked gifts.*

Whistling merrily, he abandoned his search for a book and set off for town with a spring in his step.

Within a very short time of Monty being home, it soon became clear that Freda wasn't the only one who had stars in her eyes when it came to the young master, for Eliza too fell under his spell and her eyes would follow him like an adoring puppy's whenever she caught sight of him. Pearl was surprised. Eliza had hated him when they were younger, but it seemed that was water under the bridge now. As for Monty, he wasn't at all averse to the attention she paid him, for he soon saw that she too had turned into a very beautiful young girl. Unlike Freda who was as plain as a post and whose attention made him cringe. Even so, in his experience, girls like her were always grateful for any attention they received and were happy to do anything that was asked of them, so he was willing to keep her sweet with the odd smile.

On the following Sunday after lunch, Pearl set off for her afternoon walk. Susan usually went with her, but she hadn't been too well and had decided to catch up on some rest. Pearl took her usual route through the orchard and down to the river. Now with a profusion of wildflowers growing on its banks and the sun glistening on the fast-running waters, it looked beautiful and she never tired of going there. She wandered along, picking flowers as she went, which she would put into a vase in her and Eliza's room when she got home – until she suddenly sensed that she wasn't alone. When she turned around, she was shocked to see Monty walking towards her with a friendly smile on his face.

'Hello, Pearl. Your afternoon off, is it?'

She nodded, not quite sure what to say as he stared at her. Today she was wearing her favourite dress, a cream linen sprigged with tiny rosebuds, and with her silver-blonde hair loose about her shoulders he thought she looked very pretty. He was aware that he would have to go slowly with her and so falling into step, he said, 'You seem to be doing a really good job at the house for someone so young. Do you enjoy working for my parents?'

'Oh yes . . . thank you, sir.'

'Oh please.' He waved his hand in the air. 'I'm not much older than you. There's no need to be formal and call me sir. You can call me Monty . . . at least when we're alone.'

Pearl frowned, not liking the way the conversation was going at all. She could never imagine herself calling him by his first name and in truth she had no wish to anyway. She wished even less to be alone with him. She could remember all too clearly how spiteful he had been to her before he went away to school, and anyway he was her employer's son.

'I, er . . . don't think that would be quite right, sir,' she answered in a small voice, suddenly painfully aware that there was no one else in sight. 'And now if you'll excuse me, I ought to be getting back. Susan isn't feeling too well, and I want to check that she doesn't need anything.'

Just for a second she thought she saw a spark of annoyance in his eyes, but it was gone in a flash and he was all smiles again. 'Of course, don't let me keep you. I hope Susan is soon well again. But, er . . . just before you go, I have something for you.' He fumbled in his pocket, and after a moment held out a small bag to her.

She looked inside and frowned as she saw a length of the lovely blue ribbon she had been admiring in the window of the haberdashery shop a few weeks before.

'B-but I don't understand,' she faltered as colour seeped into her cheeks.

'It's just a little thank you from me for taking such good care of my mother,' he told her gallantly, but his smile soon faded when she pressed the bag back into his hand.

'That's very kind of you, but I really don't need to be rewarded for doing a job I am already paid for,' she informed him primly – and before he could utter another word, she turned abruptly and hastily went back the way she had come.

He stood for a moment with a scowl on his face as he crushed the bag containing the ribbon in his hand. The jumped-up little tart! Just who did she think she was, speaking to him that way? She was just a guttersnipe that had arrived on the orphan ship who his mother had taken pity on.

But as he watched her disappear into the distance, a smile played about his lips again. She was tasty though, and he'd bet everything he owned that she was still a virgin. He'd never had a virgin before so he'd bide his time. What was it they said? 'Faint heart never won fair lady!' It might take a while but he'd win her in the end and in the meantime . . . he grinned as he thought of Eliza. What a difference a few years had made. He'd never understood why his mother had fawned over her when she was younger but now . . . well, now he was starting to see the attraction. She seemed to be a bit sullen, admittedly, but she was even prettier than her sister and she'd already made it more than clear on the few occasions that he'd ventured into the kitchen that she was his for the taking. Hm, she might just be the distraction he was looking for.

With a smile, he pushed the ribbon back into his pocket and set off for the house.

Chapter Twenty-Six

The following morning, much to his disgust, Monty was woken early and went down to breakfast to find his father waiting for him.

'Ah here you are.' Zack helped himself to a devilled kidney and a thick rasher of bacon from the dishes on the sideboard, then went to sit at the table, raising his eyebrow as he took in the expensive suit Monty was wearing. 'You might want to change into something a little more suitable before we leave for the sawmill,' he advised.

Monty scowled as he filled his own plate and joined his father at the table. 'Why is that?'

'Because as I told you, to learn each business thoroughly you have to start from the bottom and work up. Today I shall be sending you out with the lumberjacks that fell the trees so that you know how to tell which trees are ready to be felled and how it's done.'

Monty looked horrified. 'But I don't want to be a lumberjack!' he objected.

Zack chuckled. 'Don't worry, you won't be doing that for long. When the men can assure me that you know what you're doing on that job, you'll go into the sawmill and learn how the logs are prepared for shipping. There's a lot more to it than you think and you might even find you enjoy it.'

Monty scowled as he stabbed at a mushroom. So much for him thinking he would live the life of Riley when he came home. Already it was apparent that his father wasn't going to let that happen and he almost wished he'd stayed in London. But then, he thought glumly, he probably wouldn't have got away with a lot there either. His grandfather had been keen for him to learn a trade so he'd probably have ended up in some dead-end job anyway. He finished his meal and went upstairs to get changed, although the outfit he came back down in was not much more suitable than the suit he had been wearing originally.

'Haven't you got any old trousers and a jumper you can wear?' his father asked. The lumberjacks would fall about laughing if Monty turned up in the clothes he was wearing.

'Since when have I had the need for such clothes?' Monty replied peevishly. 'I had to be smartly dressed at school and I never realised that I was going to be nothing more than a skivvy!'

'Don't you *dare* knock the lumberjacks. They're all good, hard-working men,' his father snapped. 'And let me tell you, they are far from skivvies. They're experts at what they do and so will you be by the time they've finished with you. Although I do agree that you will need some more suitable clothes.' He thought for a moment before saying, 'Here, get yourself down to the outfitters in town and get some hardwearing breeches and a couple of thick shirts. And get a pair of good, sturdy boots while you're at it. Those soft leather things you're wearing won't last two minutes in the job you'll be doing.' Taking a small wad of notes from his pocket he peeled some off and passed them to his son. 'You'll start tomorrow,' he warned him. 'So make sure you get them otherwise you'll go dressed as you are and the men will laugh at you.'

Monty pushed the money into his pocket as his father left the room. At least he'd had a reprieve, but the thought of what he would be doing the next day filled him with dread.

Much later that evening as his mother and father were entertaining some dinner guests, Monty mooched round to the orchard with his hands in his pockets and a scowl on his face as he thought of the awful clothes he had bought that day. There was a pair of brown corduroy breeches that made his legs itch and a thick shirt and work jumper that had no style to them whatsoever. But the boots were the worst! Ugly black leather things that were so heavy he wondered how he would manage to wear them all day. And to think that tomorrow he would be doing a menial job. It just didn't seem right to him when he was the son of such a wealthy father.

In the middle of the orchard, set amongst the apple and pear trees, was a clearing with a small lake that was home to a variety of local wildlife, and as he left the shelter of the trees, he saw a female sitting with her back to him. She had her shoes off and her skirt was hitched up showing off a pair of very shapely legs as she dangled her toes in the water, humming softly to herself. Her lovely blonde hair was glinting in the late sunshine making it shine like molten silver and he stopped abruptly as a smile came to his face, thinking it was Pearl. But as the girl turned her head slightly, he saw that it was her sister, the little kitchen maid. The one his mother used to make such a fuss of. What was her name now? Ah! Eliza; that was it.

He gave a gentle cough to make her aware of his presence and when she turned to see who was there her face lit up.

'Hello, Eliza,' he said pleasantly. 'It's a beautiful evening, isn't it?'

Eliza was so tongue-tied that she merely nodded, although she made no effort to cover herself as she blushed with pleasure.

Monty approached and sat down beside her on the glass. 'It's nice to meet you properly,' he said with a winning smile. 'I've been wanting to tell you how pretty you are.'

Eliza's blush deepened as she stared back at him. He was easily the handsomest young man she had ever seen and here he was telling her that she was pretty.

He leaned forwards then and as his hand began to gently stroke her ankle, she made no move to stop him. *He must really like me*, she thought, and she held her breath, wondering what he would do next as a million butterflies began to flutter in her chest.

He smiled to himself; a few charming words and she would hopefully be like putty in his hands – much easier work than her prissy sister. But for now he would just toy with her for a while and leave her wanting more – that way she'd be that much more grateful and willing next time. Monty always got his way and would do everything in his power to do so here – so apart from chat to her he didn't go any further, and eventually he said, 'I ought to be getting back. I have to start work in my father's sawmill tomorrow. He wants me to learn every aspect of the business, but I shouldn't moan really. One day I shall inherit all his businesses and then I shall be rich and both myself and the girl I choose to marry will live like kings.' He took her hand and gently turning it over he kissed her palm, making her legs turn to jelly. 'I don't think you and I were cut out for menial work,' he said softly. 'Look how sore your poor little hands are. But never mind, I'm sure that is all about to change.'

Her heart began to beat faster. Was he suggesting that she might be the girl he chose? But before she could give it much thought, he rose and, leaning down, he helped her to her feet.

'Perhaps we could meet here the same time tomorrow evening?' he suggested and she nodded eagerly. 'Good, then I shall see you tomorrow. But perhaps it wouldn't be wise to mention it to anyone just yet. You know how jealous people can be.' And with that walked away, leaving her to put her shoes back on and wander back to the kitchen in a happy daze.

'You seem to be in a happy mood tonight,' Pearl commented, as they got ready for bed that evening.

'I *am* happy.'

Pearl stared at her for a moment, but she didn't ask her what had brought it about. It was just so lovely to see Eliza smiling again, as she used to in the months when they had first come here.

Whatever it is making her smile, long may it last, Pearl thought happily as she hopped into bed, and soon there was nothing to be heard but the sounds of the night creatures through the open window.

The next day, a grim-faced Monty set off with his father wearing his new clothes, which he detested, much to his father's amusement. 'I'm not making you do this to punish you,' his father explained. 'But if you're to take over the businesses one day it's important that you know them inside out. My father, God rest his soul, told me, when I was first starting out, "Never ask a worker to do a job that you wouldn't tackle yourself," and he has been proved right time and time again. Once you know what's involved in the chopping of the trees and the correct way to do it, then you'll move on to another job. Depending on how keen you are to learn, you'll be at a managerial position in no time. But imagine what the workers would say if I was suddenly to make you their boss. A young man fresh out of school trying to tell them how to do a job when he has no idea what the job entails.'

Disgruntled, Monty sniffed and rammed his hands into his pocket. Still, he supposed that everything wasn't all gloom and doom; he had a ready supply of young women at hand and he didn't envisage having a lot of trouble persuading Eliza to succumb to him. He only had to look at her to know that she was besotted with him. But Pearl, now she was a different kettle of fish altogether and she would be his main prize, hopefully in the not too distant future. Until he tired of her, that was – but with a bit of luck by then there would have been another ship full of vulnerable orphan girls brought to the town. Feeling slightly better, he matched his steps to his father's.

'Oh, here you are darling. How did your first day go?' his mother enquired when he joined his parents at the dining table that evening.

Monty scowled as he held out his hands. 'How does it look?' he said in a surly voice. 'My hands are full of splinters and the men have been making fun of me all day, calling me a sissy!'

Unconcerned, Zack chuckled, incensing Monty all the more. 'That's just their way when a new lad starts, don't take it to heart,' he told him. 'As soon as they see that you're pulling your weight, they'll leave you alone. They're not a bad lot.'

Monty would have liked to argue that point but knew that he'd be wasting his time. 'So what will I be paid for doing this job?' he asked sulkily.

Again his father laughed. 'You won't be paid as such but I'll restart your monthly allowance and you'll know you've earned it now.'

Monty wasn't at all pleased with this either. He'd thought that the boss's son would be allowed perks but it didn't look as if that was going to be the case.

His mother meanwhile was staring at his sore hands with a look of concern on her face. 'As soon as dinner is over, I'll get those splinters out for you,' she offered. 'We don't want them to get infected.'

'Infected!' Zack laughed. 'It's only because his hands haven't been used to hard work. They'll toughen up in no time. Try soaking them in urine from your chamber pot. That soon does the trick, I'm told.'

Emmaline fell silent and Monty looked horrified. It was obvious to them both that Zack would show no sympathy, and so they got on with their meal.

Three days later as Emmaline sat writing a letter to her mother the door burst open and Pearl told her, 'Please, Mrs Forbes. Mr Forbes has just sent word that you're to send Will for the doctor straight away. Master Monty has had an accident and they're bringing him home now. One of the men from the mill just came with the message.'

'Oh, my goodness.' The colour drained from Mrs Forbes's face as her hand rose to her throat. 'Is it serious?'

'I've no idea, ma'am. He just said that his leg was hurt. Shall I run and tell Will to go for the doctor?'

'Yes, please do . . . And, Pearl, tell him it's urgent and ask him to come as soon as possible and then turn Master Monty's bed back.'

Twenty minutes later, Monty was brought home on one of the horse-drawn carts that dragged the sawn timber to the sawmill. Two men carried him into the house between them and asked Mrs Forbes, 'Where do you want him, ma'am?'

'Upstairs, the second door on the left, please. But what's happened?'

'We were fellin' a tree an' he didn't get out of the way quick enough,' one of them answered. 'We're so sorry, we were trying to keep 'im safe – we must 'ave told him where to stand for safety at least a dozen times.'

'Never mind that for now. What's done is done,' she said, as she lifted her skirts and followed them up the stairs.

Once in Monty's room, they dumped him unceremoni- ously on the bed and left, while Mrs Forbes took control of the situation and told Pearl, 'Run to the kitchen and fetch me some scissors please. We're going to have to cut his trousers to see what damage has been done.'

She glanced at her son, who was grimacing with pain and once Pearl had returned, she began to cut through the thick corduroy until his lower leg was revealed.

'Oh, good grief,' she said with alarm as she stared at the injury. His foot was jutting at an unnatural angle, a bone had pierced the skin in his ankle and the wound was bleeding profusely. Pearl rushed away to fetch a bowl of clean water and towels. But when his mother attempted to bathe the injury, Monty screamed in agony.

Thankfully the doctor arrived as she was attempting it and, after looking at it for a moment, he shook his head and snapped open his large black bag.

Removing a bottle of chloroform, he shook some on to a piece of lint and told Mrs Forbes, 'This is a very bad break. I'm going to have to get the bone back into line before we splint it and it's not going to be nice. When I tell you, I want you to hold this over his nose. Hopefully it will help the pain some but I'm afraid it's still going to be extremely painful.' As he removed his jacket and rolled his sleeves up, he turned to Pearl and asked, 'Could you go and find me two nice straight pieces of wood. No doubt Will will know where there's some. Once we have the bone back in place, I'll tightly splint it and then all we can do is let nature take its course and hope he doesn't get an infection in it. If he does, it could mean that he'll have to have his foot amputated, but we won't think about that until we've done all we can.'

Mrs Forbes looked as if she was on the point of collapse by now, but knowing that she had no choice but to leave her, Pearl rushed away to find Will.

She was back within minutes. Will had found her two pieces of wood that were just right for a splint and he had even washed and dried them for her.

'Right.' The doctor nodded towards Mrs Forbes. 'Now!'

She quickly pressed the cloth over her son's nose as tears streamed down her face, and thankfully after a few seconds his moans became quieter. The doctor took a deep breath and then gently taking a hold of the foot he twisted it into position, causing Monty to give an inhuman scream as his back arched from the bed.

'Sorry, old chap, but it had to be done.' Once the doctor was satisfied that the foot was in the right position, he quickly threaded a needle. He then got Pearl to hold Monty's head in position while he expertly stitched up the wound, before asking, 'Have you got any whisky?'

'Yes.' It was Mrs Forbes who answered faintly. 'In the drawing room. Would you run and fetch the decanter, Pearl?'

Pearl thought it rather strange that a doctor should need a drink while tending a patient but when she returned with a crystal decanter, she realised what he was going to do with it.

Taking out the stopper the doctor held it above the ankle and instructed the mistress, 'Keep a tight hold of his shoulders now. This is going to sting like hell.'

Mrs Forbes looked as if she was about at the end of her tether, but she nodded and did as she was told. The doctor poured the liquid straight on to the wound. Monty's screams echoed around the room and he began to thrash about as the doctor began to splint the injured leg.

At last it was done and the doctor stood up and wiped the sweat from his brow. 'That's about all I can do for now,' he told Mrs Forbes, as he checked that the bandages about the splints were tight enough. 'But it's going to be a long job before he's on his feet again, even if an infection doesn't set in, and I wouldn't be surprised if he isn't left with a bad limp. That's probably the best outcome we can hope for, but we'll see.'

'Th-thank you, doctor.' Mrs Forbes was almost as pale as her son, who seemed to be only semi-conscious now. It was a blessing as far as Pearl was concerned because at least he was no longer screaming. She hurried away to fetch the doctor clean water to wash his hands, and once he was dressed in his jacket, he warned them, 'He could well have a fever tonight. It will be the shock to his body and the loss of blood. Make sure you keep him as cool as you can and try to get plenty of fluids into him. I shall be back first thing in the morning to see how he is, but should you need me before then, don't hesitate to send for me.'

'Thank you again.' Mrs Forbes dropped heavily into a chair at the side of the bed.

'It looks like you're in shock too, ma'am,' Pearl said. 'Just sit there and rest while I go and get you a nice cup of hot, sweet tea; it's supposed to be good for shock.' In fact, she was feeling more than a little queasy herself after what she had just witnessed. 'Then when you're feeling a little better, we'll change the bed and Will can come and help you get Master Monty into his night clothes.'

Pearl could see that this would have to be done; the bed looked like a butcher's block and there was blood everywhere. Some had even dripped on to the carpet. Still, that could soon be remedied. But what might happen to Monty now was another thing altogether. Much as she disliked him, she silently prayed that he would survive; no one deserved to die so young and she suspected that her mistress would not survive the death of another child. But it was all in God's hands now.

Chapter Twenty-Seven

For the rest of that day and night, Mrs Forbes barely left her son's side, and the next morning when Pearl went to check on her and the invalid, she found that Monty had spent a restless night, tossing and turning, soaked in sweat, and his poor mother was so exhausted that she was barely able to keep her eyes open. Her face was pale and gaunt, and her husband was so concerned that he took a day off work – a rare occurrence for him. He couldn't help but feel that he was responsible for the accident. After all, it was he who had forced Monty to do the job, but then as Cook had pointed out, 'Accidents happen, sir, it's no good whipping yourself, and it could have been worse. He could have been killed.'

Mr Forbes knew she was right, but it didn't lessen his sense of guilt, particularly when he saw how distraught his wife was.

'Why don't you go and have a lie-down, ma'am?' Pearl suggested kindly. 'You'll be no good to your son if you make yourself ill. I'll sit with him, and as soon as the doctor comes I'll send for you, I promise.'

'Pearl is right, Emmaline,' Mr Forbes agreed as he stood at the side of the bed. 'Pearl is more than capable.'

Mrs Forbes shook her head. 'No, I can't leave him. What if he takes a turn for the worse?'

'Then of course I would fetch you immediately,' Pearl promised.

Mrs Forbes bit on her lip. 'I suppose you are right,' she agreed uncertainly, much to her husband's relief.

'Come on, darling,' he coaxed, and as he gently drew her to her feet, Pearl took her place in the chair at the side of the bed. 'I'm going to get you tucked into bed, have a tray of food sent up to you and then I want you to rest, even if it's only for an hour.'

Mrs Forbes allowed him to lead her away after a last worried glance at her son and Pearl immediately wrung out the cloth in the bowl of cold water at the side of the bed and began to mop Monty's brow.

Once he had settled his wife, Mr Forbes returned and asked worriedly, 'Has he not shown any signs of waking at all?'

Pearl shook her head. 'Not as yet, sir. But the doctor did say to expect this. His body has had a shock, which is what has caused the fever, but once it breaks, he'll hopefully start to get better.'

There was a tap on the door then, and to their relief the doctor appeared.

'So how is the patient this morning?' he asked, as he took his stethoscope from his bag and leaned over Monty.

'I should fetch Mrs Forbes,' Pearl said.

Mr Forbes held his hand up. 'No, please don't disturb her. She needs her rest and I can pass on whatever the doctor says.'

'Very well, sir.' Pearl stood back from the bed with her hands clasped neatly at her waist. She felt distinctly uncomfortable, for she had promised her mistress she would fetch her as soon as the doctor arrived. But then she could understand Mr Forbes's concern and could hardly disobey him.

The doctor continued his examination and once he was done, he told Mr Forbes, 'Well, his heart seems strong enough. Once we can get that temperature down, he should be on the mend.' Next, he examined the splints on Monty's leg and nodded with satisfaction. 'Good, good. There doesn't seem to be any leakage from the wound and there's no smell, so hopefully there will be no infection. I don't really want to remove the splint until I have to. The longer it stays on, the quicker the bones will knit together. Just keep doing what you're doing and hopefully he'll come round before too much longer.'

He took his leave of them then, promising to return the following day and Mr Forbes went downstairs with him to see him out, leaving Pearl to care for the patient.

Freda entered the room at one point with the excuse that she wished to dust the furniture but Pearl sent her away, much to Freda's disgust. And then just before lunchtime, as Pearl was gently mopping his brow, Monty suddenly opened his eyes and looked directly up at her.

'P-Pearl . . . what's happened?'

'It's all right,' she soothed as she pressed him gently back against the pillows. 'You had an accident but you're safe at home now.'

He winced as he made to move his leg and she hurriedly explained, 'You broke your ankle, but the doctor has set it and hopefully it will start to get better now.'

He scowled for a while as he lay there but as it all came rushing back to him, he said, 'Ah, yes, I remember now. I was in the wrong place when we were felling a tree. Big Joe had told me where to stand but I must have misunderstood him.'

She nodded before asking, 'Would you like a drink now? Perhaps tea, or would you prefer a sip of water?'

He ran his tongue across his dry lips, and despite the fact that she thoroughly disliked him, Pearl couldn't help but feel sorry for him.

'W-water, please.'

Lifting his head from the pillow, Pearl held the glass to his lips and he tried to gulp at it but she told him, 'No, just sips now else you'll make yourself sick.' She dribbled trickles of water between his lips and once he had had what she judged to be enough his head fell weakly back on to the pillow. She was happy to see that he was cooler, though, and hoped that this would be the turning point.

His mother dashed back in at that moment and Pearl almost didn't recognise her. Her hair was all over the place and the clothes she had slept in were wrinkled and dishevelled.

'*Why* did you let me sleep so long? Has the doctor been? Why didn't you wake me?'

'I didn't want to disturb you,' Pearl told her. 'And yes, the doctor has been and he's very pleased with his progress. I was going to come for you, but Mr Forbes said not to; he wanted you to rest. But the fever has broken, so hopefully he'll be on the mend now, Mrs Forbes. Why don't you go and get washed and changed? You'll feel much better for it and I can manage here.'

'She can as well,' Monty said with a crooked grin. He would much rather look at Pearl sitting beside him than his mother. It occurred to him then that he had managed to get her into his bedroom a lot more quickly than he had expected, although he could have wished it had been under different circumstances.

'Very well, I shall,' his mother agreed, after catching sight of herself in his dressing-table mirror. 'But I shall be back in no time.' And lifting her skirts, she bustled away again.

'So how long have I got to lie here for?' Monty questioned as he glanced down at his leg.

'I'm afraid it could be for some time. The doctor said you must allow the bones to knit back together.'

'Does that mean I won't be able to do that job again?' he asked hopefully.

'I wouldn't know. You'd have to discuss that with the doctor and your father.'

He grinned. He still felt a little dizzy and wobbly, but it appeared that his ploy had paid off. He had hoped that by standing in the wrong place the tree they were felling would just clip him and hopefully knock him out. He certainly hadn't intended to break anything, but still, there were compensations to be had if it meant having Pearl tend to him.

Soon after his mother rejoined them, looking clean and tidy again, and Pearl was dismissed, much to Monty's disgust.

He didn't see her again until she brought a tray of food up some time later. His mother had ordered a light meal for him: chicken soup and a bowl of wobbly jelly, and he eyed it with disdain.

'How am I supposed to get my strength back eating that muck?' he complained.

His mother chuckled. He must be feeling better if he was grumbling again. 'It's good for you,' she told him, as she and Pearl gently lifted him into a sitting position and piled his pillows behind him. 'Now stop complaining and if you manage to keep it down, I'll have cook make you something a little more solid tomorrow.'

He grimaced as he tasted the thin soup, but then realised that he was actually quite hungry and cleared the dishes in no time.

'There's a good boy,' his mother praised as if she was talking to a young child, and he cringed as he wondered how he was going to cope with her fussing over him. She crossed to the window and swished the curtains shut, telling him, 'I want you to have a little sleep now.'

'But I'm not tired. Can't Pearl read the newspapers or something to me?'

'No, she cannot,' his mother said firmly. 'I think you're well enough to be left to have a little nap now, but I shall be back to check on you shortly.'

'God save me from a bloody doting mother,' Monty grumbled as the door closed quietly behind her but seconds later his eyelids drooped and before he knew it, he was in a deep sleep.

Over the next few days, as Monty continued to improve, he became increasingly bad-tempered at being confined to bed. Two days after the accident, the doctor had gently removed the splint to check on the injury and although there was thankfully no sign of infection, Monty had been sickened at the sight of his injured ankle. It had been twice the size it should have been and black and blue with bruises. The skin around the stitches was tight, and he began to worry whether he would ever be able to walk on it again.

Even so, both Pearl and his mother were endlessly patient with him and went out of their way to think of things to keep him occupied. Each afternoon, Pearl would read the newspapers to him and she enjoyed that almost as much as he did. They were shipped in regularly from England for Mr Forbes, and although they were always out of date by the time they arrived, she loved knowing what was going on back at home.

Later in the day, his mother would play chess with him and occasionally his father would visit him in the evening for a game of cards. Cook soon discovered that while Susan tried to avoid it, both Freda and Eliza would vie with each other about who should carry the young master's trays up, and although it was amusing, she also found it a little disturbing. Monty was a good-looking young man and she considered both of the girls to be very young and vulnerable, so she promised herself that once he was up and about again, she would keep a close eye on things. God forbid that he should take advantage of either of them.

A week into Monty's recovery, Mr Forbes got the local carpenter to make him a sturdy pair of crutches, and as soon as they were delivered Monty was keen to get back downstairs. Achieving that was easier said than done, and eventually they found the best way for it to happen was for him to sit with his splinted leg sticking out in front of him and slide down on his backside. The same worked in reverse when he wanted to go back up again, although that took a little more time.

'I shall have huge muscles at this rate,' Monty panted to his father, as he painfully hauled himself up step by step.

Mr Forbes smiled wryly. *The muscles certainly wouldn't be earned by hard work*, he thought, but not wishing to upset his wife, he wisely didn't say it. Emmaline still thought the sun rose and set with their son, and he knew nothing would ever change that now, especially since they had lost Elizabeth.

In no time at all, Monty got the hang of using the crutches, and at least now he could wander out into the garden and the orchard if he took his time. The doctor had already said that he doubted Monty would be able to return to hard, manual work for some time and so his father was trying to think of some other job he could do. He'd be damned if he was going to let him sit about doing nothing once he was fully recovered.

One evening, as they were having their coffee after dinner, Monty told his parents, 'I think I'm going to go outside and get a bit of fresh air.'

'Oh, then I'd better come with you,' Emmaline said immediately. She was terrified of him falling off his crutches and doing further damage to his leg.

'No . . . Mother, I shall be fine really,' Monty told her, as he rose awkwardly and pushed the crutches under his arms. 'I shall go very carefully, I promise.'

She wasn't happy with the idea, but nodded nevertheless. He was so touchy that she didn't want to upset him. 'Very well, darling, but just see that you do.'

As he hobbled out of the room, Zack said thoughtfully, 'I've been thinking about what sort of a job Monty could do until he's fully recovered, and I think I've come up with a good idea.'

Emmaline looked none too pleased. 'But surely, he's not going to be well enough to do anything for quite some time?'

Zack chuckled. 'But he isn't ill. He's just broken his ankle,' he pointed out patiently. 'I thought I could get him to do the bookkeeping at the shipyard: balancing the books and being responsible for orders, things like that. What do you think?'

'But how would he get there? He's very slow on his crutches.'

'Ah, I thought of that too. Will could take him to the office each morning in the carriage and collect him again each evening. At least it would keep his mind active, and it wouldn't impede the recovery of his ankle if he has his leg propped up on a stool.'

'Hm.' She supposed she could see the sense in what he was saying, but she didn't think Monty would be too thrilled with the idea.

Monty meanwhile had almost made it to the clearing in the orchard and was sweating profusely. The splint and the many bandages that covered his leg made it very heavy to swing back and forwards and he just hoped that when he finally got there the journey would be worth it.

He grinned to himself when he saw Eliza lying on the bank of the lake with her hands behind her head, enjoying the last of the sun. *Yes*, he thought. *It had been worth it.* She had kicked her shoes off and hitched her skirt up above the knees and he thought how pretty she looked. He had almost reached her when she turned on to her stomach and saw him. She flushed and gave him a radiant smile.

'Ah, I'm glad I've caught you.' He smiled back at her. 'I've got you a little present for all the trays you've been carrying up and down the stairs for me.'

'A present! For *me*?' She looked astounded and when he pushed the small paper bag into her hand and she peeped inside she sighed with pure delight.

'I-I . . . why, thank you, Master Monty.'

'I've already told you, when we're alone it's just Monty.'

Carefully, he lowered himself down beside her, and when she made no effort to move away from him, he knew that she was his for the taking. If only her sister was so easy to woo. But then, he consoled himself, everything came to those who waited, and for now this tasty little tart would do nicely.

Chapter Twenty-Eight

'Eh! Will you two *please* stop bickering,' Cook snapped one morning. 'Ever since Master Monty's accident, you've been at each other's throats like rabid dogs and it's getting me down. What does it matter who takes his tray in to him? If you don't stop it right now, I shall bang your heads together, you just see if I don't! And Susan will be taking all the trays.'

'Sorry, Cook,' Freda muttered as she glared at Eliza, who boldly glared back. With a last malicious grin, Freda lifted the laden tray and sailed out of the kitchen to take it through to the young master and his mother in the drawing room.

Eliza watched her go with a glum expression on her face. Freda wasn't even the kitchen maid now, so why *she* was allowed to carry the tray through she didn't know; it should have been her job. But then Cook made no secret of the fact that Freda was her favourite and she could get away with murder.

Taking the broom, Eliza went back to sweeping the kitchen floor, but her mind was working overtime. It had been over a week now since Monty had gone to their secret meeting place by the lake, even though she had waited there every night for him. Could it be that now he'd had his way with her, he was losing interest in her? she wondered, but then she pushed the thought away. Of course it couldn't be that, she thought; he loved her, she knew he did, and one day when he told his parents about their love she would be mistress here and woe betide Freda then! Suddenly smiling again, she dreamed of what it would be like to wear fine gowns and be driven around in the carriage. But she didn't have long to dream before Cook said impatiently, 'How much longer are you going to be on that floor, lass? Get a move on and make a start on peeling those potatoes.'

With a sigh, Eliza did as she was told.

She was in her room getting changed that evening when Pearl walked in and smiled at her. 'Off out again, are you?' she said pleasantly. 'I can't say as I blame you, it's a lovely even—' Her voice trailed away as she spied the pretty blue ribbon in Eliza's hair and in a wobbly voice she asked, 'Where did you get that ribbon, Eliza?'

Eliza was instantly on her guard. Monty had told her the importance of keeping their meetings a secret for now, because he said that if Pearl or Freda found out about them, they would be jealous.

'I found it outside in a bag,' Eliza lied. 'Someone must have dropped it.'

'Oh.' Pearl desperately wanted to believe her, and it was possible that Eliza was telling the truth, but the ribbon looked suspiciously like the one Monty had offered her. Although, Monty could quite easily have dropped it when she refused it, so why were alarm bells ringing? She stood silently as Eliza slipped her dainty feet into her shoes, and for the first time Pearl realised just how beautiful her sister really was.

'See you later,' Eliza said gaily, as she tripped from the room.

Pearl stared after her, worriedly chewing on her lip. Could Monty be the reason that Eliza had suddenly taken to going out for a walk each evening, and the sudden interest she was taking in her appearance? If that were the case, Pearl suspected that her younger sister might be in grave danger of being seduced; she was so young and vulnerable. *I shall have to watch her as closely as I can from now on*, Pearl promised herself, as she went to help the mistress prepare for bed. She had said she had a headache after dinner and that she was going to have an early night.

Eliza had just emerged from the trees bordering the lake when she saw Monty speaking to Freda and instantly her temper rose. What did she think she was doing? Surely she had guessed that Monty was *her* young man; she had certainly dropped enough hints. Without slowing her steps, she marched right up to them and, ignoring Freda completely, she fingered the ribbon in her hair.

'I thought I'd wear this tonight, Monty,' she said with a giggle as she put her arm possessively through his. 'Thank you so much for such a lovely gift. Shall we go for a stroll?'

Freda's mouth gaped open as Monty squirmed uncomfortably. Had he been able to, he would have run like the wind, but that would be difficult with his crutches to contend with, and so they stood in an uncomfortable silence for some moments until Monty said, 'Actually, I'm afraid you'll both have to excuse me, ladies. I just remembered I'm going to visit one of Mother's friends with her this evening.'

He turned and hobbled off as fast as his crutches would take him, leaving Freda and Eliza facing each other with hatred in their eyes.

'You just keep away from him, he's *mine*,' Freda said heatedly.

Tossing back her head, Eliza laughed. 'Is he now? Then why did he buy this for *me*?' She stabbed a finger at the ribbon in her hair. 'Did he buy *you* a ribbon?'

'He . . . he didn't need to. I *know* 'e loves me,' Freda retaliated. 'I've already given meself to 'im and he truly cares fer me!'

But it was easy to see that she was upset. Just like Eliza, she had been dreaming of becoming the lady of the house, but now she was unnerved. Surely Monty couldn't have been stringing both of them along? Unable to contain her hurt and fury any longer, Freda rushed forwards and snatched at the ribbon in Eliza's hair. With a mighty yank, she pulled it from her hair, making Eliza howl with pain – and then suddenly they were rolling on the ground with fists flying as their screams rent the air.

Having found that her mistress wasn't going to have an early night after all, Pearl had been strolling beneath the trees in the orchard, hoping to catch a glimpse of her sister – but as she heard the cries, she rushed towards the direction they were coming from.

On entering the clearing, she stopped abruptly in shock, before rushing forwards and catching the girls' arms. 'Whatever do you think you are doing? You're fighting like a pair of alley cats. Stop it this instant!' she cried.

Both girls' eyes were glazed and both had cut lips and scratched faces as Pearl did her best to keep them apart. Eliza's new dress was ripped and Freda had the beginnings of a black eye already forming. They were both breathing heavily, and Pearl had the feeling that if she were to release them they would start fighting again.

'It's *'er* as started it!' Freda gasped breathlessly, stabbing a shaking finger towards Eliza. 'She's after my chap an' I'll kill 'er afore I let 'er take 'im away from me!'

'He ain't your chap, 'e's *mine*,' Eliza retaliated furiously, as she made to lunge towards her again.

It was taking all Pearl's strength to keep them apart and her arms were beginning to ache. She gave them both a little shake. 'And just who *is* this young man you are fighting over?' she demanded.

All at once, the fight seemed to go out of Eliza and her shoulders sagged. It was obvious that she wasn't about to disclose his name.

'So *you* tell me who it is then!' Pearl turned her attention to Freda, but she too remained obstinately tight-lipped before turning about and slinking away.

Pearl looked back to Eliza and in a stern voice asked, 'So let's have the truth! Just *who* were you fighting over?' The blue ribbon Eliza had been wearing was on the ground with a good tuft of Eliza's hair in it, and again her suspicions were aroused when she thought back to the afternoon Monty had offered one just like it to her. 'It wasn't Master Monty, was it?'

'*No!*' Eliza denied grumpily, as she tentatively touched her split lip, which was already swelling alarmingly.

Pearl sighed. She could hardly beat the truth out of her sister, so she supposed that for now she would just have to accept what she was saying. 'All right . . . you'd better come with me and we'll bathe that face. I'm afraid you're going to look as if you've been in a boxing ring in the morning.'

Subdued, Eliza turned to follow Pearl back to the house, but not before she had bent to retrieve her ribbon and stuff it into the pocket of her dress.

'Just what the *hell* is going on?' Cook asked angrily as Eliza entered the kitchen with Pearl close behind her. She was sitting in a chair by the kitchen table dipping a piece of huckaback into a bowl of tepid water and bathing Freda's face. 'Why did you have to go and attack Freda like that?'

Behind the cook's back, Freda gave a sly little grin as Eliza stated angrily, 'I didn't attack 'er! It was *'er* that started it.'

'No, it weren't!'

'Stop it immediately, *the pair* of you. Enough is enough!' Pearl interrupted them. 'It doesn't matter *who* started it. You should both be ashamed of yourselves fighting like that. And about a boy as well!'

Cook's mouth gaped open. Freda could do no wrong in her eyes and to the cook she was little more than a child. Certainly not old enough to be having boyfriends. Meanwhile, Pearl fetched another bowl of water and began to bathe Eliza's face as the two girls glared at each other across the table.

'Well, this is a fine kettle o' fish,' Cook grumbled. 'I would have expected better of both of you. This is a respectable household and I'll have none of these goings-on in my kitchen, I warn you. Furthermore, you'll *both* be in trouble when the mistress catches sight of you, and serves you both right, I say!'

Both girls now had the grace to look shamefaced.

'I reckon she's loosened one o' me teeth,' Freda whined, as she moved the offending molar with her tongue.

'That's what comes of fighting. Perhaps you'll both think twice next time.' Disgruntled, Cook picked up the bowl and waddled away to the sink. 'And now I suggest you both get yourselves off to bed and let's hear no more of it.'

Both girls slunk away as Cook shook her head. 'So who were they fighting over?' she asked, when they had left the room to go and lick their wounds.

'They wouldn't say.'

Cook shrugged, but her mind was whirling. Surely not Master Monty? She hoped not, as she knew no good could come of that.

From then on, the girls studiously ignored each other, although whenever they were in the same room the atmosphere was so thick it could almost have been cut with a knife. They had never liked one another but now they were sworn enemies. Eliza had withdrawn into her shell again and stopped taking an interest in her appearance. The evening strolls stopped too, and now she went to her room when her chores were done and stayed there. Pearl just hoped that this was the end of it. But all she could do was keep an eye on things and wait and see.

Monty meanwhile was unhappy again, because his father had been as good as his word and set him to work in the office of the shipyard. Will would take him there each morning in the carriage and because Monty was limited on how far he could walk on his crutches, he felt like a prisoner there. The office was musty and reeked of ink and damp, but when he opened the window the heavy smell of tar and wet timber from the boatyard was even worse and he glumly closed it again. Mr MacArthur, the elderly gentlemen who had been assigned to teach him the ropes, was without humour, although Monty was forced to admit that he knew his job inside out. He was also a strict disciplinarian and so Monty had no chance to sit back and take it easy.

'It's slave labour,' Monty complained to Will one evening, when he came to pick him up.

Will chuckled. 'I'd hardly call it that, Master Monty. It can't be that hard to push a pen about all day.'

Monty grimaced and fell silent. Everything was going wrong for him. He hadn't dared approach either Freda or Eliza since the night of the fight in case they told his father how he had played one off against the other, and Pearl was still being distant and cold with him. But still, he consoled himself, the splints would have to come off eventually and then hopefully his life would return to some sort of normality.

In the kitchen the mood had not improved, and Cook was almost at the end of her tether. Mrs Forbes wasn't happy either. The day following the fight, she had noticed the cuts and bruises on both of them, but when questioned about how they had come by them, both girls had remained obstinately quiet. She had mentioned it to Monty and her husband that night at dinner, but Monty merely shrugged and said he had no idea what had gone on. His father eyed him thoughtfully and although he made no comment, he had the strangest feeling that Monty knew more than he was saying.

As for Pearl, she blamed Freda for the entire situation – Freda had always had a spiteful streak – and she hated the fact that Eliza had become withdrawn and unhappy again. But there wasn't a lot she could do, as she confided in Susan one day, other than keep an eye on them and pray the situation eventually improved.

The summer rolled by, and before they knew it they were into October and the weather took a turn for the worse. A strong wind blew in from the sea and suddenly it was cold again. Then, one morning as Pearl collected the post that had come in with the latest ship, she noticed a letter with a French postmark addressed to her and her heart began to pound. It could only be from Nick and she could hardly wait to read it, but she would have to be patient and see to Mrs Forbes's needs first.

She helped her mistress to dress and did her hair for her and then, while the family were at breakfast, she sneaked away to her room, unable to wait a moment longer.

Taking the sheet of paper from the envelope, she began to read.

My dearest Pearl,

I'm not sure when this letter will reach you but when it does, I hope it will find you and Eliza well. I have thought of you so often since leaving Canada and can hardly wait to get back to see you again. I am in Calais at present and due to sail for England tomorrow. Even as I write this, the ship is being loaded with cargo and we hope to set sail on the morning tide. When we get to London I intend to go and see your old neighbour, and of course if she is able to give me any idea of the whereabouts of your sister Amy, I shall let you know immediately.

I must admit I am enjoying a life at sea and hope that you are still happy in your job. Do you think you will settle there? Much as I liked Canada, I have always felt that eventually I shall settle back in England. I suppose I feel that is where my roots are, but meantime it is nice to see a bit of the world. I am saving hard and one day I would like to start my own little farm. The only drawback to my life at present is that you cannot write back to me because I am never in one port long enough to receive mail.

I so enjoyed seeing you again in the brief time I was there and wonder if you ever think of me? I hope so. I am hoping to be back in Canada for Christmas, although I can't promise it because it all depends on if the weather is kind to us. I do hope I can make it as I so want to see you again. If I do make it, I will be staying at the Bear Hotel until we leave again.

Anyway, I should go and help with loading the cargo now but just wanted you to know that you are in my thoughts. Take very good care of yourself,

With love,

Nick xxx

By the time she had finished reading, there were tears in her eyes and she held the letter close to her heart as she thought of him. She had never forgotten the feel of his lips on hers and it came as a shock to her to suddenly realise that her feelings for him went beyond mere friendship. *But that's silly*, she silently scolded herself. *You can't fall in love with someone with one kiss . . . can you?*

She crossed to the window just in time to see Monty coming up the drive, leaning on his walking stick. It looked like he had left work early again, which wouldn't please Mr Forbes at all. Ever since Monty had had the splint off his leg, he had barely worked a full day, much to his father's disgust. Though she wasn't one to gossip, Susan had told Pearl that she'd overheard his parents arguing about it.

'His father thinks he's fallen in wi' a bad crowd o' chaps about his age,' she'd confided to Pearl. 'They're into gambling and all sorts apparently, but you know what the master is like. He don't want to upset the mistress so 'e keeps 'is mouth shut fer much o' the time, bless 'im. An' o' course now Monty 'as a limp he's makin' the most of it, sayin' as a lot o' the work his dad expected him to do is too hard fer him now, an' his ma agrees wi' him!'

Pearl shook her head as she watched him swagger along. He was a bad one, was Monty, and the further he kept away from herself and Eliza the happier she would be. But the smile came back to her face as she quickly reread Nick's letter, before tucking it under her pillow to read again at bedtime. All being well, he would be home for Christmas and she could hardly wait!

Chapter Twenty-Nine

'Eh! That looks wonderful, Pearl! The missus will be right pleased when she sees it.'

'Do you think so, Susan?' Pearl smiled as she stepped back from the Christmas tree she had just been decorating in the drawing room. Will had planted it in a sturdy bucket of earth and now it took pride of place beside the fireplace, the glass baubles that Pearl had adorned it with shining in the light from the fire. 'It does look nice, doesn't it?' she agreed, with a measure of satisfaction.

'It certainly does. But tell me, when is Nick due to arrive?' Susan was looking forward to seeing him too.

Pearl's smile faded as she shrugged. 'Your guess is as good as mine.' She glanced towards the window, through which she could see the snow steadily falling. It was already a foot deep and she could see Will out on the drive trying to clear it away. It was a hopeless task really because as soon as he cleared it, it settled again. 'All I know is that he's sailing on *The Mermaid*, which is due in any time, but looking at the weather . . .'

'Oh, don't get worrying about that,' Susan said airily, as she plumped up the cushions on the sofas. 'I'm sure the weather won't slow it down. Why, he could be dockin' even as we speak.'

The words had barely left her lips when Mrs Forbes entered the room and clapped her hands with delight when she caught sight of the tree.

'That looks truly magnificent, I couldn't have done a better job myself,' she praised Pearl, who flushed with pleasure at the compliment. 'But if you are both done, girls, I'm expecting Mrs Pettigrew-Simms at any moment. If the weather doesn't prevent her getting here, that is,' she added as she too looked towards the window.

Both Pearl and Susan bobbed their knees and hastily left the room. Once out in the hallway, Susan went to prepare the afternoon tea trolley, while Pearl went up to tidy Mrs Forbes's room. She avoided the kitchen as much as she could now, for Eliza and Freda were getting on no better, although in fairness Pearl had to admit that it was more down to Freda than her sister. Freda was constantly uttering sarcastic comments and trying to get Eliza into trouble, whereas Eliza was just very quiet. During the summer she had hoped that Eliza was coming out of herself again, but then that had ended in disaster, and she wasn't sure if anything would ever bring a smile back to her sister's face.

She was beginning to wonder if she shouldn't take her back to England when they were a little older. They were very fairly treated, admittedly, but they had certainly not found the wonderful new life the orphans had hoped for before they left. Pearl was also still very keen to try to track down Amy, which would be virtually impossible if they stayed here. But that, she decided, would be something to think of in a few years' time. They were both saving every penny of their wages they could, but she knew that as well as paying for their passages home she would also need enough for them to live on when they arrived until they both found work, and that was still a long way away.

As she crossed to straighten the heavy velvet drapes hanging at the window, she caught sight of Mrs Pettigrew-Simms's fine carriage coming along the drive, so after hastily straightening her skirt and patting her hair, she hurried downstairs to admit the visitor.

'Thank you, my dear.' Mrs Pettigrew-Simms handed her coat to Pearl as Mrs Forbes came out of the drawing room to greet her.

'Oh, Eunice, I wasn't at all sure you would be able to make it,' Mrs Forbes said.

'Well, I would have been earlier,' Pearl heard the visitor say as she was led into the drawing room. 'But *The Mermaid* has just docked and it's chaos in the town. All the shopkeepers are there for the supplies they have ordered. It's a good thing, of course, because at least we know they will all be well stocked for Christmas . . .'

Pearl's heart began to pound with excitement as the door closed on the two women. *The Mermaid* was here, which hopefully meant that Nick would be, too. He had told her that he would be staying at the Bear Hotel on the high street for the duration of his stay and she wondered when she would be able to get there. Perhaps she could manage it that evening, provided Mrs Forbes didn't need her after she had helped her dress for dinner? With a happy smile, she lifted her skirts and hurried towards the kitchen to tell Eliza and Susan the good news.

She found Susan and Will enjoying a cup of tea together at the table, and when she glanced towards Cook, the woman winked at her and grinned. The two of them seemed to be getting along very well lately and both Pearl and Cook were wondering if this might not be the start of something sweet. So, saving her news for later, Pearl slipped away.

The day passed interminably slowly, but immediately after dinner Mrs Forbes pleaded a headache and declared she would have an early night, so after helping her to bed Pearl was finally free and she hurried off to her room to get changed.

Eliza was still down in the kitchen tackling the towering pile of dinner pots, but tonight Pearl didn't even think about helping her. She was too keen to see Nick. So after changing into her prettiest dress, she took the pins from her hair and brushed it until it shone, then donning her thick cloak and her boots, she rushed downstairs and was off down the drive like a hare.

It was bitterly cold and the snow was still falling thick and fast, causing her to stumble. But worse than that, in no time at all the hem of her dress was sodden and snow had crept over the top of her boots, but she was so excited about seeing Nick again that she barely even noticed.

At the end of the drive, she turned on to the lane that led into the town. She had gone no more than a few yards when a male figure loomed out of the snow ahead of her, causing her to gasp with fright. But then the figure spoke and her heart began to bang with joy so loudly that she feared he would hear it.

'Pearl . . . is that you?' a voice asked hesitantly.

She giggled like a child. 'Yes . . . yes, Nick, it's me.'

Suddenly, they were face to face and beaming at each other. 'I guessed word would have reached you that we'd docked. News usually travels like wildfire in this place so I was hoping that you'd come to see me when you could get away and I thought I'd come and walk into town with you,' he told her.

Suddenly feeling shy as she remembered the feel of his soft lips on hers, she could only nod as warm colour seeped into her cheeks.

They stood there for a moment, just staring at each other, until Nick suddenly reached out and took her cold hands in his. 'I . . . I've missed you,' he muttered. 'In fact, I've thought about you every single day since we set sail.'

'I've missed you too,' she admitted, and suddenly she was in his arms and he was kissing her again and she had the strangest feeling that she had come home. This was where she wanted to be and belonged and she knew in that moment that Nick was the man she wanted to spend the rest of her life with.

When they finally broke apart, Nick grinned happily. 'Phew! I was worried that you'd forget about me while I was gone.'

She shook her head, still holding tight to his hand. 'I could never forget about you, Nick,' she admitted. 'And I've thought about you every day, too.'

It was far too cold to stand still for long so, huddled together, they began to walk.

'I'll take you into the little parlour at the back of the hotel,' he told her. 'Mrs Baggett who owns the place doesn't mind her guests using it for visitors and she'll probably make us a pot of tea to warm us up an' all if I use me charm on her. I certainly can't take you into the bar. Mrs Forbes would go mad if she were to find out.'

Pearl smiled at the thought, but then they fell silent as they battled on through the thick-falling snow. It was no easy task to stay upright on the lane and they slipped and slithered their way into town. By the time the high street came into view they were breathless, but Nick squeezed her hand encouragingly. 'Not far now and we can get warm by a nice big log fire.'

Minutes later he led her down an alley to the back of the hotel and into a small parlour with comfy leather wing chairs dotted about and a roaring fire in the grate. Almost instantly their outer clothes began to steam in the heat, and he laughed as he helped her off with her cloak.

'Come on, come and get warm,' he encouraged.

Only too glad to do as she was told, Pearl crossed to the fire and held her hands out to it. The snow in her boots was melting rapidly so she took those off too and laid them on the hearth to dry out while Nick pottered away to request a warm drink for them.

By the time he returned, she was sitting by the fire with a dreamy expression on her face as she stared into the flames and imagined the little house they would buy one day. She would have a fire just like this one burning every night for him to come home to, and she could imagine them cuddled close together in one of the chairs after dinner as the snow fell outside.

'A penny for your thoughts?'

She started and flushed an even deeper shade of red. What would he think of her if she were to tell him about her imaginings when he hadn't even officially asked if she would be his girl yet?

'Oh, I, er . . .' Thankfully she was saved from having to say any more when the door opened and a young maid entered bearing a tray.

'Tea for two,' she said brightly and Pearl recognised her as one of the girls who had travelled on the orphan ship with her. 'Would you like me to pour it for you?' the girl asked politely as she set the cups and saucers out.

Pearl shook her head. 'Thank you, but no, I can do it.'

When the girl bustled away, Pearl lifted the strainer and began to pour the tea into the two cups. 'Sugar? One lump or two?' She smiled as it dawned on her that she was already planning their future when she didn't even know how he liked his tea.

'Two please.'

They drank the tea quickly, and then he pulled her from her chair and down on to his lap.

'So tell me what's been going on while I've been away,' he said and Pearl quickly obliged.

'It's still like living in a war zone with Freda and Eliza constantly at each other's throats,' she told him regretfully. 'Although in fairness it's usually Freda who starts the trouble. She's so jealous and spiteful to Eliza. And the master and mistress have had a few rows lately too, usually about Monty.' She shook her head. 'You can't help but hear them when they get going. Monty doesn't like working, you see, and he's been running up gambling debts. His father refused to pay any more off for him a few weeks ago but I suspect he's going to his mother for money now.' She shuddered as she thought of him. He still tried to waylay her at every opportunity, and she'd taken to glancing over her shoulder frequently to make sure he wasn't behind her. She had come to detest him but had to be polite because he was her employer's son.

'I don't trust him around Eliza either,' she confided worriedly. 'She couldn't stand him at one time but now she seems to have developed a crush on him. The trouble is, Freda is sweet on him too, and the two of them ended up fighting over him. I'm glad in a way because since then, as far as I know, he's given them both a wide berth. I dare say he doesn't want to do anything else to upset his parents.' She could have added that Monty's attentions were all now firmly fixed on herself, but she didn't know how Nick might react to that so she kept it to herself.

Nick went on to tell her of all the places he had been, including his visit to London, where sadly he'd not found out anything about Amy, but he promised he would try again when he was next there.

The time seemed to pass in the blink of an eye, until eventually Pearl's eyes lit on the clock on the mantelpiece and she jumped off his lap.

'Crikey, it's almost ten o'clock. I don't think Mrs Forbes would be any too happy if she knew I was out so late. I ought to be going.'

'I'll walk you back,' Nick offered, hurrying to fetch her cloak, and soon after they again stepped out into the freezing snow. The wind had risen alarmingly and Pearl had to cling on to his arm as they battled through the town with their heads bent. The journey took twice as long as it should have done because of the blizzard-like conditions, but at last they reached the end of the drive and he pulled her close to his chest again.

'Can I see you again tomorrow night?' he asked hopefully, but she had no time to answer because as she raised her face to look up at him he kissed her again, and just for a short while there was no one else in the world but the two of them.

'I-I should go in now,' she whispered when they finally drew apart. 'And yes, if I can get away, I'll see you tomorrow.'

And then she turned and wobbled down the drive, her lips still tingling from his kisses and a wide smile on her face.

She was laying the table for dinner in the dining room the following day when a voice behind her made her jump.

'Enjoy your little rendezvous with your sailor boy last night, did you?' a voice said sarcastically

Pearl dropped the knife and fork she was holding on to the table with a clatter, before whirling about to find Monty standing very close behind her. Flustered, her hand rose to her throat as he sneered. 'I was in the bar of the hotel when I saw you go by with him. I wonder what my mother would think if she knew you were the sort of girl to go off meeting men of an evening?'

'I-I wasn't meeting *men*!' Pearl spluttered indignantly. 'It was Nick . . . my friend . . . we came here together on the ship.'

'Hm, I *bet* you did!' He narrowed his eyes as he leaned in closer. 'Well, if you can be so nice to him perhaps it's time you started being a little nicer to *me*!'

Pearl shuddered, but somehow managed to stare calmly back at him. 'We did nothing untoward,' she said in an icy voice. 'We merely sat in the parlour and chatted.'

Thankfully the door opened and Susan appeared to tell her, 'Pearl, the mistress is ready for you to help her get dressed for dinner now. I'll finish this.'

With a silent sigh of relief, Pearl nodded at Susan and, ignoring Monty, turned and swept from the room.

However, once in the hallway, her courage dissolved and she began to shake. Would Monty really go ahead with his threat and tell his mother that she had gone to meet Nick? And if he did, would Mrs Forbes believe her if she told her that they had done nothing wrong? She could only wait and see. But one thing was for sure. Nothing would keep her away from Nick now, even if it cost her her job.

Chapter Thirty

It was much later that evening before Pearl was able to get away, and once again she found Nick standing in the lane, stamping his feet and blowing on to his hands to try and keep warm.

'You shouldn't have waited,' she scolded him gently. 'You'll catch your death of cold out here!'

He grinned. 'This is nothing compared to being out at sea in this weather,' he informed her. He tucked her arm into his and they began to walk towards the town, lifting their feet high through the snow.

Pearl's face was glowing by the time they reached the cosy parlour at the back of the hotel, and she was pleased to see that they had it to themselves again.

'Is everything all right? You seem a bit quiet tonight,' Nick commented as he helped her off with her snow-caked cloak.

Pearl forced a smile. She didn't dare tell him of Monty's threat for fear of what he might do. 'Everything is fine,' she answered, crossing her fingers, and he went away to order them some hot cocoa. Once again, they chatted non-stop and the time passed quickly, until suddenly he became solemn, and taking her hand he said quietly, 'There's something I want to ask you, Pearl.'

'Then ask away, I won't bite,' she laughed, although her heart was pounding.

Nick looked vaguely uncomfortable as he stroked the palm of her hand, before muttering, 'Well . . . the thing is, I know we're still young and all that but . . . but I was wondering if you'd be my girl . . . official, like.'

When she gazed back at him, he rushed on nervously, 'Of course I know it'll be years before we can save enough to get married but all the same, I'd like to know when I'm away that you'll wait for me because I . . . I love you, Pearl. So, will you? . . . Be my girl, I mean!'

'Of *course* I will,' she laughed, as happy tears sparkled in her eyes. 'Because I love you, too, Nick, so *very* much.'

And then there was nothing more to be said. They kissed and she felt like the luckiest girl in the world.

All too soon it was time for him to walk her back to the house, and she felt as if she was floating along because Nick loved her.

'I'll see you tomorrow,' he whispered when they reached the end of the drive.

She nodded, and stood and watched him until the thickly falling snow swallowed him up. She was almost halfway down the drive when Monty suddenly stepped from the bare trees to stand in front of her, and she almost jumped out of her skin.

'I thought I'd catch you if I waited long enough,' he growled. 'Been out with your fancy man again, have you?'

'Nick is *not* my fancy man, as you so crudely put it!' Pearl ground out, as her eyes flashed fire. 'We're stepping out together, if you must know, and I'm proud of the fact!'

Monty glowered at her. 'Stepping out! *Huh!*' He leaned menacingly towards her. 'Since when do girls like *you* court? Everyone knows that all the girls who are shipped here come from the gutter. Keeping him happy, are you? Because if that's the case, you can keep me happy, too.'

He lunged towards her, but luckily Pearl stepped aside so quickly that he lost his footing when he made a grab for her and went sprawling full length in the snow.

'You little *bitch*!' he growled as he tried to rise. But Pearl didn't wait to hear what else he had to say – she just lifted her skirts and ran like the devil himself was after her, not stopping for breath until she reached the safety of the house.

That night, she tossed and turned as she thought of the position she was in. She had avoided Monty as much as possible in the months before, but now she had an idea that his unwanted attentions would be even more unbearable. And the worst of it was she could do nothing about it, because even if she went to her mistress and asked for her protection, she was bound to take her son's side. She might even say that Pearl had led him on and then she could well find both herself and Eliza out of a job. And so she decided all that she could do was avoid Monty as much as possible and hope that soon he would transfer his attentions to some other girl. It wasn't a very satisfactory solution, but it was all she could come up with for now.

The mistress was entertaining guests the next night so Pearl was unable to get away to meet Nick. Frequently throughout the evening Pearl glanced worriedly towards the window and wondered if she would be able to see him again before he sailed, for the snow was so deep now she knew that soon they may well be snowed in.

'Whatever's the matter with you, lass?' Cook asked, as Pearl stalked up and down the kitchen. 'You're like a cat on hot bricks an' you're making me dizzy with all this pacing!'

'Ah, she's in love!' Freda said sarcastically and Pearl glowered at her. Monty had ignored both Freda and Eliza for weeks but the girl was aware that he was still being attentive to Pearl and it had made her hate her all the more.

'I hope it's not Master Monty you're mooning over, girl?' Cook looked alarmed, and was relieved when Pearl shook her head.

'I can assure you I have no liking for him,' Pearl responded frostily.

The cook frowned. 'So who is it you have a fancy for then?'

'I don't have a fancy for anyone,' Pearl retorted. 'But I do have feelings for a certain young man. We travelled here together on the same ship, as it happens, and one day we hope to be married.'

'I see.' Cook tapped her lip with a plump finger as she regarded Pearl. 'Then that's all well and good, but just remember, decent girls do no more than give a chaste kiss before they have a ring on their finger.'

'I'm well aware of that.' Pearl was so embarrassed that she turned and left the room, leaving Freda with a smirk on her face.

She had gone no more than a few steps into the hallway when Monty suddenly appeared from his father's office and stopping, he glared at her. With her chin in the air she made to pass him, but he caught her arm and swung her towards him.

'Not seeing lover boy tonight?' he taunted, as she tried to squirm from his grasp.

'Let me go this *minute*,' she ground out through gritted teeth. 'Otherwise I shall scream so loudly the whole house will hear me and I don't think your mother will like that, will she?'

He released her abruptly, his face red with rage as he bent towards her. 'You've got too big for your boots,' he said menacingly. 'But I shall bring you down a peg or two, you just see if I don't.'

With a toss of her head, she went on her way, without giving him a backward glance – but once she was out of his sight, her legs felt as if they had turned to jelly, and she leaned heavily against the wall. *From now on I shall have to be very careful never to be alone with him*, she thought. And yet she knew that this could prove to be a lot easier said than done.

Thankfully the snow stopped falling the next morning and so Pearl was able to meet Nick that evening, although he had bad news for her.

'I'm afraid we'll be sailing a lot sooner than I'd thought,' he told her, and her heart sank. 'It seems Mr Forbes has promised a cargo of timber to be shipped to England as soon as possible.'

'So when will you be going?' she asked with a catch in her voice. Now that they had declared their love for each other, she wondered how she could bear to let him go.

'The day after tomorrow,' he said miserably. Forcing a smile, he squeezed her hand. 'But never mind. I shall write to you just as soon as we dock and if we're in port long enough I'll go and see your old neighbour for you and ask her if she's found out where Amy is. Think of the money I'll earn, too. The quicker we can save enough, the quicker we can get married.'

She managed a tremulous smile, seeing the sense in what he said, but it didn't make the thought of parting any easier.

In no time at all they were saying goodbye and Pearl couldn't hold back the tears. Luckily, Mrs Forbes had asked her to get some things for her in town on the day Nick was due to sail and so she was able to go to the docks to see him off. The ship was loaded with timber and sitting low in the water with the weight as they stood face to face, enjoying their last few precious moments together.

On board sailors were dashing here and there preparing to sail and all too soon someone shouted, 'Come on, Willis, we're pulling the gangplank up now and we'll go wi'out yer if yer don't get yer arse up 'ere right now!'

Nick gave her one last hasty kiss before making a dash for it. 'I'll be back before you know it. Stay safe,' he shouted across his shoulder, and she stood there, her eyes wet with tears.

Minutes later, the huge ship began to drift away from the quay and she waved and waved until Nick was just a tiny dot in the distance on the deck. It had started to snow again and, pulling her cloak more tightly about her, she turned and headed back to the house feeling bereft. There were few people about. Most of them had chosen to stay by their firesides and Pearl didn't blame them.

After a time, she left the main street behind and the going got harder, for the snow was much deeper here, and soon she was breathless. She had gone some way when she thought she heard someone behind her and, turning, she was appalled to see Monty limping towards her. Her first instinct was to lift her skirts and run, but common sense took over. She must stand her ground and not let him see that she was afraid of him, so she continued on her way until suddenly he was beside her.

'Look . . . about the other night. I'm sorry. What I said was out of order.'

Pearl was so shocked that she almost tripped over the sodden hem of her skirt. She had half expected him to try and catch hold of her again, and yet here he was apologising!

'The thing is I'd had too much to drink,' he rushed on. 'And I'm truly sorry.'

Pearl peeped at him out of the corner of her eye, not trusting him an inch. This was just too much of a turnabout for her liking and she didn't believe a word he was saying.

'So . . . can we go back to being friends again?' he wheedled, as he tried to keep pace with her.

She stopped so quickly that he almost collided with her. She stood with her hands on her hips glaring at him.

'Let's just get something straight once and for all,' she said with a grim look on her face. 'As far as I'm concerned, we have never and will never be friends. You are my employer's son, so I have to be polite to you, but other than that I want nothing to do with you. Is that *quite* clear?'

And without waiting for an answer, she strode away, leaving Monty with a scowl on his face.

Once again she had turned him down and he wasn't used to rejection. Worse still, he now had to go and face his father cap in hand to ask for yet more money. He'd been out all night and had lost a small fortune gambling once more, so he knew his father would not be pleased – again! With a sigh, he moved on.

Within minutes of him entering the house shouting could be heard echoing from the study and Susan, who was on her way to the day room to give it a good polish, raised her eyebrows at Pearl.

'Sounds like the young 'un is in 'is father's bad books again,' she whispered.

Glancing towards the study door, Pearl nodded. She had no sympathy for him whatsoever if the rumours she was hearing were true. He hardly ever ventured into work any-more, apparently, and he had fallen in with a bad crowd, much to his father's disgust.

'Did Nick get off all right?' Susan asked then.

Pearl nodded, her face miserable. 'Yes, he did, and goodness knows when he'll be back.'

'Ah, well, that's a life on the ocean waves for yer,' Susan said, and hurried on her way. With the mood the master was in by the sounds of it, it wouldn't do for him to find her slacking.

Cook was in no better mood when Pearl entered the kitchen. 'Damn wolves came in close last night and took some more o' the chickens,' she told Pearl with a shake of her head. It wasn't the first time it had happened since Pearl had lived there. They always got hungry in the winter and ventured out of the forests looking for food. She shuddered at the thought. Thankfully, as yet she had never encountered one, although she often heard them howling in the dead of night and it always made the hairs on the back of her neck stand up.

'Hardly any eggs at all today, not that they lay well in the cold,' Cook grumbled. She had made Will build a coop for them and the chickens were her pride and joy. 'I've told Will to bring me a rifle in and if the damn things start howling again tonight, I'll go out and shoot them meself!'

Pearl stifled a grin. She couldn't imagine the cook wielding a rifle, but she didn't say it aloud.

Later that afternoon, Pearl answered a knock on the door to find a man in a smart suit standing there. 'I wish to see Montague Forbes,' he said with no preamble and looking none too pleased.

'I, er . . . I'm not sure that he's in, sir,' Pearl told him.

At that moment Mrs Forbes appeared and raised an eyebrow. 'Why, James, how nice to see you,' she said moving forwards with her hand outstretched. 'And how is your mother? Do come in out of the cold.'

Looking uncomfortable, the young man shuffled into the hall and removed his hat. 'My mother is very well, thank you, Mrs Forbes. But I'm afraid I haven't come on a social visit. I need to see Monty as a matter of some urgency.'

'I see.' Looking slightly disturbed Mrs Forbes lowered her hand. 'Is it anything I can help you with?'

When he shook his head she told him, 'In that case, Monty is in the drawing room. Do go through to him.'

As he strode away, Pearl realised that he must have been there before, because he knew where he was going.

'Oh dear, I do hope Monty hasn't gone and got himself into bother again,' Mrs Forbes muttered. Then, with a smile at Pearl, she asked, 'Would you mind organising a tray of tea and taking it into them, dear? I'm sure James must be cold. His mother is a good friend of mine and he's just reminded me that I really should go and see her.'

She pottered away as Pearl went to do as she was asked. Minutes later Pearl was back with a tray, but as she tapped on the door and entered the room, she found Monty and the young man having a furious row.

'I'm telling you now, Forbes, if I don't have that money back before ten o'clock this evening, I'll bloody *kill* you! If my father finds out I've been gambling again, my life won't be worth living and I owe him what I won off you!' The visitor had hold of Monty's cravat and was shaking him like a rat, and Pearl gasped as she wondered whether to go in or not.

The two men became aware of her standing there and, hurriedly letting go of Monty, the visitor growled threateningly, 'Remember . . . ten o'clock tonight, *or else!*'

He barged past Pearl, his face purple with rage as he almost knocked the tray from her hands. Monty barked at her, 'Well, don't just stand there! Take the bloody tray away, can't you!'

Pearl turned so quickly that she almost tripped over her skirts and ended up sloshing tea all over the tray as she fled from the room just in time to hear the front door slam behind Monty's visitor.

I wouldn't like to be in Monty's shoes, she thought as she went back to the kitchen, although from where she was standing it wouldn't be such a bad thing if someone were to take Monty down a peg or two. He was far too cocky by half!

Chapter Thirty-One

The atmosphere was decidedly frosty when Pearl served breakfast to the family the next morning, and she had a funny idea that the swollen black eye Monty was sporting was something to do with it. No doubt the visitor of the previous day had caught up with him and fulfilled his threat.

Unfortunately, that morning both Cook and Susan had been confined to bed with nasty chills and so until they were better, Pearl, Freda and Eliza were going to have to muddle through as best they could. It had been decided that Pearl would take over the cooking and waiting on table and Eliza and Freda would do the rest of the chores. It was far from ideal, especially as Pearl wasn't a particularly good cook, but it was the best they could do.

'I'm sorry there isn't the selection there usually is,' Pearl said as she brought in the breakfast.

Mrs Forbes waved her apologies aside. 'Bacon, eggs and porridge is quite sufficient,' she assured her. 'Just do the best you can, dear. I'm sure we won't starve. Oh, and by the way, I've just seen Will and asked him to go into town to fetch the doctor to take a look at Cook and Susan.'

'Yes, ma'am.' Pearl placed the rest of the dishes down and quickly took her leave, glad to escape the atmosphere.

Freda was throwing logs on to the fire and Eliza was washing pots in the sink when Pearl went back into the kitchen and told them casually, 'Master Monty has got a right shiner on him. Someone must have landed a punch on him last night.'

Instantly, both girls stared at her in horror.

'But he's all right, ain't he?' Freda asked worriedly,

Eliza glared at her. 'And what's it to do with you?'

'Everythin', 'cause if yer must know 'e still loves me an' when we're older 'e's goin' to tell 'is parents about us!' Freda spat.

'I know you're lyin' 'cause it's *me* he loves,' Eliza shot back.

Pearl looked in amazement from one to the other of them. 'Girls! *Stop it* this instant – do you hear me?' Her voice shot across the room to them as they eyed each other threateningly. 'It's bad enough having two members of staff ill without having to listen to you two arguing like a pair of fishwives!'

They were so unused to hearing Pearl raise her voice that for a moment the two girls were silent – but then Eliza muttered sullenly, 'You're only angry 'cause you want him for yourself!'

'*Me*, want Monty Forbes?' Pearl's eyebrows rose in astonishment. 'I can assure you I wouldn't touch him with a barge-pole if he was the last man on earth. I love Nick, so stop this silly nonsense immediately and get on with your work. We have a lunch and a dinner to prepare for the family.'

But despite her harsh words, Pearl was gravely concerned. She knew that for some time after the girls had fought over him, he had pointedly ignored them both, but now she could only assume that he was once more playing one off against the other, and the thought of it made her feel physically sick. Eliza was so vulnerable, who knew what he might persuade her to do? *I shall just have to watch her more closely from now on*, she promised herself and, hurrying to the larder, she began to try and find something suitable for lunch. Their stocks were sadly depleted, as due to the weather it wasn't so easy to get into town for provisions. Unlike Cook, who seemed able to produce a meal from almost nothing, Pearl was limited in her cooking abilities, but even so she liked a challenge and she got started on trying to produce something tasty.

The mood in the kitchen did not improve throughout the morning, and Freda and Eliza ignored each other, but Pearl supposed that was better than having them argue, so she left them to get on with it.

Just before lunchtime she went to set the table in the dining room and almost bumped into the cause of all the trouble in the hallway.

'Ah, Pearl, I was just coming to find you,' he told her with a charming smile. 'I'm afraid this eye of mine is giving me some gyp, and I wondered if you might have something I could put on it to soothe it?'

'No I *don't*,' she replied bluntly as she strode past him.

As he watched her go, the smile slipped away and he frowned. He had tried wooing her, frightening her and treating her as an equal, but still she was holding him at arm's length and he wasn't used to that. He had only to click his fingers and Freda or Eliza would come running to please him, but it was Pearl he really wanted and now he was sick of her rejections. *So, no more being nice*, he told himself. It was time Pearl learned her place in the house and he would teach her the first chance he got!

As it happened, the chance came much sooner than he'd expected. That evening, because Cook and Susan were ill in bed, it fell to Pearl to make sure that everything in the kitchen was safe and the doors locked before retiring, and she was doing just that when Monty strolled into the room to join her.

'Ah, still up, are you?' he said rather unnecessarily. 'I was just coming for a drink of water before turning in.'

Pearl stared at him suspiciously. She always ensured there were fresh jugs of water on the family's bedside tables each evening, so his words didn't quite ring true. Even so she continued with what she was doing, uncomfortably aware that he was watching her every move. Both girls, Will and the family had retired to bed some long time ago, which meant she and Monty were quite alone. She continued to go about the room, dousing the flames in the oil lamps until there was only the glow from the fire – and that was when he lunged at her, taking her completely by surprise and bearing her to the floor.

She landed heavily on her back, knocking the wind from her lungs and rendering her unable to do anything more than gasp for a few moments. Within that short time, he was astride her and when she opened her mouth to squeal, his hand clamped across it.

'Don't even *think* of it,' he warned her menacingly. 'Otherwise I shall tell my mother you seduced me and she'll believe me over you *any* day of the week. And where will you be then, if you and Eliza get kicked out into the snow on your pretty little arses, eh? Not only that – you would never feel safe again, because I have a way of getting rid of people who upset me. Like my awful little sister, for instance. Mother was always fawning over her. I may as well not have been here once Elizabeth arrived, for all the notice she took of me. It's a shame she ended up in the river when we went for a little stroll, don't you think!'

As the full implication of what he was saying sunk in, Pearl shuddered with horror. He had killed his little sister, but how could she ever tell anyone? As he had pointed out, it would be her word against his and who would believe her?

Her head wagged from side to side as he started to drag her skirt up her legs and, terrified, all she could do was pummel him ineffectively with her fists.

Yet even as she fought him, she knew it was useless. He was so strong and with his heavy weight pinning her to the ground she stood no chance. His hand was tearing at her blouse and appalled she felt the buttons pop and roll across the floor. And then she heard the sound of her chemise tear and suddenly his wet mouth was licking and biting at her tender nipples, making her whimper and buck with pain. Next she felt his hand on her drawers and as they too ripped he dragged them to one side and began to fumble with the buttons on his flies. And then she shuddered as she felt his hot throbbing penis rest against her thigh before he plunged it into her, making her feel dizzy with pain. She could feel the vomit rising in her throat as she lay there wishing for death, but he seemed totally oblivious to her distress as he bucked up and down gasping and grunting, his breath hot on her cheek. When she was convinced she could bear the pain no longer, he suddenly went rigid and with a cry collapsed on top of her, knocking the air from her lungs once more.

Now she lay very still, terrified that if she so much as moved it would start all over again, but after a while, when his breathing returned to a somewhat more normal rhythm, he rolled off her and, cool as a cucumber rose to his feet and began to adjust his clothes.

'You were hardly worth the wait, slut,' he growled. 'Although I won't be averse to coming back for another taste if there's nothing better available. Even your little sister is more exciting then you. At least that little whore enjoys it. In fact, she can't get enough of me.'

Pearl tried to close her ears to what he was saying as she rolled herself into a foetal position, pulling her torn clothing about her, and she knew in that moment that had she had a knife in her hand she would have killed him and suffered the consequences.

And then he was gone and finally she gave way to a paroxysm of weeping as the full impact of what he had done came home to her. He had taken her virginity! No man would ever want her now; she was soiled goods.

Oh Nick, her heart cried, as tears started to roll in rivers down her pale cheeks. *He's taken what should have been yours.*

She lay there for a long time, aching in every bone in her body, but eventually she managed to drag herself up and, crossing unsteadily to the kettle, she tipped the hot water into a tin bowl and began to savagely scrub her most private places, trying to ignore the traces of blood and semen on the piece of huckaback she was using as a flannel.

After a time it came to her that no matter how hard she scrubbed, she would always feel dirty now. Already bruises were beginning to show across her breasts, and she guessed that they would be black and blue by morning. Shakily, she lit a candle and on hands and knees began to hunt about the floor for the buttons from her blouse. It wouldn't do for Eliza or Freda to find them the next day. She would hide them in her room and repair the blouse one evening when Eliza was out of the way.

Wearily, she eventually made her way up the servants' stairs, praying that Eliza would be asleep. Thankfully she was, so Pearl quickly undressed, bundled her clothes beneath the bed and slid into her nightgown.

Shivering in the cold, she crossed to the window. Somewhere the wolves were howling as the icy wind slapped the thickly falling snow against the window and the tears came again as she remembered the day she and Eliza had first arrived there. They had truly thought this would be the start of a new life for them, but now she felt like a prisoner. Worse still, she was aware that this may not be the end of it. Monty had said he would take her again and if he did there was nothing she could do about it. What he had said was true: the mistress would never believe her word against his.

With a shuddering sigh, she climbed between the icy cold sheets, feeling more afraid than she had ever felt in her life. She had dreamed of a happy future with Nick but that was gone now. How could she ever tell him what had happened, for if she did, she knew that Nick would take matters into his own hands and who knew what he was capable of doing to Monty then? No, somehow she would have to find the courage to tell him that she had made a mistake and that she didn't love him after all. At least that way he would have a chance of finding a girl who deserved him, even if it meant breaking her own heart. The tears ran faster as she lay in the darkness, listening to the haunting sound of the howling wolves as all her plans for the future turned to ashes.

Chapter Thirty-Two

Pearl was getting dressed with her back to Eliza when she woke the next morning.

'You're getting up early, aren't you?'

Pearl turned to find her sister looking at her curiously. 'Yes, I didn't sleep very well.' She hesitated and dropping on to the bed beside Eliza she said, 'I want you to promise me something.'

Eliza narrowed her eyes suspiciously.

'I want you to *promise* me that you'll keep well away from Monty.'

Instantly Eliza was on her guard. 'Why? Is it because *you* want him?'

'*Of course* I don't,' Pearl snapped, trying hard to stay calm. 'But he's . . . he's bad – rotten to the core, and I need you to promise me that you'll give him a wide berth.'

Eliza stared up at her, stubbornly silent, until Pearl turned and left the room with her shoulders hunched, wondering where it was all going to end.

The day got worse when she went down into the kitchen to find no sign of Freda. She was usually the first up attending to the fires, but today the kitchen fire was almost out and

Pearl hurriedly raked out the ashes and threw some logs on to the dying embers as she muttered to herself.

'You'd better go and knock on Freda's bedroom door, she's overslept,' she told Eliza, when she put in an appearance a few moments later.

Eliza gave a sullen sigh and went off to do as she was told, only to return to inform Pearl, 'She says she's not feeling well and she won't get up.'

'Oh, that's great,' Pearl said. 'That means we now have to cook, clean the house *and* look after three invalids. Has she got a chill like Cook and Susan?'

Eliza shrugged. 'She didn't say, just that she was feeling bad.'

Pearl filled the kettle and set it on the range. She ached in every bone in her body today and would have liked nothing better than to have a day in bed herself, but that wouldn't be possible.

When Will entered the kitchen shortly after, he saw at a glance how busy they were. 'I'll go and light the fires in the drawing room and the dining room, you two concentrate on getting the breakfast ready for the family. And don't worry if it's a bit late. There's no way Mr Forbes will be going out today. We're finally snowed in,' he said.

Pearl flashed him a grateful smile as she carried the food she was to cook for breakfast from the pantry.

Will was as good as his word and once he'd got the fire going, he even went back to lay the table in the dining room for them.

'I didn't realise you'd have a clue how to do it,' Pearl admitted when it was ready.

He smiled sadly. 'Ah, you'd be surprised what I can do. My Esme worked here with me when we first married and she taught me how to do it.'

Pearl looked surprised as she flipped the bacon in the frying pan. Will had never spoken of his personal life before. 'Oh, I'm sorry, I didn't know you'd been married.'

He nodded, his eyes clouded. 'Yes, but only briefly. Me and Esme came here on the same boat when we were in our early teens and I think for me it was love at first sight. When we were old enough, we got married, but she died before we even got to our first wedding anniversary.'

'That's so sad.' Pearl's heart ached for him, so much so that she almost forgot what had happened to her the night before, but only for a moment. It was always there, like a niggling toothache that wouldn't go away, and she couldn't feel clean no matter how many times she scrubbed her hands.

While she was seeing to the family's food, Will prepared three trays for the invalids and once the family was served, they each carried a tray up to the servants' quarters. It had been torture for Pearl to have to face Monty in the dining room, especially when he smirked at her, but somehow she had kept her calm and not given him the satisfaction of letting him see how upset she was, although she had longed to lunge at him and gouge his eyes out.

'Are you feeling all right, Pearl?' Mrs Forbes asked. 'You're looking awfully pale.' She had dressed herself that morning, knowing that Pearl would be busy in the kitchen.

'Yes, ma'am. I'm fine, thank you.'

And with that she had gathered together what dignity she could and swept from the room, even though she had wanted to blab to her mistress about what her wicked son had done to her the night before.

'So what's wrong?' she asked Freda when she entered her room. She had thought it best if she brought her tray up; she didn't want her and Eliza bickering again. 'Have you come down with this chill Cook and Susan have got?' She had to admit that Freda did look awful. Her face was the colour of putty and her hair hung in damp rats' tails about her pale cheeks. There was a bucket at the side of her bed and Pearl saw that there was vomit in it, which would account for the vile smell in the room.

'I don't know.' Freda was clutching her stomach and was clearly in pain. 'I feel really sick and queasy.'

Pearl nibbled on her lower lip as she glanced towards the window. 'Well, I doubt there's much chance of us getting the doctor out to you today. Will said the lane is almost impassable, though I dare say he'll be going out to try and clear it later on when he's eaten. But come on. Let's sit you up so you can eat something. It might make you feel better. I've made you some nice bacon sandwiches.'

Just the mention of the food made Freda shake her head and hold her hand up to ward her off. 'Th-thanks. But I don't want *anything*. Just take it away, *please*; the smell of it's makin' me feel sick again.'

'All right, if you're sure. But won't you just try a sip of tea? You really should have something inside you.'

Freda groaned. '*No* . . . but thanks.'

With a sigh, Pearl took the untouched tray away. Thankfully it appeared that Cook and Susan were both feeling a little better, which she supposed was something at least.

The rest of the day passed in a blur as Eliza and Pearl saw to the needs of the family and the invalids, and before they knew it, it was dark again.

'The damn wolves came close again last night,' Will said with a shake of his head when they finally got the chance to sit down for five minutes for a well-earned cup of tea. 'And another two of Cook's chickens were gone this morning. There would have been more lost if I hadn't gone out with my gun to scare the buggers off! I dread to think what Cook is going to say when she finds out.'

'It's not your fault,' Pearl assured him, shuddering as she thought of the sound of them howling the night before. Thankfully she still hadn't encountered a wolf close up as yet, although she had glimpsed a pack of them through the trees in the woods once.

She was glad when it was finally bedtime and she could escape to her room, although she found an excuse to keep Eliza downstairs with her until she went up, terrified that Monty might turn up again and do a repeat of the night before. Thankfully, there was no sign of him and as they climbed the stairs together, she gave a little sigh of relief.

Once Eliza was asleep Pearl fished her torn clothes from beneath the bed and repaired them in the light from a candle, then she bundled them up again ready to go down to the laundry the next day and finally managed to sleep.

Susan was a welcome sight when Pearl went down to the kitchen the following morning. She still had a nasty cough and looked slightly flushed, but assured her that she was feeling well enough to be up and about again, although Cook wasn't and Freda seemed worse if anything.

Eliza prepared a tray each for the invalids and Pearl carried them up to them but once again Freda refused to eat, although she did manage a few sips of her tea.

'I really think we ought to try and get the doctor out to her today,' she told Will worriedly.

He nodded. 'I'll try an' clear a path just as soon as we've got breakfast out of the way,' he promised. 'And if I manage it I'll go into town and ask him to come out again.'

Pearl gave him a grateful smile and turned to say something to Susan. But she stopped as she noticed the way her friend's eyes were fixed on Will and she realised why she had been so keen to be up and about again. If she was wasn't very much mistaken, her and Cook's suspicions had been correct: Susan was sweet on him.

It was much later that day as they sat eating lunch that Pearl said teasingly to Susan, 'He's a nice chap, Will, isn't he?'

Susan's flushed cheeks told her all she needed to know. 'Yes . . . he is.'

Pearl smiled. 'And would I be right in thinking you have a soft spot for him?'

Susan's blush deepened. 'I suppose I have,' she admitted. 'Although I doubt anything will ever come of it. He's a fair bit older than me for a start off and he's never been anything but friendly.'

'Ah well, that might be because he was married once but his wife died soon after the wedding,' Pearl confided. 'It could be that he's not quite ready for another relationship just yet but who knows what might happen in the future. Why don't you let him know how you feel?'

Susan was horrified. 'Oh, I couldn't do that.'

'Then you'll just have to let things take their course, but personally I think you'd make a lovely couple and he isn't all that much older than you. Probably not even ten years or so, I should think and that's nothing.'

'We'll see.' Although Susan knew that she would wait for him forever if need be.

Their conversation was interrupted by a knock on the door, and Pearl hurried away to admit the doctor who had come to see Freda and Cook.

'Well, Cook is much better. She should be up and about again in the next couple of days,' he was able to tell them when he joined them in the kitchen shortly after. 'But Freda . . .' He shook his head as Pearl poured him a cup of tea. 'Her symptoms seem to be suspiciously like those Mrs Veasey had, so once again all I can ask you to do is make sure that she has plenty of fluids.'

'Serves her right,' Eliza said spitefully.

Pearl shot her a warning look. 'Eliza, that's a *terrible* thing to say,' she scolded, but Eliza was unrepentant and merely went on with what she was doing.

There was yet another visitor mid-afternoon. It was another gentleman to see Master Monty. But he was out, so Pearl showed him into the drawing room where the mistress was doing some embroidery. Shortly after, Mrs Forbes rang the bell for Pearl to come and show him out again and once he had gone, she made a point of finding Pearl to tell her, 'Please don't mention the visitor to my husband, Pearl.'

Pearl guessed that Monty owed money to the man, but she nodded. No doubt Monty's mother had settled the debt for him again and didn't want Mr Forbes to find out.

'Of course, ma'am,' she answered respectfully and went back to cooking the dinner. It was none of her business, but she wondered how long it would be before Monty got his comeuppance. It couldn't be soon enough as far as she was concerned.

Later that afternoon when Monty put in an appearance there were raised voices from the drawing room, and Pearl's hunch was proved correct when she heard his mother tell him, 'I can't keep digging you out of debt, Monty. Your father would be furious if he knew how much money you were gambling away!'

She hurried on her way so didn't hear Monty's answer, but she had heard enough. Just as she had told Eliza, he was bad through and through, although Eliza would never accept it and nor would Freda – they were both still completely besotted with him. As much as Pearl loved working for Mrs Forbes, she knew that somehow she was going to have to get Eliza away from him. That brought her thoughts sharply back to Nick and once again tears stung at the back of her eyes. After what Monty had done to her, they could never be together now, and so it was up to her to save enough to get them both a passage back to England. What they would do when they got there she had no idea, but something would turn up, she told herself as she went about her work with a heavy heart.

Christmas passed in a blur of misery for Pearl, and as they were snowed in, the days all rolled into one with no relief from the tedium.

In February, Pearl received her first letter from Nick and it almost broke her heart to read it. He had no idea what had happened to her and was clearly still planning their future together.

My dearest Pearl,

Well here I am back on our home turf. I hope this finds you well, my love. You are the first one I think of when I open my eyes and the last one I think of before I close them each night. I didn't realise how hard it would be for us to be apart and can hardly wait to get back to see you again.

I have wonderful news for you, I went to see your neighbour and she was able to tell me that your sister Amy is living in a market town in the Midlands called Nuneaton. She is happy and settled by all accounts and I promise when we finally come back here the first thing we shall do is track her down. I'd like to buy a little piece of land then and start a smallholding, some-thing we can work on and build together. How does that sound? I'm afraid the sea has no lure for me now. I just want us to be a family. We could perhaps think of settling in Nuneaton, if you'd like to, so that you will be close to your sister? I asked Lil to pass on your address when Amy next comes to London for a visit with Gracie so hopefully when she gets it she will write to you. I shall be sailing to New York from here on the morning tide the day after tomorrow so have no idea when I might get back to you, but I shall write again once we arrive in America.

I miss you so much and can't wait till we are together again,

Till then,

All my love

Nick xxx

A mixture of emotions swept through her as she carefully folded the letter and put it back in the envelope. There was joy and relief to hear that Nick was safe and well, and excitement at the prospect of hearing from Amy, although as far as Pearl knew, her sister had never had the opportunity to learn to read or write.

But overshadowing everything was heartbreak as she thought of the future that Monty had snatched away from herself and Nick by raping her. In her mind's eye she could see what might have been: a little cottage with roses climbing around the door and a profusion of brightly coloured flowers growing in the garden, fat chickens clucking in the yard and perhaps a few sheep and cows. A cosy fire with chairs either side of it where they would sit and speak of their day's work and a warm bed where they would retire together each night.

But none of that could ever happen now. She was too fearful of the consequences of what Nick might do if she told him what had happened and too ashamed to let him go on believing she was still pure. How to tell him it was over was the problem and it broke her heart to know that however she did it, she must lie to him.

When Eliza walked into the room to find her sister in tears, she looked genuinely concerned. 'What's wrong?'

'Oh, er . . . it's nothing.' Pearl stuffed the letter into a drawer and wiped the tears from her cheeks with the back of her hand.

Eliza frowned. 'Was that letter from Nick?' She was confused. Surely a letter from her beau should have made Pearl happy, or perhaps it had made her miss him? *Yes!* she thought, *that must be it.* 'Never mind, I've no doubt he'll be home before you know it,' she said comfortingly, which only made Pearl cry all the harder.

'We're not courting anymore,' Pearl told her dully. 'At least, we won't be when he does come home and I tell him we're finished.'

'But *why* would you do that?' Eliza scratched her head. 'I thought yer loved him?'

Pearl pulled herself together with a great effort. This was where the lies must begin. 'Yes, I thought I did too, but I've changed my mind.'

And without another word she sailed past her sister, leaving her with her mouth gaping slackly open.

Chapter Thirty-Three

It was in early February as Pearl was clearing the pots from the dining room table following breakfast that Monty sidled back into the dining room, closing the door behind him. It had been eight weeks since the night he had raped her and ever since then Pearl had managed to avoid being alone with him – but now, she was cornered.

'What do you want?' She stared at him calmly, although her stomach was churning.

'I wanted to see you, of course.' His voice was sickly sweet, but she knew him for what he was and had no time for him.

'Please step aside. I have to get these pots back to the kitchen.' Her voice was as cold as the icy wind that was blowing outside but he merely chuckled.

'There's no need to be like that.' He took a step towards her and gave her a mocking smile. 'I was thinking it was time we had another little get-together. I know you enjoyed it last time. You just don't like to admit it, do you?'

Pearl slammed the tray back on to the table so hard that the pots rattled and before she knew what she was doing she had snatched a knife up and pointed it at him.

'You step away from me *right now* or I *swear* I shall stab you!'

Monty stepped back in alarm. The look in her eye told him more than any words could have done that she meant every word she said.

'And furthermore, let me tell you that should you *ever* lay so much as a finger on me again, I shall scream so loud the whole town will hear me, even if it means your mother does throw me and Eliza out on to the street! You are *truly* the most despicable, vile man I have ever met!'

His expression was menacing now but he kept his distance as he spat, 'You *stupid* little whore. Do you *really* think I would want *you*! Why, your little sister is far more fun!'

'And the same goes for Eliza too!' Her eyes were flashing now. 'If I find out you've gone near her again, I *swear* I shall kill you!'

Without a word, he turned on his heel and slammed out of the room, his hands balled into fists. Pearl was shaking uncontrollably when Eliza appeared and asked, 'What was all that about then? You've right upset Master Monty if the mood he slammed out of here in is anythin' to go by.'

'I want you to keep *right* away from him from now on,' Pearl warned, but to her horror Eliza only grinned.

'Why, did he turn yer down?' she sneered. 'I could have told yer he would. It's *me* he wants.' And then she too left, leaving Pearl shaking her head in despair.

It was two days later when the sickness started and Pearl was afraid. Was she coming down with the same illness that was afflicting Freda? She was still ill in bed showing no signs of getting any better, if anything she was growing weaker. What if she had it too now? Who would look after Eliza if anything was to happen to her? But she kept her concerns to herself. *Perhaps it's just a little bug I've picked up,* she tried to tell herself as she went on as normally as she could.

The following morning Pearl had just come in from visiting the toilet in the yard where she had thrown up her breakfast, or what she had managed to eat of it, when she caught Cook staring at her with a strange look on her face. 'Not feeling too good, hinny?'

Pearl shook her head. 'Actually, I am feeling a bit off. But don't worry, I shall be as right as rain in a while.'

'Hm.' The cook went back to rolling the pastry as Pearl made a list of the provisions she needed Will to fetch from the town.

Mid-morning, she and Susan went up to wash Freda and change the sheets on her bed. The doctor was due to visit her later that day, although he still had no idea what might be wrong with her. Her skin was taking on the sickly yellow pallor that Mrs Veasey's had, and although there had never been any love lost between them, Pearl was feeling sorry for the girl now.

'She ain't getting any better, is she?' Susan whispered worriedly, as they made their way to the laundry with the dirty washing.

'No, I have to say she doesn't appear to be. But what more can we do for her? Even the doctor can't figure out what's wrong with her.'

They carried the washing into the laundry room and dumped it into the deep stone sink. A woman from the outskirts of town came in twice a week to do the washing now and they had certainly kept her busy recently.

'Did you hear the ruckus outside again last night?' Susan asked then and Pearl shook her head.

'Master Monty and some chap were having a right old row.' Susan grinned. She was no fan of Monty either. 'It were probably another of his gamblin' buddies that he owes money to. Somebody's goin' to knock his block off one o' these days, you just see if they don't!'

There was no time for them to talk more, though, as Will had come back with the supplies and Pearl liked to put them away herself so that she could keep stock of what they were growing short of. Thankfully it had stopped snowing some days before, but now that the thaw had set in, they were presented with other problems, and many houses and businesses in the town were flooded. The river was also dangerously high once again and had burst its banks in places, sweeping away livestock and any unfortunate wildlife that was in its way. People had been warned to keep well away from the water as no one would stand a chance of surviving if they were to slip into it.

The following week was a worrying time as Freda continued to get worse with each day that passed despite everyone's efforts.

'The poor lamb is so young,' Cook sniffed tearfully following a visit by the doctor one day. 'Surely there must be *something* we can do to help her!'

'Only what we're already doing.' Pearl was now taking it in turns with Eliza and Susan to sit with her – and even Mrs

Forbes took a turn now and again. She was so ill that they didn't dare to leave her on her own, even throughout the night.

And then almost a week later when Pearl and Susan had changed the bed for the second time that day, Freda's tortured breathing suddenly stopped and they knew that she was gone.

Susan had never been in the presence of death before and backed away from the bed with tears streaming down her cheeks and her hand clamped across her mouth.

'Oh, my dear God . . . she's gone ain't she?'

'I think so.' Pearl crossed to her and felt for the pulse in her wrist, but there was nothing. 'You'd better run down and get Will to fetch the doctor.'

Only too glad to escape, Susan took to her heels as Pearl gazed sadly down on Freda. She couldn't pretend that they had ever been friends or even that she had liked the girl, but for her to die like this at such a tender age was tragic; they'd been through so much together over the years that Pearl truly felt the loss.

Cook was absolutely distraught when she heard of her passing and sobbed uncontrollably. She had been the only person in the house who had liked Freda and she would miss her.

Freda was laid to rest in the churchyard three days later with only the people from the house and Mrs Briggs, their former teacher and travelling companion, to mourn her. It was a wickedly cold day, with rain lashing down like sharp little needles and once the service was over, they were glad to get back to the warmth of the house.

'I shall have to look for another girl to take her place,' Mrs Forbes informed Pearl, and true to her word the following week she employed another girl fresh from England who had arrived on one of the orphan ships the week before.

Sally Stuart was a mouse of a girl who looked as if a good puff of wind would blow her over. She was tiny with light-brown hair and grey eyes, but she soon proved to be a good worker and by the time they were into April, things were beginning to return to normal.

At least they were for the rest of the household – but Pearl now had grave concerns and was beginning to wonder if her life would ever be normal again. She had missed her third course and was slowly beginning to make herself accept the fact that she might be carrying Monty's child. Her breasts were tender and sore and she knew what morning sickness meant; she had seen her mother go through it many times and each time it had resulted in a baby. She was sick with fear and worry, because if her suspicions were correct it would mean she and Eliza would likely be thrown out, and then what would happen to them? She had nowhere near enough money to get them a passage back to England and worse still Nick could be back any time now. What was she going to tell him? It would be bad enough having to end their relationship without him knowing that she was carry-ing another man's child. But how much longer could she hide it? she wondered. Up to now her stomach was still flat but she was bound to start showing soon and then what? Already Cook was eyeing her with suspicion when she had to keep rushing out to the toilet to be sick, but fortunately she hadn't said anything as yet.

Things finally came to a head early one morning when she returned from the outside toilet to find Cook and Eliza in the kitchen.

Cook was turning plump mushrooms in a large frying pan and glancing at Pearl she said casually, 'Been sick again, have you?'

Pearl blushed to the roots of her hair. 'I, er . . . think I must have picked up a little bug.'

'Oh yes?' Cook turned to Eliza, telling her, 'Go and set the table in the dining room like I showed you, there's a good girl. Your sister looks a little off colour.'

Eliza scowled but went to do as she was bid, and the second they were alone, Cook raised an eyebrow. 'So . . . is there something you want to tell me, lass? I wasn't born yesterday, you know.'

'I-I don't know what you mean.'

Cook shook her head as she loaded the mushrooms on to a plate and wiped her hands on her apron. 'Oh, but I think you do. When is the baby due? Your Nick left you with a bellyful, has he?'

Pearl's mouth gaped before she snapped indignantly, 'No, he did *not*. Nick is a gentleman and it's not hi—' Realising she had made a terrible blunder, she began to chew on her lip.

Cook nodded knowingly. 'I thought as much. But if it's not Nick's, then whose is it?'

Suddenly the need to confide in someone was too much and tears tumbled down her cheeks as the whole sorry tale came out. Pearl had hoped that telling someone would help her come to terms with what had happened to her, but if anything it only made her feel worse and soon she was sobbing uncontrollably.

'The dirty young bugger!' Cook ground out. 'And to think that he did that to you in this very room. Why, I've a good mind to take a whip to him.' Cook's arms went around her and Pearl leaned into her as she sobbed.

It was only when Eliza came back into the room that the two women broke apart.

'So what's goin' on?' she asked in a surly voice.

After glancing at Pearl, Cook decided to tell her. It wasn't as if Pearl was going to be able to hide it for much longer after all.

'It's your sister. She's . . . Well, the truth of it is Master Monty has . . . he's taken her down.'

'Taken her down?' Eliza stared blankly from one to another, not quite understanding what Cook was saying.

'Yes . . . what I mean is . . . he's taken her against her will, and she's going to have his baby now.'

A dull red colour crept into the girl's cheeks as her hands clenched into fists. 'It ain't true,' she declared, as she shook her head in denial. 'Monty wouldn't touch our Pearl. It's me he loves!'

Cook was so shocked that she plonked down heavily on to the nearest chair. This was a fine kettle of fish and no mistake, but how were they going to resolve it?

Pearl was the first to break the stunned silence when she told her sister gently. 'It *is* true, Eliza, I *swear* it.'

Eliza's finger was trembling as she wagged it towards her. 'You're a lying *bitch*! I'm going to find Monty and he'll deny it, I know he will. You only want him because he loves *me*!'

'B-but I don't want him. I've *never* wanted him.'

Seeing that this was about to erupt into a full-scale row, Cook suddenly rose and told them heatedly, '*Stop it* this minute, the pair of you! Now isn't the time to discuss what we're going to do; we have a meal to get in to the family, so I suggest we all get on with it. We'll talk again this evening when everyone has gone to bed.'

Pearl lifted a dish and carried it off into the dining room while Eliza went to the sink where she began to scrub so hard at the dirty pots that Cook was sure she'd wear a hole in them, but at least she was quiet, which Cook supposed was something to be grateful for.

For the rest of the day, the atmosphere in the kitchen was strained and Eliza refused to so much as look in Pearl's direction, although Cook did manage to snatch a few minutes alone with Pearl later in the afternoon.

'We need to think about the best way to tell the mistress about this,' she told Pearl worriedly. 'But there's no need to do anything just yet. Sometimes . . . Well, nature has a way of dealing with things and it's still early days yet. How far on do you think you are?'

'I've missed three courses.' Pearl looked so miserable that Cook gave her hand a squeeze.

'God knows what the mistress is going to say, but don't worry. I'll back you up.'

Much later that evening, Pearl made her way to bed to find Eliza sobbing into her pillow and her heart went out to her.

'I'm so sorry about this . . .' she began.

Eliza rounded on her, her eyes flashing. 'No you're *not* sorry at all,' she spat. 'Everybody always likes you better than me, even Monty, and it's not fair.'

'But that isn't true.'

'Just don't go thinking he'll do the right thing by you and put a ring on your finger because he *won't*,' Eliza sneered.

'I wouldn't want him to!' Pearl turned her back and began to undress. 'In fact, I'll never marry anyone now,' she said with a catch in her voice, and then she climbed into bed and extinguished the candle as an uneasy silence descended between them, and eventually they fell asleep.

Chapter Thirty-Four

The sound of Will's raised voice woke them both very early the next morning and Pearl tumbled out of bed and dragged her clothes on, wondering what could possibly be wrong, before rushing downstairs to find Will speaking to the master in the kitchen.

It was still dark, but even in the gloom Pearl could see that Mr Forbes, who was wearing his dressing robe, was as pale as lint, while Will was standing by the back door as if to prevent the man leaving the room.

Scrubbing the sleep from her eyes Pearl asked, 'Whatever's wrong?'

Will was clearly shaken and she saw that his hands were trembling. 'It's Master Monty . . . he's lying outside . . . and I think he may be dead. We need to fetch the doctor.'

At that moment Emmaline Forbes, also in her dressing robe, appeared looking anxious. 'What's all the commotion about?'

Her husband instantly went to her and, pressing her back towards the door, he urged, 'You go back up to bed, darling. I'll handle it.'

'Handle what?' She pushed his hands from her arms and asked again, 'What's happened?'

'I-it's Monty . . . he's injured and Will is just going to go for the doctor now.'

'What do you mean – *injured*? Where is he?'

They could all see the panic on her face.

'He's lying outside, ma'am, but I wouldn't go out there if I were you,' Will warned.

'Then we must carry him in.' Completely ignoring his advice, she made for the back door and Will flew into a panic.

'No, *please* . . . don't go out there . . .' His words trailed away as she shouldered past him and she was off out of the door like a shot from a gun.

As her husband made to follow her a scream rent the air and Will lowered his head. Monty was not a pretty sight.

Seconds later Mr Forbes half dragged and half carried his hysterical wife back into the kitchen and snapped at Will, 'For God's sake, run for the doctor – *NOW*!' Yet already he knew that his son was beyond any doctor's help and what he had just seen would haunt him till his dying day. Mrs Forbes's robe was soaked with blood and mud and her hair was plastered to her head from just the few seconds she had spent out in the rain that was lashing down and bouncing off the ground.

Taking a deep breath, Will sprinted for the door and disappeared into the darkness.

Susan, Sally and Cook had appeared by that time, also in their nightclothes, and with her hair encased in a nightcap, Cook looked a comical sight.

'Eeh! What's all the to-do about? The shouting were enough to waken the dead,' she grumbled as she moved towards the table to light the lamp.

'It . . . It's Monty . . . something's happened to him,' Pearl explained just as Eliza too appeared. At Pearl's words, her sister's face drained of colour and she leapt towards the back door before Pearl could stop her. Pearl had no choice but to follow her, but she stopped abruptly and stifled a scream as she saw Eliza fling herself across what was left of Monty. He was lying on his back in the mud in a pool of blood, his eyes staring sightlessly up into the dawn sky, but that wasn't the worst of it. It was evident he must have been lying there for some long time, because during the night creatures had attacked and feasted on his body.

Pearl swallowed and, leaning to one side, she was heartily sick, as Eliza's wailing echoed around the yard. Pearl had never seen anything so gruesome in her whole life and prayed that she never would again as Cook appeared to drag Eliza back into the kitchen. Then, taking control of the situation, she snatched the cloth from the table and rushed back outside again to throw it across the corpse.

'W-we should try to get him inside,' Pearl suggested in a wobbly voice.

Cook shook her head. 'There's nowt we can do for him now, lass. We'd best leave that to the men.' She set about filling the kettle. From the poor mistress's screams that were still issuing along the hallway it was clear that she was in need of a good strong cup of sweet tea, not that Cook held out much hope of that calming her. The doctor would have to give her something stronger. Cook shook her head as she choked back tears. Poor soul, first she had lost sweet little Miss Elizabeth and now her son. *How would she survive this latest tragedy?* she wondered.

Eliza was sitting at the table with her head on her arm sobbing broken-heartedly, but when Pearl went to comfort her, she rounded on her like a wild animal. 'Don't you *dare* touch me! This is all your fault.'

'B-but . . .'

Eliza rose so suddenly that the chair she'd been sitting on crashed to the floor, and without another word she fled with tears pouring down her cheeks.

'Let her go, pet,' Cook advised as Pearl made to follow her and she obediently sank down on to the settle at the side of the fire.

Susan made a large pot of tea and was just pouring it when Will and the doctor appeared and rushed straight out to the yard.

'As you thought, he is dead,' the doctor said gravely, feeling quite queasy himself. 'And I would think he's been there for most of the night. It looks suspiciously like someone hit him on the back of the head and possibly knocked him out, but until I examine him properly it's hard to say now that the wolves have . . .' As his voice trailed away, they all shuddered. 'Anyway, I think the best thing we can do is to inform the police and then I'll do a proper examination at the undertaker's. I shall recommend a closed coffin if the mistress wants him to come home before the funeral. He isn't a pretty sight, I'm afraid.'

Will's chin sank to his chest as he shook his head. 'Like most places around here I've been having problems with the wolves and rats in the stables for some time, but I really didn't hear anything last night. If only I had I might have been able to . . .'

'You mustn't blame yourself, Will,' the doctor told him kindly, as he gratefully took the tea Susan offered. He was used to seeing death – it was a natural progression of life – but he had never before seen anything as horrendous as the face he had just seen, or what was left of it.

'I don't suppose you have a drop of something stronger to top this up, do you?' he asked Cook.

She nodded and fetched a bottle of brandy from the cupboard on the dresser and sloshed a generous measure into his cup, before doing the same for her own. She had never seen the doctor touch a drink in all the years she had known him, but then these were extenuating circumstances.

'Ah, that's better,' Dr Lark said when he had drained his cup. 'I'll just go through to your master and mistress and give them something to calm them down, poor devils. And don't worry, after what Will told me I guessed there would be nothing I could do and I asked the undertaker to bring his hearse before I came. He should be here any minute now. In the meantime, I would advise you all to stay indoors until the body has been removed.'

Pearl was only too happy to do as she was told, and as the doctor went to tend to Mr and Mrs Forbes, she hurried up the steep, narrow staircase to check on Eliza. There was no sign of her upstairs and Pearl bit her lip, wondering what she should do. Her first instinct was to put her cape on and go and search for her but she decided against it. Eliza clearly wanted to be alone and she would respect her wishes, unless she was away for too long, that was.

Soon after, the undertaker and his assistant arrived with the hearse, and the black stallion that pulled it stood patiently as they loaded Monty's body on to the back and pulled away. Mrs Forbes's screams and sobs were still echoing through the house and everything began to take on an air of unreality as they all sat about in the kitchen. There would clearly be no breakfast needed this morning.

'I bet you any money it was one of the chaps he owed money to who did for him,' Cook said shakily, as she sipped at yet another cup of tea liberally laced with brandy; she felt in need of it. She had known for some long time that the young master was a nasty piece of work, but even so she had known him all his life and it was hard to believe that he was dead. 'But fancy leaving him lying there like that for the wolves to—' She gulped and took another swallow of her drink as Pearl glanced worriedly towards the door, praying for Eliza to come home.

'Do you think they'll involve the police?' Susan piped up.

Cook nodded. 'Oh yes, no doubt about it. I just hope that all those he owed money to have got good alibis else it might be a case of God help them. We haven't had a hanging here for a long time but . . .'

They stopped talking as Mrs Forbes's screams ceased abruptly and seconds later Dr Lark appeared in the doorway again.

'I've given Mrs Forbes a very strong sedative,' he told them gravely. 'But her state of mind is very fragile so it might be as well if she isn't left on her own for the next few days. I shall call in again this evening after surgery but should you need me before then please send Will for me and I will come immediately. Good day, ladies.'

They inclined their heads and looked at each other. With their routine completely disrupted, they had no idea what they should do.

It was Pearl who eventually broke the silence. 'I'm going to get some clean dry clothes for the mistress and see if I can change her; she was soaked through when she came in and the last thing we need is for her to be ill too,' she told them. 'Could you bring a bowl of warm water and a towel into the drawing room for me please, Sally?'

Sally nodded and hurried to the sink, as Pearl headed for the drawing room. She found Mrs Forbes lying on the settee in a semi-conscious state and her husband sitting in the chair opposite with his elbows on his knees and his head sunk in his hands.

'I, er . . . thought I'd try and get the mistress out of her wet clothes, sir.' Pearl hovered uncertainly, ready to run if he told her to clear off, but he merely nodded numbly and, rising from his seat, walked unsteadily from the room. He too was in shock, but there was little Pearl could do for him.

The police were the next to arrive and they questioned each of them in turn, apart from Eliza who was still missing.

'Did you hear anything untoward last night? Did you hear young Mr Forbes cry out? Did . . .' The questions went on and they all answered them mechanically, wishing they had heard something. Perhaps they could have prevented this tragedy if they had. And then at last the back door opened and Eliza returned, wet and bedraggled.

'You'd better go up and get changed, the police will want to speak to you,' Pearl told her gently, and without a word her sister went to do as she was told.

When the doctor returned that evening, he was able to inform them that he thought it was the blow to the back of the head that had killed Monty. It wasn't good news, but it was better than knowing that he had been alive when the wolves attacked him. 'The police are questioning everyone who knew him. I'm sure they'll get the murderer,' he said gravely, before going through to attend to Mrs Forbes. She had lain in the drawing room all day without saying a word.

At Mr Forbes's request, Pearl wrote a letter to Mrs Forbes's parents in London informing them of their grandson's death and the next morning she took it to the post office. From there it would sail on the first ship to leave the port. Eliza still hadn't said so much as one single word to her, and Pearl left her alone to grieve in her own way.

The funeral was arranged for three days' time and Cook was glad to have something to do again as she began to prepare the food for the wake. The Forbeses were very well respected in the town and she was expecting a good turnout, although how Monty's poor mother was going to get through it, she had no idea. She seemed to be locked away in a world where no one could reach her and they were all tiptoeing about the house like ghosts, afraid to disturb her.

The police arrived to give Mr Forbes an update daily, but as yet no arrests had been made and the longer it went on, the more doubtful it was that they would ever catch who had done it.

'Everyone he knew that we've spoken to have had cast-iron alibis for that evening,' the constable told him with a shake of his head.

Numb with grief, Monty's father could only nod. He was suffering all manner of guilt now for he and Monty had never had the best of relationships. In fact, he had always had a suspicion that Monty had had a hand in his little sister's death. Monty had been jealous of Elizabeth and had resented her from the day she was born. But now he wished he had tried a little harder with him. Perhaps he shouldn't have pushed him so hard to work in the businesses? Perhaps he should have shown him a little more affection? But it was too late to make amends now, and he daily whipped himself for what he saw as his failings.

And then all too soon, it was time for the funeral – an event every parent prays they will never see. It was a dark, dismal, day to match their moods and Pearl helped Mrs Forbes into her black mourning clothes as the woman stood mute, her eyes dull and staring, before leading her downstairs to where a carriage pulled by two magnificent jet-black stallions with black plumes on their heads was waiting to take her and the master to the church.

The second it pulled away from the door, everyone ran about laying out the magnificent banquet Cook had slaved over, and preparing the cups and saucers for when the mourners returned. In no time, the house seemed to be bursting at the seams as people stood about eating and drinking and talking in hushed voices. But at last, as darkness fell, the final mourners departed and the staff breathed sighs of relief.

'Phew, I'm glad that's over,' Cook remarked, as she sank into the chair at the side of the kitchen fire and kicked her slippers off. 'Me feet are killing me and I'm having a nice cup o' tea before I do anythin' else. Put the kettle on, Sally, there's a good lass. And all of you lot have one, too. The clearing up can wait for a bit.'

Soon they all sat sipping tea. It had been a terrible day. If truth be told, none of them had had a lot of time for Monty – he had never had time for them, after all, except to treat them all as menials – but they felt heartsore for the poor master and mistress.

'I reckon the mistress brought a lot of this about,' Cook confided to Pearl. 'She always spoiled him and let him have his own way, but then I suppose that's what mothers do. Never having had any of me own, I'm no expert on the matter.'

Pearl nodded as she glanced at Eliza. Not one word had she spoken to her since the morning they had found Monty's body lying in the yard, despite all Pearl's efforts to draw her into conversation. The last few days had been horrendous for everyone, but the funeral was over and once more Pearl was forced to think of her predicament. Monty might be gone but his child was growing inside her, and the thought of it filled her with dread as she wondered what the mistress would say when she found out. Her hand subconsciously dropped to her stomach as she chewed on her lip. One thing was for sure, she wouldn't be able to put off telling her for much longer. It was a daunting thought.

Chapter Thirty-Five

In May, the weather finally changed for the better and at last spring was in the air after all the long cold months of rain and snow. Tender green buds began to unfurl on the trees and spring flowers pushed through the earth. Suddenly Pearl's waistbands were growing a little tight and one morning as she cleared the dining room table, Cook said quietly, 'You're going to have to tell the mistress about the bairn soon, hinny. You'll not be able to hide it much longer.'

Ignoring the look of contempt that Eliza was flashing her, Pearl nodded. 'I know, Mrs Drew; I've been meaning to but after what's happened I need to pick the right time.'

Susan burst through the back door then, beaming from ear to ear, and dumped the basket of shopping she had just fetched for Cook on to the table. 'I think I've got some news that will make you smile,' she told a bemused Pearl. 'I've just heard in the hardware shop that the ship Nick is on is due into port today.'

Pearl leaned heavily on the edge of the table as the colour drained from her face, and Susan frowned. 'B-but I thought you'd be pleased.'

'I-I would have been not so long ago.' Pearl's voice came out as a squeak. 'But I, er . . . I've decided that we're too young to think of settling down yet awhile.'

'*Really?*' Susan was amazed. 'But I thought you loved each other.'

'I did too, but you can't get it right all the time and I've changed my mind.' Pearl forced a smile and hoped that Susan wouldn't notice how her hands were shaking. Without another word, she left the room as Susan stared after her.

She found Mrs Forbes sitting in her seat by the window, gazing blankly out, just as she did each and every day now. She rarely spoke anymore and even when she did her voice was dull and lifeless.

Pearl's heart was thumping so loudly that she was sure her mistress would hear it. Nick was home! She would have to tell him that it was over between them now. Better that than see the look of contempt on his face when he eventually found out that she was carrying someone else's child.

'It's time for your medication, ma'am,' she told her mistress gently, but when she brought it to her with a spoon, Mrs Forbes pushed it away.

'Don't want it! It makes me tired.'

'But the doctor said—'

'I don't *want* it,' the woman repeated stubbornly, so with a sigh Pearl placed it down and quietly left the room. She could hardly pour it down her throat, after all, and perhaps it was a good sign that she didn't want to be drugged up anymore?

She hurried upstairs to snatch a few quiet moments to herself as she tried to think of what she could say to Nick. The thought of hurting him was tearing her apart but what else could she do? Far better for him to sail away not knowing what had happened. At least then he stood a chance of meeting someone who deserved him.

The rest of the day dragged by painfully slowly and as usual the mistress retired early, leaving Pearl free to do as she chose. The master and mistress rarely ate together in the dining room anymore, which meant a lot less work for the staff. The mistress usually had a tray sent up to her room, which almost always came back untouched, and the master had started to eat out. Pearl couldn't blame him. There was no laughter or joy in the house anymore, so who could blame him for staying out of it as much as he could? Now was her ideal opportunity to go and meet Nick and let him down as gently as she could, and yet when it came to it, she found that she couldn't do it.

I'll go and tell him tomorrow, she promised herself as she wearily climbed the stairs to her room.

Eliza was out, but then since the weather had improved, she often went for a walk by the river in the evening. Pearl wasn't entirely happy about it, knowing how dangerous the river could be should anyone slip into it, but Eliza was a big girl now and she was no longer able to tell her what to do. With a sigh, she slipped out of her dress and lay on the bed, listening to the sound of birdsong through the open window as she thought of Nick and what might have been.

Eliza meantime was walking purposely towards the town with a grim expression on her face. She knew that when Nick was ashore, he would normally come to meet Pearl and she hoped that he would this evening. Sure enough, within minutes of setting off she spotted a figure striding towards her. It was Nick and she smiled with satisfaction. It was time to get her revenge for what she considered to be her sister's betrayal.

'Hello, Eliza,' he greeted her cheerily. 'Are you well? I was just coming to meet Pearl.' He was carrying a large bunch of flowers and looked happy and healthy.

'Oh!' Eliza put on a suitably tragic expression. 'Then I-I'm afraid you've had a wasted journey.'

'Really?' He frowned. 'She isn't ill, is she?'

Eliza shook her head setting her blonde curls bobbing. 'No . . . but . . . well, you've probably heard about Master Monty being murdered? It was a few weeks ago and the police still haven't caught his killer. It's looking highly unlikely that they ever will now and—'

'Look, just tell me where Pearl is,' Nick butted in impatiently.

Eliza pursed her lips. 'The thing is, Pearl left soon after he died. She went on a ship back to England and none of us have heard from her since. To be honest, I think she and Monty had something going between them and once he was gone, she couldn't bear to stay here. She asked me to tell you the next time you came back and to say sorry for her.'

'*No!*' Nick stared at her in stunned disbelief. It couldn't be true. He and Pearl were promised to each other.

But then common sense kicked in and his shoulders sagged as the flowers slipped from his hand to land in the dust. Why would Eliza lie to him? She had no reason to and everyone knew what a lady's man Monty had been. Perhaps he had wooed Pearl after he sailed the last time and she had fallen for his charms? If so, she couldn't have cared for him that much. She hadn't even bothered to leave him a letter.

Eliza reached out to touch him, but with his eyes dangerously moist, he backed away. 'Then if that's the case I shall sail on *The Dolphin* with the tide tomorrow. I was planning to be here for a while but there's no point in staying now. I should still have time to sign on if I get straight back.'

'I'm so sorry, Nick,' Eliza muttered, her eyes downcast.

He nodded. 'Aye, and so am I, Eliza. Goodbye.' And with that he turned and strode away, his shoulders slumped.

Once he had gone, Eliza picked up the flowers and shaking the dust and the loose petals from them, she turned back to the house with a spiteful grin on her face. That had been so much easier than she had thought it would be. But she hadn't finished with Pearl yet, not by a long shot, and by the time she had, her sister was going to wish she had never been born.

Suddenly changing direction, she struck out for the church and once she had passed through the lychgate she picked her way through the tombstones until she came to Monty's grave. The mistress was having a fine marble headstone carved for him but until it was ready a simple wooden cross marked his resting place. As she stared down at the bare earth, it was hard to believe that the young man she had adored was laid there.

'I miss you so much,' she whispered as tears streamed down her cheeks. 'And don't worry, I shall make sure Pearl is punished for all the lies she's told about you. I realise now that it must have been her tempting you and I forgive you for what you did.'

She gently laid the flowers down and, with her heart breaking, turned and slowly trudged back to the house.

'Oh, you're back then. Did you have a nice walk?' Pearl gave her sister a weak smile as she entered their room but Eliza ignored her. Pearl's eyes were swollen from crying but Eliza didn't even seem to notice. 'Look, can't we be friends again?' Pearl implored. 'This is getting silly now. Neither of us can change what's happened and we are still sisters. We should stick together.'

But her words appeared to fall on deaf ears as Eliza quickly undressed, climbed into bed and turned her back on her. With a sigh, Pearl stared towards the window and as she thought of Nick, so close and yet so far away, the tears started again. *I've been a coward*, she thought miserably. *He at least deserves to know the truth of what's happened and I shall go into town first thing in the morning and tell him.* Feeling slightly better now that she had reached a decision, she eventually fell into an uneasy sleep where once again she dreamed that she was on the kitchen floor with Monty raping her.

She woke drenched with sweat in a tangle of damp sheets and sobbed with relief when she realised that it had only been a nightmare. But now there was no time to lose. She would go and see to Mrs Forbes's needs and get straight off into town.

The poor woman was lethargic with no energy whatsoever. It seemed to be an effort for her to just help Pearl to get her dressed and it took twice as long as it should have. But at last she was ready and Pearl asked, 'Will you be wanting any breakfast, ma'am?' Mr Forbes would already have had his and be on his way to work by now.

'No, thank you, perhaps I could just have a tray of tea sent up?'

'Of course.' Pearl hurried away to fetch it as Mrs Forbes sank into the chair by the window where she could watch the garden. She seemed to spend much of her time there now.

Soon after Pearl was back with the tray to tell her cheerfully, 'Here's your tea, ma'am. And I've brought you some nice buttered toast as well. Perhaps you might fancy just a little bite or two? You really must start to eat more.'

She placed it within reach of her but got no response from the woman, so she crept from the room and within minutes was heading down the drive after telling Cook, 'I shall be back as soon as I can; I have to go into town.'

'Aye, all right, lass.'

Pearl failed to notice the smirk on her sister's face as she left the room.

Once in town, Pearl headed for the hotel where Nick always stayed and after approaching the desk, she told the receptionist, 'I'm here to see Nicholas Willis. Could you tell me which room he is in, please?'

The woman opened the book that lay on the desk and after running her finger down a list of names she looked up and informed her, 'Ah yes, I remember now. I'm afraid Mr Willis checked out a few hours ago. He only stayed the one night.'

Pearl shook her head. 'B-but there must be some mistake. He only arrived yesterday.'

The woman nodded in agreement. 'So he did, but he said that he was sailing out again on *The Dolphin* this morning.'

Without waiting to hear any more, Pearl lifted her skirts and raced down the street in a most unladylike manner until she emerged on to the docks where she paused to look around and get her breath back. There were a number of ships either loading or unloading cargo and after a time she rushed up to a burly sailor and, catching his arm, she asked him breathlessly, 'Please – can you tell me which of these ships is *The Dolphin*.'

'I certainly can – that's her there, look.' Raising his finger, he pointed out to sea, where Pearl could just make out a ship on the horizon. She was too late! Nick had sailed without her even being able to explain what had happened.

'Oh! Thank you.'

Tears sliding down her cheeks, she turned and retraced her steps. Why hadn't Nick come to find her? And why had he left again so soon? Could it be that he had tired of her? She could think of no other explanation. But then common sense kicked in and she realised that if this was the case, it was probably for the best. At least she wouldn't have to worry about breaking his heart now. It was too late for hers; it was already broken.

Chapter Thirty-Six

'You really must speak to the mistress soon, pet,' Cook urged Pearl again one sunny morning early in June. 'You're beginning to really show and I've no doubt if she wasn't still in mourning, she'd have noticed before now. As it is the poor soul barely seems to know what day it is.' She shook her head sadly. She hated to see her mistress so low. 'I know the master is gravely concerned about her. She's all but shut herself away but there's nothing we can do till she's ready to face folks again. She isn't even entertaining visitors anymore.'

'I know I have to.' Pearl's expression was thoroughly miserable as she looked at Cook's beloved chickens pecking outside in the yard. 'It's just that I hate to add to her troubles.'

Cook shrugged her plump shoulders. 'Well, it can't be put off forever, hinny.'

Eliza, who was washing dirty pots at the sink, glared towards her and Pearl's heart sank even more. Eliza never even spoke to her now apart from when she had to, and this, added to the gloomy atmosphere in the house, was getting her down.

'You'll need to think about what's to be done with the bairn once it's arrived an' all,' Cook went on as she measured flour on to the table for the pastry she was about to make. She was doing the master his favourite steak and kidney pudding for his dinner, not that he was eating much nowadays. 'Are you intending to keep it?'

Without hesitation, Pearl shook her head. She hated what was growing inside her with a vengeance and knew that she would never love the child. How could she when it was a result of rape? No, she decided, she would have to go to see Mrs Briggs and arrange for it to be admitted to the home. There were always childless couples who would adopt a baby and so she had no doubt Mrs Briggs would find it a home. There were times when she wanted to tear open her stomach and rip it out of her, but of course that couldn't happen and with each day that passed, as her stomach grew, she hated the tiny being inside her a little bit more. On top of that, she was still mourning the life she might have had with Nick and was wishing that she had stayed in the workhouse back in London. If she had, maybe none of this sorry mess would have happened.

'The doctor was saying when he came to check on the mistress yesterday that he still isn't happy about the way Mrs Veasey and Freda died,' Cook commented as she kneaded the pastry into a ball. 'He says if it was some sort of virus that it's funny none of the rest of us got it as well. Still, there's nowt to be done about it now, God rest their souls. I reckon this house has seen enough heartbreak in the last few months to last a lifetime. But still' – she smiled then – 'at least there's one bright spot on the horizon. Have you noticed how well Susan and Will are getting on? They went out for a walk together again last night and I wouldn't be surprised if we didn't hear wedding bells soon. Not before time either. Will's young wife, Esme, was a lovely little lass, but as I told him, he can't mourn her forever. Life is for the living and he could do a lot worse than young Susan. There might be a bit of an age gap a'tween them, but what does that matter if they love each other? You should take your happiness where you can, that's what I say.'

Pearl gave a wry smile. Perhaps Cook should have listened to her own advice after she had lost her husband, but she never had.

At that moment the bell above the door tinkled and Pearl hurried to the door. 'I'll just go and see what the mistress wants. Hopefully she'll be ready for something to eat.'

'Aye, and pigs might fly,' Cook snorted, for up to now all the tasty titbits she had lovingly cooked for her had been sent back to the kitchen untouched. 'And don't forget what I said,' she reminded Pearl.

Pearl nodded. She knew Cook was right so perhaps now would be a good time to make her confession?

She found Mrs Forbes sitting in her usual place in the chair by her bedroom window and asked, 'Is there something I can get for you to eat, ma'am? Or perhaps you feel well enough to get dressed?'

Mrs Forbes shook her head. 'No, just some tea, if you would please, Pearl?'

'Of course, straight away.' Pearl hesitated for a moment then with her hands tightly pressed into her waist, she plucked up the courage to do as Cook had advised. 'And perhaps if you feel up to it, I might have a word with you?'

The mistress looked towards her with dull eyes. 'Yes, what is it, Pearl?'

The words that needed to be said stuck in Pearl's throat and beads of sweat had broken out on her forehead, but after taking a deep breath she managed to blurt out, 'The thing is . . . I-I'm going to have a baby.'

For the first time since Master Monty had died, the mistress seemed to come out of her trance-like state as her head whipped around to stare at Pearl. *'You're what?'*

Pearl bowed her head as shame washed over her. 'I'm going to have a baby.'

There was silence for a time until Mrs Forbes finally asked, 'Have you told your young man? Is he prepared to stand by you?'

'The baby isn't his,' Pearl answered dully, and now she really did have her mistress's attention.

'Then whose is it?'

Pearl gulped. 'A few months ago . . . I was raped.' There, it was said – but how could she tell the woman that it was her son who had raped her?

Mrs Forbes looked horrified. 'But why haven't you said anything before? We could have had the culprit brought to justice. And how far along are you?'

'I think the baby will be born sometime in September . . . but don't worry. I'm going to see Mrs Briggs now. I'm going to ask her to arrange an adoption for me.'

'I see. And who did you say the father was? Does he know that you're with child?'

'He . . . he isn't here anymore, ma'am, and so no, he doesn't know. He'll never know.'

Pearl waited with bated breath for Mrs Forbes to tell her she was dismissed, but instead the woman suddenly said softly, 'It would be nice to have a baby in the house again after all the sadness we've had to endure. Are you *quite* sure that you wish to give it away, Pearl?'

Pearl was so shocked at this reaction that for a moment she was rendered temporarily speechless, but then she said in a croaky voice, 'I'm *very* sure. I couldn't possibly contemplate keeping it after . . .'

Unable to go on, she hastily knuckled a tear from her cheek as her employer continued to stare at her thoughtfully. This was not the reaction she had expected at all, and she didn't know what to make of it.

'Very well. Do go about your work and let me think about this.'

Heart hammering, Pearl bobbed her knee and fled to fetch Mrs Forbes her tea.

The instant she entered the kitchen, Cook saw how upset she was and asked, 'So you took my advice and told her then?'

Pearl nodded numbly as Eliza turned from the sink with a smirk on her face.

'An' has she chucked you out on your ear?' she asked spitefully.

'Not as yet but I dare say she will when she's had time to think of it,' Pearl muttered miserably, as she prepared a tea tray.

'Well, you've only yourself to blame.' There was not a trace of sympathy in her sister's voice and it was like a stab in the heart to Pearl. 'If you hadn't flaunted yourself at him and flirted, he'd never have looked at you twice,' she said with vitriol. 'Monty told me it was *me* he loved!'

'Aye, you and a few dozen other lasses,' Cook said scathingly. She could see how upset Pearl was. 'Now get back to work, girl, and keep your caustic comments to yourself else you'll feel the back of me hand. Things are bad enough without you adding your two'pennorth!'

In a sulk, Eliza turned back to the sink. With shaking fingers, Pearl carried the tray up to her mistress.

'Do you know, Pearl, I think I will get dressed after all,' the mistress told her as she placed the tray down. 'I think I'd like to have a word with my husband when he comes home for lunch. Get my black gown out for me, would you?'

'Yes, ma'am.' Pearl went to the armoire and lifted out the gown that Mrs Forbes had worn for her son's funeral, and once she had helped her to dress, she brushed her hair into a neat chignon on the back of her head. She was appalled to see how much weight the woman had lost. The gown hung slackly on her now but it was nice to see her making the effort to be dressed again at least. Mrs Forbes added pearl earrings and a matching strand of pearls to her ensemble, and then on legs that were weakened by weeks of lying or sitting down, she made her shaky way down to the drawing room, instructing Pearl to bring the tray of tea with her.

'You say she's up and about?' Cook was delighted when Pearl told her. 'Well, the master will be pleased when he gets back. Poor man has been worried sick about her but let's hope this is the start of her recovery. And did you tell her whose baby it was?'

As Pearl hung her head Cook had her answer and she sighed with exasperation. 'But *why* didn't you tell her?' She looked annoyed. 'None of this was your fault.'

'I couldn't bring myself to in case she didn't believe me,' Pearl admitted.

With a snort Cook took off her apron and flung it across the back of a chair, then patting her mob cap she made for the door. 'Then if you won't tell her, I will!' she declared. 'Just 'cause Monty has gone don't make him a saint, and she needs to know. Once she tells the master the condition you're in, he'll have you out of here like a shot from a gun and it ain't fair! They both need to know that this is their grandchild you're carrying.'

She found the mistress in the drawing room and the woman gave her a smile as she entered. She was very fond of the cook and always made time to have a word with her.

'It's nice to see you,' Mrs Forbes told her, patting the seat beside her. 'What can I do for you, Mrs Drew, dear?'

Cook tentatively perched on the edge of the seat like a rabbit about to take flight. 'Well, the thing is, I know Pearl just told you about her predicament, but there's something else I think you should know.'

Quietly, she went on to tell her story to Mrs Forbes, and when she was done the woman's eyes were stretched wide.

'Are you quite, quite, sure about this?'

Cook gave a vigorous nod. 'Oh yes, ma'am. Pearl ain't the sort of girl to go telling lies and I saw her the morning after it had happened. In a rare old state, she was.'

'Then you have done right in telling me.' Mrs Forbes was clearly shaken, but she managed a weak smile. 'Thank you,

Cook. Please leave it with me. I shall have to discuss with my husband what we're going to do about it.'

With a nod, the portly woman made her way back to the kitchen, happy that she had done the right thing.

That afternoon when Mr Forbes came home for his lunch, as he did each day now to check on his wife, he was delighted to find her up, dressed and waiting for him.

'Darling, what a wonderful surprise.' He instantly crossed to her and dropped an affectionate kiss on her forehead. 'It's so lovely to see you up and about again and—' He stopped talking abruptly as he saw the expression on her face before asking, 'But there's nothing wrong, is there?'

'Not wrong exactly, Zack. But something *has* happened and I need to talk to you about it. I have a feeling you're not going to be very pleased when I tell you what it is, but I feel we could turn it to our advantage.'

'Then tell me what it is by all means.'

Flicking his jacket tails to either side of him, he sat down beside her, and haltingly she began to relate what Pearl and Cook had told her.

When she had finished, his face was set in a grim mask and he slapped his knee. 'Good Lord, this is all we need,' he exclaimed in horror.

'But don't you see?' Emmaline grabbed his hand and shook it up and down, her face animated. 'This could be the best news we've had for some long time. You see, what I was thinking was . . .'

She began to ramble on, and the more she told him of what she was proposing to do, the more horrified he looked.

'Have you gone stark staring mad? Why, darling, you *must* see that this could never work.'

'Oh, but it *could*! I *know* it could! Please tell me that you will at least consider my idea. This baby is our grandchild. And if we were to take it as our own, we would still have a piece of Monty here with us.'

As he looked into the face he adored, his heart sank. How could he refuse her anything after all she had been through? 'Very well . . . I'll think on it. But that isn't a yes,' he warned.

Her smile lit up the room as she rose to follow him to the dining room and he felt as if he was caught in a trap.

Chapter Thirty-Seven

Pearl spent the next two days veering between anxiety and despair as she waited to hear her fate. Then finally one morning, as she helped Mrs Forbes dress, the woman said, 'I think I may have found the perfect solution to all your problems, but before I tell you what it is I must first ask you, are you *absolutely* without any doubt sure that you do not wish to keep this baby?'

'I'm positive, ma'am.' Pearl's voice was dull. 'How could I even if I wanted to? I have nowhere to go, no home to offer it, nothing.'

'In that case, here is what I propose we should do.' Mrs Forbes took a deep breath. 'As you know I have not ventured out of the house for some time now, nor have I received any visitors. And so, we shall immediately begin to put it about that I am with child. Fortunately, I am still of a childbearing age and no one will know any different, only the people who live in this house, and they are all utterly trustworthy. We will, of course, have to confide in the doctor, but it would be more than his job is worth to break the confidence of a patient. From now on, you too will be confined to the house, and when the child is born my husband and I will adopt it as our own. Once the birth is over, it will be up to you whether you wish to go or stay. If you should decide to leave, we shall make sure that you have a free passage back to London with enough money to keep you for some time. I can even arrange for you to have a position in my mother's house, if you so wish. She need never know that the baby isn't truly mine; it will have my blood running through its veins, after all. Then you would be able to put all this behind you. So, what do think of the idea?'

Pearl was so taken aback that she plumped heavily on to the nearest chair. She felt as if all the breath had been knocked out of her. And yet the more she thought of it, the more she realised this could be the perfect solution for both of them. Having the baby to love would give Mrs Forbes something to live for again and it would certainly put an end to her problems.

'M-may I give it some thought, ma'am?'

Mrs Forbes nodded graciously. 'You may. But please try to be sensible when you reach a decision. Remember, by your own admission, you have nothing to offer a child, whereas we would ensure that the child never wanted for anything. Boy or girl, it really doesn't matter to me.'

As Pearl saw the longing in her mistress's face she nodded. 'Thank you. I will of course bear that in mind.'

'Just one thing,' Mrs Forbes said. 'Until you have reached a decision, I would ask that you don't mention this to anyone. Not even anyone in this house. If you do decide that this could work then I shall call a meeting and tell them myself.'

'Yes, ma'am.'

Pearl left the room on legs that felt as if they had turned to jelly as the mistress's plan raced through her mind. And it was at that moment that she had the strangest sensation in her stomach as the child let her know it was there. She shivered with revulsion as a picture of Monty's face flashed in front of her eyes. A part of him was growing inside her, getting stronger by the day as it prepared for its birth, and she didn't know how she was going to bear it. But here was Mrs Forbes offering her the perfect solution. She knew then that she was going to accept her offer.

Mrs Forbes was elated when Pearl told her of her decision and clapped her hands. 'Wonderful. Then, if you are quite sure, I shall call a meeting of the staff immediately. They must all know that they cannot tell a soul outside of these four walls what we are going to do. And now I must insist that you go and have a lie-down, dear. I couldn't bear for anything to go wrong now.'

Already, her head was full of the things she would need. Miss Elizabeth's crib would have to be brought down from the attics. She would get Will to paint it for her. And she would write to her mother immediately with a list of baby things that she would need to be sent over from England. The nursery would need airing and given a fresh coat of paint too. Oh, there was so much to do and not a lot of time left to do it, but the birth couldn't come quickly enough for her. Her mother had not been able to attend Monty's funeral, but she could just imagine how delighted her parents would be when she wrote to tell them that they were about to become grandparents again. She could hardly wait to put pen to paper to begin the subterfuge, but first she must have a strong word with the staff and they must all know in no uncertain terms that should any of them disobey her instructions it would mean instant dismissal for them.

To say the staff was stunned when she gathered them together to tell them of her plan later that afternoon would have been putting it mildly. They gazed at her in disbelief.

'Now, have each of you clearly understood what I have said?'

'Yes, ma'am.' Their heads bobbed in unison and with a satisfied nod and a swish of silken skirts Mrs Forbes left them to mutter amongst themselves.

'But why didn't Pearl tell us she was carrying Master Monty's baby?' Sally said. Mrs Forbes had consciously decided not to tell them that the child was a result of rape. 'I didn't even think she liked him.'

Cook remained tight-lipped; it wasn't her place to tell them. Eliza didn't say anything either, she was too busy fuming. *Once again Pearl was going to land on her feet, just as she always did*, she thought jealously.

And what about after the birth? Mrs Forbes had told them that Pearl would be free to return to England if she so wished, but what about her? Was she to be left here scrubbing pots for the rest of her life? Had Pearl even given Eliza's future a thought? Her mood dark, she stormed from the room and headed for the riverbank; she needed time to think.

It seemed that she wasn't the only one, because when she got to the river, she saw Pearl staring into the swirling waters with a thoughtful expression on her face.

'Well, you certainly came out of that all right as usual, didn't you?'

Pearl started and swung about to see her sister stamping towards her, her gleaming fair curls swirling about her shoulders like a golden cloak. 'Oh . . . Mrs Forbes has told you what we intend to do, then?'

'She's told us, all right,' Eliza answered scathingly. 'What I don't understand is how you can give Monty's baby away as if it means nothing! I would have done anything to have his child!'

'How many times must I tell you, I *never* wanted Monty,' Pearl said in exasperation, but Eliza simply wheeled about and stalked away, leaving Pearl to stare sadly after her, wondering if they would ever be close again.

Once she'd made her announcement, suddenly Mrs Forbes began to take an interest in things again. In the nursery the cobwebs that had accumulated over the years were swept away and it was scrubbed from top to bottom, then Will moved in to give it a fresh coat of paint, and the crib was fetched down from the attic. A chimney sweep came to sweep the chimney and gay-coloured rugs were laid across the floor. Mrs Forbes wrote to her mother to inform her of the impending arrival and within weeks baby clothes began to arrive in readiness for when the child was born. Cook began to knit tiny coats and bonnets and Mrs Forbes, who was an excellent needlewoman, spent much of her time embroidering tiny nightdresses. Pearl, meanwhile, was no longer allowed to work.

'I don't want you overdoing things,' Mrs Forbes explained, terrified that something might happen to the baby. She was aware that her husband still had grave reservations about the adoption but because his wife seemed to have come out of the shell she had hidden away in, he said not a word. His main fear was that Pearl would change her mind about giving the child away once it was born. He had heard of this happening but his wife assured him that Pearl had had no intentions of keeping the baby, even if they had not offered to adopt it.

Pearl seemed to grow bigger by the day, and by the end of July she could hardly wait for the birth to be over. She was the only one who knew she was bearing the child of a murderer but it was a secret she would take to her grave, for how could she ever tell her mistress that her son had murdered his own sister?

And then some very happy news further heightened the mood in the house, when Will and Susan confided to them all that they intended to get married.

'About time too!' Cook told them with a wide grin. 'Why, a blind man on a galloping donkey could have seen how fond you were of each other. I'm just shocked it's taken you both so long to realise it yourselves.'

Susan smiled shyly as they all offered their congratulations.

'So, when is the happy day to be?' Cook asked in her usual forthright way.

'We thought the end of next month, providing the mistress doesn't mind. I mean, we know she is still in mourning and we wouldn't want to upset her.' Will gave his new fiancée a warm smile. 'But now we've decided to do it there seems no point in waiting, so if the mistress does give her permission, we're going to see the vicar today.'

'I'm sure she wouldn't want to stand in the way of your happiness,' Cook said. 'But that don't give us much time to organise everything,' she fretted.

'Actually, we only want a very quiet wedding,' Susan told her hastily. 'We'll just go to the church and get married and then I'll move into Will's rooms over the stables with him.'

'But you'll need a nice new dress,' Cook told her. 'And I'll put a little spread on here for you. I'm sure the mistress won't mind.'

Knowing that it would be useless to argue with Cook when she had made her mind up about something, the couple agreed.

'But only a very small do for the people here,' Susan told her.

'Right, then if you don't mind, I'm going to go through and tell the mistress the happy news and put your minds at rest,' Cook declared, as she took her apron off – and before they could stop her, she was off with a spring in her step.

She found Mrs Forbes busy sewing in the day room and when Cook told her about the wedding she beamed with genuine pleasure.

'They're just concerned that it might be a bit soon after . . . you know with Master Monty . . .' Cook faltered.

'Not at all, it's just wonderful.' Her face became sad for a moment. 'After all the sadness, we now have two happy events to look forward to, don't we? It's funny, isn't it? They say that life's circle is a birth, a marriage and a death. We shall have had all three within a year, even if they have been in the wrong order. But now, what is Susan planning to wear? We must have her looking her best. Send her in to me, would you, Cook? I'm sure I shall have a gown that would be suitable for her upstairs, and a bonnet too, no doubt. My gowns will probably be a little large for her but we can alter it to fit. I'm just sad that I won't be able to attend the church and neither will Pearl. But never mind, we can see them before they set off and when they get back.'

And so shortly after, Susan and the mistress went upstairs and when she came back down Susan had a beautiful shot-silk gown across her arm and a large smile on her face.

'The mistress insisted I should have it,' she told Pearl, her eyes shining like stars. 'And she's given me a bonnet trimmed with silk flowers and a tiny veil to match it too. She's even going to alter it to fit me. Oh, I'm *so* happy.'

Pearl was pleased for her too, and yet as she witnessed Susan's joy, she felt a pang of regret as she thought of Nick. She would never know what it was to be a bride now because if she couldn't marry him, she would never marry anyone. She deeply regretted that she couldn't be at the wedding as well, but that was out of the question. Until after the birth, both she and the mistress would be virtual prisoners in the house. But still, she consoled herself, at least she would be able to help Susan get ready for her wedding on the day and she would be here to celebrate with her when the happy couple got home, so that was something.

The next four weeks passed in a blur and finally the day of the wedding dawned. A bright sunny day with not a cloud in the sky.

Downstairs, Cook was putting the finishing touches to the wedding breakfast as Pearl helped Susan to get dressed. Finally, she was ready and as Pearl tied the ribbons of her bonnet beneath her chin she was choked with emotion. 'You look *so* beautiful,' she whispered. And it wasn't just the grand dress that made her so, it was the glow that emanated from her. Mrs Forbes tapped on the door then and as she entered the room, she too was emotional as she stared at the bride.

'Why, you look just stunning, my dear,' she whispered as she handed Susan a bouquet that she had ordered for her.

Susan gasped with pleasure as she stared at the sweet-smelling freesias and cream roses surrounded by delicate, snow-white baby's breath.

'Oh, ma'am . . . you shouldn't have. The dress and the bonnet were more than enough.'

'Nonsense.' Mrs Forbes waved her thanks aside. 'Every bride should carry a posy.'

'Thank you, ma'am.' Tears glistened in Susan's eyes as her mistress stepped forwards to give her a hug and pull the wispy veil that was attached to the hat over her face. 'Now, be off with you. You have a wedding to go to,' Mrs Forbes told her with a smile. 'And we shall all be waiting here for you when you get back. I only regret that I can't be there with you.'

The happy couple arrived back at the house an hour later to a shower of rice and rose petals and a feast fit for a king laid out for them. Even Mr and Mrs Forbes were there to greet them and they looked genuinely happy for them.

'We've never had two members of staff get wed before,' Mr Forbes said as he accepted a glass of wine from Pearl. 'So may I raise a toast to the happy couple. May you always be as happy as you are today and may all your troubles be little ones!'

As Susan blushed, everyone laughed.

'Poor lass, give her chance,' Cook chided as Will stared down at his wife adoringly. After losing his darling Esme, he had thought he would never love again but Susan had wormed her way into his heart and he felt whole again.

'I don't want any of you doing any more work today. This is a day of celebration; we can all do with cold cuts for dinner this evening,' Mrs Forbes told them, and everyone was more than happy to oblige.

It was a truly happy day, even Eliza managed the odd smile, and by the time the newly-weds retired to their room, they were all in a happy frame of mind. It was a wonderful balmy night with the sky full of stars and Pearl was tempted to stroll by the river before going to bed, but because her ankles were swollen, she decided against it. She was just weeks away from giving birth now and was so big that she waddled rather than walked. The warm weather wasn't helping either and her back ached almost all the time.

She found Eliza already in their room by the time she had puffed her way upstairs. Mrs Forbes had offered her a room in the main house, but Pearl had opted to stay close to her sister, not that Eliza had any time for her anymore.

'It's been a lovely day, hasn't it?' Pearl said as she struggled into her nightgown – but as usual there was no response from her sister, so with a sigh she climbed into bed and tried to get comfortable, which was proving to be more difficult by the day.

I wonder what Nick is doing now? she thought, as she stared towards the window. She still missed him but had accepted that she would never see him again. It broke her heart, but she knew that it was something she was going to have to learn to live with for the rest of her life.

Chapter Thirty-Eight

'I really must insist that you have a bedroom in the main house now, Pearl,' Mrs Forbes told her one day early in September, as they sat together sewing yet more baby clothes. Pearl was sure that between them they must have made enough for at least six babies. 'Your labour could start any day now and I would feel safer knowing I was close by, so I've asked Susan to prepare a room for you on the same landing as me. I also have the doctor on standby. The midwife here is known to be a bit of a gossip, so I'd rather the doctor attend the birth; we know we can trust him.'

Knowing that she was about to leave the room she shared with Eliza, Pearl suppressed a sigh. She supposed Mrs Forbes was right, so she reluctantly agreed. After all, she could hardly give birth with Eliza there. 'Very well, I'll get Susan to help me move my things in a while.'

Mrs Forbes looked relieved. She was as nervous about this birth as Pearl herself was, and terrified at what she thought of as her last chance at happiness being snatched away from her.

'Have you thought of any names for the baby yet?' Pearl asked.

Mrs Forbes smiled. 'I have, as it happens, but I've decided to wait until after the baby is born to make my final decision.'

Pearl had no problem with this. If Mrs Forbes was going to take the child as her own, then she thought it only fair that she should choose its name. As something else occurred to her, she asked tentatively, 'And what about, er . . . feeding it?'

'I've already discussed this with the doctor,' Mrs Forbes surprised her by saying. 'And he did suggest that perhaps it would be best if you were willing to feed the baby, for the first few days at least. Apparently, that's when the child draws its goodness from the mother. Ordinarily I would hire a wet nurse but of course in these circumstances that won't be possible. Once we get the first few days over, the doctor can see no reason why the child can't be bottle-fed. Do you think you could do that for me?'

'I suppose so,' Pearl agreed, although the thought was abhorrent. Just thinking of it conjured up images of Monty sucking and biting at her tender breasts. But then she supposed the child couldn't be blamed for the sins of its father.

'Excellent. Then I think we are all prepared, and once you've moved into your new room, all we need is the baby.'

'Will you be hiring a nanny to care for it?'

Mrs Forbes shook her head. 'Oh no, dear. I intend to care for it myself, and Susan has promised to help too. I'm sure we'll manage very well between us.'

'I'm sure you will.' It was strange to think that this dear woman was looking forward to having the child as much as Pearl was dreading delivering it. Now that her time was close, she was alternately looking forwards to getting it over with and dreading the birth. She had seen her own mother bring two of her siblings into the world, so she knew exactly what lay ahead of her. Not something to look forward to at all. But she supposed the sooner it happened, the sooner she could get on with her life.

She was in the process of packing the last of her clothes that evening when Eliza appeared in the doorway and raised an eyebrow.

'Mrs Forbes wants me to move into the main house until after the birth,' she explained.

'How very nice for you. I wonder if you'll be in the room I had while I was the favoured one,' she sneered. 'If you are, I shouldn't get too comfortable, because as I know Mrs Forbes can lose interest in you very quickly.'

Pearl bit on her lip, not quite sure how to reply. Eliza was right up to a point, and Pearl knew how difficult it had been for her sister to be suddenly abandoned by Mrs Forbes after getting used to being pampered and waited on.

'I'm sure it will only be until the baby is here,' she told Eliza. 'I'll be back here with you before you know it and then we can decide what we want to do – whether we wish to stay here or go back to London.'

'Huh! As if *you* care what happens to me,' Eliza snorted with contempt.

'Of *course* I care!' Pearl stared at her. 'You *know* that I've always cared about you.'

'*Do I?*' Eliza ripped her apron off and threw it on to the bed before storming out, no doubt to go off on one of her wanders along the river again.

With a sigh, Pearl collected the rest of her things together. At the door she took one last glance at her old room, before going down the stairs to get settled into her new one. But she couldn't stop thinking about her sister and eventually she decided to go and find her. A bit of fresh air and a gentle stroll would do her good. She hated to be on bad terms with Eliza.

She had wandered for some way along the riverbank when she spotted Eliza ahead, skimming stones across the turbulent water.

'So what do *you* want?' Eliza asked sullenly.

'I want us to be friends. I can't bear it when you're angry with me,' Pearl told her with a tremor in her voice.

But her words only seemed to incense Eliza all the more. 'No, of course you can't. You want to be everyone's best friend, don't you? Little Miss Goody Two-Shoes!'

'That's so unfair.' Pearl was getting angry too now. There seemed to be no reasoning with Eliza and she wished she hadn't come. She'd developed a dull backache and just wanted to go back now. 'Have it your own way then,' she threw over her shoulder as she turned to retrace her steps.

Suddenly, Eliza gripped her arm and flung her around with surprising strength for one so small and slight.

'No, it's not fair!' Eliza cried, stabbing a finger at Pearl's swollen stomach. 'It should be *me* not you carrying that baby!' Her face was so contorted with rage that Pearl barely recognised her, as she struggled to free her arm from Eliza's grip. Then suddenly Pearl felt a warm gush between her legs and, shocked, she looked down to see a small puddle of water on the ground.

'Oh no, I think my waters have broken!'

Eliza looked shocked too, but then she was in a fury again as she cried, 'I can't let you have this baby! It should be mine. You've always spoiled everything for me, *always*!'

'Stop being so stupid!' Pearl was beginning to panic now. 'This isn't the time for your petty tantrums. Do you understand what's happening, Eliza?'

'I understand perfectly.' Suddenly Eliza's voice held a note of malice. 'In fact, I've always understood far more than any of you ever gave me credit for.'

'What do you mean?' Pearl's hand was cradling her stomach as if she was afraid the baby might pop out at any minute.

'You and Ma always thought you were better than me, didn't you? But in fact, I was a lot brighter than you were. While you were at home skivvying, I was off out of it because Ma wrongly assumed I was stupid. Same at the workhouse; you worked twice as hard and I barely had to lift a finger. Then we got here and Mrs Veasey favoured you and felt I should be working as hard. Well . . . I had to make her pay, didn't I? The same way I had to make Freda pay for the way she treated me and tried to steal my Monty from me. It was so easy to poison them both, slowly, bit by bit. I took poison from the stables a bit at a time and I enjoyed watching them die. Then there was Monty . . . I was so angry with him. He'd chosen you when he could have had me, so I found a rock and . . . well, the rest you know.'

Seriously frightened now, Pearl broke free and backed away from her. There was a strange gleam in her sister's eyes and it dawned on her in that moment that Eliza was insane.

'You mean it was *you* that . . .'

Eliza laughed, a wild laugh that sounded almost inhuman and made the hairs on the back of Pearl's neck stand on end. 'Yes, it was me. Rat poison for Mrs Veasey and Freda and a blow on the back of the head for Monty. He never even knew what hit him. Mind you, I never meant to kill him, just teach him a lesson. He was alive when I left him, I *swear* it. How could I have known that there were wolves about? And now it's *your* turn – you and that bastard you're carrying.'

Pearl was crying now as she shook her head in stunned disbelief. She didn't want to believe what she was hearing; she felt as if she was caught in the grip of a nightmare. Her little sister, the one she had loved and looked out for since the day she was born, was a murderer, and wasn't even sorry.

'I-I think you need help, Eliza,' she whispered in a strangled voice, as she held her hand out to her. 'Come back to the house with me now and we'll get the doctor to come and see you.'

'You won't be going back to the house ever again.' She glanced across her shoulder at the fast-flowing river and it dawned on Pearl what Eliza was planning to do.

Pearl turned to run, but the weight of the child made her ungainly and, losing her footing, she fell heavily, knocking the air from her lungs. Eliza was on her in a moment and grabbing her skirt she began to drag her sister towards the river's edge.

Arms flailing helplessly, Pearl screamed, terrified for her life and the life of the child she was carrying, but there was no one to hear her. '*P-Please*, Eliza, stop for a moment and think what you're doing. You're not well. You can't really want me dead.'

'Oh, but I do,' Eliza cackled.

They were almost at the edge of the riverbank and the sound of the turbulent water was drumming in Pearl's ears. There was a drop of about five feet to the water below now that the river had subsided slightly, but Pearl knew that no one who fell in would stand a chance – the currents were too strong, especially for someone in her condition.

And so, with one last superhuman effort, she kicked out. The kick caught Eliza squarely behind the knees, knocking her forwards and making her relinquish her hold on Pearl's skirt. With a look of shock on her face, she turned slightly as she teetered on the edge of the river. Pearl tried to reach out for her hand, but it was too late, and as she finally lost her balance, Eliza fell backwards and there was a loud splash as she hit the water and disappeared beneath it.

Sobbing, Pearl crawled towards her and held out her hand as Eliza surfaced, coughing and spluttering, her face a mask of terror. '*Grab my hand*,' she screamed as Eliza stared up at her, but it was too late. Already the currents were carrying her sister out of reach and she was being swept towards the middle of the river. And then suddenly another strong current sucked her under and she disappeared.

'*NO, NO!*' Pearl's hysterical screams made a flock of birds in the trees take flight as she watched helplessly for a sign of her sister resurfacing. It was then that the first pain struck and she dropped back to her knees.

'Oh, please God, no,' she whimpered as she somehow managed to stand. 'Don't make me give birth here with no one to help me.'

With a last look at the river, she turned and began to slowly make her way back to the house, but she had gone only a few feet when another pain brought her to her knees again. She waited for it to subside, then began to crawl towards the orchard. The next minutes – or was it hours? – seemed to pass in a blur. The pains were coming quite closely together and yet Pearl had understood that first babies usually took their time. Every now and then she stopped and tried to scream for help, but she was exhausted and beginning to feel dizzy.

After what seemed like a lifetime, she saw the orchard ahead of her. The trees were laden with fruit and the large tabby cat that Cook had taken in to try to keep the rats down was lying in the shade washing himself. He gave her a cursory glance as she painfully crawled past him before curling into a ball for a nap. Pearl's skirt was in ribbons now, trailing behind her, and her knees and the palms of her hands were bloody, but still she kept going. If only she could reach the yard, someone would surely spot her then?

And then she heard the welcome sound of Susan's voice and with the last of her strength she began to shout. '*H-help! Please . . . help me!*'

'Did you hear something?' Susan had taken a mug of tea out to Will, who was grooming the horses and she looked towards the orchard.

'Actually, I think I did.' Placing his mug down, he made for the trees as his wife cautiously followed him, eyes darting all around.

Suddenly, she pointed. 'There, *look* . . . over there! Someone is lying beneath the trees.'

Will sprinted ahead to Pearl, who was now only semi-conscious.

'E-Eliza . . .' she whispered brokenly as tears streamed down her face. 'Th-the river. Eliza . . .'

'Stay here with her,' Will ordered. 'She's trying to say something about Eliza and the river.' He sprinted away as Susan sank to her knees beside her friend and lifted her head into her lap.

'Whatever has happened?' she asked, but Pearl could only shake her head and as another pain tore through her she rolled into a ball.

Will was back in seconds shaking his head. 'There's no sign of anyone on the riverbank.'

'Never mind that for now. We need to get her inside,' Susan told him. 'I think Pearl is having the baby. Can you manage to carry her if I run ahead to tell the mistress?'

'Of course.'

Susan sprinted away, and Will lifted Pearl in his strong arms and began to stride towards the house. As he reached it, both Mrs Forbes and Susan appeared in the doorway and, taking control, Mrs Forbes told him, 'Carry her up to her new room, and then would you run for the doctor for me, Will?'

He nodded as he strode up the stairs and laid Pearl gently on the bed.

Mrs Forbes shook her head as she stared down at the state of her hands and knees. 'We'll get her undressed and get these bathed before the doctor comes,' she told Susan, who was staring at her friend wide-eyed. 'Pop down and tell Cook we want hot water and towels, please, Susan. Lots of them!'

Pearl's eyes were rolling but every now and again, as another pain started, she would groan and draw her knees up, which made getting her undressed very difficult. Even so, once Susan was back, they managed it between them and sat on either side of the bed watching Pearl carefully.

Every so often she opened her eyes but all she kept saying was '*Eliza . . . w-water.*'

'Run and see if you can find her, would you?' Mrs Forbes asked as she gripped Pearl's clammy hand. 'Perhaps having her sister here will calm her.'

But when Susan returned some minutes later, she shook her head. 'There's no sign of her, ma'am. When I found her in the orchard she was trying to say something about Eliza and the river.'

A cold hand closed about Emmaline Forbes's heart. Surely the river hadn't claimed yet another victim? But there was no time to think of it for long, because it was clear that Pearl's baby was in a hurry to be born.

'I just hope the doctor can get here in time,' Mrs Forbes said worriedly, as she glanced towards the window. 'Otherwise it looks like you and I are going to have to deliver this baby, Susan.'

Susan paled at the thought, but thankfully at that moment they heard someone clattering up the stairs, and the next second the doctor appeared in the doorway.

After hastily washing his hands, he took his jacket off and rolled his sleeves up before crossing to the bed to examine Pearl. 'Hm.' When he was done, he straightened with a frown on his face. 'I have an awful feeling the baby is breech. It was when I checked her last week but I was hoping it would turn before the birth. But she's early, isn't she? At least a couple of weeks by my reckoning.'

Mrs Forbes nodded, her face a picture of dismay as she thought of this longed-for child being snatched away from her. Preparing for the birth was all that had kept her going over the past few weeks and she didn't know how she would cope if she was to lose the baby now.

'But why is she in this state?' the doctor asked as he stared at Pearl's grazed hands and knees.

'We don't know. Susan found her crawling from the direction of the orchard some time ago. She was clearly in a very distressed state and kept going on about her sister and the river. You don't think Eliza might have fallen in, do you?'

He pursed his lips. 'Well, something has clearly upset her and made her go into early labour. Have you checked where Eliza is?'

Mrs Forbes shook her head and wrung her hands together, getting more agitated by the minute. 'I sent Susan to look for her just before you arrived, but she isn't in the house.'

'Then I suggest you get Will to go down to the river and check that she isn't there,' he told her, as another sharp contraction had Pearl arching her back. 'Meanwhile, I'm going to do what I can to turn this baby, but it isn't going to be pleasant and if I don't succeed . . .'

Susan ran off to pass instructions to Will to start searching for Eliza, as the grim-faced doctor leaned over his patient.

Soon Pearl's screams were echoing through the house as he struggled to manoeuvre the baby into the right position, and within minutes sweat was standing out on his brow.

But all his efforts were in vain and after what felt like a lifetime, he told Mrs Forbes, 'We're going to have to try and bring it as it is. It should have been born by now and if I leave it any longer there's a strong possibility that we'll lose both mother and child. But I'm going to need your help.'

Mrs Forbes began to chew on her knuckles as she stared down at Pearl's flushed face. The poor girl was exhausted and clearly in agony. But then after taking a deep breath, she swallowed and said, 'Very well, tell me what you want me to do.'

'I need you to stand here and keep her legs open while I try to get hold of the baby.'

With a nod of her head, Mrs Forbes took her position and began to pray.

Chapter Thirty-Nine

It was now darkest night, and in the bedroom Pearl was hovering between life and death, with still no sign of the baby being born.

Both the doctor and Mrs Forbes were almost as exhausted as the mother-to-be, but at last the doctor cried, 'I think I have hold of the baby's leg. Now this isn't going to be nice but whatever you do don't loosen your hold of her.'

Minutes later, after a few gentle tugs from the doctor, the child slithered out of its mother to lie in a bloody heap between her legs.

Mrs Forbes began to cry tears of joy. 'Oh . . . it's a little girl . . . But why isn't she crying?'

Expertly, the doctor cut the cord – then, lifting the baby aloft, he slapped its back sharply. There was no response, so he laid her on the bed and gently cleaned out her mouth, but still no response. Once more he lifted her and sharply slapped her back again – and this time, he was rewarded with an indignant mewling cry.

'That's better!'

He smiled for the first time since he'd arrived in the room and passed the child to Mrs Forbes, who hastily wrapped her in a towel she had ready and kissed her downy curls.

Both Cook and Mr Forbes, who had been hovering anxiously on the landing, began to hammer on the door, and with a proud smile Mrs Forbes took the baby to meet them while the doctor turned his attention once more to Pearl, who was lying so still she might already have been dead. She was bleeding profusely and the doctor worked valiantly to stem the flow, knowing that if he couldn't, and quickly, Pearl had little chance of surviving.

'Are Susan and Will back yet?' Mrs Forbes asked as her husband and her beloved cook billed and cooed over the new arrival. She had sent them out some hours ago to search for Eliza and no one had seen them since.

Cook shook her head. 'Not a sign of them yet, hinny. But come along now. you look all in. I'll make you and the doctor a nice hot cup o' tea and then we'll get this little madam bathed and dressed. Eeh, she's a right little beauty and no mistake, but what about her poor mother? From what we could hear of it, the poor lass has had a hard time of it.'

Suddenly tearful, Mrs Forbes nodded. She passed the baby to Cook and leaned heavily against her husband. 'She's had a terrible time of it and I don't think she's out of the woods yet,' she confided, and solemn now they slowly descended the stairs.

Susan and Will had just arrived back from their search when they reached the kitchen and they quickly told them that they had found no sign of Eliza, before turning their attention to the baby.

'We'll start searching again in the morning,' a weary Will promised. 'But it's too dark and dangerous to do any more tonight; we could end up in the river ourselves.'

By the time the doctor appeared, the new addition had been washed and changed and Cook was dripping milk into her tiny mouth from a pap bag.

'I think she'll make it,' the doctor told them, as Susan pressed a steaming cup of tea into his hand. He certainly looked as if he needed it. 'I've managed to stop the bleeding and provided she does as she's told she should recover, although it will take time. She's very weak.'

Mrs Forbes breathed a sigh of relief. 'Thank goodness. Thank you. Now remember, we need to spread the word that I have given birth and no one need be any the wiser.'

The doctor didn't altogether agree with the plan his patient and Mrs Forbes had made, but it was none of his business and so he had no option but to go along with it. He hastily checked the child over then and to everyone's relief declared that although she was small, she appeared healthy.

'Isn't she just *perfect*, darling?' Mrs Forbes said as she stared down at the little girl adoringly.

Her husband nodded. It was strange to think that this little soul was his granddaughter, for he couldn't see anything of Monty in her. The baby had blonde hair just like her birth mother's.

The second Cook had finished feeding her, Mrs Forbes took her into her arms and gently kissed every inch of her that wasn't covered. 'I suppose we should think of a name for her now. I thought we might call her Elizabeth.'

Mr Forbes's face darkened and pain briefly flashed in his eyes. 'I don't think that is such a good idea. There could only ever be one Elizabeth for us, and she is gone,' he reminded her gently. 'What about calling her Mathilda, after my mother?'

Mrs Forbes looked thoughtful and then gave him a radiant smile. 'That's a lovely idea, and we could call her Tilly for short. I think it quite suits her.'

He smiled at her indulgently. 'That's settled then. But now I really think we should all try and get some sleep, although someone should stay with Pearl.'

'I'll do it,' Susan volunteered without hesitation. 'I can keep my eye on her from the chair at the side of the bed and cat nap.'

The doctor nodded his approval. 'Excellent. I've given her a very strong sedative so she shouldn't wake until morning, but if she does, give her two drops of the painkiller that I've left for her on the table beside the bed. No more, mind.'

'Yes, sir.'

The doctor stifled a yawn as he struggled into his coat. He had been up since five that morning and felt as if he could have fallen asleep standing up. 'Goodnight then. I shall be back after surgery in the morning.'

Once he had gone, Susan settled in the chair beside Pearl and the rest of them drifted off to their rooms. Mrs Forbes carried Mathilda to spend her first night in the crib, which was placed ready at the side of her bed.

'I was hoping that Pearl would be able to feed her for the first few days,' she fretted to her husband as they undressed, 'but I doubt she will be strong enough now. Still, if she doesn't thrive on the milk she's getting, I suppose I could always get a wet nurse in. I could say that I hadn't made enough milk to satisfy her, couldn't I?'

'Let's face each problem as we come to it,' he suggested. 'She seems quite happy with the feed Cook has given her so far.'

'You're right.' She smiled as she hopped into bed, not a bit tired. She was too excited about having the baby at last and felt as if she could have just sat and looked at her all night. It was worrying about Eliza, though. *Where could she have got to?* she wondered, praying that her fears would not be confirmed. If the girl had fallen into the river, she would have stood no chance of getting back out again, but only time would tell.

The cockerel crowing woke everyone early the next morning and, still in her dressing robe, Mrs Forbes lifted the infant and took her down to the kitchen for Cook to feed her, while she went to check on Pearl.

The poor girl looked positively ghastly. There were large dark circles under her eyes and her head was moving restlessly on the pillow. She was frighteningly pale and every now and again she cried out, '*Eliza . . . Eliza . . . no, nooooo!*'

Will had already gone to continue the search for her and Mrs Forbes urged Susan to go and get some sleep, but the girl shook her head, reluctant to leave her friend.

'Eliza didn't come home last night and I'm getting seriously worried about her,' Mrs Forbes whispered to Susan, keeping one eye on Pearl.

'All we can do is wait,' Susan said glumly. 'But how is the baby this morning?'

Mrs Forbes glowed as she smiled at her. 'Oh, she's absolutely beautiful and she's been *so* good. Once we get Pearl well and word is about that I've had her I shall start to receive visitors again and no one will ever know that I didn't give birth to her.'

Susan didn't say a word. She was pleased for Mrs Forbes but heartsick that Pearl would never be able to acknowledge the child as her own – not that she had ever wanted to admittedly, so perhaps things would work out for the best after all.

The doctor's face was grim when he arrived sometime later and he ushered Mrs Forbes out on to the landing to tell her, 'I'm afraid I have just heard some very disturbing news. A young woman was fished out of the river about five miles downstream this morning, and from what I heard she matches Eliza's description.'

Mrs Forbes gasped as her hand flew to her mouth. 'Oh no. But what will this do to Pearl if it proves to be Eliza?'

'First, I think one of you should go and see if it is her,' he advised. 'And I certainly wouldn't tell Pearl yet, whether it proves to be Eliza or not. She's far too weak to take another shock at the moment.'

Mrs Forbes nodded. 'I understand. I'll ask Will if he wouldn't mind going. I can hardly go myself when I'm supposed to have just had a baby, can I?'

Somewhat reluctantly, Will agreed to go while the doctor examined Pearl. She was slipping in and out of consciousness and was still crying out but the bleeding had not started again, which the doctor assured them was a good sign.

'Something has clearly traumatised her other than the birth,' he told them. 'And if indeed it is Eliza's body that's been fished out of the river, that will explain it. But all you can do for now is keep her cool and try to get plenty of fluids inside her. I shall come back again tomorrow. And now I should perhaps take a look at the baby. Is she doing well with her feeding?'

'Oh yes.' Mrs Forbes instantly lit up at the mention of her. 'She's taking her milk and we've decided to call her Mathilda. Mathilda Mary Ellen to be precise.'

'Charming.' The doctor smiled as he snapped his bag shut. There was one little one he wouldn't have to worry about, he thought to himself, after he had taken a quick look at her to make sure that all was well. Even Zack seemed to be taken with her, so all in all things just might turn out for the best, for them at least – but he wondered how Pearl would cope with her sister's death, if indeed the body that had been found was hers. With a sad sigh at the complexities of life, he went on his way.

Some two hours later, Will returned, and one glance at his solemn face told them all they needed to know.

'It was Eliza, all right,' he said, with a catch in his voice. He would never forget the sight of her laid out on that cold mortuary slab for as long as he lived. She had looked so young and beautiful, with her fair hair fanned out about her, almost as if she was just asleep and might wake at any minute.

'God rest her soul!' Cook quickly made the sign of the cross as tears sprang to her eyes. It seemed so cruel when one so young was taken. 'Goodness only knows how Pearl will take it. And what do we do about a funeral for the poor lass? The mistress won't be able to go and Pearl is in no fit state to.'

'No, but we can and so can Mr Forbes,' Susan pointed out. 'And the least we can do for the poor girl is give her a decent send-off.'

'Well, that'll be for the master and mistress to decide, but I've no doubt that will be what they want too.'

Cook was proved to be right and Eliza's body was brought back to the town and laid in the chapel of rest until the funeral in three days' time.

During that time, although Pearl had begun to improve, she had yet to regain full consciousness, so on the day of the funeral Mrs Forbes stayed with her while her husband and the members of staff attended the service. It was a quiet affair, although Mr and Mrs Forbes had insisted she should have the finest mahogany coffin the undertaker could provide, and once Eliza had been laid to rest beneath the branches of a towering red oak tree in the tiny churchyard, they all felt that they had done right by her. But their mood was sombre as they made their way home.

'*Eliza . . .*'

Two days after the funeral, Susan was sitting at the side of the bed when Pearl suddenly sat bolt upright, her eyes wild as they searched the room. 'Where is she? She fell into the river and I couldn't help her . . .' She began to cry as the sight that had haunted her nightmares came back in full force. And the things that Eliza had said . . . they were so awful; how could she ever forget them? She had admitted to killing poor Mrs Veasey, Freda and Monty!

'Aw, sweetheart!' Susan was beside her in a sigh and wrapped her arms about her as she began to sob.

'Is she . . . is she . . .?' Pearl couldn't bring herself to say the word.

Susan solemnly nodded. 'Yes, she's gone, but she's at peace now. When you're better I'll take you to put some flowers on her grave.'

'*What?* You mean she's been buried already? But how long have I been asleep?' As Pearl's hand fell to her stomach, a look of shock passed over her face. 'And what about the baby? Where is the baby?'

'Shush now,' Susan crooned. 'You'll do yourself no good at all getting into a state. You've been unconscious for some days, but the baby is just fine. Beautiful, in fact. You gave birth to a lovely baby girl.'

'*I did?*' Pearl became quiet as she tried to take it in, but her mind was in a spin and she looked stunned. All she could remember was the pain and then there was nothing but darkness.

'Wh-where is she . . . the baby?'

'Oh, don't you go worrying about her,' Susan told her, as she gently smoothed the hair from her forehead. 'She's being well taken care of.'

'But I was supposed to feed her,' Pearl said fretfully.

Susan nodded. 'I know you were, but you were in no state to after the birth. Anyway, she's thriving and already has all of us wrapped around her tiny finger, even Mr Forbes is taken with her. She looks just like you.'

'*Like me?*' Pearl was shocked. Somehow, she had never thought of the baby as being anything to do with her and she had imagined that it would be the double of its father. Even so, she was glad the birth was over and she had no wish to see the child. There was so much to take in but already her eyes were growing heavy again and within minutes she was fast asleep. But this time it was a healing sleep and Susan sighed with relief as she crept from the room. Hopefully now Pearl would start to get better.

The next morning a letter with an English postmark arrived addressed to Pearl and Mrs Forbes took it up to her.

'A letter for you, dear,' she said, as she handed it over and began to straighten the counterpane.

Pearl eyed it curiously. 'For me?'

Mrs Forbes laughed. 'Why don't you open it? It won't bite you, I'm sure.'

And so Pearl carefully slit the envelope and within minutes tears of joy were rolling down her face. It was from her sister, Amy; she must have learned basic reading and writing since she'd started work.

Avidly, she started to read.

Dear Pearl,

I ope this leter finds you an Eliza well. I was so pleased to get your adress from Lil an just wanted to rite to give yu mine. I live in Swan Lane in Nuneaton with Gracie. It's a nice place, a market town an I ave a good mistres what is good to me. Yur bloke left yur address with Mrs Hewitt and she passed it on to Gracie when she went ome to see her ma. He sounds nice. Are you two goin to get wed? An as Eliza got a bloke yet? I don't know if we wil ever see each other again but at least we can keep in touch now. I wud like to ear ow things are with you. I stil ain't very good at writin as you'l see but its nice to know that we are in touch again. Pleese rite back soon,

    Yur luving sister,

    Amy xxxx

'I hope those are happy tears?' Mrs Forbes looked concerned. Pearl had gone through so much lately, she hoped it wasn't more bad news.

Pearl gave her a weak smile. She was propped up on pillows today and feeling better by the hour. She knew now that Nick had kept his promise to put her in touch with her sister again, and it was thanks to him she had received the letter. But her joy was tinged with sadness as she thought of the wonderful future they might have had together had things turned out differently, and it only made her miss him more.

'It is good news. It's from my sister, Amy. I know where she is now.'

'I see, then that's excellent. And I have some good news too. My mother is coming to visit. She's on the way even as we speak to meet her new grandchild. Did Susan tell you that we have called her Mathilda?'

Pearl shook her head. 'No, she didn't, but it's a lovely name.'

Mrs Forbes looked slightly embarrassed as she asked tentatively, 'Would you like to see her, Pearl?'

Pearl was silent for a moment as she considered it. She was still feeling happy about receiving the letter from Amy; at least she still felt that she had some family left now. The problem was when she replied to her she would have to tell her of Eliza's death; she would tell her that her death had been accidental, as everyone here believed. How could she tell them all that Eliza had wanted to kill her and that she was already a murderer three times over? That was a secret that she would take to the grave, she decided. And also, Amy's mention of Nick had cut deep and reminded her how much she missed him.

'I, er . . . no, thank you. I don't feel quite strong enough just yet,' Pearl answered and she was sure that she saw a look of relief pass across her mistress's face.

'Very well, but when you do feel ready . . .' Mrs Forbes smiled. 'Now get some rest, dear. It's time for Mathilda's feed so I must go, but Susan will be bringing you some soup up in a minute. Cook is determined to get you well again, as we all are.'

After she'd left, Pearl stared towards the window and thought of Nick, Amy and Eliza, as tears of sorrow and loss trickled down her cheeks. Would she ever be able to feel happiness again? she wondered.

Chapter Forty

'I've been thinking,' Mrs Forbes said the following day, when she was doing her daily check on Pearl, 'that if you were considering going back to England now that Mathilda is here, you could perhaps travel back with my mother? I'm sure she would give you a position in her household if I asked her, and as she's staying for a month the doctor thinks you should be fully recovered by the time she leaves. What do you think, dear?' She looked slightly uncomfortable as she asked this.

In actual fact, Pearl hadn't given her position much thought – she was still grieving for Eliza – but now with a jolt she realised that perhaps it would be for the best. After all, she had nothing to keep her here now.

'You don't have to give me an answer right away,' Mrs Forbes assured her. 'But if you do decide you want to go I shall make sure that you don't go empty-handed. You have given me the most precious gift in the world, after all.'

'I don't want anything from you,' Pearl said dully as tears sprang to her eyes. 'It would make me feel as if I was selling my baby to you.'

'Nonsense. She does have our family blood running through her veins. It feels right that she should stay with us.'

At that moment, for the first time, Pearl heard the baby cry through the open bedroom door and it gave her a shock. Of course, she was quite aware that the baby was in the house somewhere, but it was the first time in the four weeks since she had given birth that she had actually heard her and it made her realise that Mathilda was a real living, breathing little person.

'Oh, that's her ladyship crying for her feed.' Mrs Forbes laughed. 'She might be small, but I assure you, she has a very good pair of lungs on her.'

She turned to leave to attend to the baby's needs, but Pearl's voice stayed her at the door.

'I, er . . . think I'm ready to meet her now.'

Mrs Forbes looked panicked for a moment, but after fixing the smile on her face again, she nodded. 'Of course, if that is what you wish. It's the least I can do for you. I shall bring her up directly after I've fed her.'

Pearl nodded as the woman left the room, and peeped down at her swollen breasts. They had been extremely painful but now that she hadn't fed the baby her milk was drying up and thankfully, they weren't leaking anymore.

She wondered then if she had done the right thing by agreeing to see the child, but decided it might be for the best. It would be some time before she could leave – if she decided that was what she wanted to do – and she was bound to see her once she was up and about again, so best to get it over now.

She found herself holding her breath as she watched the door, and almost an hour later Mrs Forbes appeared with a bundle wrapped in a fine lace shawl in her arms. She approached the bed cautiously, almost as if she was afraid Pearl might snatch her from her.

'So, here she is,' she forced herself to say cheerfully, and without further ado she held the baby out to Pearl, whose arms automatically opened to take her.

The child was full and content, having just been fed, and as Pearl stared down at her in awe, the strangest thing happened. A feeling she had never experienced before pierced her heart and a lump formed in her throat. The little girl was quite utterly beautiful. Her soft blonde curls formed a downy little halo around her head and her long fair eyelashes were curled on her plump little cheeks. Her tiny fists were curled beneath her chin and her rosebud mouth was working as if she was still feeding. *But how can she possibly be so lovely when she was conceived in violence?* Pearl found herself thinking. Throughout the long months she had carried her, she had hated her with a vengeance and yet now . . . The realisation hit her like a blow – this was *her* child, her own flesh and blood, and such a surge of love pulsed through her that it threatened to choke her.

'She's just perfect, isn't she?' Mrs Forbes said softly, and Pearl could only nod in reply, too full of emotion to speak.

The woman hovered, clearly keen to take the baby back at the earliest opportunity, and at last Pearl handed her over.

'Right, I'll just go and settle her down for a nap.' Mrs Forbes was backing towards the door as if she couldn't leave the room quickly enough.

And then she was gone and Pearl broke into devastated sobs. It felt as if all she had done on and off ever since she had woken was cry, and now she knew there would be yet more tears to come as she thought of the little girl she could never claim as her own. She had given up that right when she had agreed to let Mrs Forbes take the child and it would surely break the woman's heart if she were to go back on her word now.

What could she offer her anyway, compared to what the Forbeses could? With them she would be dressed in fine clothes and have the best education that money could buy. She would be spoiled and pampered and never know what it was like to go without as Pearl had. No, the deal was done and, much as it hurt, Pearl knew that she could never renege on it now. It was this that finally helped her to make her decision about her future. It would be torture to stay here and watch the child grow, knowing that she could never claim her as her own. But in England she still had a sister, so she would go there and try to make a life close to her.

'I think you have made the right decision,' Mrs Forbes said, trying to hide her relief when Pearl told her the next day. 'When my mother returns to England, I shall book you a passage too. But are you quite sure that you don't want a position with her in London?'

Pearl shook her head. She had felt well enough to get out of bed and sit in the chair by the window for a short time today. 'Thank you for the offer, but no. I would rather try to find work close to Amy. She's all I have left now, you see?'

'I understand.' Mrs Forbes nodded. 'In that case, I shall write you an excellent reference. That should help when you begin to seek work.'

Pearl nodded numbly. There could be no changing her mind now.

Mrs Forbes's mother and her lady's maid, Sophie, arrived two weeks later, heartily glad that the sea voyage was over. She had never been a good traveller. Pearl was up and about by that time and it had been agreed that she should resume some of her duties so that it wouldn't look suspicious to the visitor. Mrs Forbes had also started to receive visitors again and it was now commonly known within the community that she had given birth to a baby girl, who was duly admired by all.

When first introduced to the baby, Laura Kennedy-Scott stared at the child for some time, before declaring she was just beautiful. 'Although I will admit to being shocked when I heard that you were with child again,' she told her daughter, who had the grace to blush. 'You had such a hard time with Elizabeth that I thought your child-bearing days were well and truly over?'

Emmaline's cheeks grew rosy as she squirmed uncomfortably. 'So did I.'

'And was it a difficult birth? Are you feeding her yourself or do you have a wet nurse?'

Her daughter was growing more uneasy by the minute. There were so many questions. 'No, it wasn't a difficult birth and no, I'm not feeding her myself; I didn't have enough milk,' she answered a touch coldly. 'And no, I don't have a wet nurse, or a nanny for that matter. I want to look after her myself. I feel I missed far too much of their infancy when I had Monty and Elizabeth.'

'But my dear, whatever will people think?' Mrs Kennedy-Scott had a heart of gold beneath her bossy exterior, but she was a hopeless snob. Thankfully the conversation went no further, for the subject of their attention woke at that moment and gave a lusty yell to let everyone know she was due for a feed.

That afternoon, while Mrs Forbes spent time with her mother and settled her in, Pearl took a walk to the church-yard. She was very much better now but still tired easily, and by the time she got there she was glad to sit down for a while on the little wooden bench that nestled in the shadows of the tiny church's walls. It was now early October and once again the prospect of a long, hard winter was looming. *Not that it will bother me*, Pearl thought, as she looked towards the simple wooden cross that marked her sister's grave. She would be leaving for London in four weeks' time when Mrs Forbes's mother returned and it felt strange to think that she would never come here again.

Eventually she wandered across to the grave and gently laid the posy of evergreens she had picked on to the pile of earth that marked Eliza's resting place. As always, her heart was heavy as she pictured the little sister she had always loved and tried to protect. Even now it was hard to accept that her love had never been returned.

'I shall be going away soon, Eliza,' she whispered, but the wind snatched her words away. 'I shan't be able to come here again, but rest easy knowing that, wherever I am, you will live on in my heart.' The afternoon was fast darkening by this time and so after a few more minutes of silent contemplation she turned and wearily made her way back to the house.

It was decided that the three women should return to London aboard *The Neptune*, yet another of Mr Forbes's ships, that was due to deliver a cargo of timber to London early in December, and from then on the time seemed to pass in a blur. Mrs Forbes insisted that Pearl should visit the dressmaker for two more new gowns before she left, and despite her mistress's kindness Pearl had a funny feeling that Mrs Forbes would be glad to see the back of her. She could understand why. Once she was gone, the baby would be completely hers.

Pearl had tried her best not to be near the baby but it was hard to avoid her sometimes, and each time she saw her she had to resist the urge to pick her up and nuzzle her soft skin. She had moved back into her old room in the servants' quarters and it brought back painful memories of Eliza each time she entered the room and saw her empty bed.

Susan was also beginning to get upset at the thought of Pearl leaving. They had been close since they first met in the workhouse, and become even more so during their journey to Canada, and she knew that she would miss her.

She was cheered somewhat when Susan shared some happy news the week before Pearl was to sail. 'I think I might be with child,' she whispered, when they sat in the kitchen together one evening. Cook and the family had all gone to bed and Will was snoozing in the fireside chair with his feet stuck out on the fender. 'I'm not sure yet, I've only missed one course so I won't raise Will's hopes yet awhile but I fought yer'd like to know afore yer left.'

'Oh, how wonderful!' Pearl was genuinely pleased for her, and gave her a quick hug. 'Little Mathilda will have a playmate.'

Susan grinned. 'I doubt that. Can yer really see Mrs Forbes letting her mix wiv the child of a servant?'

'I don't see how she could stop it if they both live here,' Pearl responded.

Suddenly Susan's eyes became moist as she went on, 'I'm going to miss yer *so* much.'

'I'll miss you too. But we can write to each other regularly. I want to hear about everything that's going on here and all about . . .' Her voice trailed away, but they were both aware of what she had been about to say.

'Don't worry, I'll make sure yer know how Mathilda is,' Susan promised, her face solemn. Knowing Pearl as she did, she realised just how much it was going to cost her to leave her child there.

'Perhaps one day when you and Will have saved up enough, you could come to England for a holiday,' Pearl said, hoping to lighten the mood.

Susan nodded enthusiastically. 'I'd love that, but I fink it will be a long time away yet. Me and Will are saving hard now and when we've enough put by, he wants to start a little horse farm of his own.'

Knowing how much Will loved the horses, Pearl thought it was an excellent idea. He stirred at that moment and pulled his shoes on, and soon after he and Susan retired to their rooms above the stables, leaving Pearl to lock up for the night.

Before she knew it, it was the morning of their departure, and while Mrs Forbes helped her mother's maid to pack her last-minute things, Pearl crept into the drawing room to say a final goodbye to her baby daughter. She was lying in her crib, cooing and gurgling as she waved her chubby arms and legs in the air.

As Pearl bent over her, she gave her a gummy smile that set Pearl's heart racing. 'Goodbye, my sweet darling,' Pearl whispered brokenly. 'Please forgive me for leaving you. You'll have a much better life here than I could ever have offered you, so please be happy.' She planted a tender kiss on the baby's cheek, savouring the feel of the soft skin on her lips. Then she hurried from the room without looking back, for she knew if she did, she would not be able to leave her.

'Ah, Pearl.' Mrs Forbes hurried towards her and pressed an envelope into Pearl's hand. 'I was hoping to catch you on your own. Please take this . . . it's a sort of little thank you for all you've done for me.'

Pearl shook her head. 'No, please. You've done more than eno—'

But Mrs Forbes frowned and wagged a finger at her. 'I don't want to hear another word. There should be enough there to cover your travelling expenses to the Midlands once you get to England and keep you going until you find employment. And don't worry, I promise that when you are settled, if you let me have your address, I shall keep you updated on Mathilda's progress.'

Swallowing the lump in her throat, Pearl moved on to the kitchen without another word.

Susan was just putting her coat on – she had insisted that she come to the quay to see her off – so Pearl went to Cook to give her a last hug and kiss.

The woman's eyes were watery as she told her, 'You just take care of yourself now, hinny. And don't forget us. We shall want you to write regularly to let us know how you are.'

'I will,' Pearl promised with a catch in her voice as she turned blindly to the door. She would say her goodbyes to Will once he had taken them to the docks in the carriage, which was now loaded with their luggage and waiting at the door.

She had said goodbye to the master that morning before he had gone to oversee the loading of the timber on to the ship, so now all that remained was to go and take her seat in the carriage. Once she had leaned back against the soft leather squabs, she stared at the house from the window, knowing deep down that she would never see it again. She and Eliza had gone there with so much hope in their hearts, thinking that this would be the start of their for-ever future, and in fairness she had to admit that she had known a deal of happiness and contentment there, but it didn't outweigh the heartbreak she had also suffered. Now she watched numbly as Mrs Kennedy-Scott, her maid and Susan came out to join her.

The older woman waved at her daughter as Will drove the carriage away, and soon the house was lost to sight and they were rattling through the town. She allowed herself a last quick glance at the church as they passed it. Susan had promised that she would tend Eliza's grave for her, which gave her a measure of comfort. Almost before they knew it, they were at the docks, and as they got down from the carriage, sailors appeared as if by magic to spirit all the luggage away up the gangplank.

'Half an hour until we sail,' a sailor shouted from the deck, as Susan sidled up to her and took her hand.

'This is it then,' she said softly as she and Pearl stared into each other's eyes, each knowing how much they were going to miss each other. Mrs Kennedy-Scott and her maid discreetly started up the gangplank leaving them to have a few precious moments alone.

Will joined them and all three of them were tearful.

'You just make sure you look after her for me,' Pearl told him in a shaky voice.

He nodded and placed a protective arm about his young wife's shoulders. 'You need have no fear on that score. It's you we're more concerned about. We wish you were going to work for Mrs Forbes's mother. At least we would know you were safe then instead of going off galivanting to pastures new all on your own.'

Pearl smiled through her tears. 'I shan't be galivanting, as you put it,' she assured him. 'I know exactly where my sister is now and it's important to me that I find her. She's all the family I have left now apart from Mathil—' The name died on her lips as a sharp pain pierced her heart, but they said nothing as they nodded in understanding.

But then someone was shouting for all to come aboard, and Will gently nudged her towards the gangplank.

'Go on and stay safe, just remember we're always here for you if you should need us.'

Pearl nodded and blindly began to climb. Soon she was on the deck, and already the gangplank was being raised. This was it; there could be no going back now.

Very slowly, the enormous ship began to move, and they all waved to each other until soon Susan and Will were nothing more than distant specks on the shore.

Slowly Pearl turned and went to find her cabin. She discovered that she was in the one next to Mrs Kennedy-Scott's maid and was pleased to see that it was slightly bigger than the one she had shared with Eliza when they had travelled to London before. It all seemed such a long time ago now and so much had happened since. With an enormous effort, Pearl pulled herself together. There was no point in looking back. What had gone before could never be changed. From now on she must look to the future.

She began to unpack her clothes and make herself as comfortable as she could. Thankfully, Mrs Forbes had supplied her with a good selection of books to read on the journey, so at least she knew she wouldn't be bored. Once it was done, she wrapped up warmly and went up on deck, just in time to see the coastline of Canada fading into the distance as the rain fell.

'Goodbye, Eliza; goodbye, Mathilda; goodbye, Nick,' she whispered, glad that the raindrops disguised the tears on her cheeks.

Chapter Forty-One

A week into the voyage, the weather took a drastic turn for the worse and everyone was confined to their cabins. Mrs Kennedy-Scott's maid informed Pearl that her mistress was suffering from a severe bout of seasickness, but thankfully up until then Pearl had been well, possibly because she had kept herself busy reading and not given herself much time to think about anything else.

'Eeh, the poor woman's been as sick as a dog,' the maid informed her, wrinkling her nose in distaste. 'The cabin smells like someone's died in there, despite all my best efforts to keep it clean.'

Her words brought back memories of Eliza being the same way on their last sea journey, but she hastily pushed them away.

'No doubt she'll feel a lot better when we get through this storm,' Pearl told her encouragingly. The poor woman didn't look all that well herself and her face was the colour of lint.

'I hope you're right,' the woman sighed, as she tried to catch her plate again.

They were seated in the dining cabin eating a surprisingly tasty meal of stew and dumplings, although it wasn't easy when with each swell of the ship their plates kept sliding away from them.

Thankfully, the next day the storm abated, and once more they were able to go up on deck to get some fresh air, although no one ventured outside for long because it was bitterly cold. In fact, Pearl had overheard the first mate say that he was sure he could smell snow in the air.

It was early one evening as she stood on deck, watching the mighty ship slice through the waves, that someone came to stand beside her. Glancing over, Pearl saw that it was Mrs Kennedy-Scott. She was still decidedly pale but looking much better than she had.

She smiled. 'So how are you, my dear?' she asked pleasantly as she gripped the iron railing. She clearly wasn't feeling very confident out there.

'I'm very well, thank you.' Pearl returned the smile. 'And I'm pleased to see that you're looking a little better too. Your maid told me how poorly you've been.'

'Hm, it was that wretched storm. I've never really found my sea legs, which is why I don't visit Emmaline as often as I would like to,' she confided. She peeped at Pearl out of the corner of her eye then as she went on quietly, 'Of course, I could hardly avoid this trip when I had a new granddaughter to meet, could I? Baby Mathilda is quite delightful, isn't she? A real little beauty.'

'Yes . . . yes, she is,' Pearl agreed, feeling the colour rush into her cheeks.

They stood in silence for some seconds, but the woman's next words made Pearl's head snap around and her eyes widen with shock.

'It couldn't have been easy for you to give her up, my dear.'

'*Wh-what*? I, er . . . don't understand what you mean,' Pearl stammered.

'Oh, come now.' Mrs Kennedy-Scott chuckled. 'I knew the second I clapped eyes on the child that she was yours. I have a sneaky feeling that Monty had something to do with it too.'

Pearl clamped her lips together as panic coursed through her. If Mrs Kennedy-Scott had suspected her and Mrs Forbes's deception, why had she waited until now to say anything?

The woman reached out and laid her hand across Pearl's. 'Don't worry. You don't have to confirm my suspicions, but I've lived a long time and I'm no fool, my dear.' Her voice held a trace of sadness as she stared out across the waves. 'I loved Monty – he was my grandson – but I also know that he was no angel. When he was living with me, it was no secret that he sought out female company often. I think this baby will be the making of my daughter, although I do realise what it must have cost you to leave her back there. After losing both of her children, I feared for Emmaline's sanity. No mother should lose a child, let alone both of them. But now that she has little Mathilda to focus on, I think she will survive. Just tell me one thing – were you in love with Monty?'

'Oh no . . . I . . . we . . .' Pearl faltered, shaking her head in denial.

Mrs Kennedy-Scott nodded. 'It's all right, you don't need to say anymore. I think I have a picture of what happened now, and although I mourn his death, I have to admit that he had a bad streak in him. I just pray that little Mathilda takes after you.'

Pearl was at a complete loss for words, but Mrs Kennedy-Scott patted her hand. 'We will say no more on the subject, but just know that if ever you should need anything in the future, you can always come to me. You have given my daughter the most precious gift in the world and I thank you, and apologise on my grandson's behalf for all you must have gone through. Goodnight, my dear.'

And with that she turned and walked away, her back straight and the feathers on her hat dancing in the wind.

Pearl stood there, shocked to her core. She and Mrs Forbes had thought they had done so well keeping the true parentage of the baby quiet, but it seemed they hadn't reckoned on Mrs Kennedy-Scott's astuteness. Still, at least Pearl felt confident that she would never share the knowledge with anyone else, and that was some comfort. She would have hated for Mathilda to ever find out the deception, for then the child would know that she had abandoned her and Pearl couldn't have borne that.

After a time, she slowly turned and made her way to her cabin, and for the rest of the journey she barely ventured out except to visit the dining cabin when she was hungry.

At last land was sighted and Pearl began to pack her few belongings. She was feeling a mixture of emotions: sadness for the baby she would never see again, heartbreak for the loss of Eliza and Nick, but also a growing excitement that very soon she might be reunited with Amy. It was only then that she thought to open the envelope Mrs Forbes had pressed into her hand before she left Canada, and what she found inside made her gasp. There were fifty crisp one-pound notes; more money than Pearl had ever dreamed of having, an absolute fortune, and tears swam into her eyes as she thought of the woman's generosity.

Had she known how much was inside it she would have refused it point-blank, but it was too late for that now, so she began to make plans. She had thought that she would immediately have to find work, but now there were endless possibilities. She could perhaps even afford to open her own little business, although what she might do, she had no idea as yet. She was sorely restricted in skills apart from those of being a servant. She took out two of the notes and tucked the rest safely down into her valise, and after carrying it on to the deck she stood and watched as the shore of her home-land grew closer.

At last it was time to disembark, and as Pearl made her way to the gangplank, she briefly glimpsed Mrs Kennedy-Scott and her maid. The woman raised her hand in fare-well and after waving back, Pearl squared her shoulders and descended on to dry land.

The docks were teeming with people: sailors rolling barrels and shifting heavy cargo, well-dressed ladies and gentlemen waiting to greet passengers, as well as heavily made-up prostitutes parading up and down. Pearl flushed as she saw their rouged cheeks and the way they flaunted themselves, but she also pitied them. She knew that many of them had turned to their profession because there was no other option open to them. Most of them probably had children to feed or elderly parents to care for, and as she passed one such woman she fumbled in her bag and pressed some loose coins into her hand. The woman's face was pockmarked and she smelled strongly of stale sweat, but as she glanced down at the gift, she smiled. 'Thank you, me dearie. You've a 'eart o' gold. God bless yer!'

Pearl hurried on, stepping across the coils of rope that littered the quay and weaving in and out amongst the throngs of people until she reached the street where she hailed a cab to take her to Euston Station.

It was only when she was settled in a carriage on the train that she began to relax a little. She had never travelled such a long distance on her own before and found it quite nerve-wracking. But very soon now she would hopefully be reunited with Amy and the rest of her life could begin. As she stared from the window, a lump formed in her throat as she thought of Nick and the baby she had left behind, but she pushed the thoughts away. They were her past now and it was time to look to the future.

As the train chuffed on its way, the view from the window began to reveal fields covered in frost with horses, sheep and cattle grazing in them. It was nothing like the vast open spaces she had seen in Canada, but all the same it was very different to the crowded streets of London where she had been brought up and she watched with interest.

It was dark and bitterly cold by the time the train drew into Trent Valley railway station in Nuneaton, and as Pearl stepped down on to the platform, she experienced a moment of panic. She was in a strange place with nowhere to stay, but then as she thought of the money tucked safely away in her bag, she relaxed a little. It was far too late to try to find Amy that evening; that was a pleasure she would save for the following day. For now she would have to find a hotel where she could rest for the night.

The kindly porter directed her to one in the marketplace, and soon she was shown to a room where she thankfully kicked her shoes off and lay on the wonderfully comfortable bed. She was very hungry by then, but the thought of going to find something to eat seemed to be too much of an effort, and before she knew it, she had slipped into an exhausted sleep.

The following morning she rose and, after having a thorough wash, she went down to the hotel dining room to enjoy a hearty breakfast. Excitement was beginning to build by then, and after asking directions to Swan Lane, she set off with a spring in her step. It was market day and Pearl strolled past pens full of farm animals that the ruddy-faced farmers had brought to sell. There were chickens squawking indignantly in their cages and cattle, pigs and sheep who gazed at her dolefully as the farmers heatedly bartered and argued their prices. Once she had passed the cattle market, she came to stalls selling everything from fish to buckets and brooms, but she was too excited to linger and hurried on.

Swan Lane proved to be a prosperous-looking road with rows of imposing three-storey houses, and after checking the address that Amy had given her, she stopped to eye the snow-white lace curtains that hung at the windows. There was a deep front garden with well-tended lawns and a red front door that gleamed in the cold, early December sunshine. A large gate stood to one side of the house, which she assumed would lead to stables and the servants' entrance.

She paused uncertainly then. She could hardly knock on the front door when she was merely the sister of one of the maids. Making a hasty decision, she entered the gate and took the path that led round to the back of the house, hoping that she was right in her assumption that this would lead to the kitchen.

She was proved to be correct when she came to a stable block and a large cobbled yard. To the other side of the yard was a room which she thought might be the laundry room from the amount of steam that was issuing from it, and next to that was another door. She approached it and paused. Through the window to one side of it she could see a young maid scrubbing away at a sink full of dirty pots and for a moment it made her think of Eliza and a lump came to her throat. But she forced herself to stay calm and after a moment she raised her hand and tapped on the door.

Almost instantly it was opened by another maid in a starched white mop cap and a frilly, snow-white apron, who smiled at her.

'Hello, can I 'elp you?'

Pearl returned her smile. 'I'm hoping so. I believe my sister Amy works here, and I wondered if it might be possible for me to see her for a moment?'

The maid's smile broadened as she took Pearl's arm and almost dragged her into the room. 'Why, you must be Pearl! Amy never stops going on about you but we thought you were in Canada. Oh, this will be such a lovely surprise for her won't it, Cook?'

A plump, rosy-cheeked woman who was rolling pastry at the table paused to look up and give her a gummy grin. 'It certainly will,' she agreed. 'But get our visitor a cup o' tea, Becky. An' you, Mildred, go an' find Amy an' tell 'er to get her arse down 'ere. She's strippin' the mistress's bed, I believe.'

Pearl perched sedately on the chair that the cook motioned to, while another girl shot off towards a dark wooden door that Pearl guessed must lead to the main house.

'An' don't get tellin' 'er why I want her,' the cook shouted after her retreating figure. 'We don't want to go spoilin' the surprise.'

Becky poured a cup of tea from a huge brown teapot that stood close to the range and Pearl thanked her as she kept her eyes firmly fixed on the door, her heart hammering. A few minutes passed and the door opened as Becky reappeared, followed by Amy, whose mouth gaped at the sight of her sister.

Amy was now fifteen years old and had grown so much that Pearl barely recognised her, although she still had the same cheeky grin and twinkling blue eyes. And then suddenly she let out a whoop of joy and Pearl just had time to balance her cup and saucer on the edge of the table before Amy threw herself into her arms, almost knocking her from the chair.

'*Oooh*, I can't believe it!' Amy's voice was thick with emotion. 'There were times when I was sure I'd never see you again . . . but what are yer doin' 'ere? Are yer on a visit?'

Pearl laughed as she returned the hug. 'No, it isn't a visit. I've come to live here,' she told her with a grin. 'Well, not here in this house, of course, but somewhere close by. I just have to find somewhere to live. I stayed in a hotel in the marketplace last night but it's quite pricey so I don't want to have to stay there for long.' Then, looking apologetically towards the cook, she told her, 'I'm sorry to come and interfere with Amy's work but I couldn't wait another minute to see her.'

'No need to apologise, luvvy.' The cook gave her a warm smile. 'The bedrooms can wait for a while. And I'll tell you what, bein' as you've come so far, I'll let her have this evenin' off so you can meet up an' have a proper catch up.'

'Thanks, Cook,' Amy said gratefully and, turning back to Pearl, she asked, 'Where shall I meet you an' what time?'

Pearl shrugged, not knowing the area at all. Then she had an idea. 'Why don't you come to the hotel? It's far too cold to be walking the streets and I'm sure they won't mind me having a visitor in my room, providing it isn't a gentleman.'

Amy tittered, her eyes shining. 'Eh, yer don't 'alf talk posh now,' she teased. 'But that's a good idea, shall we say about seven o'clock?'

And so, after a few more minutes during which they barely stopped talking, Pearl took her leave; she didn't want to take advantage of the kindly cook's good nature.

She was pacing the floor that evening as she waited in anticipation for Amy's arrival, and spot on time there was a knock on her door.

'I'm still 'aving to pinch meself to believe yer really 'ere,' Amy told her, as she took her coat off and slung it across the chair. Then glancing about the room she whistled through her teeth. 'Eeh, fancy you bein' able to stay in a posh place like this. 'Ave yer come into some money or sommat?'

'Let's just say I'm comfortable,' Pearl hedged.

Amy sighed as her face became sad. 'I got yer letter about our Eliza drownin',' she said with a catch in her voice. 'I could 'ardly believe it; she were so beautiful.'

'Yes, she was,' Pearl agreed. A maid appeared with a tray of hot chocolate and biscuits that Pearl had ordered, and the sad mood was broken as Amy chuckled.

'Look at us bein' waited on like toffs, eh? I reckon I could get used to this.' Reaching out, she took a biscuit as Pearl handed her a steaming mug of chocolate. 'But now tell me all about this chap of yours. It's Nick, ain't it? Is he 'ere an' all?'

'Actually . . .' Pearl licked her lips as she avoided her sister's eyes. 'It didn't work out between us in the end, so we decided to go our separate ways.' She was determined that Amy would never know the real reason for her and Nick parting, or the truth about Eliza's death, and definitely never anything about Mathilda.

The next hour passed in a blur as they caught up on all that had happened since their separation and all too soon it was almost time for Amy to return to the house in Swan Lane.

'So, what sort of job are yer lookin' for?' she queried as she pulled her coat back on and wrapped a thick scarf about her neck.

'Actually, I was wondering if I couldn't open a little shop of some sort,' Pearl admitted. 'Perhaps something with living quarters attached.'

'Crikey, bein' a lady's maid must 'ave paid good wages,' Amy commented, impressed. Pearl didn't reply as her sister stared thoughtfully into space for a moment, before suddenly saying, 'Stone the crows! I reckon I might know just the place that might suit yer. An' I 'appen to know that it's goin' fer a song an' all!'

Chapter Forty-Two

'Go on then! Tell me about it,' Pearl urged excitedly.

'It just so 'appens' that my mistress is also a great seamstress,' Amy informed her. 'She's allus sewin' or embroiderin' somethin' or another so she often sends me into town to fetch embroidery silks, cottons an' stuff like that. Anyway, the old woman that owns the 'aberdashery shop, Mrs Wilkinson, 'as been poorly an' 'as decided to sell the shop an' go an' live wi' her son an' his wife in Bournemouth. She's a dear old soul an' we get on well, which is why she told me she's lookin' to make a quick sale. It might be worth you payin' 'er a visit. I'll write the address down for yer, shall I?'

Pearl nodded. It sounded like something she could do. After all, how hard could it be selling sewing materials?

'I shall go and see her first thing in the morning,' she promised Amy as she saw her to the door. 'And I'll meet you on Sunday afternoon, shall I?'

'Can't wait!' Amy went off with a spring in her step. Having her sister back was like having all her birthdays and Christmases come at once, and she was humming merrily as she hurried home through the frosty streets.

Bright and early the next morning, Pearl dressed up warmly and hurried back to the main street in search of the little shop that Amy had told her about. When she found it, she stood outside examining it for a moment. The window was so dirty that she could barely see through it and the paint was peeling from the door. The sign above it had faded until it was unreadable and there was a hotchpotch of things displayed in the window. Reels of cotton, embroidery silks, loose buttons – all covered in a thick layer of dust. She took a deep breath and entered the gloomy interior, setting a little bell above the shop door tinkling merrily. There was a long wooden counter that stretched almost the length of the back wall, which was untidily piled with all manner of things, and as she looked about a door behind it opened and a little old lady leaning heavily on a walking stick and with a thick shawl about her shoulders appeared. Her hair was silver-grey and pulled into a tight bun on the back of her head and her face was lined, but her eyes were friendly as she said, 'Hello, me dear. May I help you?'

'Actually, my sister advised me to come and see you. She visits your shop regularly to get things for her mistress. Her name is Amy.'

'Ah, young Amy.' The woman nodded. 'I can see the likeness now you've said it. She's such a lovely girl. But what can I do for you?'

And so, Pearl hesitantly told her about Amy saying that the shop was up for sale, and when she was done the woman narrowed her eyes and frowned. 'But aren't you very young to be thinking of buying a shop, dear?'

'Not at all and I do have the money, I assure you,' Pearl answered. 'Well . . . that's depending on what you're asking for it, of course. This would suit me down to the ground, particularly as Amy tells me there are living quarters attached?'

'There are but they're very small,' the woman warned. 'There's a bedroom and a little sitting room above, which is what's causing me trouble, you see? Getting up and down the stairs isn't as easy as it used to be. And then the kitchen is out the back here. Would you like to take a look?'

'I'd love to,' Pearl told her.

After placing the closed sign on the door, Mrs Wilkinson led her upstairs. At the top of them was a small square landing that led directly into a tiny sitting room, which again was in rather a squalid condition and as Pearl looked about the old woman squirmed with embarrassment.

'I apologise for the condition it's in. There was a time when the whole of this place gleamed from top to bottom and the shop was neat as a new pin, but it's all got too much for me now, I'm afraid.'

'Please don't apologise,' Pearl said with a smile. 'It's very cosy.'

A door in the far wall led into what proved to be a bedroom, but again it was in a very sad state of disrepair. Even so, Pearl could see how it could be improved with some tender loving care, and she could picture herself living there.

'It's really charming,' she told Mrs Wilkinson after a tour of inspection. 'And if I could afford it I would be very interested in buying it. What are you asking?'

The old woman eyed the girl pensively for some moments as she leaned heavily on her walking stick. She certainly seemed genuine enough, even though she did seem very young to be starting a business. And then she named a price that made Pearl blink with surprise. It seemed to be remarkably cheap, and as Pearl quickly did calculations in her mind, she knew it would leave her more than enough to get the place back to rights and restock the shop. She would even be able to afford to close the shop while all the redecorating was done.

'In with that I'll leave you all the furniture and whatever stock there is,' Mrs Wilkinson told her. 'I know the furniture ain't up to much, but I dare say it'll do you till you can afford to change it. All I want is to walk away and get on the train with a suitcase, and the sooner the better. Have a think about it, eh?'

'I don't have to.' Pearl made a hasty decision. 'It's a deal!'

Mrs Wilkinson beamed. 'In that case I'll have my solicitor draw the papers up this very day and once they're signed, happen I can be gone by the weekend.'

'That would be marvellous.' Pearl shook her hand. She couldn't believe how quickly she had found something that she hoped would be just right for her, and she felt as if the angels were smiling down on her.

'Right, then I think we should celebrate now with a cup of tea,' the old lady said with a grin as she sank into the faded wing chair at the side of the small fireplace where a cheery fire was burning. 'I'll let you go down into the kitchen at the back of the shop to make it. You may as well start to feel your way around while I rest me old legs.'

Pearl was only too happy to oblige, and while she was waiting for the kettle to boil on the small stove she peeped out into the yard and was pleased to see that it was a fair size with a little coal house and an outside toilet. There was a tin bath hanging on a nail in the wall and the yard was full of empty boxes and rubbish, but already she was picturing it in the summer when it would be swept clean and have tubs of geraniums scattered about.

Once the tea was made, she placed a cosy over the teapot and carried it back upstairs on a tray.

'Now, I'm not going to lie to you,' Mrs Wilkinson said as Pearl poured the tea into two pretty rose-patterned china cups and saucers. 'Business hasn't been as brisk as it used to be just lately, but that's only because I haven't been able to keep the shop properly stocked up. What I'd advise you is take note of what your customers ask for and don't stock anything too expensive. You have to remember this is a market town, so the majority of your customers will be farmers' wives and working-class women who make their own clothes. It might be worth stocking some bolts of reasonably priced material as well to see how that sells. I always intended to do that but never got around to it.'

'I'll do that,' Pearl promised, glad of any advice she could get. They chatted about the area for a little while, and then arranged a day for Mrs Wilkinson to move out.

'I shall only need a day to pack my personal things,' she told Pearl. 'And providing my solicitor can get everything signed and sealed I could catch the train to Bournemouth on Friday. Or is that too soon for you, dear?'

'Oh no, not at all, that would suit me just fine,' Pearl assured her and smiled as she thought of Amy's face when she met her on Sunday and brought her back here.

'In that case, come back tomorrow afternoon and hopefully I should have the papers all ready for you.'

'Thank you, I'll be here,' Pearl promised and she almost floated back to the hotel in a fog of happiness. It was now Tuesday, which meant that if all went well, she would only be sleeping for three more nights at the hotel before moving into her very own home. It was an exciting thought.

The following day, as arranged, Pearl signed the paperwork that Mrs Wilkinson's solicitor had prepared and he shook her hand.

'If you would care to come and pay the agreed price at ten o'clock on Friday morning, I will then hand you the keys to your new property, and may I congratulate you, Miss Parker. I'm sure you will make your new venture a huge success.'

'Thank you, sir.' Pearl blushed prettily as she stepped out into the market and began to stroll amongst the stalls, wishing the time away until Friday rolled around. She so wanted to tell Amy the good news, but somehow she was going to have to contain her excitement until Sunday.

During the night on Thursday it began to snow, and Pearl awoke to a white world that made the streets and roofs glisten like diamonds. She had her breakfast and paid her bill, then set off for the solicitor's. Once the money for the business had duly changed hands, she was given the keys and she made her way to her new home, pausing outside to study it. She had to admit that the frontage looked in a sorry state, but the night before when she had called in to say goodbye to Mrs Wilkinson, who would already be on the train and heading towards her new life in Bournemouth, the dear old soul had given her the number of a reliable odd-job man, so Pearl was confident that if there were any jobs that she couldn't tackle herself she would have someone to help out.

Once inside and with the closed sign on the door, she made her way upstairs and was pleased to find that a few glowing embers were still alive in the grate. Hastily she threw some nuggets of coal on to the fire and wandered about. True to her word, the old lady had left every stick of furniture for her, and although the wing chairs and the curtains were somewhat faded, she was pleased to discover that the mahogany sideboard and the dresser were actually very sturdy and just needed a good clean and polish. From there she wandered into the bedroom and again she was pleased to find that the chest of drawers and the wardrobe were of good quality. She realised, though, that she must concentrate her efforts on downstairs first so that she could reopen the shop, and so back down she went, to decide where she should start.

Beneath the counter were countless small drawers to accommodate the buttons and cotton reels but they had become mixed up and there was no order to them at all. With a smile she rolled her sleeves up and went into the small kitchen to put the kettle on for some hot water, and soon after she was scrubbing the floors as if her life depended on it. She then went out to purchase some paint for the front door and some limewash for the inner walls along with some new bedding. She also did some food shopping and, by the end of the day, her efforts were beginning to pay off. She had emptied everything out of the front window and scrubbed the glass until it shone and the display shelves sparkled. She would have liked to tackle the walls next but realised with a yawn that it was very late and as yet she hadn't eaten. *Never mind, Rome wasn't built in a day*, she told herself, and wearily went upstairs to spend the first night in her new little home.

On Sunday she could hardly wait to meet Amy and when she saw her sister swinging towards her, she hurried to greet her.

'You'll never guess what I've done.' She grinned as she slipped her arm through Amy's. 'I went to see Mrs Wilkinson and I've bought the shop from her!'

'You've *what*?' Amy was astounded but delighted for her. 'Why, that's wonderful. When are you moving in?'

'I already have. That's where we're going now and I can't wait to show you what I've been doing.' They hurried on through the snow, and once they arrived at the shopfront and Pearl unlocked the door, Amy stared around in amazement.

'Crikey, someone's been busy. It looks so clean and fresh!'

Pearl nodded. 'I certainly have. I only have that wall there left to paint and then once I've restocked, I shall be ready to open. There's still a lot to do upstairs, mind, but that will have to wait and be done when the shop isn't open. I want to make a go of this, Amy, and I'm sure I can if I work hard enough.'

'I'm sure you will.' Amy was very impressed, even more so when Pearl showed her the living quarters upstairs.

'I was thinking that if I did make a success of things you might be able to come and help and live here in time – but only if you want to, of course. It would be a bit of a squeeze, admittedly, and we'd have to share the double bed, but it wouldn't be the first time, would it?'

Amy shook her head as she thought back to the squalid living conditions they'd been brought up in in London. Small this place might be, but it was a palace compared to that.

'I'd love us to be properly together again,' she admitted with a catch in her voice. 'Not that I'm not 'appy where I am, you understand? The mistress is fair and we never go short of decent food and a clean bed, but it isn't the same as being with family.'

'Then that's what we'll aim for,' Pearl declared and leaving Amy to have a good look around she went off to put the kettle on, feeling as proud as Punch!

They sat for a time chatting and catching up on all the years they had been apart, although Pearl was careful not to mention any of the people she had loved and lost. It was still far too painful. But then once they had drunk their tea, Amy rolled her sleeves up and declared, 'There's no point in sitting here when there's work waiting to be done. Lend me an apron to cover me dress an' we'll go down an' tackle that last wall in the shop. We should get it done between us if we stick in now before I have to go back. We can chat down there just as well as up here.'

Pearl felt guilty. 'But it's your afternoon off. Wouldn't you rather put your feet up and rest?'

'There'll be time aplenty fer that when I'm old an' grey. Now where's that apron?'

And so for the rest of the afternoon, armed with paint brushes, they worked side by side and as darkness fell, the job was done. 'I reckon you'll 'ave to wait till the weather improves a bit afore yer try to paint the front door,' Amy said sensibly. 'We'll 'ave to just give it a good rub and a scrub fer now, eh?' Just like her sister, she was keen to see results when she set her mind to something and as well as tackling the door, she also cleaned the outside of the shop window, even though she was up to her ankles in snow.

'There then!' She smiled with satisfaction as she surveyed their afternoon's work. 'I reckon you can start to get the shelves stocked up now and then you'll be all ready to go. By the time I come back next Sunday, you could well be open.'

Amy was right, and the following Friday, just a week after moving in, Pearl turned the sign on the door to open and the first few customers began to trickle in. She had taken Mrs Wilkinson's advice and purchased some bolts of good, serviceable but inexpensive material, and to her joy it was selling like hot cakes, particularly to the farmers' wives who went more for serviceability than fashion. Admittedly, Pearl realised, before she went into profit, she would have to get back all the money she had spent on stock, but the signs were promising and she had every hope that the shop would be a success.

She wrote to Mrs Forbes to tell her of her new address, for she was longing to hear how Mathilda was. Even though almost every hour of her day was busily occupied, Pearl still thought of the child constantly and when she saw a mother with a baby of a similar age to Mathilda, it was like a knife in her heart. Thoughts of Nick were still painful too but she doggedly went on with what she was doing, determined to make a new life for herself and her one remaining sister.

She had chosen her path and now she must stick to it.

Chapter Forty-Three

December 1881

Almost exactly a year to the day Pearl had taken posses-
sion of the shop, Amy left her employment in Swan
Lane and joined her. The shop had proved to be a huge success and Pearl was now confident that it was earning enough
to keep both of them comfortably, even after paying Amy
a modest wage. As neither of them knew the exact date of
their birthday, they each decided that they would settle on
the middle of the month they were born in and so, on the
day Amy moved in, they celebrated Pearl's birthday with an
iced cake that Amy had bought for her from the baker just
along the street.

'I can't believe you're nineteen,' Amy giggled. 'And still
no sign of a young man. You'll end up an old maid if you
don't get your skates on.'

A cloud passed across Pearl's face as a picture of Nick
flashed in front of her eyes, but she quickly forced a smile
again as she told her sister, 'I'm quite happy as I am, thank
you very much. I have you and my shop – what more could
I want?'

'Ah, but I won't always be here, will I?' Amy had a dreamy
look in her eye. She had recently met the son of one of the
local farmers and from what Pearl could see they seemed to

be quite taken with each other. It could be that Amy would be living with her for only a short time if their relationship did develop, but she didn't begrudge Amy her happiness. Robert Chetwynd was a nice young man and she just wanted to see her sister happy. Meantime, Amy being there was going to make her life a lot easier. From now on she would be able to leave Amy in charge of the shop while she went off to buy stock, and it meant that she wouldn't have to work six full days a week with no help. 'Anyway, happy birthday.'

Amy's voice brought her sister's thoughts back to the present and she smiled. Over the last year, Mrs Forbes had been as good as her word and she had received three letters from her telling her all about Mathilda's progress. Pearl now knew the date she had cut her first tooth, that she was able to say 'mama' and 'dada' and the last letter had informed her that she was now crawling and pulling herself up the furniture. *We expect her to take her first steps any day now*, Mrs Forbes had written, *and she really is into everything, although we wouldn't change a hair on her head. She really is such a sweet child and the whole household adore her.*

They were all such milestones in a child's life and Pearl was sad that she hadn't been with her to share them; and yet she still felt that she had done the right thing. Susan had also written to tell Pearl that she was now mother to a bouncing baby boy, and Pearl was pleased that her friend seemed so happy and content.

Amy had once read one of the letters that Pearl had left on the table upstairs and had commented, 'Ain't it a bit strange for your former employer to go on about 'er baby daughter to you?'

Pearl had felt her colour rise but she had remained calm as she answered, 'Why should it be? I was still living there when Mathilda was born, so it's nice to hear how she's coming along.'

'Hm, I suppose so,' Amy had said and thankfully the subject had been dropped; but Pearl promised herself that she would make sure she put the letters away in future.

'I was wondering,' Amy said hesitantly, after she had gobbled down two slices of cake, 'whether you would mind very much once I've settled in if I went out a couple of nights a week?'

Pearl eyed her with amusement. 'Not at all but would this have anything to do with a certain young man?'

Amy's face was as red as a beetroot. 'Well, actually Rob 'as asked me if he could take me out. But I won't go if yer don't want me to.'

'Of course you should go,' Pearl told her good-naturedly. 'Just so long as you behave in a ladylike manner.'

Amy tittered. 'Ooh our Pearl, even Ma would never 'ave said that. But don't worry, I ain't daft. No chap will 'ave 'is way wi' me till there's a ring on me finger.'

'I'm pleased to hear it, but now don't you think you should put your things away? I've left half the wardrobe space for you and the bottom two drawers in the chest are empty. Will that be enough room for you?'

'More than enough,' Amy assured her, and she went to do as she was told while Pearl took the pots down to the kitchen to wash them.

Soon the two girls had settled into a routine and Pearl enjoyed having someone to talk to again. Her days had always been busy, but until Amy had moved in the nights had sometimes felt very long and lonely. Within a very short time of her being there, however, Amy began to go out two nights a week and every Sunday afternoon to see Robert, and by the end of January she shyly told Pearl, 'Rob 'as asked me if I'll officially be 'is girl an' 'e's asked me if I'd like to go to 'is parents farm with 'im fer tea next Sunday. What do yer think, Pearl?'

'I think if you like him and it's what you want, you should do it,' Pearl told her.

It was a clear as the nose on Amy's face that she was besotted with him, and Pearl was pleased that she'd met someone nice, although she did realise that this might mean she was going to be all on her own again at some time in the future. 'And you should invite him here for tea as well,' she went on. 'I'd like to meet him properly and get to know him.'

'Hm, I wonder if I could get that dress I've been sewin' done in time for Sunday?' Amy mused.

Pearl laughed. She could take a hint, especially one as big as a house brick. 'I'm sure you could if I help you with it,' she said obligingly, and so every spare minute they had for the rest of the week was spent working on the new gown.

It was finally finished late on Saturday evening and after Amy had tried it on and given a twirl, Pearl had to admit that she looked beautiful in it. The material was a very fine soft-green wool that showed off Amy's eyes to perfection, and although the style was simple it looked classy and elegant.

'You can borrow my navy cloak and my blue bonnet to wear with it,' Pearl offered.

Amy could scarcely wait for the next day to arrive. Robert was bringing the horse and cart to take her to his family's farm on the outskirts of Attleborough at three o'clock, but long before then Amy was ready and watching anxiously from the upstairs window for him.

'What if something 'appens an' 'e can't come,' she fretted.

Pearl tutted as she looked up from the newspaper she was reading. She bought one every day now and loved reading about world events. 'Will you please stop looking for problems where there are none? If he said he'll be here then he will.'

And sure enough, shortly before three o'clock they heard the rattle of the cart's wheels on the cobblestones outside and there was Rob, all done up in his Sunday best suit.

'Are yer really *sure* I look all right?' Amy asked for at least the tenth time, and in that moment, she looked so like Eliza that a lump formed in Pearl's throat and she had to blink back tears. 'You look absolutely lovely. Now just go and enjoy yourself.' She hastily adjusted the ribbons of the bonnet beneath Amy's chin and nudged her towards the door. Then, hurrying to the window, she watched as she climbed up on to the cart beside Rob and they drew away, chatting nineteen to the dozen.

When Amy got home later that evening her face was glowing. 'Rob's ma an' dad made me so welcome,' she gushed, and within minutes she had told Pearl all about what they had had for tea and how wonderful the farm was. 'There's a little cottage set back from the main house,' she told Pearl, blushing prettily. 'And Rob's ma told me that one day when Rob gets married that's where he and his wife will live.'

The following Sunday Rob came to their little rooms above the shop to have tea there and Pearl had to admit that he did seem a very nice young man. With his shock of curly dark hair and his vivid blue eyes, he was undeniably good-looking and hard-working, and she knew that Amy had chosen wisely.

The weeks passed quickly, and before they knew it they were into spring again and the long cold winter was becoming just a distant memory. The tiny yard was transformed into a riot of colour by pots full of gaily coloured geraniums and chrysanthemums, and now that she had more time Pearl had whitewashed the living quarters and sewn some flowered curtains for the windows. The old wing chairs now sported pretty cushions, gay peg rugs were scattered across the floors and the furniture was polished until Pearl could see her face in it.

And then early one morning in April, as Pearl went into the tiny kitchen to make them both a cup of tea before they started work, she found the back door swinging open and when she went to close it she heard a noise coming from the outside toilet. It was Amy being violently sick and Pearl's heart sank into her shoes. She knew what it might mean and was terrified for her sister. Even so, she forced herself to wait until Amy entered the room, looking as pale as a ghost, before asking quietly, 'Is there anything you'd like to tell me?'

Amy gulped and wrung her hands together as she avoided her sister's eyes – and then suddenly, she burst into tears and threw herself into her sister's arms.

'Eeh, our Pearl I've been *such* a fool,' she sobbed. 'I know I said I wouldn't let Rob touch me till we were wed but I love him so much that it just sort of 'appened. We couldn't 'elp usselves an' now I reckon I might be 'aving a baby. What am I goin' to do?'

Pearl's first instinct was to rant and rave, but common sense took over and she realised that this would do no good at all. 'How far gone do you think you might be?'

Amy sniffed. 'I've just missed me second course, so about two months.'

'And have you told Rob yet?'

Amy shook her head. 'No, I daren't. What if 'e won't stand by me?'

'You won't know what he'll do until you tell him, will you?' Pearl said sensibly. 'So, I suggest you do just that as soon as possible. When are you next seeing him?'

'This evenin' as it 'appens.'

'That's your chance then, there's no point in putting it off, because if you are having a baby it's not going to go away is it?'

'I suppose not,' Amy answered miserably, and for the first time since she had met him, suddenly she dreaded seeing him.

'When he arrives, I'll make myself scarce,' Pearl told her. 'At least that will give you both the chance to talk in private. I'll go for a walk.'

She left that evening just as Rob was arriving and went for a wander around the Pingle Fields. It was a beautiful evening and the hedgerows were full of spring primroses and clumps of daffodils. After a couple of hours, she slowly made her way home wondering what she would find. When she climbed the stairs to the little sitting room, she found Rob and Amy hand in hand waiting for her.

'She's told you then?'

Rob looked shamefaced. 'Yes, she has, an' I'm so sorry, Pearl. But the thing is I really love 'er, an' this will just mean we 'ave to get wed a bit sooner than we'd planned.'

Pearl sighed with relief. At least Rob was prepared to do the decent thing and make an honest woman of her. 'And what do you think your parents will say?' she asked.

'They'll probably give me an earful, an' I well deserve it,' he admitted. 'But I know they love Amy. We've got somewhere to live at least, an' I promise I'll do right by 'er an' the baby when it comes.'

'In that case we'd best get the wedding arranged,' Pearl said quietly. 'Where would you like to get married?'

'Me ma an' dad go to the Holy Trinity Church in Attleborough, when they can. I was christened there, so it would be nice if we got wed there.'

Pearl nodded. 'Then I suggest you tell your parents what's happened and we'll get it arranged as quickly as possible. Luckily not many people need know. Amy is only a couple of months on so she won't be showing yet awhile and when the baby comes, we can say it was early.'

'Huh! People ain't daft, they'll know we're lyin',' Amy said tearfully.

'So what? They can think what they like, and don't forget, while they're gossiping about you they'll be leaving some other poor devil alone. It'll just be a nine-day wonder,' Pearl said.

Rob nodded and after saying his goodbyes he took his leave.

His parents took the news surprisingly well. 'You're both young an' only human at the end o' the day,' his mother told him stoically. 'You can tell Amy's sister we'll put a bit of a spread on here for you in the front parlour after the service. Meantime you'll 'ave to give the cottage a good spring clean. It ain't been lived in fer some time so I've no doubt it'll be musty an' full o' spiders.'

Every evening after that, Amy and Rob worked together to get the little cottage ready and three weeks later, on a Monday morning, after the vicar at the Holy Trinity Church had read out the banns, the wedding day dawned bright and clear.

Pearl had insisted that Amy should have a new gown and bonnet, and once she was ready to leave for the church carrying a posy of sweet-scented freesias she looked truly beautiful. Her dress was a lemon cotton sprigged with tiny cream rosebuds, which fit tight into the waist before billowing out into a wide skirt held in place with starched cotton petticoats. The bonnet was of the same colour trimmed with cream silk roses and a yellow ribbon, and Pearl was sure she had never seen a prettier bride.

'You look stunning,' she told her sister as Amy stared at her reflection in the mirror. 'But I'm going to miss you so much!' They had had such a short time together, but she knew that Amy's place was with Rob now.

And then suddenly Amy was crying as she hung her head. 'I'm so sorry I've let yer down, Pearl,' she whimpered.

'You haven't let me down at all.' Pearl gave her a stern look. 'A baby is a blessing, just remember that, and actually I'm quite looking forward to being an aunty.' She dried Amy's tears and, arm in arm, they went out to the carriage that was waiting for them outside. Rob had ordered it for them and they were thrilled to see it had been decorated with flowers and ribbons.

Word of the wedding had spread quickly once the vicar began to read the banns, and Pearl had had quite a few curious customers who never usually came in enter the shop to ask casually, 'It's a bit quick, this wedding, ain't it?'

To each of them she had given a serene smile before saying calmly, 'Do you think so? I don't blame them. They're young and in love, so why should they wait? I'm sure they're going to be very happy together.'

Not at all happy with Pearl's answer, most of them had left the shop disgruntled, but Pearl didn't care. As long as Amy was happy, she could put up with any amount of tittle-tattle.

The wedding was a very quiet affair, as Amy and Rob had requested, with only Pearl, Rob's parents and grandparents, plus a few very close family friends attending, but even so the service was lovely and as they emerged from the church to the peal of bells, the newly-weds were glowing with happiness.

Back at the farmhouse, Mrs Chetwynd had laid on a mouth-watering spread and the mood was light-hearted as laughter echoed from the farmhouse beams. As the afternoon progressed, Rob's father went to get into his work clothes. He had animals to attend to, be it his son's wedding day or not, and this was the signal for the guests to leave.

'I'll get Rob to run you home in the trap,' Amy offered but Pearl shook her head.

'You'll do no such thing, Mrs Chetwynd. The walk will do me good. You just get off to your new home and see to your husband's meal.'

Amy giggled – it felt strange to be addressed as Mrs – but then, becoming solemn, again she clung to Pearl's hand as she whispered, 'I'm going to miss you.'

'Me too! But it's not as if we're hundreds of miles apart anymore, is it? We can see each other all the time.'

She gave Amy a little push towards the cottage where Rob stood in the doorway, waiting for her. And then she turned and went on her way, not looking back once, for she didn't want Amy to see the tears on her cheeks.

Chapter Forty-Four

July 1885

It was market day and the street outside the shop was bustling with people as Pearl stood behind the counter, fanning herself with a newspaper. The heat outside was so oppressive that she had propped the shop door open, but it was still stifling inside and she was looking forward to closing time when she could go and sit in the backyard with a nice big glass of lemonade.

Amy had not long left with Stanley, her little boy, and his new baby sister, Dorothy, who was a little beauty. Amy often popped in whenever she was in town, and sometimes Pearl visited the farm to see her niece and nephew, although not as often as she would have liked to because of the hours she worked. Amy and Rob were happy and clearly adored each other, which made the loneliness Pearl had felt since her sister left a little easier to bear. Admittedly her days were full and she didn't have much time to think, but it was when she put the closed sign on the door that the loneliness descended. Mrs Forbes, Cook and Susan still wrote to her regularly, and even though she still thought of Mathilda constantly, she had accepted now that she would never see her again.

The year before, the yearning for a child that she could love had become so intense that she had accepted a young farmer's offer of an evening out. He had been bereaved the year before when his wife had died in childbirth with his second child, and made no secret of the fact that he was drawn to Pearl. Tall, dark and handsome, Pearl was aware that there were probably many young women who would have happily stepped into his late wife's shoes, but after two very pleasant evenings spent with him, she knew that she was wasting his time. He was a truly lovely man – but he wasn't Nick, and Nick was and always would be the love of her life. Pearl knew she was spoiled goods and the thing that kept her and Nick apart still hung over her. Monty had taken so much from her that night and she knew she could never be wed because of it.

Sometimes she wondered where Nick was now and what he was doing. Was he married? Did he have children? She had no way of knowing, but it didn't stop her thinking of him and mourning what might have been. She still suffered from the nightmares that had plagued her following Eliza's death, although thankfully not as often now, but when they did come, she would wake up in a blind panic, thinking she was back on the riverbank with Eliza spitting hate and abuse at her. And yet still she retained the love she had felt for her and accepted that, whatever her sister had done, she always would.

At that moment, someone entered the shop and, putting aside her memories, she turned to serve them. The woman had her back to her and to one side of her stood the most beautiful little girl Pearl had ever seen. She was dressed in a charming little dress with a nautical design in blue and white, with a wide green ribbon exactly the same colour as her eyes fastened in her hair. Pearl froze, for there was something about the blonde-haired child that struck a chord in her, and then the woman turned to smile and Pearl felt as if all the breath had been sucked out of her body as her hand flew to her throat. It was Emmaline Forbes, which meant that the child standing beside her must be . . . Mathilda!

'Hello, Pearl, dear. How are you?' The woman smiled brightly as the child held tight to her hand. Gently nudging her forwards, Emmaline told her, 'Say hello to Miss Parker, darling. This is the lady I told you used to live with us some years ago back at home. We're on a visit to my mother at present, so we've come all the way from London to see you, haven't we, sweetheart?'

The child nodded and stepping forwards she bobbed her knee as she said politely, 'How do you do, Miss Parker.'

'I . . . I . . . Oh, this is such a lovely surprise,' Pearl stammered, as she blinked back scalding tears. 'I didn't even know you were in London.'

'Father's been unwell so it was rather a spur-of-the-moment decision to visit,' Emmaline told her. 'And while we were here . . . well, I thought you might like to see how much Mathilda has grown. She was just a baby the last time you saw her, wasn't she?'

'Oh, Mamma, look.' Something had caught Mathilda's attention and she skipped towards the counter, so close that Pearl had to stifle the urge to reach out and drag her into her arms. 'These buttons are like little crowns. May I have some for my new jacket, Mamma?'

'Of course, you may,' Pearl said in a wobbly voice before Mrs Forbes could answer, and she dropped a number of them into a tiny brown paper bag and handed them to the little girl, who beamed and clutched them to her chest as if they were treasure. 'B-but please . . . let me put the closed sign on the door. You must be thirsty after that long train journey.' Before Mrs Forbes could object, she hurried to the door, closed it and switched the sign, and led them through the door behind the counter.

'I live in the rooms above the shop,' Pearl said as she ushered them upstairs, and all the time her eyes were fixed on this adorable little girl as her heart raced faster than the train they had arrived on.

'That's very kind of you, but we can't stay too long,' Mrs Forbes said. 'The train back to London leaves in an hour and a half so this is just a flying visit really.'

Now that the little girl had got over her initial shyness, she began to chatter away like a magpie about anything and everything her eyes settled on, as Mrs Forbes smiled indulgently.

'I'm going to start learning my lessons an' have a teacher when we get back home, aren't I, Mamma?' she told Pearl proudly. 'But I can already count to ten. Daddy teached me to.'

'Taught!' Mrs Forbes corrected her fondly.

'An' for my birthday, Mamma an' Daddy bought me a big rockin' horse, almost as big as the ones in Will's stables.'

'Really? Well, how wonderful!' Pearl watched as Mathilda crossed to the window to stare down at the shoppers below, which kept her quiet for the whole of two minutes.

'Did you like living in our house?' she asked then, with a child's innocence.

Pearl nodded. 'Oh yes, yes I did, very much.'

Mathilda grinned, and Pearl suddenly remembered that she had not offered them a drink and shot off to the kitchen to fetch a jug of lemonade.

'This is very nice, thank you,' the little girl said politely when Pearl handed her a glass. 'Did you make it all by yourself? Cook makes me lemonade back at home an' jam tarts.' Mathilda grinned as she rubbed her tummy. 'But sometimes she lets me have too many and Mamma tells her off, don't you, Mamma?'

'Yes, I do,' Mrs Forbes told her indulgently. 'Too many are bad for your teeth.'

'I've already got one wobbly one, look.' She showed the offending tooth to Pearl proudly as she wobbled it to and fro. 'But I don't mind, 'cause Daddy says when it comes out the tooth fairies will come and fetch it from under my pillow an' leave me a present.'

She began to explore the room then as Mrs Forbes looked towards Pearl and said quietly, 'I hope I did the right thing bringing her? I thought you deserved to see her.'

'Oh yes, you did,' Pearl assured her. 'She's such a credit to you . . . and she seems to be so happy.'

'Thank you, that was all we both ever wanted for her, wasn't it? But what about you, Pearl? Are *you* happy?'

Pearl lowered her eyes. 'Yes, of course. My business is doing well and I see my sister regularly . . .'

'But you never met another young man that you felt you could be happy with?'

'Oh, I've met quite a few, but none that took my fancy. I'm quite happy as I am,' Pearl told her, with a false smile.

Mrs Forbes looked sad, but then Mathilda was chattering away again and the next hour seemed to fly by.

'I'm so sorry, but we really should be going now,' Mrs Forbes said, as she glanced at the small ormolu clock on the mantelpiece. 'We don't want to miss our train, do we, Mathilda? But it's been so lovely to see you, Pearl.'

'And you too. I'll never be able to thank you enough for what you've done today.'

An unspoken message passed between the two of them as Mrs Forbes embraced her. At least now Pearl would be able to carry a picture of the little girl Mathilda had become in her heart.

'Shall I come to see you off at the station?'

Mrs Forbes shook her head. 'Better not to. Let's say our goodbyes here, shall we?'

Pearl nodded as she bent down to Mathilda's level, and almost instantly the child's plump little arms wrapped themselves about her neck and she planted a sloppy kiss on her cheek. 'I *like* you,' she said solemnly.

'And I like you too . . . very much,' Pearl whispered, as she breathed in the sweet scent of her.

But then Mathilda was skipping towards Mrs Forbes again. 'Come on, Mamma. I want to see the chickens in their cages on the way back to the train,' she said bossily and, laughing, Mrs Forbes allowed herself to be yanked off down the stairs with Pearl following close behind.

The two women stood awkwardly staring at each other for a moment when they reached the shop door, before Mrs Forbes leaned forwards and gently kissed Pearl's cheek.

'Thank you,' she said simply and her words held a wealth of meaning.

Pearl somehow managed to unlock the door, which was no easy feat when her hands were trembling so much, and then with a final wave Mathilda and Mrs Forbes were gone and Pearl could finally allow her tears to fall as she thought of the delightful, happy and contented child who had just left. And yet although her heart was aching, she also felt a huge sense of relief, for now she had seen with her own eyes how close Mathilda was to her mamma – and Mrs Forbes really *was* her mamma; Pearl was just the vessel that had carried and given birth to her.

Blindly, she stumbled back upstairs. There was no way she could reopen the shop that afternoon. She wanted to just sit quietly and savour every moment she had spent with Mathilda.

However, it seemed that someone else had other ideas for almost an hour later there was a hammering on the shop door. Swallowing her annoyance, Pearl curled up in the chair and tried to ignore it – but whoever it was was clearly persistent for the banging went on, until with a disgruntled sigh she rose and started down the stairs, intending to give them the length of her tongue.

There was a man standing with his back to the door as she marched across the shop floor and, after throwing the door open, she snapped irritably, 'Can't you *read,* sir? The sign on the door clearly says *closed*!'

But then very slowly he turned, and as she found herself looking up into eyes that still haunted her dreams, the breath caught in her throat and she had to hang on to the door jamb for support.

'*Nick!*'

'Well, aren't you going to invite me in then?' he asked, with the same cheeky grin – and without waiting he strode past her and closed the door firmly behind him. A tall, well-muscled and very handsome man stood before her and she had to blink to make herself believe that it was really him.

'Hello, Pearl.'

It was the second shock she had had in a day and she was rendered temporarily speechless as she gawped up at him.

'B-but how . . . how did you know where to find me?' she asked eventually.

'Ah well, luckily I was docked in Canada recently when I bumped into Susan and Will and we got to talking and . . . the long and the short of it is, they told me what really happened with you and Monty. Eliza had told me that you loved him, which is why I didn't bother you again. But *why* didn't *you* tell me what had really happened? Didn't you trust me enough?'

Pearl started to cry softly. 'How could I tell you that I had been raped and that I was carrying another man's child?' she said brokenly. 'I was too ashamed and too afraid of what you might do if you knew. It seemed kinder to just let you go and forget about me. I was soiled goods and I couldn't face you.'

'You little fool! You could *never* be soiled goods; it wasn't your fault,' he scolded her. 'Although you were

465

right to worry about what I might have done, I admit. I'd have killed Monty with my bare hands if I'd known. As it was, he got his comeuppance anyway. But once I knew the truth, wild horses wouldn't have kept me away, so when I discovered that Mrs Forbes was travelling to England, I got on the boat with her. She told me that she was intending to come and see you and I needed to know how the land lay before I turned up. After all, you might have been about to get married or something!'

Smiling, he reached out to gently stroke a strand of damp hair from her cheek, and at the touch of his hand her heart began to thump so loudly she was sure he would hear it.

'You can probably guess the rest,' he went on. 'I travelled here with Mrs Forbes and she agreed to come and see you first to see if there was still a chance for me. I don't mind telling you, it was the longest hour I have ever spent, but thankfully when she and Mathilda arrived back at the station just now, she was able to tell me that you were still footloose and fancy-free. You see, I've done quite well since the last time I saw you and I've got enough saved up for that little smallholding I used to talk about. Of course, I can see that you have your own thriving little shop now and perhaps the thought of being a farmer's wife doesn't appeal to you?'

Pearl glanced around at the little business she had built up. It had taken years of hard work and long hours and yet now she realised that it meant nothing compared to what he was offering her. Looking back at him she smiled through her tears. 'Actually, I've always quite fancied living on a farm. But you'd have to make an honest woman of me first!'

'Oh, I think that could be arranged.' He grinned and then she was in his arms and as his lips pressed down on hers, her heart swelled with love and she knew she was finally in the place she was meant to be.

Acknowledgements

First of all I would like to say a massive thank you to my lovely editor Sarah Bauer, Katie Lumsden, Eleanor, Kate and all 'the Rosie team' at Zaffre who have worked so hard to keep everything on track throughout the awful pandemic. Special thanks also to the designer for the wonderful covers for my new series, and to my amazing agent Sheila Crowley, and my brilliant copyeditor Gillian Holmes. I know it can't have been easy for any of you having to work from home and we've all had to adapt to the changes, but somehow you've managed it, so many thanks and well done to you all.

Finally, a huge thank you to my wonderful family and all my lovely readers for all the smashing reviews – love to you all!

MEMORY LANE

Hello everyone,

It seems like no time at all since I was writing to you in the hardback of *An Orphan's Journey* and now here we are with the paperback on the shelves. Thank you so much to all those of you who've taken the trouble to get in touch to tell me how much you liked it! It spent quite some weeks in the *Sunday Times* bestseller list so I was thrilled. I'm so glad I've had my writing to keep me occupied or I think I would have gone crazy over the last year. It's been such a difficult time for everyone but hopefully we are now seeing light at the end of the dark tunnel. I really feel for those who have lost friends and loved ones to the pandemic, I'm afraid life will never be quite the same again for them, I lost a dear friend last April and miss her every day but we all have to keep going.

At least now we can all get out into the garden and it's so lovely to be able to potter outside again, isn't it? I've been busily working on the next book, *A Simple Wish*, which will be out in October and you'll find a little sample of it in the back of this book. In this one you'll meet Ruby and I do hope you'll all love her as I did while I was writing about her. Your lovely messages and reviews have helped to keep me focused during the last year so please keep them coming; I do so look forward to hearing from you all.

We did have a very happy family event in February to lift the sense of doom and gloom with the birth of my very first little great-granddaughter Jaiah-Rose. Sadly, because of complications, she had to be delivered eight weeks early weighing only two pounds one ounce, and needless to say she gave us some worrying times in the early days, but I'm thrilled to say she's doing marvellously now and both mother and baby are fine. She is such a beautiful little poppet, not that I'm biased, of course!

Now that the lockdowns are easing, we've also managed to spend a little time at our holiday home with our fur babies, all six of them, and that was lovely too. There's nothing like a little sun, sea and sand to put you in a better frame of mind so I hope all of you are going to manage to get away on holiday this year too. I know that many people's holidays had to be cancelled last year because of the lockdowns and bans on foreign travel etc., which must have been so disappointing! Still, here's to better times ahead, we have to stay hopeful and optimistic.

Meantime, I hope you all stay safe and take care of yourselves, and I look forward to meeting some

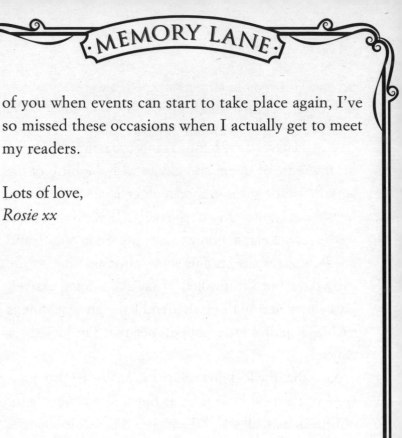

of you when events can start to take place again, I've so missed these occasions when I actually get to meet my readers.

Lots of love,
Rosie xx

Read on to learn more about Rosie Goodwin's other books,
and for an exclusive sneak peek at her upcoming novel,
A Simple Wish . . .

Prologue

December 1870

'There we are, luvvie, it's a little girl.' As the old woman straightened up from the bed with a newborn whimpering softly in her hands, the doctor glanced at her and solemnly shook his head. The child was tiny and weak and if he couldn't stop the flow of blood coming from the mother soon, it was doubtful either of them would survive.

'You should have sent for me sooner,' he scolded gently. 'Another *niece* of yours, is she?' The doctor was no fool and he had a good idea where the young women came from, but on the odd occasion Mrs Bradley had called him out, she always introduced them as her nieces.

She nodded and sniffed, avoiding his eyes. She'd only sent for him when she could see that the young mother was slipping away. Doctors cost money, which bit into her profits from dealing with these girls whose babies she delivered, and the madam at the whorehouse who sent them paid her little enough as it was. Even so, she was saddened to see the state of the young woman on the bed. She shook her head. She'd delivered dozens of babies in her time; how could things have gone so terribly wrong?

Almost four months this girl had been staying with her now and she seemed to be a cut above the girls who had preceded her. They came with frightening regularity despite the birth control methods they practised, and as far as she was concerned most of them deserved no better. The girls would come once they became too big with child to earn their keep, then, once the birth was over, she would find homes for the babies – which meant yet more money for her – and continue to care for the mother until she was fit to return to work. Usually it wouldn't be long before the next one arrived and the cycle would start all over again.

But this girl had not come from the whorehouse and the old woman could only assume that she came from a good family who had turned their backs on her until she had got rid of the baby. Now, as she wrapped the infant in an old towel, she looked at the little face approvingly. She'd have no trouble at all placing this one – if she survived, that was.

'I-is the baby all right?' the young mother asked weakly as she sagged limply back against the pillows.

Mrs Bradley smiled, displaying a mouthful of tobacco-stained and rotting teeth. 'She's better than all right; a right bonny little piece. Just look at this shock of red hair, an' she's got the bluest eyes I've ever seen. I reckon she'll grow into a little beauty.' Noting the tears that were slowly trickling down the girl's pale cheeks, she didn't tell her of her concerns about whether the child would survive.

'Can I . . . see her? J-just for a moment . . . *please?*'

Mrs Bradley frowned. She had explained to the girl that the babies were usually taken away as soon as they were born. It was easier that way because if the mothers didn't see them, they couldn't bond with them and it saved a lot of heartache. Yet how could she refuse the request if the girl was about to die?

Tentatively she approached the bed and pulling back the corner of the towel she leant towards the girl who lifted her hand and tenderly stroked the baby's cheek. 'I want her to be called Ruby,' she said softly. She was shocked at the feelings that were coursing through her. For months she had longed to just get the birth over with so she could get on with her life, and yet now she had glimpsed this beautiful little human being, she didn't know how she was going to be able to bear to part with her.

Mrs Bradley sighed. It was usually left to the adoptive parents to name the child but then, what harm could there be in going along with her wishes – for now at least – if it gave her some comfort? She nodded and as she left the room to bathe and feed the newborn, the girl on the bed turned her head to the wall and began to sob quietly, oblivious of the doctor as he battled to save her life.

Some hours later, looking haggard and weary, the doctor went downstairs. 'I've managed to stem the blood flow but there is nothing more I can do for her,' he told Mrs Bradley. 'It's all in God's hands now. I shall call back tomorrow.' He glanced at the baby, who was now lying quietly in a drawer lined with a coarse blanket at the side of the fire.

'Is that really necessary?' Mrs Bradley looked disgruntled as she shuffled over to a tin on the mantlepiece to get his fee. Another visit meant yet another payment. 'I'm sure as I can see to 'er now if the bleedin's stopped. She'll just want peace an' quiet an' feedin' up to get 'er strength back. A few bowls o' my chicken broth will 'ave her back on 'er feet in no time.'

The doctor shrugged. Mrs Bradley could be a stubborn old devil when she had a mind to be. 'Very well, but if you have any concerns whatsoever you are to send for me immediately.' His steely blue eyes stared sternly into her faded grey ones and she nodded, setting her double chins wobbling.

'O' course I will, it goes wi'out sayin',' she spouted indignantly and following him to the door she saw him on his way before snuggling into the old wing chair at the side of the fire for a bit of a rest. It had been a long day and an even longer night.

Two days later, Mrs Bradley opened the door to Ruby's prospective parents. Despite her initial concerns, the baby seemed to be thriving, which was more than could be said for her mother, who was still hovering between life and death.

The Carters were a middle-aged couple and compared to most folk in the town were very comfortably off as Mr Carter owned his own thriving bakery in Queens Road in the centre of the bustling little market town of Nuneaton. They had approached Mrs Bradley some time before, expressing an interest in adopting a baby boy, but she had no doubt that Rita Carter would take little persuading to accept a girl, especially one as bonny as little Ruby. It was a well-known fact that Mrs Carter had suffered numerous miscarriages throughout the course of their married life and now she was desperate for a child.

'Come in,' Mrs Bradley encouraged. 'The baby I got word to you about is over there, fast asleep in the drawer.'

Rita Carter was a plump, kind-hearted soul and she hurried across the room to peep at the baby. The instant she saw her, tears sprung to her eyes and her face softened.

'Oh, Bill, come and look at him, he's just beautiful.'

'Ah . . . well, that's the only thing.' Mrs Bradley looked slightly uncomfortable as Bill Carter raised an eyebrow at her. 'It's a little girl. Her name is Ruby, although o' course, should yer decide to take 'er yer could always change it to a name o' yer own choice.'

'But I distinctly told you we wanted a boy to take over the business when I get older.' Bill looked less than pleased but it was already clear that his wife was quite smitten with the child, judging by the way she was looking at her.

'Oh, Bill. *But please* just come and look at her!' his wife implored.

Looking less than happy, he crossed the room to do as she asked. 'She's bonny enough, admittedly. But what good will a girl be to us? I thought we'd agreed to wait for a boy who could carry on the family business.'

The old woman held her breath. Unlike his wife, who was a charitable soul, Bill Carter was known to be a hard man and she suddenly saw the fee for Ruby disappearing out of the window. But she hadn't reckoned on Rita Carter's desperate need for a child.

'I *beg* you to let me take her.' Rita was openly crying. 'Just think of the help she could give in the bakery when she's a little older,' she went on cajolingly. 'We can teach her how to make the bread and see to the ovens and all sorts of things.'

Bill scowled. 'An' how much are yer askin' for her?' he snapped at Mrs Bradley.

She licked her lips, which were suddenly dry. 'I thought two guineas would be a fair price . . . it'd be three if she'd been a lad.'

'*Two guineas!*' He looked shocked, but then seeing the tender look on his wife's face as she gazed down at the infant, he knew he had lost. She would never forgive him if he didn't let her have the child.

'Very well.' Fumbling in his pocket he extracted some coins and flung them begrudgingly onto the old scrubbed table, then looking at his wife he snapped, 'Well, gather the child and her bits together then, woman. I haven't got time to stand about here all day. There's work waiting to be done.'

'Yes, of course, dear.' Rita gently lifted the child from the drawer and after wrapping her tightly in her blanket she scurried towards the door.

Once they had gone, Mrs Bradley snatched up the coins and smiled. But then as she glanced towards the ceiling the smile was replaced with a frown. She was sorry for the baby's mother, but the fact of it was that when the girl died, she would have to spend some of the money she had just made to pay for a funeral – and that consideration far outweighed any pity she felt for the girl who had shared her home for the last few months. Still, she told herself, she already had another girl lined up for a stay so she'd worry about that when she had to.

Humming happily to herself she went to put the kettle on, the coins jingling merrily in her pocket.

Roast Pork Dinner

A dinner of pork and vegetables is the first meal Pearl serves in the Forbeses' household, in chapter thirteen.

You will need:

1 leg of pork
8 large potatoes, peeled and cut into quarters
6 carrots, peeled and cut in half
4 turnips, peeled and cut into wedges
4 parsnips, peeled and cut in half
1 cabbage
2 tbsp flour
2 tbsp butter
500ml stock or water
Salt and pepper, to season

Method:

1. Lightly score the pork, then rub salt and pepper into its score lines. Place on a baking tray, cover with foil, and leave to roast at 180°C for 1 hour (or 25 minutes per 500g, depending on the weight).

2. Meanwhile, peel and chop the potatoes. Boil them for 25 minutes, until soft. Separate into two bowls of equal sizes, then pour the contents of one bowl into

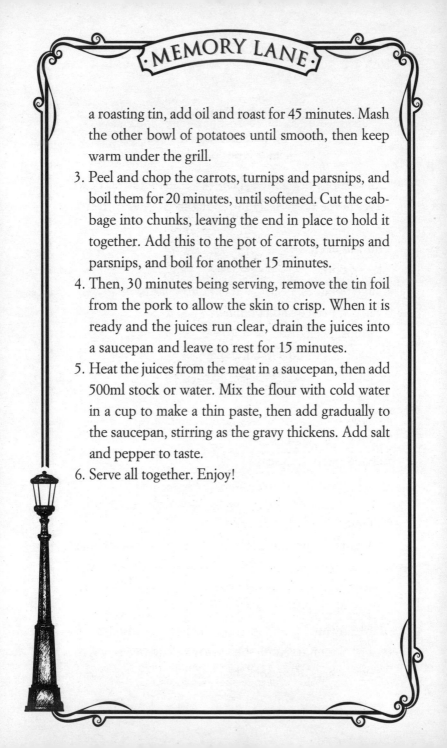

a roasting tin, add oil and roast for 45 minutes. Mash the other bowl of potatoes until smooth, then keep warm under the grill.

3. Peel and chop the carrots, turnips and parsnips, and boil them for 20 minutes, until softened. Cut the cabbage into chunks, leaving the end in place to hold it together. Add this to the pot of carrots, turnips and parsnips, and boil for another 15 minutes.

4. Then, 30 minutes being serving, remove the tin foil from the pork to allow the skin to crisp. When it is ready and the juices run clear, drain the juices into a saucepan and leave to rest for 15 minutes.

5. Heat the juices from the meat in a saucepan, then add 500ml stock or water. Mix the flour with cold water in a cup to make a thin paste, then add gradually to the saucepan, stirring as the gravy thickens. Add salt and pepper to taste.

6. Serve all together. Enjoy!

An Orphan's Journey is the second book in Rosie Goodwin's Precious Stones series – if you enjoyed it, why not try the first in the series, *The Winter Promise*?

1850. When Opal Sharp finds herself and her younger siblings suddenly orphaned and destitute, she thinks things can get no worse. But soon three of them – including Opal – are struck down with the illness that took their father, and her brother Charlie is forced to make an impossible decision. Unable to afford a doctor, he knows the younger children will not survive. So, unbeknownst to Opal, Charlie takes their younger siblings to the workhouse. When she finds out, Opal is heartbroken.

Charlie starts taking risks to try to support what's left of the Sharp family and earn Opal's forgiveness, but he takes it too far and finds himself in trouble with the law.
Soon, he is sent on a convict ship to Australia.

As poor Opal is forced to say goodbye to the final member of her family, she makes a promise to reunite them all one day. Will she ever see her family again?

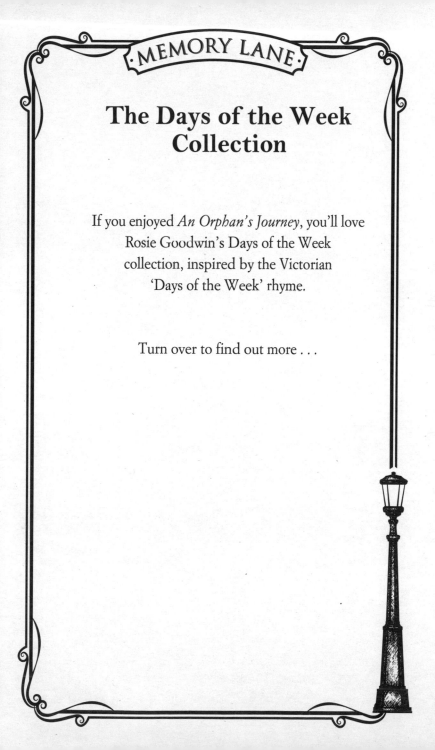

MEMORY LANE

The Days of the Week Collection

If you enjoyed *An Orphan's Journey*, you'll love
Rosie Goodwin's Days of the Week
collection, inspired by the Victorian
'Days of the Week' rhyme.

Turn over to find out more . . .

Mothering Sunday

The child born on the Sabbath Day,
Is bonny and blithe, and good and gay.

1884, Nuneaton.

Fourteen-year-old Sunday has grown up in the cruelty of the Nuneaton workhouse. When she finally strikes out on her own, she is determined to return for those she left behind, and to find the long-lost mother who gave her away. But she's about to discover that the brutal world of the workhouse will not let her go without a fight.

The Little Angel

Monday's child is fair of face.

1896, Nuneaton.

Left on the doorstep of Treetops Children's Home, young Kitty captures the heart of her guardian, Sunday Branning, and grows into a beguiling and favoured young girl – until she is summoned to live with her birth mother. In London, nothing is what it seems, and her old home begins to feel very far away. If Kitty is to have any chance of happiness, this little angel must protect herself from devils in disguise . . . and before it's too late.

· MEMORY LANE ·

A Mother's Grace

Tuesday's child is full of grace.

1910, Nuneaton.

When her father's threatening behaviour grows worse, pious young Grace Kettle escapes her home to train to be a nun. But when she meets the dashing and devout Father Luke, her world is turned upside down. She is driven to make a scandalous choice – one she may well spend the rest of her days seeking forgiveness for.

The Blessed Child

Wednesday's child is full of woe.

1864, Nuneaton.

After Nessie Carson's mother is brutally murdered and her father abandons them, Nessie knows she will do anything to keep her family safe. As her fragile young brother's health deteriorates and she attracts the attention of her lecherous landlord, soon Nessie finds herself in the darkest of times. But there is light and the promise of happiness if only she is brave enough to fight for it.

A Maiden's Voyage

Thursday's child has far to go.

1912, London.

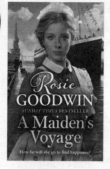

Eighteen-year-old maid Flora Butler has her life turned upside-down when her mistress's father dies in a tragic accident. Her mistress is forced to move to New York to live with her aunt until she comes of age, and begs Flora to go with her. Flora has never left the country before, and now faces a difficult decision – give up her position, or leave her family behind. Soon, Flora and her mistress head for Southampton to board the RMS *Titanic*.

A Precious Gift

Friday's child is loving and giving.

1911, Nuneaton.

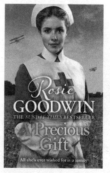

When Holly Farthing's overbearing grandfather tries to force her to marry a widower twice her age, she flees to London, bringing her best friend and maid, Ivy, with her. In the big smoke, Holly begins nurse training in the local hospital. There she meets the dashing Doctor Parkin, everything Holly has ever dreamt of. But soon, she discovers some shocking news that means they can never be together, and her life is suddenly thrown into turmoil. Supporting the war effort, she heads to France and throws herself into volunteering on the front line . . .

Time to Say Goodbye

Saturday's child works hard for their living.

1935, Nuneaton.

Kathy has grown up at Treetops home for children, where Sunday and Tom Branning have always cared for her as one of their own. With her foster sister Livvy at her side, and a future as a nurse ahead of her, she could wish for nothing more. But when Tom dies suddenly in a riding accident, life at Treetops will never be the same again. As their financial difficulties mount, will the women of Treetops be forced to leave their home?

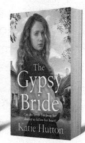

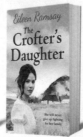
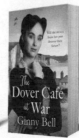